BOLD STROKES

BOLD STROKES

JANE BOON

Regan Arts.

Regan Arts.
Copyright © Jane Boon, 2024
All rights reserved, including the right to reproduce this book or portions thereof in any form whatsoever. For information, contact internationalrights@reganarts.com.

First Regan Arts paperback edition, July 2024.
Library of Congress Control Number: 2024902161
978-1-68245-228-8 (Paperback)
978-1-68245-229-5 (eBook)

Cover design by Richard Ljoenes
Design by Neuwirth & Associates, Inc.
Author photograph by Natasha Gornik

Printed in the United States of America

10   9   8   7   6   5   4   3   2   1

For professional dominatrixes:
Your brave work in darkened
rooms deserves a spotlight.

WITHOUT CRUELTY, THERE IS NO FESTIVAL.

—*Friedrich Nietzsche*

PART 1

INSPIRATION

INSPIRATION: The initial stage of an artist's
work, where ideas and themes are conceived.

1

LITTLE RED DOTS

June 2008

To see the look I get when I have an orgasm, watch me peel off a little red dot and apply it next to one of the works in my gallery. I don't want to admit it to anyone, because they wouldn't understand and they might even be insulted, but sticking those dots is better than sex.

I have a method, even, to heighten my excitement. I walk up to the piece that's been sold and stand in front of it for a moment. It's like foreplay, to examine the work and try to better understand what aroused the buyer. Then I pull out my sheet of stickers and pause, savoring the moment. I'm basically teasing myself as I pull the little dot off its mount and then carefully apply it to the card.

My stickers were ready. Everything about the evening said it was going to be a blockbuster show. It was perfect. The artist, Cassidy Smith, was a recent MFA from Yale—a very pretty, pink cheeked, blue-eyed blonde. Originally from New Jersey, she looked like she'd been airlifted from a farm in Idaho; she was that wholesome. She made exquisite oils filled with fetishistic and violent imagery. There was blood, skin covered with ligature marks, leather, latex and all sorts of garments not worn in polite company. The contrast between her presentation and her work thrilled me. I felt like it would open wallets, and the money would come gushing out.

My clientele was mostly bankers and lawyers, but the kinds of buyers who liked to imagine they still had an edge, even if it had been dulled and softened through decades of buffing and care. They wanted emerging works, but they didn't want to visit Bushwick. They wanted something that smacked of danger, but they didn't want to travel above the Upper East Side, or east of Tribeca. They wanted their frisson wrapped in convenience, to be mounted on the walls of their exquisite SoHo lofts, and my Chelsea gallery delivered.

The day was coming together. My favorite piece, the largest, was one I had outlined for Cassidy. It had taken the artist a few tries, but she finally got the black latex to gleam on the canvas. Photorealism is not for the faint of heart. It requires technical mastery to execute so that all the details are precisely conceived and rendered. It's a challenge to make these works possess conceptual depth; they can be cold and superficial. Fortunately, Cassidy had created exactly what I wanted. It was a woman's face, oversized, wearing a shiny black hood. The only skin you could see was her heavily made-up eyes and her mouth, with blood-red lips and a glimpse of teeth. The painting's uncanny sneer followed you around the room. Passion oozed from the canvas.

There were already a couple of presales. Michael, a longstanding client and collector, had ponied up for a painting of a black patent stiletto tied in coarse hemp, but the bulk of the works would be available. I'd set the prices high, but not stratospheric. In contemporary art, pricing is as much about signaling as it is about money, and I wanted to signal that Cassidy was a woman to be taken seriously.

Certainly, her works were to be enjoyed, but they also represented excellent investments.

Cassidy was bouncing around the gallery like a child who'd eaten too much candy. That nervous energy appealed to me, but it had to be channeled. I took her aside. "What are you wearing tonight?"

"This?" She was wearing faded jeans, white sneakers and a man's white shirt, rolled up at the sleeves. She looked attractive, but I wanted her to smolder. It was her professional debut and she would have an audience who'd seen that tired look before.

"No." I shook my head. "That's too casual and too common. You are neither. Do you have a little black dress, or something sexy?"

"I don't want to look like I'm trying too hard. How about a blazer over the shirt?"

"No. That won't do, unless you ditch the shirt entirely." They don't teach these lessons at Yale. "You've painted sexy works, you're a gorgeous, sexy woman. The collectors want to see that the artist who made such outrageous works is someone who awes them . . . that she knows things they don't, and that she can see and feel things they only dream about. Wear something short and tight. You do have something short and tight, don't you?"

"Uh, not exactly." Cassidy fidgeted in disappointment. Her cheeks grew pink, as she blushed.

"Follow me." I took Cassidy upstairs to my apartment—I lived above the shop. She was about my size, which meant my closet held hope.

She stood in the middle of my dressing room, as I pulled out a stack of cocktail dresses, still wearing plastic bags from the cleaners or sheathed in the garment bags they'd come in. "You should be the center of attention. How about white or red?"

"White, then." She wrinkled her nose. "I've never liked wearing red."

"Okay. Your comfort is key. I want you to feel like a goddess. How do you feel about Alaïa?" I grabbed one of his short dresses from my small stash of white dresses and held it in front of her. "This should fit you!"

"Alaïa? I adore his designs. He treated clothing as an art form." Cassidy's face had relaxed. She even seemed intrigued.

"Yes. His outfits are technical and sculptural and gorgeous. I hope this suits you. And if it doesn't, darling, we'll try something else. Let me give you some privacy while you put it on." I stepped out of the room while Cassidy stripped. "Let me know if you need a hand!"

"Erika?" She called from the room with a slight giggle.

"Yes?"

"I'm unsure about the zipper."

"It goes in the front." Sometimes, the obvious needed to be said.

"I know that, but how low should it go?" Cassidy's voice had a pleading quality, one I knew all too well.

"Oh, now that's my kind of question. May I come in?" I've always been maniacal about consent. If I'm alone with someone, especially if they're not fully dressed, it's because I'm welcome.

Cassidy stood there in the stiff white dress, with the zipper down to her rib cage. Her pink lace bra was visible where the dress lay against her skin. She moved the zipper up and down, trying different heights. She paused, with the dress zipped up to her neck. "Too prim?"

"If you want to woo collectors, it is." I cocked my head and assessed Cassidy's ensemble. "Pull it down six inches."

Cassidy must have been feeling more comfortable, because then she got saucy and unzipped the dress to her waist, so that her cleavage was on full display. "Would this close deals?"

"Depends on what you're selling. But yes!" This show of spunk appealed to me. "Now close that dress up. We're selling paintings today. Let me tell you, darling, the collectors will adore your attitude."

We settled on a zipper placement that revealed just a hint of lace. I found Cassidy some shoes and a few accessories. I put her in front of my makeup mirror. "You should put on a little eyeshadow and a pretty pink lipstick. Go demure with the makeup. The crowd will eat it up." That's one good thing about painters, they know how to wield a makeup brush, and if you tell them what to do, most will comply. I watched her get ready, nodding with delight as she transformed into a fresh-faced beauty, through the addition of only a little bit of war paint. I found a simple black leather sheath dress by Jitrois for myself, which I embellished with a corset-style belt in patent leather.

Once we were both dressed, I sat Cassidy down on my couch to brief her on what to expect. These opening nights could be intense, and we had many things to cover. Virgins demand extra care before they get sacrificed on the altar of commerce.

"So, I've presold a couple of your pieces already to collectors I know. I'll put the red dots on them before the doors open. This will cultivate an aura of scarcity. The message being, the paintings are going fast, so you'd better buy yours while you can."

"I like that message. I'm buried in student loans." Cassidy's mood shifted and she grew pensive.

"We've all been there. Unless someone else pays, getting a fancy education is crushing. You would not believe the things I did to pay off my Harvard debts."

Cassidy looked me in the eye. "So, what's the deal with *Latex Hood*, the painting you had me do? I mean, it's huge."

"Yes, it's fucking enormous. So, there aren't many people who can put that in their living room, but I have a collector who loves the imagery and who has the space to hang it. I showed him a photo of your hood, and he went bonkers. The guy's in town this week, so he's going to look at it. I think he'll scoop it up. He's also a big fucking deal, a known collector with a great eye, so if people see that he's buying, there will be copycats." Cassidy nodded, so I continued. "What *Latex Hood* does is anchor your other works. It's the most extreme. It's also the most expensive. It will make the other paintings seem more approachable and less pricey. All of a sudden, that painting of biceps covered in ligature marks seems plausible and spicy. Alone, without the hood for context, it might feel too wild for some milquetoast hedge funder. With *Latex Hood* nearby, those ligature marks suddenly seem accessible and relatively safe."

"Oh wow, I never thought of my works that way. I'm so glad you're representing me, you're so smart about this stuff, Erika." Cassidy grew serious. "Who's coming, anyway?"

"Well, I sent out lots of postcards and emails, and we worked the phones, so I've had a lot of RSVPs. But the yield, for evenings like these, is highly variable. Is the weather okay? Yes, thank goodness. If it were rainy? We'd be fucked." New York crowds were cruel. Any excuse would keep them at work or at home. "There should be some serious collectors in attendance, a few members of the press. I hope you invited some friends and family—they're good for emotional support—and it's great for them to see you shine. But, I should warn you, there will also be some cruisers."

"What's a cruiser?"

"Oh, these are people who just love openings. They love the drama. They love being near artists. They love free booze. They love being able to brag to their friends that they were there. They like to cruise in . . . but they *never* buy. They just fill the room, and then they move on to the next event. I need cruisers, even if I don't like cruisers; they are the Big Mouths that add to the buzz."

"They sound harmless enough." Cassidy shrugged.

"Well, most of them are harmless. They're basically vampires. You're gonna get cornered by a cruiser or two tonight. They'll ask you questions about your process. You won't recognize they're not serious, so you'll talk to them. These assholes get off on talking about art. They'll basically be having multiple orgasms while you discuss your brush technique. Just so we're clear, I prefer the assholes who get off on actually *purchasing* art."

"I'm with you, Erika. Buyers, not cruisers."

"Just know every minute you spend talking to a cruiser is a minute you're not spending talking to a potential patron. Your time and attention are precious. Especially tonight. Sure, you might convert a cruiser to a patron, but that's a long, tough slog. With emerging artists like you, the excitement for the collectors is buying from your first or second show. This gives them bragging rights, because it affirms their taste and eye. Cruisers, however, lack the confidence or the cash to take the plunge. But darling, they want to talk. They'll talk your ear off."

"Oh boy. Don't let me get cornered by a cruiser. Rescue me if you see someone wasting my time." Cassidy's wish was my command.

"Will do. Okay." I was desperate to rescue her from the wine-guzzlers who never buy, and I was ecstatic to have her invitation to intervene. "Another word of warning: someone's going to show up—maybe that guy from studio class, you know that guy . . . he's the one whose work was never great, but who always had cutting things to say under the guise of criticism. Or maybe that jerk you dated as an undergrad who teased you for studying something useless. Well, that guy is going to show up and he's going to diss you. Probably to your face. He'll see you charming critic Jerry Saltz and it'll piss him off. Don't let him phase you. Just know there are people out there who think talent needs to be put in its place. These jerks lack the creativity and the courage to do what you're doing. You are putting yourself and your work out for the world to see, and that, my darling Cassidy, takes guts. These assholes will resent you for having balls bigger than theirs."

"Are you serious?" Cassidy fidgeted on the couch. "Jerry Saltz is coming?"

"He said he is. Be ready. And he won't be the only critic tonight. But be yourself. You've been working on these pieces for years now. You know your paintings and you know what to say about them. Jerry Saltz will be putty in your hands."

"Speaking of putty . . ." Cassidy squirmed in a way that warmed my heart. "I hope this isn't too personal, but I've heard rumors you're a dominatrix. Is that how you put these guys in their place?"

"You've heard rumors?" I laughed, even as I worried my laugh sounded strained. The prospect of this kind of gossip was horrifying as I did my best to preserve my privacy. "That's a myth, but it's a useful myth." I shook my head as I stood up and showed off my leather dress to full effect. "I've cultivated this persona for years and it's intentional. I want the collectors, the clients and the cruisers to be afraid of me. If it's because they're worried I'm going to spank them? What do I care, so long as they do as they're told? I had way too many assholes try to grope me when I was starting out. Never again. Looking stern and demanding works for me, but it's just the persona I cultivate." I leaned in and whispered, "But keep this to yourself. I'd hate for it to get out that I'm all bark and no bite."

"Oh, I understand. It's just between you and me. Frankly, I was hoping the stories were true. The face behind the latex hood is actually yours. I used one of your headshots as inspiration."

"Seriously? That's amazing, I'm flattered you painted me. If you'd told me you wanted me to model for the piece, I'd have come in and put on a hood. Seriously. I've been collaborating with artists since I was a teenager. It's such an intimate act. You really have to put your trust in the artist. Do you remember Piotr Adam's *Cadaver* series?"

"The one that got him in trouble with the police for desecrating human remains? Those paintings were amazing. So vivid and dark. He really captured something profound in them."

"Yeah, that series. But confidentially, the bit about desecrating human remains was bogus. It was something he milked for publicity." Then I paused for dramatic effect. "Next time you're looking at one of those works, look closely. *I* was the cadaver."

"That body was yours? But, like, that body hung from a meat hook. In another, it was sliced open. He did garish things to that body."

"Well, clearly he didn't cut me. The series was my idea. He wanted something Dalí-esque, bold and ghoulish, but with enough Renaissance style to class it up. Et voilà, a woman is decapitated while lying on a bed of lilies. Another woman is disemboweled while petting a greyhound. And so on. That was one crazy week."

"Oh my god. I can't believe that was you."

"I wasn't going to let him do that to some innocent little figure model. I admire the guy, but he'd have fucked that girl up. Just because someone consents to something doesn't mean they understand what they're getting into. After all, there can be a huge asymmetry of power between the artist and the model, which can lead to outright exploitation. As for me, it took a few sessions with my massage therapist and another few with my therapist-therapist before I got back to normal."

"That sounds crazy intense." Cassidy's jaw gaped.

"It was, but it was also a collaboration between us, as equals, and we shared something meaningful. Piotr respected my vision and also my limits. There were some ideas he proposed that I didn't want to be part of."

"Oh my goodness. I can only imagine . . ."

"Yeah, his imagination can be pretty extreme. That said, I thought the finished works highlighted something unsettling about the male gaze, and also, how oil paint can transform depravity into beauty. Pinault agreed and bought a piece for his collection."

"No kidding. Well, now I definitely want you sitting in my studio. Your headshot won't be enough, next time."

"That's perfect. It's a pleasure for me to help my artists in any way I can. And although I normally prefer to keep my participation secret, please share this tidbit with Edouard de Grenet. He's the collector I think will love the work."

"Okay! Whatever you want. I'm beyond excited and so grateful for this opportunity. But clearly, I have a lot to learn."

"Cassidy, your trajectory is going to stun you. I can't wait to see what happens. Of course, you'll have to figure out what works for you, because that glare of attention is going to start in about an hour."

"Oh my god. So soon."

"Yes, so soon. And here's something else they probably didn't teach you at Yale. Some of these guys are going to make a pass at you. You'll get more than the male gaze tonight. Looking at great art releases dopamine, and yours is fantastic, so the room will be *awash* in dopamine. But dopamine is also released during orgasm. We're all just animals at core, and some of the animals in the gallery will act out." Cassidy rolled her eyes. "Thankfully, they're not like dogs, so at least they won't try to hump your leg. Instead, they'll want to put their arm around your waist or try to give you more than just an air kiss. If you're not feeling it, don't let them. If you're feeling it? Do whatever you like. Just know that I'm not one of those dealers who's going to expect you to fawn over potential buyers. Be polite, be enthusiastic, be engaged. But only do what feels comfortable to you. You're allowed to have limits. Exercise them."

"No, they didn't teach that at Yale. I feel like I'm an expert in art theory, but a child when it comes to practice."

"This stuff takes time. You'll learn how to deflect and dodge. But don't forget, we're selling arousal and emotion today. And once these factors are on the table, strange things happen. The fact that you're a beautiful woman only heightens matters because at some level, prospective buyers figure this sexualized subject matter gives them permission to be forward and to fantasize. The men who produce explicit works don't face the same shit we women do. I bet you were warned off fetishism as a subject matter."

"How'd you know? My advisor and my parents all suggested I find something else. I just happen to find these materials gorgeous and misunderstood. The prospect of spending days looking at a canvas covered in flowers? Just shoot me!"

"Understood. We're on the same page. The tame stuff doesn't move me, either. Just know that things can get weird. So, if you get cornered or anything strange happens, catch my eye, and I'll come over. And if you don't see me, look for one of my associates. We all know what to do."

"Will do, Erika. And thanks, again." Cassidy stood up and arranged the dress around her body before raising the zipper an inch.

"You're welcome, now let's go downstairs and sell some fucking paintings." I took Cassidy's hand and led her down to the gallery.

Josh, one of my assistants, handed me the show's catalog with his discreet notations, indicating which works had already been sold and which were being eyed by potential collectors. Cassidy and I toured her works as I applied little red dots next to the four paintings that had already been scooped up. "Four down, only twenty to go!" I tried to convey enthusiasm because I didn't want to deflate Cassidy on the cusp of her art world debut, but I was disappointed. We were exhibiting two dozen paintings of varying sizes, and I had expected to presell seven or eight of them. I'd had shows where I'd presold over half the works, which, for an emerging artist, was extraordinary.

Thanks to my reputation for putting on exciting exhibitions, there were people queued up outside the gallery when the doors opened at seven. They streamed in to see the works, but it felt like most of them were just there to throw back my canapés. I fantasized about the black-clad gallery-goers being little baby birds, mouths agape and squawking, while I threw worms at them, in the form of pigs in a blanket. Each appetizer represented a hit to my bottom line, and a hot dog unavailable to actual patrons. I hated having to feed imbeciles who had no intention of buying, but it was the nature of the business.

Fortunately, about fifteen minutes in, Edouard arrived. He said he'd show, and he did. The guy lived in Switzerland, and he had learned to be punctual from the best. Although he was born in Paris, he embodied the Swiss banker. He was tall and lean. His look oozed precision. His charcoal-gray suit was sharp and perfectly tailored, his white shirt had a spread collar, and his navy tie had a hint of sheen. I grabbed a glass of champagne for him and made my way to his side. "Here, I have something to show you." Edouard followed as I led him to the main room. "Behold." I pointed at *Latex Hood* and saw him inhale sharply.

"*C'est magnifique.*" He stood rooted in place, as he took the face in.

"Yes. Stunning. Cassidy Smith just graduated from Yale, and this is her first gallery show. I wanted you to take in this work in person. The photos don't do it justice."

"No. It's wonderful, the way the latex gleams. And is that a tiny bit of saliva on her front tooth? *Fantastique.*"

"Let me fetch Cassidy, so she can tell you a bit about the work." I waved at Cassidy to come over. "Cassidy, tell Edouard what you told me about your inspiration."

Cassidy giggled in a way that made me melt. "The face behind the mask belongs to Erika. I wanted to capture ferocity from within the hood, and I couldn't think of anyone with more intensity."

"Erika, get out your stickers. I want it, and I want to watch you apply that red dot."

"Deal." I slid my arm into Edouard's, and we walked up to the little card next to *Latex Hood*. He stared at me as I slowly removed the dot from its mount and carefully applied it to the card. I may have flushed.

"Does applying a red dot always have that effect?" Edouard had a slight grin on his face.

"Only when it involves a sale. Applying a dot to my coffee cup isn't going to cut it."

"Oh, I can imagine how it could excite you." Edouard was now smiling broadly. "You've sold the coffee cup as an ode to Duchamp and the readymade, and somebody's about to give you a large check."

"You're absolutely right." I had to laugh. He understood me and my fetish so well. "Now tell me, Edouard, am I going to see more of you on this visit? I have some time on Thursday."

Edouard shook his head. "I'm afraid not. I must return to Geneva, and I'm not sure when I'll be back. The markets are strained, and it's taking everything I've got to keep my world upright."

"I'm sorry to hear that. I was looking forward to testing out some new gear. It's made of latex . . ."

"You're such a tease, and I'm tempted. I'll tell you what, if you ever want a few months in Switzerland, let me know. I have a big house right on the lake, lots of contacts in galleries in Geneva and Zürich. When was the last time you visited a Freeport? It could be fun."

"That sounds great, but all my businesses need care and feeding, too."

"I understand." Edouard gently laid his hand on my bicep and focused on my eyes. He leaned in and spoke softly. "I hate to be the bearer of bad news, but your gallery is going to come to a standstill very soon. And as for your other business? Who knows. We're on the brink of a recession and I'm worried."

"You're not the first person who's told me that, but I don't think a Geneva trip is in the cards even though it's an intriguing offer. To be honest, I'm also a bit worried. My sales have slowed. Emerging artists aren't favored at the moment."

"No, they're speculative. You're selling potential and the likelihood of future returns. The market for these works is Wall Street, right?" I nodded. "They're feeling the same forces I'm feeling in Geneva. The markets are going sideways for now, and then they're probably going down."

"Edouard, you sure know how to burst my bubble."

"No, Erika, I didn't mean it like that. But seriously, if you find you have time on your hands, let me know. My fall is going to be wretched, and I'd love the company. I have a spare wing in the house. It's yours. We can play a couple of times a week. It boosts my mood and my focus; it makes me better at what I do. And when you're done, I'll give you a Hirst to sell."

"Show me the Hirst." Edouard pulled out his iPhone and flipped to a photo of a modestly sized black painting littered with a few iridescent butterflies and other odds and ends. I knew the series even if I didn't know the work, and it screamed "property of a hedge fund asshole," making it easy to flip. "This isn't your style. What happened? Drug bender?"

"Hah! No, I won it from a colleague. We were betting on *le football*." Edouard smirked.

"Football? It figures. Let me think about your offer, darling. I don't see how I can make it work, but you just never know."

"I understand. Well, I hope the show is a huge success. Miss Cassidy is very talented. I also hope she realizes how fortunate she is to be working with the great Erika Grieg, Mistress of Chelsea."

"That's me, and somebody ought to spank you." I gave his ass a playful swat.

"Not somebody. *You*. Come to Geneva. Please. It could be a year before I'm back in Chelsea and that's far too long."

We both sighed. "Darling, you're the best, and thanks. Your friendship means so much." I kissed Edouard good night and returned to the crowd, trying to find a collector with a taste for the outrageous, or even some Wall Streeter with a big checkbook, a large couch and an empty wall.

I made the rounds, we made a few more sales, but it wasn't the blockbuster I'd hoped it would be. Some critics showed up and took notes. Cassidy looked pleased by the attention, and after two hours of intense mingling, the exhibition was over. Josh and I tallied up the sales for the evening. It wasn't hard, there were only three more, including Edouard's. We hadn't even sold half the works, when six months earlier, I would have sold out my entire inventory and gotten to utter my favorite words, "Nothing is available." Edouard was one of the smartest people I knew, and he was worried. Unlike the case with many of my peers, there was no trust fund or rich spouse supporting my gallery. If I wanted to make payroll and Chelsea-overhead, the gallery and I had to produce.

After the cruisers and the collectors had left, and as the caterers were cleaning up the napkins and the wine glasses, we all had a chance to debrief.

"Josh, any fence-sitters likely to buy in the next few weeks? Any way to nudge them?" Josh was my deputy, and he ran the gallery when I was occupied.

"Maybe? I gathered some contact info for follow-up, but they didn't seem serious." Josh ran his finger down his notepad, as if it might suddenly reveal something unexpected or profound.

"What was your take, Cassidy?" I asked. "Anyone say they'd like to follow up with you or visit your studio? Anything like that?"

"No. I got quite a few business cards, but I think they were looking for a date, not a painting." Cassidy reached into the pocket of the Alaïa and pulled out a half dozen business cards, which she fanned between her fingers, like a magician doing close-up work.

"I told you that would happen! The neurochemicals released when people enjoy art are intoxicating, which means I'm also a matchmaker. Gallery shows are great for your sex life." Josh snorted at my comment. "What a pity no one wanted to impress you with their great taste and their fat wallet."

"No. Sadly, there was nothing like that. There was one old guy, though. At first, I thought he was a buyer, so I paid him extra attention. I realized he was a cruiser when he said the strangest thing to me." Cassidy smoothed her long blonde hair with her fingers.

"Oh, don't tease us, what did the guy say?"

"He said I had hair like Grace Kelly. Then he wished me great success."

"Grace Kelly? How wonderful." I tried to keep my tone neutral and not betray my anxiety. The art press had nicknamed me Erika the Great. I was the Mistress of Chelsea. And yet suddenly, I was a gawky preteen again. "What did this man look like? How old do you think he was?"

"He was older. Maybe seventy. Silver hair, but the kind of perfect silver you pay tons to a colorist to get." I nodded. "He didn't linger, though."

"Sounds like no one important." The group all nodded in agreement with me, even though I was lying. "Anything else interesting or strange happen? Any new prospects?"

There was little more to discuss. Cassidy and I climbed the stairs to my apartment, and she stripped out of the Alaïa and into her jeans. "Erika, I'm sorry we didn't sell more. I hope I didn't let you down."

"We didn't do as well as I'd hoped, but you did great. You've been a joy to work with. We'll sell more in the next few weeks, but I've had a few clients warn me the economy is about to turn bad. I'm not ready for this, darling, but I hope you are."

"Erika, don't worry. Truly, how bad can it get?" Cassidy buttoned up her shirt and gave me a hug. She must have realized I needed reassurance.

"You're right, Cassidy, how bad can it get?" I didn't want to transmit my fears to her, but my estranged, criminal father had shown up at my show, cornered my artist and mentioned Grace Kelly. I'm not superstitious, but that was a portent. Things could get really fucking bad.

2

NEED TO KNOW

October 1995

I had lied to Cassidy about not being a dominatrix, but that information was something I shared only on a need-to-know basis. And unless you're Damien-Fucking-Hirst, you don't need to know.

Being a dominatrix was my big secret, although it felt like word of my deviant interests was starting to seep out. So far, it was only at the level of rumor and innuendo, which I did my best to squelch. What gentleman wants to be seen going into an art gallery and have his motives questioned? My basement dungeon was my private sanctum, and I shared it only with a select few.

When I think back to what I was like when first starting out in the business, I can't help but shudder. I was reckless and unskilled, but what choice did I have? It was the nineties, and I was in college. It's not like Harvard had classes in how to give a spanking or how to tie up a cock, so I splurged on a couple of books. There was a sleazy store in Central Square with bongs up front, latex dresses in the back, and one rack featuring a jumble of erotica and how-to-kink books and another rack crammed with porno magazines. I'd read *Story of O* in high school, but in college, while my classmates read Howard Zinn or Michel Foucault, I devoured *SM 101*. That store is also where I found out about the local BDSM scene.

There was a rundown nightclub not far from the Harvard campus and on Fridays they hosted Fetish Nights. I remember the first time I went to Club MantaRay. I scrounged together the entry fee from my earnings working in Harvard's dining services, used my tried-and-true fake ID, made my hair Medusa-like, with black tendrils swirling out and around my face. My short black dress was paired with fishnet hose and black sneakers. My wardrobe was ready for a funeral or a meeting of a coven, it was so full of black, but it served me well. I batted my heavily made-up eyelids at the pierced guy at the door, showed him the borrowed ID, and once I'd paid ten bucks, I joined the throng inside.

The music was loud and techno, there were strobe lights pulsing, and there was even a little stage where a bored woman wearing a red leather catsuit flogged a man wearing little more than a pair of combat boots and a black leather jockstrap. I'd been to Club Fuck! back home in LA, so none of this fazed me, and I certainly wasn't impressed, but it was the best Boston had to offer. A sweaty guy with a buzz cut and wearing a chest harness sauntered over to my side. "Mistress, may I rub your feet?"

I looked at him, realized I didn't want him touching my toes, but it occurred to me he might be useful in a different way. "No, but you can buy me a drink. Get me a rum and Coke."

"Yes, mistress." He scurried over to the bar, as I continued to explore. Another man announced he was a human carpet and invited me to walk on him. "Seriously?" He nodded, so I pointed to the ground, picking a spot where someone had sloshed their drink, just to see if he'd avoid the puddle. He lay down in the middle of it. I crouched a bit, pretending like I was going to jump on him. He flinched but lay still. I decided to be careful, because I had no idea how much his body could take. I placed my right foot on the fleshy top of his thigh. He lifted up his arms, inviting me to grab his hands for balance. His fingers were warm and soft—a poet's hands, not a plumber's. With practiced efficiency, he helped me up as I put my left foot on his other thigh. Once installed, I stood there, looking down at his face and then out at the room. I'm five ten in my bare feet. Atop his thick body, I loomed over most of the crowd.

A small group had gathered around us, and I began to inch my feet forward, so that I was standing on his stomach. A few more steps, and I was atop his chest. "Give me your hand again." He balanced me, and this time, I put my sneaker to the side of his face and with my toe, I pushed down on his cheek, nudging it so that he was looking at the back wall instead of up at the ceiling. His body was steady, as was his breathing. He moaned softly as I shifted my weight.

Feeling emboldened and figuring someone would say something if I were about to kill him, I put some weight on my foot, so that he would feel his head crushed against the floor. I bent my elbows and put my hands on my waist, as if I'd just reached the peak of the Matterhorn. I was practically daring the carpet to move or say something, but he remained still, his right cheek stuck to the floor by a mix of Budweiser and sweat, while his cock pushed against his black jeans, erect from the public exposure.

After a few moments, enjoying the gaze of the crowd, I jumped off the carpet, never looking back at him. Another shirtless middle-aged guy in dark jeans handed me a deerskin whip and asked me to hit him. I had no idea what I was doing, but I knew what I wanted to do, which was to savage him. His slicked back dark hair pissed me off. If not for his bare chest, he looked like he could have been the father of one of my friends from middle school, or maybe even my own dad, before he went to prison.

With all the strength I could muster, I hit him repeatedly with the flogger. I was putting everything I had into it, and I was strong from hauling trays filled with dishes, but nothing was happening. Each blow elicited a thump-like noise from his back and a sigh from his mouth. I wanted to hear wails. I was desperate to hear cries, but there were only contented moans. I upped the intensity, striking his upper back, ass and thighs repeatedly. A different crowd formed, but they were invisible to me. My cheeks burned from the humiliation—I was trying to hurt this man, to make him suffer, and all I was doing was arousing him. I gave him a few more strokes, as hard as I could, and then I hid in the bathroom to calm myself down.

I hadn't expected to feel so full of hatred again. It had been two years since I first left LA, when I last felt an anger that extended from my stomach to my fingertips and that burned through my lungs. I'd gotten into Harvard, my dream school. I was getting good grades. I even had a few friends. But the darkness and the venom had returned, almost as if it had never left. It took a few splashes of cold water out of the tap in the dingy bathroom before I felt ready to return to the club floor. I should have stayed in there longer, because the nameless, faceless guy I had tried to beat was waiting for me.

"Hey, honey, you did a great job with that flogger." I looked at him more closely—he had a bit of silver stubble on his face, and short dark hair.

I snorted. "No, I didn't. You hardly felt it. I wanted it to hurt."

"You're new, aren't you? The whip is made of deerskin, it's never going to hurt! See?" He motioned toward an empty couch, so I sat down beside him. He put his hand on my knee, and I moved it back into his lap. As a peace offering, he handed me the whip and gave me a quick lesson on the physics of floggers. "Feel this." He held up the tails of the whip and ran a few of the burgundy leather strands across the skin of my forearm. They were soft and thin. I had been so full of rage, I hadn't even noticed.

"What does it take to hurt you?"

"A single-tail does the trick, or maybe a cat-o'-nine-tails, but these soft floggers feel like a relaxing massage." He turned his body toward mine and grabbed my hand. "It's actually really rare to find a woman who can hit hard enough. Sometimes, I'll have men flog me. I like to be hit with some oomph."

I extracted my hand from the whip, irritated by how forward this guy, who was old enough to be my father, was being. "What's the point of being hit by an instrument that hardly leaves a mark and that you can barely feel?"

"It relaxes me. And what's wrong with that?" I shrugged and moved on. I wanted to hurt somebody.

"Excuse me, miss, I've been looking for you all over the place. Here's your rum and Coke." It took me a moment to remember that this was my wannabe foot slave. "Is there anything I can do for you?"

"I want to make someone suffer. Like, really suffer." I was staggered at how the words came out of my mouth, but it was the truth. My anger at the world had been simmering for years, and it was coming to the surface at that shitty bar in Cambridge. I was studying art history and every day it felt like I was sitting in a class being compelled to study some gorgeous depiction of rape or violence against women. Renaissance art was filled with gory shows of misogyny. Oil paint has a way of making the most vile topics seem enticing and important. I had grown tired of my delicate feminine martyrs. It was time for the ladies to strike back. "If you can find something for me to hit you with, I'll let you suck my toes, afterward."

He handed me my drink and then scurried off. It felt odd to be so close to school, and so removed from all my classmates. I didn't care if any of them saw me thrashing some willing victim, but it never occurred to me that anyone I knew would come to a place this decrepit.

MantaRay felt like an absurdity. Its slogans were "Our tails sting" and "Surrender to the sting," despite the fact that manta rays are gentle filter feeders with wimpy tails. But MantaRay, with its moody lighting and dark corners, was the closest thing Cambridge had to a fetish club. Most nights, it was a gay club. I imagined hot, hard bodies grinding up against one another, but on Fetish Nights, it was a motley crowd, whose flab bulged out of their fetishwear encasements. Half the place looked like refugees from a Dungeon and Dragons convention, while the other seemed like they'd stopped by after a PTA meeting. Where were my fellow weirdos? Where were the goths and the punks I'd danced with at the Viper Room or blown in the bathroom of the Burgundy? I struggled to find anyone enticing in the crowd—male or female.

My prospective victim returned in the company of a petite, short-haired brunette. "This is my friend Snapdragon." Her name might have been ridiculous, but she was boyish and cute. She wore a white tank top so tight across her chest that her breasts were contoured, and her nipples pointed through. She wore combat pants and high-top sneakers. Her eyebrow was pierced, and I later learned that her nipples were as well.

What I had assumed was a prop, the black hooked cane that she'd been using as she walked, was actually an implement. "Loki says you want him to suffer." He called himself Loki? I struggled not to laugh. He was no Norse god. "What's your name?"

"I'm Erika, and yeah, I want to inflict some misery. Can I borrow your cane?"

"Sure, but we can't do this here, or we'll get thrown out. There's a back room for shit like this." Snapdragon took me by the hand and led me to a door I hadn't noticed while Loki followed behind us, not wanting to miss his opportunity with two women. Snapdragon pushed the door open and we entered a small, weird space. The walls were painted purple and there were hefty benches, large wooden crosses and people engaging in hardcore activities, instead of the tame stuff I'd been seeing on the main floor. There was a backdrop of grunting and whacking.

Snapdragon motioned to Loki, who promptly bent over a black leather-padded bench. She handed me her cane. I landed a couple of blows over Loki's jeans. "Drop your pants, Loki." Loki lowered his jeans to midthigh, revealing a pair of gray jockey shorts. With the tip of the cane, I nudged his pants lower, and then I stepped back and began tapping his ass with the tip of the cane while I got a feel for things. There was a bald man using a paddle with holes in it, on the ass of a woman whose kilt was pulled up to reveal a round, pink bottom. I felt sorry for her, as she tried to keep her balance in black high-heeled shoes. He aimed for a range from the middle of her cheeks to the tops of her thighs, so I followed suit with Snapdragon's cane.

Each blow elicited a yelp from Loki. I thrilled as the stripes became apparent and the welts started to form. They were an invitation to hit harder and faster, so I did. For a beginner, my aim was decent. All those years of Beverly Hills tennis lessons were paying off. I left parallel marks over his thighs and ass. I began to hit in tune to the music. It was something moody and alien, all synthesizer and hypnotic beats. It was a blur, as I began to strike him, timed to this crazy electronica. I was barely noticing his ass or his howls, until Snapdragon stopped me because I was on the verge of drawing blood.

She held my arm back, as I was winding up for another strike of the cane. It was noisy in the room, so she pointed at Loki's oozing bottom. In the dim light, preoccupied by rage and adrenaline, I hadn't noticed he was getting fucked up. Or rather, that I was fucking him up. Snapdragon gave me a sour look and snatched the cane from my hand. Loki, however, was floating. He winced as he pulled up his pants over his battered skin, and then he dropped to his knees in front of me. He sobbed as he kissed my feet.

I was standing there awkwardly, when I spotted a place to sit. "I said you could suck my toes if you took a beating. I'm a woman of my word. Crawl to me." I sat down and began to untie my sneakers.

Loki scurried to me on his hands and knees, and before I could remove my left shoe, he said, "No, allow me." He opened up my sneaker with delicacy and reverence, and he buried his nose in the sweaty canvas, still adhered to my foot. I could feel his tongue, probing and licking my skin through the fishnet hose. He slid the shoe off, and then proceeded to take my toes, down to the ball of my foot, into his mouth as if he were a porn star, deep-throating cock.

Snapdragon sat down beside me. She seemed far more interesting than Loki, and far more appealing, too. I slid my arm over her shoulder and moved her body closer to mine. The irritation she'd transmitted only moments earlier had disappeared, and she snuggled into the side of my body. I whispered to her, "Take off your boot. Let's give Loki something to think about."

She gave me a sly smile, as she liberated her foot from her Doc Martens. Snapdragon wore a white sport sock, stained from boot leather and sweat. Loki caught sight of what was happening, and he began to caress her foot with his hands at the same time as he slobbered over mine with his tongue.

While Loki kept busy with our feet, I got curious about Snapdragon, who was now nestled close. "So, what's your thing? What brings you here?"

"I'm a switch. I like to play." Snapdragon was now looking up at me, her eyes glistening in the dim light. "Sometimes I'm a top, and sometimes I'm a sub. Usually, I sub to women." She batted her eyelashes at me.

"Oh, is that so? Then kiss me." I didn't move. I wanted to see what would happen. Snapdragon pulled her foot away from Loki, and then she sat astride my lap. Loki had paused to check things out, so I wiggled my toes at him. "Get back to work."

Snapdragon was slim and petite, I hardly felt her weight on my thighs. She gave the side of my cheek a gentle peck, with a pair of very soft lips. I turned my head, so that she could kiss the other cheek, which she did. I flashed back to Culver City, and my only friend in high school, Megan, and how we messed around together. That delight in soft, smooth skin came back to me, and I wanted more.

Snapdragon's lips hovered by mine, and all it took was a gentle push from my hand to the back of her head and our lips made contact. She wasn't the first girl I'd kissed, but she was the first girl I'd kissed since arriving in Cambridge.

We began necking like teenagers in the back of a car, groping one another, lips moving along skin, tongues caressing ears, fingers sliding under shirts and bras. This is how I discovered her nipple piercing. Before things could progress, however, Loki released my foot and cleared his throat. Snapdragon and I disentangled, and we both looked down at the floor.

"Are you okay?" I asked.

"Oh, don't let me interrupt." Loki had a dreamy look on his face. His cheeks were flushed and his eyelids drooped with contentment. "I'm still floating on dopamine and endorphins. No one has ever done that to me before. Feel free to ignore me. I'll just sit here and watch."

The moment had passed. I didn't want to give Loki, or anyone else in the room, a show, so I helped Snapdragon off my lap and stood up. "I have to go home and study. Are you guys gonna be around the next Fetish Night?"

They both nodded, and Loki offered to walk us to the T station in Central Square. The neighborhood around the club was dodgy late at night, so I accepted. The three of us wound up walking arm in arm out to Mass Ave. I left them once I got to the station.

Snapdragon had mentioned she was a grad student at Boston University, and Loki worked in IT, but I wasn't ready to reveal that

I was just a junior, and I really didn't want to drop the "H bomb," which is what we called a casual reference to Harvard. Mentioning Harvard had a tendency to stop conversations and prompt assumptions, and I really didn't want to do that with the pervs. I was already using a last name other than the one I was born with; I didn't want to pick a different first name for MantaRay. As for candor? That's only for people without secrets.

3

THE MARGIN CALL

April 1988

I still have nightmares about the morning the FBI came to the house. At the time, my family was living in Brentwood in a sprawling mid-century modern house. I was eating breakfast in the kitchen— Lucky Charms, drowned in milk. My mother hated the stuff, but my dad shared my taste for cereals laced with candy, so there was always plenty in the cupboard.

Even now, whenever I eat Lucky Charms, I do this thing where I sort out the marshmallows with my spoon and push them all to one side of the bowl. There was a loud knock at the front door just as I was finishing off the bland oat morsels and getting ready to reward myself with the tiny colorful marshmallows.

My father, already wearing his navy suit and obligatory red tie, told my mother to answer the door and to tell whoever it was he wasn't there. He hustled to the master bedroom as my mother, still wearing a pink floral housecoat, walked slowly to the front door.

There were two men at the door, one with black hair, one with red, but they were both wearing sunglasses and dark suits. I heard my father's name, and then some more murmurs, as the two men came inside the house. My mother was getting exasperated. "There's been some kind of mistake. Go to Jacob's office, and he'll straighten things out for you. *There*."

"If it's okay with you, Mrs. Warnock, we'd like to wait for him. *Here*. We have a warrant."

"It's not okay with me. You should really go to his office. I don't know anything about his work. I have to take my daughter to school."

The red-headed agent came into the kitchen, where he saw me eating breakfast. He sat down opposite me, while I did my best to ignore him. "Hey, we're looking for your dad. Do you know where he is?"

I stared into my bowl, as if it held the answers to some great mystery. I was thirteen, teetering on the brink of puberty and feeling captive to hormones and parents. I'd seen enough television to know that no sensible person should cooperate with the cops when they invade your house. "No."

My mother tried to get them back outside, but she was ineffectual. Both agents sat down at the table. I looked at the clock, and an idea occurred to me. "Mom, I'm gonna be late for school."

The black-haired agent introduced himself. "Hi. You must be Erika. I'm Special Agent Peterson. You're probably gonna be late for school today. We're hoping your dad can help us with an investigation. Do you know where he is? His car's here. Did he go for a walk?"

I had a math test that morning, so I looked at my mother, and then reflexively, I looked toward the master bedroom where my father had gone. Realizing my glance might help the FBI, my Lucky Charms got my full attention. Unfortunately, the agents had recognized the significance of what I'd done. They then gestured to my mother, and the three adults spoke in hushed tones. My mother nodded and pointed back toward the master bedroom.

The agents weren't gone for very long, but when they returned, my father was in handcuffs being led out to their oversized black Buick. As Dad was being put in the back seat, he yelled out to my mom, "Call my lawyer, Mike Mitchell. Tell him what happened."

Sylvie Shapiro, my friend Karen's mom, was out on the street walking Luna, the family poodle. Both Luna and Mrs. Shapiro stood glued to the road as they took in the spectacle of my father's arrest. I was both horrified and terrified. Things had been weird at home for the past few months, but how was I supposed to know just how bad they'd become? I was a kid. They didn't tell me anything.

For instance, they didn't tell me that Dad needed money fast. I had to figure that out for myself in the fall. I got home from Westlake one afternoon and discovered half the paintings on our walls had been removed. "Mom, were we robbed? Where'd the art go?" I looked around more closely. A small metal mobile, which normally bobbed and swayed on its base in the corner of our living room, was also missing. "Where'd the Calder go?" When I was seven, I'd helped them pick it out.

Mom's face was blotchy. I could tell she'd been crying, so I started to cry too. "Your dad got a margin call yesterday, and so we're selling some of the pieces."

"Who's Margin? Why's he calling Daddy?"

"A margin's not a person, it's a thing. Our investments went down in price. You read about Black Monday, right?"

"I guess." I read the *Los Angeles Times*, but not the boring business section. "What's that got to do with us?"

"Well, a margin call is what happens if you borrow money to buy stocks, and the stocks go down in value. The bank can make you pay so they don't lose money. Or they can make you sell the stocks."

"Oh. Why are we borrowing money to buy stocks?" We lived in a big house in Brentwood. My dad drove a Porsche and Mom, a Mercedes. I attended the Westlake School for Girls, with all the other daughters of families like mine. We had art on the walls. Hell, I even had art in my bedroom. I knew people borrowed money to buy houses or cars, but stocks, too? My dad was a CPA, and so I felt like I understood financial planning better than most kids. Clearly, I had much to learn.

"It's common, honey. And Dad did it. He had a lot of confidence in his stock picks. He never anticipated that the whole market would crash." Mom sounded like she was parroting something Dad had said to her. I couldn't help but look around at the gaps on our walls, where the paintings and prints we owned were nowhere to be seen.

I ran to my bedroom, to see if my babies were still there. My prized possession was a collage by Picasso, featuring nine identical babies in different positions. I loved staring at it as I lay in bed. It was a sweet work, featuring a beige top layer of paper, torn in such a way that the holes revealed adorable line drawings of fat little babies. Their arms and legs were askew, as if they were dancing.

My parents had taken me with them when they went shopping in Beverly Hills one day. We'd stopped at one of those glitzy galleries that sells overpriced works in the secondary market. Basically, it was a painting store offering only name-brand artists and designed to separate rich people from their money. It's the kind of place I'd avoid now, because I have standards. When I was nine, however, as soon as I saw those dancing babies, I planted my feet on the floor and pointed at the work. Where other kids wanted a puppy, I wanted a Picasso. At the time, I had no idea it was an unimportant work, but I craved it all the same. "Can we get this for my room? I'll take good care of it. I promise."

"You've got great taste. I bet Princess Grace had a Picasso in her bedroom." My father was obsessed with Grace Kelly, but I beamed anyway. It was affirming, to have such a grown-up assessment of my artistic sense. My mother never treated me that way, and my father never said anything like that about her, either. Dad looked at the card by the work and nodded approvingly. "Let me see what I can do for you, princess." Dad went off to talk to the saleswoman while I stared at the babies, transfixed by the simple work. I wanted to climb inside the collage and play with the infants. I wanted to enter their simple, paper world and join those jolly, bouncy babies where life was stress free, and absent the angst of girlhood.

My babies were still on the wall beside my bed, but I became paranoid. I took to hiding the Picasso around the house. For weeks, I'd sneak to wherever I had last left the collage—say, the back of the broom closet, or behind some boxes in the garage, and I'd check on it, and then move it to a new hiding spot. Things were disappearing from the house. My mom's mink coat evaporated. The Porsche went to the shop and never returned. And each day, I'd stash my babies somewhere else in the house before I left for school, and then I'd check on them when I got back.

Where school had once been my favorite place, after my father's arrest and the news coverage where he was accused of stealing client funds, I was no longer the Queen of the Blondes, my nickname from my little gang of girls. In a city where beauty was prized, and blonde hair was especially valued, I had both, and I reveled in the status that came with it. I had been the alpha of the playground, and at the top of the list for every birthday party and playdate. My mother was basically my social secretary, organizing whose house I would go to on a Saturday night for a sleepover, when there were two competing offers.

I wasn't a bully, exactly, but I liked to get my way. And if a girl— or a boy—didn't give me what I wanted, I was known to shun them from the group. They'd feel my wrath in the form of exclusion and quiet, giggly gossip they were sure was about them, but that they could never quite pin down. Girls can be rotten, and I was a fucking princess. Somehow, I'd figured out the key to popularity was indifference. My peers wanted my company more than I wanted theirs, and that had put me on top.

When I was in second and third grade, I had a habit of tying up my foes with my jump rope. I'd make a game of it, until it was too late and they were stuck. I didn't tie them so tight that their lives were in jeopardy, obviously, but tight enough that they couldn't get out. Even then, I knew my knots. I'd be lying if I said I didn't take pleasure in the fact that the odd one wound up sobbing, pleading for mercy. What's great about eight-year-olds is how they can toggle between desperation and delight in mere moments, and as quickly as my victims were brought to tears, I could untie the knots and offer solace. Despite feeling like a powerless child, I had the capacity to make an ache appear, and then to make it go away. The jump rope would then be used as designed, and we'd go off skipping to our next adventure.

The day after my father's arrest, however, the ground shifted at school. I became a pariah. Word had gotten around, and kids can be mean. And maybe I felt like I deserved what was coming to me after years of practiced indifference toward my classmates. Being a girl is about constantly wondering about your place in the world, and I had overstepped.

What I didn't realize at the time was that my father had stolen money from all the wrong people. When you grow up in the rarefied, Bel Air adjacent neighborhood of Brentwood, the local currency is celebrity or proximity to celebrity. My father's accounting firm had all the right clients—studio heads, Oscar-winning actors, actresses and directors. They were mostly creative people who lacked the acumen or the patience to manage their own money, and my dad's firm did as much as they required, from overseeing their portfolios and recommending investments, to paying the nannies.

We were part of a fancy ecosystem, and I reaped the rewards. Everyone knew my dad, because his firm did their taxes.

When Black Monday occurred in 1987, and the markets tanked by 40 percent in two days, he wasn't able to continue with his usual stunts. Between the margin calls on multiple accounts, and the panicked calls from unlucky clients who noticed they were missing money, he could no longer hide how he had been funding our lifestyle. Dad claimed it was all a misunderstanding, that the transfers from client accounts to his personal accounts were lapses in controls, not evidence of theft. The simultaneous margin calls had resulted in confusion. He promised he would make good on any missing funds. He was innocent.

When I look back at that time period now, I can see the warning signs, flashing bright red. I was twelve when the mayhem began, and I had no idea what was going down, I just knew my father was acting strangely.

That fall, I had started at a new school, Westlake, a tony private school filled with the bright daughters of the Los Angeles elite. Dad started pressuring me to make the right friends.

"Princess, Jemima Stein's in your class, right?"

"Yes, Daddy. Why do you ask?"

"I'd like to get to know her family better. Can you get her to invite you over to dinner?"

"I dunno. Maybe?" So, I went to school and cozied up to Jemima, whose father ran one of the studios. I still had the aura of being a queen bee about me, and within a week, I was her new best friend and she invited me over for a sleepover. I liked to show off, and a sleepover was far better than a mere dinner. My dad seemed impressed.

It was an amazing Saturday night. There were three of us from school, and one huge house. There were at least two pillow fights and we each made up the other while sitting in Jemima's extravagant bedroom. She had a massive collection of makeup, and we must have tried it all. The Stein's cook made us paninis to order— and fresh caramel popcorn, which we devoured while watching an early version of *Three Men and a Baby*."

That Sunday morning, I was surprised when my dad drove over to the Stein's home in Bel Air to pick me up. Mom usually took care of such chores. He arrived a little early, so I hadn't packed up all my clothes and books yet. Mr. Stein appeared, and I overheard the two men talking.

"Who manages your money?" asked my dad.

"Price Waterhouse. I work with Benny Goldsmith in their private client group," replied Mr. Stein.

"Yeah, Benny's good. But those big accounting firms, they're not great for individual clients."

"He's been my guy for a decade."

"I get it. But most of my clients are refugees from big firms like Price. They like the focus and attention we bring to their family and their unique financial issues."

"Yeah, I suppose. But I'm happy with Benny."

"Well, if anything changes, let me know. Here's my card and one of my brochures." I watched my dad give Mr. Stein his business card and a pamphlet on tax avoidance he'd written, which featured a picture of Dad shaking hands with President Reagan. This was something Dad had clearly prepared for, and he had used me to cozy up to the Steins. When we got into the car, I was seething.

"Daddy, why'd you do that?" I asked.

"Do what?"

"You know what." I took out my anger on the controls of the seat. "You asked Mr. Stein to be your client."

"Yeah. So what? That's what grown-ups do, princess. He understands it's business."

"Daddy, it's gross. Jemima's gonna find out and it'll be weird. Don't do it again, please."

"Mr. Stein gets this sort of thing all the time. Don't think twice about it, princess." But I did. I thought about it a lot. I went to a different classmate's house in Beverly Hills for a sleepover, and the same thing happened when my dad appeared to pick me up. He hit that father up for accounting work. Again, I was mortified.

There were other changes I noticed but didn't understand. His behavior became wilder. Instead of having the guys over for poker once a month, he was hosting a poker game every Thursday night. He'd call me over to the card table and introduce me to these new buddies. He loved calling me his "Little Princess Grace" and when you're nine, that sounds wonderful. I loved princesses, although I preferred queens. But when you're twelve? The effect was different. I hated having to show up for the old men who stank up our living room with their cigars.

He'd ask me to bring snacks to the table, which I did, and then he'd preen over me to his pals. "This gal's gonna be a heartbreaker, fellas. Check out this blonde hair—she's like Grace Kelly. And look at her eyes—they're blue like the water around Capri." I had started having a growth spurt, so I was all spindly legs and arms. I felt awkward and absurd being shown to these guys like some prized filly. I hated having their eyes on me, as they sized me up and imagined me a few years older.

Dad got noisier and he spoke faster. The phone conversations in his home office became audible and angry, where the house used to be quiet. I remember, just before Christmas, hearing him scream into the phone: "Tell the fucking Andersons they're not liquid right now! They got creamed on Black Monday because they picked the wrong stocks and I had to clean up their fucking mess." Or maybe it was the Rosens, or perhaps the Cellinis. There were so many similar conversations, with the phone being slammed into the receiver, that I was sure his desk would collapse.

And then there were the late nights, where I'd hear him pacing in the living room. Mom would have extra glasses of wine with dinner, so she'd be passed out early, but Dad would roam. I got up a few times to see what he was doing. Once I found him with an enormous teak salad bowl filled with Lucky Charms, that he was shoveling back without pausing between mouthfuls.

"Hey, want some?" He waved the box at me as he summoned me into the kitchen.

I took the box from him, realized it was empty and shrugged. "No, I'm not hungry."

"Princess"—he swallowed another large spoonful of cereal—"we're not gonna go to Hawaii this Christmas. Things are too crazy at work. Is that okay?"

"Of course. Can we go see Granny and Grandpa in Oxnard, instead?"

"No. Why would you want to spend time in that dump? We're just gonna stay home. Take it easy. Maybe enjoy a simple holiday where we can hang out, just us three. You'd like that, right? Something simple? Back to basics. That'd be nice, right, princess?"

"Sure, Daddy. But Jemima's going skiing in Utah. Maybe we can do that this year, instead?"

"Hotels are booked up months in advance, princess. There's no point to it. We're just gonna stay put and save some money."

I was too young to understand that the point wasn't simplicity or nurturing closeness; it was saving money. Years later, I took an introductory psych class. We learned the symptoms of mania, and I recognized them immediately. At the time, I understood things were off, but all I knew to do was protect my babies. Every day I stashed the Picasso somewhere else. It was the one thing I controlled, and I wasn't going to let it get disappeared, along with the rest of our belongings. Boy, was I naive.

4

PAWN SHOPPED PICASSO

March 1988

It was some time after our quiet Christmas at home, with only a paltry exchange of gifts, and before my dad's arrest. We were down to little more than our beds, a table and chairs in the kitchen, a couch and our television set. Basically, we were left only with the essentials. Unfortunately, my parents had both liked to be surrounded by antiques and valuables, and those antiques and valuables were all awaiting buyers at consignment stores throughout Los Angeles. From the street, we looked fine. From inside, we looked ravaged.

One Thursday, I was delayed because I wanted to ask Mrs. Kelly some questions about my English homework. When I got home, I went straight to the pantry to check on my Picasso babies. They weren't there. I looked under my bed. They weren't there, either. I checked all the places where I usually hid the collage—behind some boxes in the garage, beneath a blanket in my closet, behind a bookshelf in the spare bedroom. It was nowhere. I was working myself up, even as I wondered if I had forgotten some new hiding spot.

I raced around the house, looking under and behind things. My mother was in the kitchen, sitting at the table, smoking a cigarette. "Your dad took it," she said flatly.

I wasn't quite ready to admit my scheme. "Took what?" I asked with as much innocence and calm as I could muster, even though I knew exactly what she was talking about.

"The Picasso. We knew what you were doing, and I kept your dad from taking it for as long as I could, but he said he really needed the money."

"Why didn't you stop him?" I stared at her, my eyes filled with tears.

"Do you think I like living like this?" She took a long drag on the cigarette. It had been years since I'd seen her with a pack of Virginia Slims in her hand. She was still wearing her bathrobe, with its delicate pink roses embroidered on the lapels. She hadn't bothered to put on clothes, and it was almost time for dinner.

"I hate it. I want my babies."

"Well, they're gone." Mom looked at me, and then stared at the cigarette as she flicked some ash into a coffee cup. Her voice didn't waver. "Your father says once he gets the mess at work cleaned up, we'll get my jewelry and your painting back." I hadn't realized Mom's expensive baubles had gone missing as well. I looked at her elegant hands, and her engagement ring, with its substantial solitaire, was missing.

"Where'd your ring go?"

"It's all at some pawn shop in Beverly Hills. Frankly, I'd like the nice couch back, too, but I think it's been sold already. It was a Nakashima I ordered straight from the guy's workshop in Bucks County."

"I don't care about the couch. I care about my painting." I was getting worked up, and her flat affect only heightened my emotions.

I ran to my room and slammed the door as hard as I could; not once, but twice. I collapsed into my bed and bawled. My world was being destroyed, bit by bit. Along with my innocence, things I loved were being stolen from me. I wanted to blow up the house. I fantasized about running away. I imagined sneaking onto a train and watching Los Angeles grow smaller and smaller as we chugged down the tracks. Only I had just turned thirteen and had no way of escaping. I was stuck. My rage and I had nowhere to go.

Dad didn't come home for dinner that night, so Mom brought two grilled cheese sandwiches to my room, and we ate them on top of my purple bedspread. "I'm sorry, honey, but I don't think things are gonna get better for a while. Your dad says he'll have it straightened out in a few weeks . . . but he's been saying that since October."

"What about school?"

"We paid most of the tuition in September, so you're set for this year. But it's going to be public school next year if your dad doesn't come through."

I sat, stunned, on my bed, as I nibbled away at the gooey center of the sandwich. I always left the crusts until the end. "But the public schools suck. I've heard you say so."

"Many of them suck, but we'll find one that doesn't. Westlake is expensive, and we just don't have the cash."

"Mom, how can you do this to me? All my friends are at Westlake."

"Look around, Erika, there's nothing left for us to sell."

I didn't know I was about to become a pariah, but I knew my status had shifted. Girls have antennae that pick up on slight shifts in the social hierarchy, and I was trending downward. It brought me relief, the prospect of leaving Westlake. The girls at the bottom of the pecking order suffered, and I preferred to induce misery, rather than take it. As an angry thirteen-year-old, I wasn't going to let my mom off easily, so I lied. "But I love Westlake. My teachers are great. I won't get into a good college if I go to some shitty public school."

"Don't use that language, Erika. It makes you sound cheap, and it makes it seem like your parents don't care."

"All you care about is what people will think. What about what I think?"

"I'm doing my best." She looked depleted. Instead of her trademark radiant skin, buffed and polished every week by some Romanian facialist in Beverly Hills, there were wrinkles and even the odd blackhead. "Besides, you'll be fine. Not everyone goes to Dartmouth or Yale. I didn't go to some Ivy League school."

"I know. You went to UC Santa Barbara and majored in surfing." I'd seen the photos of my mother balanced on a surfboard, her long blonde hair streaming behind her, mangled by the wind and the water into elegant tendrils. She'd been a fearless pioneer in a hot-pink bikini, at a time when there were few women vying for the big waves off Silver Strand Beach.

"No, I *majored* in communications. I *minored* in surfing." My mother smiled at me and stroked my hair. We finished our sandwiches in silence. As she got up to leave my room, she said, "We'll get through this, sweetie, but it's gonna take some sacrifices from all of us. Your dad's working hard to fix things."

I wanted to believe her, but later that night after my dad got home, I could hear their voices, loud and tense. The conversation ended with my dad screaming, "Woman, I didn't marry you for your brains. Cut it out with the advice. I'm doing everything I can, but Black Monday hurt the firm. Half my clients are gone, and the other half are threatening to sue. I'm fixing things, but it's fucking hard. All I want is a little support and understanding at home. What do I get? Fuck all. You do your job and I'll do mine." I turned out the light in my room and lay still on my bed. I wanted support and understanding, too. Instead, I got robbed.

5

TRASH TALKING KLIMT

Spring 1992

"Would you like me to put your mail on the table, Mr. Kovac?" The postal carrier had shoved a stack of letters into the mail slot, and they had scattered across the cement floor of the garage turned art studio. Mr. Kovac lived three doors down from my mom and me.

Not long after Dad was arrested, my mother borrowed some cash from her parents, who didn't have much themselves, and rented a tiny two-bedroom bungalow on the LAX side of Culver City. Because my father had hidden in a closet when the FBI came to arrest him, he'd been deemed a flight risk. He'd gone straight to jail, and he would not be released until the end of his seven-year sentence. Judge Michener had found him guilty of one count of money laundering, one count of wire fraud and one count of plain vanilla fraud.

It could have been worse, I suppose, but the interviews in *People* magazine and in the *Los Angeles Times* of his celebrity clients who'd lost millions to him were horrifying. Oscar-winning actresses are trained in eliciting sympathy. But if you rob a ninety-nine-year-old widow? People hate you. And my father had pulled millions from her trusts. If only she'd died at ninety-eight, his problems would have been solved and I could have stayed at Westlake, ignorant and popular. He must have planned to raid the estate upon her death, because her only heirs were a bunch of animal rights organizations, and what were they going to do? Sue the old woman's accountant if the bequest wasn't as big as they were expecting?

Of course, studio executives, actresses and widows weren't his only victims. My mom and I were as well. I got taunted at Westlake, especially since the parents of two of my classmates had been fleeced. My mother struggled to find work. She even took to using her maiden name, Grieg. The biggest blow to both of us was the realization that someone we loved and trusted had lied to our faces every day, and we had never even realized it.

Mr. Kovac barely looked up from the canvas as he waved me toward the back of his studio. I made a tidy pile with the various unopened envelopes, sorting them into stacks of letters that looked serious, like bills, and letters that looked casual. Anything with a handwritten address went into the second pile.

I'd only been working for the guy for a month, but I needed the money. Fortunately, the tasks weren't difficult. I swept the floors and tidied the studio, and most important of all, I cleaned the brushes. I've always been precise about my work, so I took great care in getting all the little bristles straight and correct.

Some brushes I only had to wipe off and then dip in poppy seed oil to prepare them for use the next day. But Mr. Kovac always had brushes that needed thorough cleaning. There were harsh solvents that chewed up the skin of my hands, and then special soaps that I would carefully work into the bristles, gently pulling the soap through the hairs with my fingertips. After multiple rinses, where I'd carefully examine the water for any trace of color, Mr. Kovac's tools were ready for future use. He didn't seem to mind when I asked him questions while we worked.

As I was blotting the water out of its bristles, I held up a fan brush with bristles arrayed in a flattened semicircle. "What's the purpose of this brush?"

Mr. Kovac glanced up from his canvas. "Some use it for hair, but I prefer to use it for feathering colors." Kovac was an artist of modest reputation, whose specialty was painting stylized portraits of beautiful women, doing very "LA" things. I found the images cheesy. His glamorous ladies were always getting out of gull-wing Mercedes, marching down Rodeo Drive with their hands full of fancy shopping bags, or slathered in cream for an indulgent facial. No self-respecting LA local would have one on their walls, but he had loyal collectors in places like Fort Wayne and Tampa.

For an after-school job, mine wasn't bad; it was certainly superior to working at McDonald's like so many of my high school classmates. Instead of coming home smelling of grease, I got to enjoy the slight buzz that comes from sniffing paint thinner. For two hours, four days a week, I had a steady gig occupying my time and attention. The money kept me in black dresses, black eyeliner, and the pitch-black hair dye my mom abhorred.

I didn't mind the work, and I learned to like Mr. Kovac, who only bothered to be charming when he was talking to his gallery or to his collectors and was otherwise terse.

One day, as I was cataloging his completed canvases, making note of *Lady Wearing Sunglasses #26* and *Manicure #12*, Mr. Kovac looked up, paintbrush still in hand, and said, "Your dad stole a lot of money. I wasn't sure if I could trust you, but you're doing good work."

I was taken aback, it had been almost three years since the trial, and I had hoped most people had forgotten about it. "Thanks, I guess. I prefer not to think about it."

"I don't blame you. It must have been awful."

"Yeah. And it still is. My dad's serving time, and my mother won't let me see him." I played with the pockets of my jeans.

"Do you want to?" Mr. Kovac tilted his head and lowered his bushy gray eyebrows at me.

"Not exactly." I was curious about the place, certainly, but I could hardly tell my boss that every time I got a letter from my dad, with his lies and denials, I wanted to break something. A glass, a vase, a face—something. Fortunately, I had sufficient discipline that I took my venom out on myself, and I'd tack an extra mile or two onto my runs just to feel my body ache.

"He's at Lompoc?"

"Yes." I paused. Dad's location wasn't common knowledge. "How'd you know that?"

"The case interested me, so I followed it. And then you moved in down the street, so I followed it more closely."

"Does everyone on the street know?" I asked, thinking Mom and I had been pretty discreet about our proximity to criminality.

"No. It's not that kind of street. People don't care so long as you mind your own business. But lemme tell ya, just a few blocks over, there's a drug house. I'll take you and your mom over that, any day." He smiled at me, his grin was warm and toothy. "You're a good student, right?"

"Yeah. Culver City High is easy compared to Westlake. I hardly have to try and I get straight As." I shrugged.

"I see you lugging those heavy textbooks back and forth every day. You don't fool me."

"You got me, Mr. Kovac." I smiled sheepishly. "It would be embarrassing to get a B at a school like CCHS. I have my pride." I liked to pretend that I didn't make an effort, but I was extremely diligent about my studies and maniacal about my grades. By immersing myself in my schoolwork, I could forget about my dad's theft, and high grades might help me get scholarships. Work was my salvation.

"You're a junior?"

"Yeah."

"Good scores?"

"Great scores, actually. I'm thinking UCLA." It was the best local school and the only one where I could figure out the finances without being up to my eyeballs in student debt.

"Ever think about going east . . . going Ivy League?" Kovac got my full attention.

"I'd love to escape this place. You have no idea how mean and mediocre my classmates are. But the cost . . ."

"Harvard has lots of scholarships."

"You crack me up, Mr. Kovac." But even as I said that, I hoped he'd tell me more. If there was a path upward and out, I wanted to take it.

"I'm serious. You should apply. I went there. I wish there'd been girls like you at the school when I was a student."

"Well, they weren't far. Wasn't Radcliffe right next door?"

"True. But they were a type. The really interesting girls went to Barnard. You'd have been a Barnard girl, not a Radcliffe girl."

"A Barnard *woman*, Mr. Kovac."

"Of course, Erika, a Barnard *woman*." He chuckled and resumed painting while I began cleaning the paintbrushes he had set aside.

"By the way, Mr. Kovac, I organized your sales records and happened to read some of the notes from your dealer in Minneapolis. Did you notice that your Rodeo Drive works sell faster than your other works? You haven't done one in a while."

"Perhaps it's time for another."

"Perhaps. And with the Cartier store in the background, not the Tiffany's. Tiffany's reads New York to me, not Los Angeles."

"I'll do that next, Erika. Great idea."

Working for Mr. Kovac was a kind of refuge. My mom and I barely spoke. She'd gotten a job at a real estate company, working with the brokers and writing up their listings. It was obvious to me she felt above the work. On those rare occasions when we weren't hissing at one another in our microscopic kitchen, she spoke dismissively about the brokers as she mocked the ad copy she wrote for the firm's brochures. "When are people going to figure out *cozy* is a euphemism for *tiny*, and *hidden gem* means *shitbox*." The one thing we had in common was a feeling of superiority over the people we were forced to spend our days with.

I realize now that Mom was as trapped as I was. Dad sent us both letters. Where mine fueled my anger, Mom's sent her into a tailspin. He asserted his innocence to us both. He pleaded with us for understanding. Where I'd get letters addressed "My Beautiful Princess" or "My Young Grace Kelly," and promises about what life would be like once he was released, Mom would get requests for money for the prison commissary or for a subscription to some magazine or newspaper that had caught his attention. I don't know what she was telling him, but we had nothing to spare. I made the mistake of mentioning college once or twice to her, and she'd immediately retreat into her bedroom and sob.

The only other adult who'd taken a consistent interest in me was Mrs. Kelly, my English teacher at Westlake. After my dad was arrested, she was very kind. My friend Jemima had turned on me, and I was suddenly the target of schoolgirl ire. "Your dad's a criminal." "Cell blocks for Warnocks." "A diamond earring went missing at my sleepover. Did you steal it? Are you a thief like your dad?"

It was horrifying, facing the mean girls in class every day. I spent hours pondering how to get out of school, and my schemes involved throwing myself down stairs or tripping on the street in front of a car and being taken to the hospital. I wanted my classmates to like me, as before, or at least, not to hate me. Where I'd once been queen, I had become desperate for acceptance. Mrs. Kelly must have realized I was struggling when she found me eating my sandwich in a bathroom stall. She invited me to join her in her classroom, and we'd eat our sandwiches in peace.

Once I'd moved to Culver City, I'd take the city bus to Beverly Hills every few months and meet Mrs. Kelly for a snack at Nate 'n

Al's, where she'd indulge in a thick, rich pastrami sandwich while I picked at a plate of french fries. She'd bring books for me to read—"This is what you'd be studying if you were still at Westlake; it'll help with your ACTs"—and we'd discuss my classes and my plans. Like Mr. Kovac, she thought I should apply to Harvard or Yale. "You've got the grades, and you'd be challenged at a top-notch school. And wouldn't it be nice to start fresh?" She didn't laugh when I told her about my passion for art history that I'd caught, like an infection, from Mr. Kovac.

One afternoon, Mr. Kovac had spied me leafing through one of his reference books, so he started telling me outrageous stories about famous artists. He loved describing their fuckups and failures, which he brandished defensively as a way, I guessed, to validate his modest career.

Fortunately for me, he was a connoisseur of the macabre, and maybe he was trying to tell me that talent wasn't an inoculant; bad things can happen to anyone. He'd say things like, "Klimt. Great artist, but a total nutjob." He'd shake his head as he worked on some canvas while riffing about Klimt. "He was basically a crazy cat lady. He was so obsessed with cats, he let them piss on his sketches. If anyone noticed, he'd tell them cat piss was a fixative. Can you imagine how smelly his works must have been?" How could I not listen to a story like that? As I swept, he'd tell me his theories about Mark Rothko's death. "It was a murder, you know, not a suicide. The razor didn't have blood on it." I was rapt. Artists lived lives that were eccentric and bold. They created works that inspired passions long after their deaths. And they all seemed fucking weird.

One day as I was mopping his floor, Mr. Kovac asked, "What are you doing this summer?"

"I dunno. Mom thinks she can get me something at her office. Their receptionist is pregnant. But I really don't want to work with her." Our relationship had been tense ever since she caught me coming home at three in the morning after a night out with some guitarist who was too old for me to date, from a club on Sunset Drive that shouldn't have let me in. I was angry at the world, so I took it out on myself. And her, of course.

"I need extra help this summer, Erika. I want to try something new with my work, and I need a sitter. Could you do that for me? This would be in addition to your usual work."

"A sitter? Whose kids?"

"No, not that kind of sitter. Someone who can sit for me. You know, model. All you have to do is keep very still for an hour or so at a time and hold the pose.

"A job where I sit still for an hour or two? I can do that." I had plans to return to that club on Sunset and fuck that guitarist again. A job that let me chill during the day seemed perfect.

"Yes. There will be sitting, and some standing. Also, one of the poses I'm imagining would have you lying on your side."

"That sounds even easier. What's the catch?"

"There's no catch. I just want to return to my roots, work with a live model, and see what happens. I'm in a rut."

"Okay, Mr. Kovac, whatever you say."

6

MY BASIC INSTINCT

Summer 1992

The summer between my junior and senior years wound up being more pleasant than I had anticipated. For a couple of hours every day, I'd pose for Mr. Kovac, work that was embarrassing in its simplicity. He had me wear a plain, beige bathing suit, because he wanted to "see the way my muscles elongated and the way my curves formed in each position." It was odd, having my elderly boss staring at me with such intensity during the day, but I enjoyed the attention. Nights, I had to myself. Mom worked late, and sometimes she wouldn't come home till midnight herself, so there was nothing stopping me from going out.

I would often take the bus into Hollywood and use my fake ID to go solo to places like Whisky a Go Go or the Burgundy Room. Grunge, punk, hard rock all moved me, as did the musicians. I loved mosh pits because there was an undercurrent of violence where I could flail my arms with abandon. Slamming and being slammed left me battered and ecstatic. My antics got me noticed, and soon I was fucking musicians. In retrospect, I wonder what those grown men were doing with me, since I was barely not a child, but I had just reached my full height and bust, so I could easily pass for a woman in her twenties. I was so desperate to not be myself or a high schooler, that I lied about everything.

One Sunday night, a drummer took me to Club Fuck!, the notorious Silver Lake hangout. I think he wanted to shock me with its pansexual go-go dancers and S&M demos. I was fascinated, only I had an algebra test first thing in the morning, and I hadn't told the musician I was still in high school. I feigned having my period when he suggested screwing in the bathroom. "Let me blow you in the car, instead," I said, so he'd drive me home in his shabby gray Mustang.

Normally, I had nothing to do with my classmates from CCHS. I found them uncouth and dull, and they hated me in return. One Thursday I was at the Fox Hills Mall stocking up on black T-shirts, when I heard my name. "Hey, Erika. Erika? Is that you?"

I looked around, embarrassed to have been caught at the local mall, when Scott Redfern sidled up to me. Scott was in my year, and he was one of those prom king kind of guys, only he was truly the captain of the football team. His sandy brown hair was perfectly fluffy, and his teeth were straight and white. I knew he had abs, because he'd show them off in American History class. I wasn't a bouncy, blonde cheerleader; I was an angry outcast with strong nerd tendencies—the kind of classmate who elicited insults and cool kid ire. I fell far outside his demographic. Surprised, I answered, "Hi, Scott. What's up?"

"Nothing much." Scott was hot, but he wasn't a deep thinker.

"I thought you'd be out of town this summer. At training camp, or something?"

"Nope. Not this summer. My ACL got torn. Gotta mend if I wanna play in the fall." He pointed at his knee, which was trapped in a brace. "Doctor says I only need this for another week."

"Oh, I'm sorry about that. How are the Centaurs gonna manage without your leadership?" My voice dripped with sarcasm. I hated football, but Scott seemed not to notice.

"I dunno. Probably not too well." Scott looked down for a moment, and then tilted his head as he looked at me and flashed some dimple. "Wanna catch a movie tomorrow?"

Normally, muscle-ridden football players weren't my type. Until then, most of my boyfriends had been skinny guitarists in shitty bands. These were guys who thought they were more edgy than they really were, but at fifteen they seemed impressive. Mom had given up on trying to tame me. I was getting As, and that was sufficient. She might have put her foot down if she'd known the guys I was dating were already in their twenties, but keeping that secret was early practice for me. I was already learning to parcel out the truth strategically.

It was one of those jerks who gave me a copy of *The Story of O*, and spoke of putting a collar on me. I found the book gothic and sexy, but narrow in scope. By sixteen, I was sick of all that posturing and preening. I was not going to be a satellite orbiting some narcissistic asshole. I wanted the narcissistic assholes to orbit me.

Perhaps I was bored and a little lonely, because in the harsh light of the food court, Scott looked enticing. So, when he asked me out, I said, "Sure." I was even taken aback that a big man on campus knew my name, but my reputation as a good student gave me a certain profile in the school. Scott was no guitarist, but I figured it might be fun to mess with his head. "I think *Basic Instinct* is still playing. Have you seen it?" I'd read that Sharon Stone was beyond sexy in the film, and that she toyed with Michael Douglas. Everything about that scenario appealed to me. And Scott seemed eager, too.

Scott met me the next day in the lobby of the cineplex. He was early, and he looked surprisingly handsome in his khaki shorts and white crew neck T-shirt. I was wearing my typical black cotton dress, black strappy sandals, and even black nail polish. It was as if a golf pro at Hillcrest Country Club had picked up a witch on the back nine, our pairing was so incongruous.

All the same, Scott seemed thrilled to see me. "Erika, you look fantastic." He gave me a quick kiss on my cheek as he put his hand on the small of my back and steered us up the escalator. "I got our tickets. Hey, do you want some popcorn?"

"Sure." It felt unfeminist to let him pay, but my own funds were tight, so whenever a guy offered, I didn't quibble. This evening would be on him.

We settled in for the movie, seated at the back of the near-empty theater. He did that yawn-like move, where his right arm went around my shoulder in one slick, nonchalant motion. I rewarded his initiative, by nestling into his body, and purring, when he ran his thumb behind my ear lobe, making goose bumps form on my skin. "I like that. Don't stop," I whispered to him, and he continued to play with the sensitive skin at the back of my head while I adjusted my body, like a cat, so that his fingers hit just the right spot.

Sharon Stone had barely come on the screen when Scott and I were making out. There was only one other couple inside, and they seemed oblivious to our panting. Scott was all tongue, and I enjoyed the feeling of his broad chest and the thickness of his arms. The presence of muscles and that sense of solidity excited me, even as I imagined making him weak.

Scott must have been used to pushing cheerleaders around, because he tried some hackneyed moves on me. With one hand, he guided my fingers onto his crotch, where I could feel his cock hard and straining against the zipper of his shorts. It was almost disappointing. I had expected something with more style and finesse. My skinny musicians had more game than the athlete. I whispered to him, "Do you want me to stroke your dick?"

He seemed startled that I actually said the words. Maybe cheerleaders did as they were told, silently and without question. "Yeah."

He shifted and undid the button at the top of his shorts as he eased down the zipper. He wasn't wearing boxers or briefs, so the taut flesh of the head of his cock and his auburn pubic hairs were right at my fingertips. I wondered if that were his typical deal, when he went out on a date, to forgo underwear.

I toyed with his prick, as his hips tried to maneuver it into my hand to get greater pressure and contact. He strained, his injured knee held at an odd angle to his body as he shifted. But I would give him no relief, as I played with the head, applying only the lightest pressure in small, circular movements. He groaned, but leaned back passively, his breathing fast and hard as we both resumed watching Sharon Stone toy with Michael Douglas.

There was one scene in the movie that was prescient. Sharon Stone as the sociopathic Catherine Tramell seduces the cop who's investigating her. As she tied him to the bed with white silk scarves, I felt Scott's cock twitch hard. It was *Story of O*-lite, but with the power switched in the direction that seemed most appealing to me, and apparently, most natural to Scott. I purred into his ear. "I bet you'd love to be tied to a bed like that and forced to take whatever it is I wanted." Scott looked away, but his cock spoke for him. He came into my hand, leaving my fingers covered in cum.

My default state in those days was anger, and he had pissed me off. So I snaked my hand out of his shorts and held my fingers up to his mouth. "Clean up this mess, you filthy slut. Can't you control yourself?" One of those scrawny musicians liked to call me his slut whenever I sucked his veiny cock, so I figured it was time to turn the tables. Scott shook his head side to side, like a petulant little boy. I gauged his response, and he seemed oddly passive, so I pushed further, amused that this big burly football player was disgusted by a little cum. "I bet girls have eaten this for you. Well, it's your turn." Scott pursed his lips together, and shrunk back into his seat, as if my fingers were repulsing him. "If you're not willing to eat it, you're going to wear it. Your choice." Scott let out a short gasp, and I felt his tongue lapping away at the ejaculate growing cold and sticky on my hand. "That's a good boy." I purred into his ear, as I wiped whatever residue lingered on my fingers onto his stubbly cheeks, before I licked my fingers clean.

After that movie, Scott became puppylike in his affection for me. He'd pick me up from Mr. Kovac's in his bright-yellow Civic hatchback, and then we'd park on one of the dead-end streets near the airport. I enjoyed feeling his cock inside me, and the way his bulky arms held me during sex. But football players often moved in packs, and somehow, we were always alone. It took me a month or so, but I realized he was keeping me to himself. I wasn't interested in his buddies, but I was offended, all the same. He was my guilty secret. I wasn't supposed to be his.

We were in the back of his hatchback with the rear seat flattened, and I was stretched on top of his thick body. I'd brought an extra pair of tights with me, and with great flourish, I pulled them out and proceeded to tie his hands above his head and secure them to part of the front seat assembly, in a move straight out of *Basic Instinct*. While he watched, I gave the hose a hard yank, and nothing budged. I'd opened his pants and eased them down around his hips, so it was obvious he was fully engorged, but he was also stuck. I gripped his cock and straddled his legs. Between my weight and his bad knee, he wasn't going anywhere.

I began fondling him, while he squirmed. "So, when am I gonna meet your friends?" I didn't really want to hang with them, but I wanted to see Scott squirm, and maybe I wanted to see him scared. He seemed puzzled, and unsure what to say. I stroked him even more vigorously as he slowly formulated a response.

"You know them. You've met them." His voice was strained.

"I know. But not with you." I brought my mouth down to his dick, putting my lips and tongue mere inches from his organ. "Is there something I don't know? Is there another girl?" I paused, pretending like it mattered, and ran my tongue along the length of his shaft. "Another guy?" I put his dick in my mouth and gave it a proper suck, running my teeth along the head, and then lowering my mouth as far as it would go, so that he was inside my throat. Hearing nothing, I released him, sat up and stared at Scott, tied uncomfortably beneath me.

"There's someone else. Another guy, right? I'm just your side-piece." He shook his head no, while I feigned caring. "Really? There's no one else?" My fingers wrapped around his dick and I began stroking him slowly as he lay beneath me, his hands still stuck in the bonds I'd tied earlier. I pulled off my panties, and shoved them in his mouth, in a move I'd hated when the scrawny guitarist had done it to me. "If you're not going to be honest with me, I don't want to hear anything from you."

He stared at me, his eyes widened in the dim light. I wondered if he would struggle or lash out, or even spit the panties out of his mouth, because there was nothing stopping him. He weighed a hundred pounds more than I did, so it's not like I could force him. Instead, he lay there, immobile, his eyes hungry and hard. The prospect of such a big, burly guy submitting to my whims was intriguing. He might crush opponents on the field, but he remained pinned beneath me. I was winning the war of the sexes.

"Maybe I should just leave you here." I taunted him, delighting in the look of anguish that had appeared on his face. I put my hands to his throat and gave it a squeeze. "You do realize how helpless you are? You're stuck, and with just a little more pressure, it could all be over." I wasn't threatening to murder him, exactly, but I was toying with the feeling of being all-powerful, and I liked it. He made desperate noises into the half-assed gag filling his mouth. I ran my fingers inside his opened shirt and toward his cock, alternately stroking and scratching him with my fingernails. "Okay. You got me. I won't kill you. But maybe I should just get out of the car and walk home. How long do you suppose it would be before someone discovered you?" I paused, he howled despite his mouth being full as he pulled at the bonds at his wrists. "How would you explain the position you're in?"

I pulled the panties out of his mouth. Scott whimpered, "Please, don't leave. I'll do anything you want. *Please.*"

"Anything, Scott? You'll do *anything* I say." His entire body moved as he bobbed his head in agreement. "You're gonna introduce me to your football friends next week. I'm tired of those assholes hassling me. Got it?" He nodded again, then I crawled up to his face, raised my dress, and pushed my pussy onto his mouth. He had been criminally negligent in getting me off, and it was time to fix that situation. "Lick."

Scott burrowed his tongue into me as if his life depended on it, and when he couldn't quite hit my clit, I reached back and slapped his cock. "It's up and to the left, you dumb ox. If you don't improve, I'll tear your balls off." I wasn't serious, but how could he know that? The anger in my voice was authentic. It crept out at odd times, and it had surfaced in the back of the Honda. The threat seemed to focus his attention. He found my clit, and then he did what was necessary. I had to brace my forehead against the driver's side headrest, my orgasm was so intense.

It didn't happen right away, but Scott kept his word, and we met up with two of his friends from the team at the Olive Garden at the Fox Hills Mall. Scott was the quarterback and his best friends, Sammy and Petey, were the two linemen most responsible for keeping him from getting tackled. While we waited for them to arrive, I decided to mess with Scott. "You said you'd do anything I said. Did you mean it?"

"We're here, aren't we? We're gonna hang with Sammy and Petey tonight." He stroked my hair and my face. "You'll like them."

"I have one more thing for you to do." I opened my purse and slid a pair of panties over to him. I leaned in and whispered in his ear, "Go to the bathroom and put these on. You might want to hurry, so you're back before the guys arrive."

"You're not serious." Scott gave me a pained look, but one that said he'd do as he was told.

"Oh, come on, it'll be fun. I'll find it hot, and I'll even chew them off later." I can't say that the prospect of seeing him in something black and silky appealed to me, but I can say that the prospect of seeing him bite his lip during dinner, whenever I ran my hands along his shorts to feel evidence of the silk, delighted me. If I couldn't destroy the men in my life, keeping them on a short leash might suffice.

Scott stuffed the silky garment into the pocket of his khaki shorts and disappeared for a couple of minutes. He came back with a silly grin on his face. Moments later, Sammy and Petey arrived, and we all started chowing down on bottomless salads and breadsticks.

That night, after dinner, Scott and I were alone in the basement of his family home. As I pulled the black lace panties down his thighs before mounting his thick cock, I told him, "I just want you to know, this is our secret. If you won't tell, I won't tell."

"Don't worry, Erika, I won't tell." And as always, he was a man of his word. He must have known, given my outsider status at CCHS, that I had no one to tell.

7

CON IN THE DNA

Fall 1992

The fall of my senior year was miserable. It was all test prep and tests, and applying to colleges I couldn't afford to attend. My mother had sat me down over the summer and shared how there was no college fund. Unlike my former classmates at Westlake, there were no wealthy grandparents or trust funds to help. Student aid was going to be essential, and I would surely end up deep in debt. Mom recommended community college to save money.

Over her favorite pastrami sandwich, Mrs. Kelly had a different take. She advised me to aim high, because the Ivy League had enormous endowments and lots of scholarships. She walked me through the applications, and then she blew my mind. "You have a secret weapon, Erika. Things have happened to you, and you have persevered. Put all that into your essay."

I sat there, stunned. I wanted to bury my dad's criminality as deeply as I could, and then forget about it. Just thinking about the theft made my mood vacillate between anger and outrage. "You think I should write about what happened? That's insane. I want to change my name, even, so his shit doesn't follow me."

"That should be the lead sentence of your essay. And then describe all the ways you've demonstrated strength and resilience." It seemed crazy, but when I discussed it with Mr. Kovac, he agreed, and then he volunteered to write letters on my behalf as well. My teachers at CCHS were similarly enthusiastic. If the smartest adults in my life were all telling me the same thing, I figured I might as well heed their suggestion. Maybe this would be *my* con? Using my father's con to secure my future.

Mr. Kovac began completing his new series of works, the one where I had been his model. There were a dozen canvases reminiscent of Klimt, each featuring a woman lying on her side with her long, dark hair swirled over her body. We'd had lengthy discussions about how I should style my hair—pulled back and away from my face, like in Flemish portraiture, or something loose and wild, like Botticelli. We'd settled on flowing and art nouveau, a look I could replicate for every sitting, where I'd style, fluff and position my locks into artful tendrils that draped across my shoulders and body. I studied Renaissance art for ideas on how to position my hands and legs, and we fussed with minor adjustments to my fingers and shoulders. I didn't think of myself as just his model, I was his collaborator.

The first work he completed, the woman's eyes were closed, and she wore a discreet smile. Her eyelashes were lush and visible against her pale, high cheeks. She wore a celadon nightgown with spaghetti straps, and you could see the curve of her breasts and hips beneath the thin silk. He'd titled it *Erika Dreaming*.

It was unlike his usual works, which hewed graphic and stark. His LA ladies had big sunglasses in sharp contrast with their faces. The bags they held in their hands were bright and bold. *Erika Dreaming* was lush and sensual. I hardly recognized myself in the work, but I wanted to curl up next to the dreamer. "It's spectacular,

Mr. Kovac. What does your gallery think? Are they in, or will they want more Rodeo Drive? They'd be crazy to miss out on this series."

"I'm not sure I'm gonna send these to Minneapolis. I may show them here."

"When can I see more?" I knew he'd been working on the rest of the series, only they were in varying stages of completion. Mr. Kovac didn't like people looking at his works in progress.

"Soon. Oh, and I have some letters for you. I hope they help." Mr. Kovac handed me several sealed envelopes for my college applications. "I'll miss you, but you deserve to go to a great school."

With all the work I was doing getting ready for college, I was at home most evenings, instead of screwing around with some guitarist. Scott had reverted to type, and he was dating a cheerleader. But whenever we'd cross paths in the hallway at school, he'd give me a shy smile. Sometimes, I'd whisper in his ear about how hot he'd looked with his arms tied above his head or wearing my black panties, and that always made him blush. He was a decent guy and not the obnoxious knucklehead I'd believed him to be before.

One afternoon, I arrived home from my job with Mr. Kovac just as my mom was buzzing around the house, with her blonde hair in hot rollers and a face full of makeup. I sat down on our blue and white striped couch and called to her. "You look pretty. Gotta date, tonight?"

Mom blushed but denied that she was going out with anyone. I'd seen her on several afternoons, when she'd rushed home from the real estate agency. She'd remove the black pencil skirt and sorbet-colored blouses that were her daytime uniform, and she'd don a DVF wrap dress in a groovy seventies pattern, and her best pumps. She'd even go for full hair and makeup for the evening, so I figured it had to be for some guy. She didn't like to talk about her sex life with me, but I knew she had one. We had achieved a truce. She stayed out late, and I didn't ask questions. I stayed out late, and she didn't pry either. We both got our work done and neither of us brought anyone home.

"Oh, come on, Mom," I teased. "You don't get dressed up like this for no reason. Who is he? I hope he deserves the full Anette!"

Mom looked younger than she had in years. Her high cheekbones were expertly contoured with a pretty pink blush, and her lips seemed even fuller, with the frosted lipstick she'd chosen. She sat down on the couch beside me and relaxed for a moment. "I'm just going out for dinner. Nothing special."

"You're not fooling me. You've got plans. Where ya goin'?"

My mother gave me a sly smile. "The Polo Lounge."

For once, she'd surprised me. "What? The Polo Lounge? We haven't been there in years. Not since Daddy, well, you know . . ."

"I miss it, so I go sometimes." She adjusted the dress so that it fell open, revealing just the right amount of cleavage.

"I miss it, too. Take me with you." I was picturing their hamburger and the fatty, salty bacon that came on the patty. I could practically taste their fries. When I was ten, I'd save the thick bacon strips for last, I loved them so much. It dawned on me that once I graduated, it could be years before we had another Polo Lounge meal together.

Mom leaned forward on the couch, clearly taken aback. I had blown off her occasional overture to go out, so this was unexpected. She inhaled deeply and paused, taking care to formulate a response. "You can come with me, but you can't come like that." She gestured at my torn-up black jeans and my black and red striped T-shirt, worn tight against my body. Mom nodded toward her bedroom. "Come on, let me dress you. It'll be fun. Like old times, when you liked the clothes I picked for you."

I rolled my eyes, but followed her into her tidy bedroom, with its blue floral bedspread and lace-trimmed pillows. Mom opened up her closet and hunted around before she pulled out a wrap dress similar to hers, in a deep amethyst. "This will look nice on you. But we have to do something with your hair."

"Whatever you want, Mom. Let's look like sisters."

"Yes, let's look like sisters, Erika." She got out her brush and got to work on me, styling my long black hair into a messy chignon. "I miss your blonde hair; it was so pretty." She ran her fingers through my waves.

"Blonde looks better on you than it ever did on me, Mom. I hated the way Dad always compared me to Grace Kelly." It was the truth. I remained angry at my father, and he had adored my blonde hair.

"If your dad had preferred brunettes, my life would have been much simpler. But I wouldn't have you in it. You're my most important accomplishment." She sighed as she blasted my head with Aqua Net.

"Yeah, his obsession with blondes was pretty clear. I visited him last month, and he was not impressed."

"You what? Darling, you didn't go to Lompoc . . . I didn't want you to see that awful place."

"I know, Mom, and it went really bad. The whole time I was there, when he wasn't railing at his attorneys or denying what he did, he ragged on my hair. It was embarrassing."

"I'm so sorry, Erika, but you know how your father is." My mother shook her head.

"Mom, he wouldn't let my hair color go. It was like *I* was the criminal, not him."

"Well, he'd probably boasted about his beautiful blonde daughter to all the other inmates, and lo and behold, you've got black hair, now."

"Oops! It was ridiculous. You know how hard it is just to get to Lompoc, and that was what he wanted to talk about?" I tried to lighten things. "I just hope he's gotten over the shame of one less blonde in the family."

My mother nodded as she examined my face. Then she cocked her head, like an artist examining her creation. "This black eyeliner is harsh. Let's just clean it off and start fresh." It was unlike me, but after telling her I'd ignored her wishes about visiting my dad in jail, I was willing to be compliant. I got out a washcloth and gave her a blank canvas. She applied burgundy eyeshadow to my lids, subtly lining them with a darker shade from the same compact. She then handed me a tube of pink lipstick and told me to put it on.

We stood side by side in the bathroom, eyeing ourselves in the mirror. We really could have been siblings.

Mom drove us over to the Beverly Hills Hotel, and valet parked her sky-blue Chevy Cavalier. I took her lead as we marched into the hotel's bar and perched on the tall seats farthest from the bartender. Mom leaned over to me and spoke softly, "Whatever happens, play along. Okay?" Curious, I was only too happy to agree.

Mom ordered us both martinis, which made my jaw drop. She whispered to me, "Nurse that drink, because you might not get another one." When the bartender handed me my martini, I played with the cocktail glass, swirling the toothpick with its two perfect olives, in a slow figure eight, like I'd seen on television. "You're doing great," she said, and I beamed with pleasure. I wasn't sure what was going on, but I loved seeing this gangster side of my mother.

It didn't take long, but two men joined us at the bar, and bought us fresh drinks. The tall dark-haired one smiled at me and asked me what we were doing at the hotel.

I looked at my mother, who tilted her head and grinned. She spoke up, realizing I didn't know the game. "It dawned on me that Erika and I hadn't been here for a while, and I wanted to make sure the place was still standing. And you gentlemen?"

"Client meeting. We're agents at CAA."

I gazed up at the tall one and took a sip of my fresh martini. "Impressive."

My mother focused on the shorter guy, wearing a gray suit, blue shirt and gray tie. "You must have interesting clients with fascinating issues. I'm in real estate, and houses bore me. You must have a strong appetite for making deals."

"Haha. Yeah, I'm fucking ravenous. This guy here"—the short guy punched the tall guy in the arm—"now this guy is basically a Pac-Man, the way he gobbles back deals."

I laughed, enjoying the slight buzz from my second martini. I turned to the tall one. "What's your name? I'm Erika."

"Marco, and my colleague here is Ethan." We shook hands, and I resumed sipping my drink. Marco turned to me and asked me what work I did.

"I'm in school, still. It's my senior year."

"Oh, a co-ed. I still fantasize about the women I went to college with." I nodded, letting the error go unacknowledged.

My mother moved in for the kill. "Speaking of ravenous, Erika and I have been craving the burgers here. You guys should invite us to join you."

The two men looked at one other, and Ethan spoke first. "Deal. Let's have some burgers and discuss life. See what happens."

Mom gave me a look out of the corner of her eye, and when the two men were making arrangements with the host at the Polo Lounge, I whispered to her, "You've got style, Mom! Anette for the win!"

After our ritzy dinner, complete with another round of cocktails and even dessert, I was awestruck by my mother. "How'd you size those guys up? How'd you do that?"

"They were both married, but they thought they might score a little action. I knew what I wanted—a nice meal and some fun company. They knew what they wanted—the potential for more. And what we all wanted was close enough to merit a meal together. I do this all the time."

"No way!" I sat in the front seat of the Cavalier, astonished by what she'd shared.

"The last thing I want is a relationship, but I miss the flattery and the attention. And I really miss the burgers."

"I love you, Mom." I reached over and stroked her dress, as she drove us home to Culver City on the 405. She clutched my hand, so tightly I could feel the blood pulsing in her grip.

"I'm going to miss you, Erika. I love you, too."

The peace didn't hold, but the intensity of our snarls diminished. We both knew it was only a matter of months before I went to college, and both our lives would change.

8

LIBERATING THE NUDE

Spring 1993

Mrs. Kelly was prescient. Harvard must have loved my essay about being the daughter of a fraudster, because they offered me a spot in the class of 1997 with enough loans and scholarships to make it happen. I was dumbfounded that my dad's con had worked on them, when it hadn't worked on his clients. Cambridge was in my future.

Mr. Kovac was thrilled for me, too. I was still cleaning his brushes and sweeping his floors, and every month or so, he'd complete another work from his Erika series. First there was *Erika Dreams*, then there was *Erika on the Waves*. He depicted me lying languidly on a surfboard, my body always in the same position, with a halo of foam above my head. This time, I stared out from the canvas while my hair flowed suggestively over a violet bikini, in mermaid-like waves.

"It's gorgeous, Mr. Kovac. I can see the hint of Klimt in this one, too."

"Oh good. I want the influences to be discreet but there for the discerning eye."

He'd switched galleries, to a prominent one in Santa Monica, for his Erika series. They weren't going to be shipped off to Minneapolis for his midwestern collectors. The dealer clearly figured these works would appeal to the locals. As the date of his show grew closer, he hastened his pace. He'd done a lot of preliminary work, so the canvases were completed in quick succession. It was odd to see so many versions of me, in different clothes with different facial expressions, but they were all so flattering and wonderful.

Next, was *Erika Studying* where the painted me wore denim shorts and a small pink tank top, with a black bra strap peeking out. My hair fell in waves over a massive art history textbook, open in the foreground. There was an *Erika Watching TV*, where I was depicted with a brownie in hand and my eyes gazing out and looking rapt. There were a dozen canvases, all variations on the same theme. I was shown lying on my side, in various clothes and contexts, and I could see how Mr. Kovac was practically daring collectors to buy two or three of the works, as a witty way to fill a wall.

I was thinking about ways to transform myself once I got to Harvard. I resolved to get serious. I'd use my mother's maiden name, Grieg, instead of Warnock. I'd keep my dad's story to myself, where it was hard to escape at home in Los Angeles. And maybe I'd even give up on guitarists. I was working on all the details, when Mr. Kovac showed me the final canvas of his series, *Erika on the Football Player*.

"You're the first to see this . . . ahead of the gallery, even." Mr. Kovac beamed as he displayed the finished work. I gasped. It was dreamy and gorgeous. I looked fantastic. But I was also naked. He'd depicted me lying on my side, as usual. And even though I'd known this was a classic odalisque pose, so named because it often depicted harem girls, it hadn't occurred to me that Mr. Kovac might imagine me this way.

Instead of the usual me, this time there was another person in the image. My eyes were half-open, there was a glimpse of tongue in the gap between my lips, and my top leg was bent and draped suggestively over a muscular man lying beside me on his back, wearing white boxers. His face and cock were hidden, but my breasts were fully exposed, and there was even a hint of my pubic hair. It was clearly and identifiably me. The work was even named after me, only I'd never posed naked, and I would never have agreed to being shown that way. I was not Olympia, and he was not Manet.

I dropped what I was doing and ran home, I was so furious. I couldn't recall mentioning Scott to him, but I must have. Mr. Kovac hadn't sought my consent for something that could conceivably follow me for the rest of my life. That it was the most spectacular work of the series, and a series that would probably reinvent his reputation as an artist was immaterial. He'd stared at me for weeks, never once suggesting that his works would be erotic. I felt betrayed by someone I had trusted, but I didn't know what to do or say.

Mom wasn't home when I raided the freezer and found a full container of chocolate ice cream. I devoured it, hoping that the cold would bring my temperature down. Once I felt more self-possessed, I returned to Mr. Kovac's studio.

"Erika, what's the matter? Don't you like the work? You're beautiful in it."

"Mr. Kovac, I'm naked in it."

"Yes."

"I lay there for hours, and you never said anything about doing a nude. I should have the right to say whether I'm going to be shown naked on a wall somewhere."

"Erika, nudes are common. Yours is lovely. I don't understand the problem."

"It should be my decision whether or not I show my tits. Not yours."

"They're not your tits. It's just a painting."

"People will assume they're mine. They'll think I posed like that, when I didn't. They'll wonder who the football player is. They'll also wonder if you and I fucked."

"Erika, don't be a child."

"Mr. Kovac, you may have forgotten, but I am a child. My mom could see this painting. People will think you're a pedophile when they learn who your model is." He stared at me, taken aback. He must have forgotten I was still only sixteen when he'd begun the series. "You need to destroy this canvas."

"You need to calm down, Erika."

I walked up to the painting and tucked it under my arm. "Well, if you're not going to destroy it, I'm going to keep it. Your reputation is too valuable to blow it all on something so nonessential to the series. Paint another version, but put me in a bra, or something. You're not getting this one back."

I gave him a look that all but dared him to stop me as I walked out of the studio. He remained rooted in place, as he looked at me, stupefied.

When I got home, I carefully wrapped the work and slid it under my bed, and then I waited. Would Mr. Kovac say something? Would he call the cops? Would he call my mom? I wondered if I should go back to his studio and apologize, but that would have required me to return the painting, and I had no intention of doing so, even as I couldn't bring myself to destroy it.

What I couldn't explain at the time was how, in the painting, I could see the power of my sexuality. Mr. Kovac had captured it, but he had also appropriated it without my permission. He'd stolen it from me, and I had refused to be helpless. There would be no trafficking in images of my body. At least not without my consent.

That was the last day I visited his studio, although I read about Mr. Kovac's opening night with great interest. The art reviewer from the *Los Angeles Times* marveled:

For years, Dennis Kovac pumped out saccharine-sweet visions of Los Angeles for people who had probably never visited the city. This year, something changed. It was like he got a blood transfusion that included some of Gustav Klimt's DNA.

Kovac's suite of "Erika" oils are lush and moody. They show a side of the city that should be explored more often. His young muse is depicted lying on a surfboard, on a sofa, and on her boyfriend, in evocative, dreamlike poses, each more stylish than the next. It's rare for an artist in his sixties to reinvent himself, but Kovac has managed. Visit the Ambling Gallery in Santa Monica to see for yourself.

9

COMMENCEMENT SURPRISE

Spring 1997

I kept going back to Club MantaRay. Although I was unable to vent my anger on the person who inspired it, it was easy to find enthusiastic proxies. At the same time, I was also collecting gear and clothes from eager benefactors. It took me a couple of weeks to figure out the game, but then I put a small post on Knots and Crosses, an online bulletin board dedicated to the Boston BDSM scene. Soon, I was buried in queries.

There was one IT pro who wanted to take me to Neiman Marcus and buy me stilettos. That seemed pleasant enough, so I let the soft, mousy-haired fellow buy me a pair of Gucci pumps with a metal heel. It was a five-hundred-dollar acquisition, and he bought them without hesitation. Once we were finished at the store, I had him take me to his small apartment in Back Bay, and then I ground that heel into his cock, like it was a dagger. And when he came, I dipped the heel into the puddle, and had him lick himself off my exquisite shoe. I was thrilled to have the pumps, they were something chic to wear to graduation, with a wicked, secret provenance. The ragged clothes of my teens had given way to a taste for things I'd seen in magazines like *W* and *Vogue*. I might not have been able to afford designer wares, but I coveted their artistry and style, and then I found some guy to buy them for me.

Another gentleman, an executive at Fidelity, had a thing for latex, so we scanned specialty websites, and I ordered a few custom dresses on his dime, while he sat bound by my side. "What do you think, Marty? Purple or red trim?" I batted my eyelashes at him, as I yanked hard on the leather parachute that encircled and squeezed his testicles.

"Definitely the purple." He had to struggle to say the words, while I applied tension to a very sensitive spot.

"You're right." I released the chain connected to his balls. "Purple."

"Thank you, Mistress," he said while exhaling in relief.

"Just think of how many men will come when they see me wearing it. I wonder if I'll let you." Marty let out the most wonderful squeak, so I continued. "Oh, and I need the stockings to match."

"Yes, Mistress." The look on his face while he sat tied to his Shaker dining chair, when I fished out his credit card and input the numbers, was delicious. It was agony mixed with anticipation, which meant he almost had an orgasm when I announced the total cost of the order would be close to a thousand dollars.

"I'm glad you're single, Marty. If you had a wife, she'd kill you for blowing your money on latex dresses for the woman who takes a whip to your cock and stretches your balls until they're practically on the floor."

"I know . . . I know . . ." The shame of the idea only got him more aroused. It was win-win. If I was irritated at a professor, I could take it out on Marty. If I was anxious about my application for doctoral programs, I could take it out on someone else. And when I learned I'd gotten into Harvard's art history program with full funding, I could celebrate in style.

Graduation was a relief. Mom came for it from Vegas, where she'd moved after I finished up at CCHS. Like me, she'd wanted a fresh start, and maybe she wanted to make it harder for my dad to track her down.

Foolishly, I'd shared my Cambridge address with him, so my father would write me these promise-filled letters every month, about what would happen once he was out of Lompoc. He'd erase my student debt. He'd take me to London and Paris, so I could visit all the best galleries. He had so many extravagant ideas about his life post-jail and the extraordinary things he'd do for me, that it was hard not to buy into his fantasies a tiny bit. There was so much about those letters that I wanted to believe, and I hated myself for every moment when hope erased doubt. My skepticism was justified because once he was released in January, things went quiet again. That peace was short-lived. He showed up at my dorm, the day before my Harvard graduation.

"Hey, princess." I recognized my dad's voice immediately, as he stood on the stoop outside my dorm. He wore a tan suit and blue shirt, looking as sharp and successful as he had before the FBI encounter, only with much grayer hair. I couldn't help myself. It had been over seven years since I'd last seen him, so I ran up and hugged him.

"Hey, Daddy. You're here!" His presence stunned me.

"I wasn't going to miss my princess's graduation from Harvard." I didn't have spare tickets to the commencement ceremony, so my mind churned through the possibilities.

"Does Mom know you're here?"

"Why would I tell her? She divorced me."

"I didn't know you were coming, or I would have scored you a ticket. They're scarce, you know."

"Don't worry about me, princess, I'll take care of it. But I'd like to take you to dinner to celebrate. I made reservations tonight at the Capital Grille. Do you know it?"

"Yeah, I know it, Daddy." That was my favorite restaurant for hustling martinis and steaks off Boston's finance crowd. Mom had taught me well at the Polo Lounge of the Beverly Hills Hotel.

I called my mother to explain what had happened. It was such a brazen move, but wanting to avoid drama, and also, to avoid her ex-husband, Mom decided to let me dine without her. She had become a dealer in Vegas, and the casinos frowned on their employees spending time with felons. I suggested hooking her up with my friend Amy's family. Amy's parents were visiting from Vermont, and they'd always been incredibly generous and welcoming to me, but Mom preferred to dine alone. "Mom, the Regatta Bar at the Charles Hotel might be a good place for you to find dinner."

"Thanks, darling. We'll celebrate tomorrow. And then you can tell me what he's up to." She sighed into the phone.

"Will do, Mom. And thanks. I'm sorry this had to happen."

"Me too. I should have known he'd reappear at the worst possible time. That man has a knack. Be careful. He's working some angle."

"Oh, Mom." But I couldn't help but wonder if she was right. When he was at Lompoc, I got these elaborate letters, describing how he was innocent of the fraud, that it was all just a big misunderstanding. He'd describe how he was going to get back to where he was before. I couldn't decide if his plans were evidence of optimism or delusion, but it seemed cruel to challenge him, so I kept my doubts to myself.

The taxi hadn't hit much traffic between Cambridge and Boston, so I arrived early at the Capital Grille and took my preferred spot at the bar. Before I had a chance to order a martini, my dad appeared and sauntered up to the bar and gave me a bear hug and a sloppy kiss on the cheek.

"How's my princess?"

"Great, Daddy, great. But woah, you sure know how to make an entrance. Why didn't you call?"

"I wanted to surprise you on your big day. I've been waiting for this for years. Your successes kept me going"—he paused, obviously referring to his time in Lompoc—"and now I'd like to celebrate them."

"Should we go somewhere else for dinner? This place is a bit fancy . . . There are some cute little places in the North End you'd like. Real red sauce Italian joints and very well-priced." Who wants to ask their father if he has the cash for a steak dinner?

"No way, princess! I'm craving steak and a very dry martini. We're not going anywhere. Besides, we have much to discuss."

And Dad wasn't kidding. Although there was no one back in LA who'd hire him, he had somehow found a benefactor in NYC—an Armenian guy setting up a wealth management firm who needed help with business development. The work was safe enough, in that Dad wouldn't be handling client money, but I was amazed that Dad had a plan for convincing high net worth individuals to come on board as clients. I was doubly amazed when that plan included me.

"In addition to all the usual financial services we'd offer the clients, I was thinking an art advisory service might be appreciated, and that's where you come in, princess. You could help me find prospects, and then you could help the clients build their collections."

"Cool idea, Daddy, but I'm a little green for serious collectors. They'd want someone with a graduate degree and maybe even time at a place like Sotheby's. Those auction houses are basically finishing schools."

"You're selling yourself short, princess. It's not the degree that matters, but the initiative and the hustle. You're fast on your feet. The clients would eat you up." He took a big gulp of his martini, while I stared at mine, trying to collect my thoughts.

"Daddy, that's gross." Was he imagining me as some kind of nubile lure to be dangled in front of wealthy men? The prospect made me shudder. "Besides, I've already been accepted into Harvard's art history doctoral program. Maybe in four years . . ."

"I need your help *now*, princess. Some of your classmates could be clients. Or their parents. You're graduating from fucking Harvard. There's so much money around here, and we could mine it." He pounded the table, animated by the prospect of piles of cash.

"Oh look, our steaks have arrived." The waiter appeared at the perfect moment and deposited the plates in front of us. "I'm too excited about my research. I've already committed to studying with my supervisor. She has some provocative ideas about the Impressionists. Maybe when I'm finished?"

"All right, princess, I understand. But don't say I didn't offer you a ground-floor opportunity. This advisory business is gonna be huge."

"I understand, Daddy. And I'm grateful you want me to be part of it with you. But I've got momentum, and I want to keep going with my research. Did you know my work on Manet won the award for best undergraduate thesis in the history of art and architecture? I was up against a really strong thesis about Le Corbusier, and I crushed that guy."

My father reached across the table and grabbed my hand, clutched it hard and wouldn't let go. "You can't blame me for wanting to spend time with my princess, can you? Those assholes robbed me of seven years with you, and I'd like to make up for all that lost time . . . Seven years of dinners, play dates, proms, college trips . . . all because of one shitty week in '87. All because of a misunderstanding."

"Yeah, I was robbed, too." It was exhausting, being angry at my dad. I wanted things to be like they were. I knew people who had great relationships with their parents, and I envied them. My friend Amy, for instance, had supportive parents. They called her every Tuesday night. They sent care packages filled with homemade oatmeal cookies, bottles of maple syrup, and her favorite snacks. Amy was so confident there'd be more, she'd share her bounty with me. Could I become an Amy? Was it even safe to ask that question?

"We'll spend time together, now that you're out. But I'm determined to get my doctorate."

"Okay, princess, I can take no for an answer. But I just want you to know how proud I am of you. You showed so much grit and hustle and look at you now . . . about to graduate from Harvard. You and your classmates are members of an elite club."

I didn't have the heart to tell my father that Harvard had plenty of elites, but social life on campus was stratified. When you get financial aid, all those hours spent working at Dining Services cuts into time that could be spent schmoozing with the sons and daughters of CEOs and heads of state. The wealthy kept to themselves. Certainly, they studied with me. They borrowed my class notes. They appreciated my help with their essays, but I was not one of them. I knew it. And so did they.

10

A DOCTORATE IN DEVIANCY

Summer 1997

After commencement, I helped Amy pack up her things for Manhattan. She'd been one of my only friends at Harvard. She had this sense of calm about her; a levelheadedness that seemed preternatural. Amy was one of those people who could size up a situation and calculate, in an instant, the optimized response. This didn't make her fun or exciting, but she was a helpful counterbalance to my erratic passions.

Amy was also a fellow "poor" on campus, getting by on student loans and scholarships. I never had to turn down an invitation to Gstaad from her. There was a comfort in never having to explain my strained circumstances to her. She didn't ask, and I didn't tell. Which is why I was so taken aback when she mentioned my father, as I was emptying the socks from her bureau.

"Erika, I really got a kick out of your father."

"You met my father? When?" I put the box down and stared at her. I'd tried to keep my father far away from everyone at Harvard, because I didn't trust what he'd tell them and I worried it would reflect poorly on me.

"At commencement, of course. He came up and introduced himself."

"Seriously? I missed that. I think he was giving my mom lots of space. Their divorce wasn't amicable." I tried to be as nonchalant as possible, but I was baffled and extremely concerned.

"He was doing the rounds. He spoke to everyone. I think he was really proud of you and wanted to boast about your success. And who can blame him? You got that big prize!" Amy looked at me and gave me a broad smile. She'd always been generous in her enthusiasm and support, but she was also painfully naive. She'd never been betrayed by a family member. She'd never known how quickly her circumstances could be reversed. She had faith in the universe, because it had never bitten her in the ass.

"Did he say anything else?"

"Why didn't you tell me he'd consulted for the International Monetary Fund? That must have been a fascinating experience. What else are you holding back from me?" Amy was joking, but she was correct. There was a lot I hadn't told her. But at least I hadn't lied to her. It took every ounce of muscle control not to reveal my horror, because it was clear my father was up to no good.

This became a trend. Dad would reappear intermittently over the next few years, with unusual requests. He had me look at the odd painting or photo of a painting. He never told me what he wanted to know, but I did my best to give him some background on the artist or the work, and a ballpark notion of their value in the marketplace. Most of the works were fine, but one had been listed in the Art Loss Register, a database of stolen and missing artworks. My blood pressure spiked when that connection surfaced. Even being in proximity to something so dodgy made my heart race. I warned him away from the work and whoever it was who possessed it, and I tried to obliterate the memory of the conversation from my mind.

I craved a normal relationship with him, but whenever he popped into my life there was always something off-putting. It wasn't clear if he wanted a coconspirator or a patsy, but I had no intention of being either.

Ironically, as my father became more and more of a criminal, so did I. I submitted to capitalism and professionalized my BDSM adventures, becoming a full-fledged outlaw—a sex worker. I no longer bartered for gear. Instead, I got paid to play. The transition was seamless. There was no handwringing as I embarked on my life of victimless crime. I needed the money. Most of my classmates had parents who were renting them apartments and buying their plane tickets. I got a pittance of a stipend from Harvard. When I considered the debt I'd accrued and my hunger for experience, it was clear that kink offered a path.

I can't say I was without worry, but I persevered. To my astonishment, there was even case law in Massachusetts—*Commonwealth v. Appleby*—that made hitting someone with a crop tantamount to assault with a dangerous weapon. A crop was no baseball bat or gun, and yet in Puritan Massachusetts, it was called out as something especially dire. The lawyer I consulted warned me that *everything* about a professional BDSM practice put me at risk of being arrested, but I decided if I kept things very discreet, no one would be the wiser. That said, I kept her business card on me at all times.

At first, it was mostly outcall to hotels. It was efficient, but I worried about becoming too familiar to the concierges at the Copley Plaza or the Four Seasons. These were clients who wanted convenience—delivery domination—but they weren't the most savvy. There was one guy who announced as I was emptying my heavy bag of gear that he wanted to have his cock pierced, then he handed me a clear plastic box of sewing needles.

"You want me to put these into your dick?" I asked, incredulously, as I tried to decide if I should bail on such a bizarre request. I'd read about piercings, but I'd never performed one.

"Yes, Mistress. I do it myself, sometimes." The curly-haired accountant looked at me sheepishly. I didn't want to admit to him I'd never done anything like that before. It was a five-hundred-dollar booking and I'd already spent the money in my head. Art history textbooks each cost about a hundred bucks. Instead of fleeing, I went into the bathroom and grabbed a few towels.

"Do you have anything to disinfect these with?" I pointed at his box.

"No. The needles are brand new. The box has never been opened" I resisted the urge to roll my eyes. Besides, if he wasn't worried about infection, why should I? In that moment, if I'd even thought about it at all, I probably figured he could take it up with his urologist. My only concern was keeping his blood away from me.

His genitals received a cursory wipe with a moist, soapy face cloth, but that was it. I put on a pair of gloves—I wasn't insane—and I plunged one of his needles into the head of his cock without any further hesitation. The guy howled, but he became erect and pleaded for a second needle. I repeated the task, sticking another needle about a quarter inch into the engorged head. While I threatened him with further needles, scratching at his shaft, he jerked himself off. "How about a third? Maybe a fourth? Is your cock even big enough for five?"

Everything was fine until I removed the needles, when bright red blood came gushing out of my improvised piercings. I grabbed the white towels, which were quickly covered in red blotches, and used them to apply pressure. The mess horrified me. Would the maids think there'd been an animal sacrifice? But mostly, I was unnerved by the needless risk I had subjected both of us to. My consent had been given impetuously. I followed up with the accountant afterward, relieved there'd been no infection.

It had been a lucky break, and not evidence of stellar technique on my part, that both of us had escaped from that suite with our health. I resolved to do better. There was a submissive doctor who'd once hit on me, so I called him up and got a private tutorial on sterile technique. All it required was for me to kick him in the balls a few times while berating him. It was gratifying really letting him have it. There's something profoundly pleasing about watching an asshole writhe on the ground after my toe had landed at just the right spot for maximum misery but minimum damage. "What did you think was going to happen? Did you think I'd go easy on your pathetic body?" There were quite a few men I had fantasized about kicking into a fetal position. That afternoon, he was a useful substitute.

The next step in my professional evolution was investing in a proper dungeon. I rented a small two-bedroom apartment in Cambridge and transformed the master bedroom into a play space while relegating myself to the tiny, spare room whose only decor was the painting of Mr. Kovac's I'd liberated. That room was mine, alone. No one was ever invited into it. I'd lull myself to sleep, staring at my painted self, and imagining what other paintings I could get to keep it company.

Once I was settled into the apartment, with extra carpets layered on the floor to muffle the sound of my high heels, and a dozen mirrors mounted on the walls, so my supplicants could see themselves beg, I placed an ad in the preeminent BDSM contact magazine, *Domination Directory International*. The cost was nominal, and the ad brought in a higher tier of clientele than I could get from little display ads in the local alternative paper, the *Boston Phoenix*. I hated my *Phoenix* inquiries. They were often just guys looking for free phone sex, and I could hear them jerking off as I answered questions about my gear or my clothes.

"Tell me, Mistress, what kind of paddles do you have?" There'd be a rustling in the background that I'd come to recognize as the guy stroking his dick. "Do you have hard metal paddles? How about hard *wooden* paddles? And just how *hard*, exactly?" They always wanted excruciating detail, in a pathetic effort to draw out the conversation for as long as possible, hoping to have an orgasm to my voice.

"Call a 900 number; don't call me." Was my standard response. I couldn't call them "pathetic losers," even if that's what they were, because that would only heighten their arousal. Instead, I let them hear the sound of my phone hanging up. It was depleting, weeding through the wankers and the wannabes in an effort to identify the best, most enticing prospects, but it was part of the job. I spent hours on the phone at night, when I wasn't studying for exams or working on my qualifying paper.

I also had a discreet website with the come-on, "Bold Strokes: Let your body be my work of art." I never showed my face, but glimpses of my torso clad in leather and latex were enough to pull them in. I called myself Miss E, but once someone became a repeat client, they learned that the *E* was for Erika. I worried a lot about getting caught. There were stories of professors learning their students were escorts or dancers, and it never ended well. Funding could be canceled. There was the possibility of getting expelled. To pursue a PhD was to bind yourself to the beliefs and systems of academia. We students were pursuing the life of the mind. Bodies, needing things like money for food and shelter, were inconveniences at the Church of Harvard. And being a sex worker and dealing with bodies pursuing orgasms—or perhaps the odd kick to the nuts— would be a clear sign I didn't take my education seriously enough.

As usual, I reverted to secrecy, with only my clients having any clue about my part-time job. If no one knew I was a dominatrix, they couldn't punish me. Worst-case scenario, I figured I could claim it was a performance art piece, reminiscent of Marina Abramović. It wasn't true, but it would confuse the right people.

The money was solid and predictable, and the sessions didn't interfere with my doctoral studies. Traditional academic robes had a place for alms. Was my approach so different? Without sex work, I wouldn't have been able to visit the museums in Paris that housed the objects of my fascination, and I wouldn't have been able to begin buying the pieces that formed the foundation of my personal collection. And without the work, I wouldn't have met Michael.

There was a loose network of dominatrixes around the nation, all about the same age, same attractiveness and same level of gear. I had no interest in networking with other local women, but I could network discreetly with counterparts like Irene Boss in Pittsburgh, Amanda Wildefyre in Minneapolis, or Midori in San Francisco, and we would exchange referrals and ideas. After a year or so, I was known to them, and they were known to me. We all positioned ourselves as monopolists, as we were the only ones who could provide time with ourselves.

It was one of those women who sent Michael to me. Clients ask around, he was going to Boston, and somebody suggested I was up to snuff.

Michael called and one week later he appeared. He had a fondness for gear—especially being outstretched. Between my black leather-topped bondage bed and a vast arsenal of paddles, crops and whips, I had plenty to keep him amused. And he kept coming back. He concocted business trips to Boston, meetings in New Hampshire, all sorts of pretenses that would give cover to twice-monthly side trips to my play space in Cambridge.

"You're studying art history, aren't you?" Michael asked after we'd finished his session. I'd mummified him in Saran Wrap, and then applied electrodes to his genitals, zapping him until he had an orgasm.

"That's right. Ask me anything about Manet." I smiled. We were long past the point of polite disinterest.

"I thought that's what you were up to. If you have a taste for contemporary works, come visit me and I'll hook you up with Jeffrey Deitch or Larry Gagosian. I'm a client of theirs."

"Are you trying to lure me to Manhattan? Be careful what you wish for!"

"I'm running out of excuses for Boston visits." Michael took a long sip of water from the bottle I'd handed him. "Why don't you come to the city some weekend I'm free. I'll put you up in the SoHo Prime, near my favorite galleries, and we can play in your suite. Or maybe you can rent someone's dungeon?"

"A hotel scene could be decadent. I'd bring some of my gear and make it special."

"Yes. Bring that leather body bag you've been threatening me with. I'd like to try that."

"Sounds easy enough. Let's figure out a weekend. Maybe there'll be an opening for me to check out."

"Perfect. My wife is heading up to the Yukon for the season. She's obsessed with Inuit art and we're founding a school that teaches the youngsters the old ways. I'll have lots of flexibility once she's gone."

"What a fantastic project. She must feel great, doing such important work. I hope you're not too lonely, in the process."

"Don't worry about me. I know how to keep myself busy. She's got her things going on, and I've got mine."

"A satisfying partnership?"

"Very." Michael nodded, and the subject was closed. One month later, I was packing my body bag, an assortment of hoods, electrical toys and other odds and ends, into a large rolling suitcase for the train ride to New York. The Yukon had finally warmed up enough for Michael's wife, so Michael was free to play, and there were exhibitions and openings I wanted to catch.

After checking into the SoHo Prime Hotel, I put on a sleek black knit dress with a neckline that bordered on improper and a pair of cordovan boots, with laces up the front and very high heels. A fetishist had purchased them on an excursion to Ralph Lauren. Before heading over to Balthazar for dinner with Michael, I pulled out the digital camera I kept in my purse and took a picture of the boots. I planned to email the fellow proof they had been enjoyed.

There was only a handful of clients I chose to spend time with beyond our appointments in my dungeon. Michael was my favorite, because he never tried to turn dinner into dessert. He never tried to fuck me. Since visions of me inhabited so many of their quiet moments, and it's my voice they'd hear in their fantasies, clients would project their own longings onto me. Once they'd left my space, I rarely thought about them. I was as busy as they were, and my fantasies were different from theirs. The hole in their lives was erotic. They craved an energy transfer or a very specific type of taking. They longed to serve, but only under specific constraints to a very specific woman. They had enough money and initiative to find an outlet that didn't turn the rest of their lives upside down.

My fantasies were very different. I could fuck anyone I wanted, any way I wanted. Top? Bottom? Man? Woman? Both? I'd tried them all, and enjoyed everything, but that wasn't what I craved. And perhaps the act of monetizing arousal had changed it for me, from a source of delight to a fountain of funds. The thing that excited me most was the abundance sex work offered. There was so much money floating around, and if I were canny, some of it would flow my way.

My clients dreamed about me. I dreamed about their cash. I fantasized about a stock portfolio with millions and a bank account with even more. I imagined swooping into a gallery and buying out a show I liked, just because I could. The thing that got me hottest was the prospect of not wanting for anything and of keeping anything I adored. I had lost so much already.

There's a lot of time and energy wasted in the BDSM scene wondering who's really in charge. Some say it's the dominants, because moment to moment, they call the shots. Others say it's the submissives, because they constrain the action and they can stop things at any time just by uttering their safeword. I've always believed the person with the power is the person who wants something less than their counterpart. I became studious in transmitting this indifference to my clients, so they always wanted me more than I needed them. Clients could sniff out weakness, and I never wanted them to feel it from me. So even if my rent was due or I needed the five hundred bucks, I acted like that session was of no particular consequence.

When I first started out in the business of fulfilling erotic fantasies, I gave myself permission to indulge my own. It seemed hypocritical to deny myself. Of course, because I'd started young, there wasn't a lot of fresh turf to explore, but I tried. For the first six months or so, I was awash in arousal—theirs and mine. By day, I was reading up on Manet and his use of courtesans to depict outrageous scenarios, and by night, I was like a courtesan, enacting outrageous scenarios of my own with wealthy men.

I had an affair with the president of a local university who'd picked me up at Grill 23 one night when I was hungry for steak. After a few dates, I whispered in his ear how much I'd love to visit a massage parlor with him. For my birthday, he arranged a four-handed massage at a sleazy place in Allston. The ambiance might have been lacking, but the two women who slathered me in oil while the president watched, were delightful. One was a tall immigrant from Senegal whose graceful fingers were deft and fearless. The other, a bouncy Brazilian with bleached blonde hair, caressed my nipples while I stared at the president. He sat there smoking a cigar, taking in the sordid tableau. My orgasm was long and furious, earning the ladies their hundred-dollar tip.

After it was over, and I was alone in my tiny bedroom in Cambridge, I stared at the painting of young Erika, nude on my wall, and felt disappointment. I'd given away such a memorable and indecent moment for free. Was the fantasy really my own or had I surfaced some notion of the president's and claimed it as mine? I was long past knowing as I'd basically become an erotic vacuum cleaner, hoovering up fantasies and collecting them for later use.

I even wondered how much of my time on the massage bed had been performance—for him, for the ladies, and for me. The ten hours of sessions I booked with clients every week were beginning to seep into my own head, making it hard to discern between arousal and theater. And maybe, it didn't matter since I was getting paid handsomely for both.

If a client inquired about my sexual preference, I'd tell him it toggled between omnisexual and sapiosexual, suggesting that anything could happen if the client were only smart enough. But I was more a plutosexual, turned on by wealth and riches. I wondered if my best partner would be an eighteen-karat gold vibrator shaped like a dollar sign.

MICHAEL WAS ALREADY installed at a back booth at Balthazar when I arrived. The place was buzzing, so I knew he must have tipped the maître d' handsomely to secure such a prime seat.

"Hi there, darling. How are you?" I slid in next to Michael on the banquette, and we looked out at the room.

"So much better, now. You look fantastic, Erika."

"Thanks. Do you like the boots?" I contorted my body to give Michael a close view of my boots, from under the table. "A crazy little fetishist got them for me last month at Ralph Lauren."

"Very chic. He's got great taste." Michael seemed amused by the fact I was wearing someone else's gift, but I liked to let the men know their peers deemed me worthy of spoiling. It was a way of challenging them to up their game as they opened their wallets. "How's school going?"

"Really well, thanks. One year down. So far, so good. My professors seem happy, and I'm approaching Manet from a different angle going forward. I'm not going to write about him. Instead, I'm going to write about his models. This may surprise you, but I have grown fascinated by the role of sex workers in Impressionist art. I have an idea for a thesis, even."

"Isn't it early to be thinking about your dissertation? Shouldn't you be wallowing in art and seducing your professors?" The clients liked to imagine me as some kind of ravenous beast, bedding men and women whenever the mood struck. And I suppose there was some truth to that—it's just that I was rarely inclined. There was only so much space in my head or in my libido, and I was operating at capacity.

"It's never too early to begin thinking about a dissertation. I look at some of my classmates, and they have the luxury of mulling over different topics and different ideas. There's so much mental masturbation in my field because they have mummies and daddies who pay their bills. Not me. I'm focused."

"Good for you, Erika. My niece took seven years for her doctorate in history."

"That happens all the time. And the number who start on a doctorate, and who give up? It's about half. I'm not going to be one of them, or one of those people who takes seven or eight years to finish. I'm giving myself four, possibly five years. So, thank you, Michael, for being a member of my unofficial scholarship board. I hope you're suffering enough for my success."

"I'm hardly suffering at all, except during the day. I'd like to fire some clients. And maybe a partner or two." Michael then shared the details of a complicated case he was involved in as he devoured his steak frites, medium rare, and I enjoyed my coq au vin. The waiter arrived with some tarte tatin, compliments of the house. Michael gave him an enthusiastic nod as he deposited the plates in front of us.

"You're reminding me that the demimonde has some advantages over the real world. If I'm angry with a client, I can beat him. You can't."

"There are definitely some clients I'd like you to correct. But why should they have all the fun?" Michael leaned back against the leather banquette.

"Precisely. The dungeon is for decent people. Assholes can get their due somewhere else."

"I like your style, Erika. But I'd also like your advice on something." Michael paused midbite and put down his fork. "There's a show about to open at Tederich. I'm thinking of getting a piece and I'd appreciate your opinion."

"The Cecily Brown show? I adore her work. When would you like to go?"

"How about now? I have the time, and the owner is expecting us."

"Oh? Pay the check and let's march."

"I have an account here. We can leave whenever you're done with dessert." Michael grinned at how he'd finessed the moment.

"You're giving me a choice between another bite of tarte tatin and a private viewing at Tederich? Tederich will win every time." I ignored the apple tart still lingering on my plate and stood up. "Do I seem too eager?"

"Not at all. I love getting beautiful women excited."

"You've got game, Michael. I bet you left a trail of broken hearts behind you before you settled down." He shrugged. "Let's go look at some paintings." Michael held out his arm and I slipped my hand into the crook of his elbow as we walked the six blocks to the gallery, while I goaded him. "Ever tried bastinado?"

"On the feet? No!" Michael looked at me with horror as we walked down Greene Street, the cobblestones administering their own punishment to my feet, clad in my high heel boots chosen for style, not comfort.

"I had a client who craved it. And judicial canings. He told me the craziest story, once. He said he went to Tehran on a business trip and deliberately drove around with liquor in the back of his car, hoping the cops would stop him. Eventually, they did, and he got the nonconsensual caning of his life."

"That's remarkable. Was he for real?" Michael paused, shaking his head. "How'd he seem, otherwise?"

"As normal as you or me. A very serious academic. Big reputation in his field. Anyone else, and I'd think he was lying through his teeth about such a crazy caper."

"Do men lie to you?"

"Of course! You're a lawyer, don't your clients lie to you?" I asked, baffled he'd think his clients would be much different from mine.

Michael laughed. "Point taken. Clients lie all the time, at first, anyway, before they smarten up and realize how expensive dishonesty can be."

"Yes, lies are a waste of time and money. But they're part of the job."

"What lies do yours tell you?"

"Oh. Maybe they're embarrassed they have no experience, so they embellish. Maybe they're embarrassed they like something unusual, so they conceal. Maybe they're just living their fantasy, and the untruths are part of their game. I had one guy tell me he was a spy. If he were really a spy, he wouldn't tell, now, would he?"

"No, Erika, I suppose not. Do you know his real profession?"

"No. Haven't a clue. If it works for him, who am I to burst his bubble? If he wanted me to call him 007, I'd probably call him 008, instead. But I try to honor the fantasy, so long as it falls within my limits. That one? It felt harmless, and it gave me ideas to work with."

"If they're lying to you about silly things, how do you know they're not lying to you about serious things . . . like your safety."

"That's a worry, of course. It's not like there's some central registry of Johns. When there's a referral, like with you, I feel more comfortable with a gentleman. Otherwise, it's a very long phone conversation and then I try to fact check as best as I can before that first meeting. So far, I haven't had a problem."

"And then you tie them down."

"Yes. Or undress them. I always have the advantage. There are easier targets for assault. The bigger problem is stalkers."

"Yes, well you ladies are charming. And you are experts at things few women have even considered. It's hard to find fault with those poor lads who fall head over heels."

"That's why I prefer men like you, Michael. Men who are married, who don't want to fuck things up by getting infatuated with the woman who tortures their body."

"Exactly. And that's what I adore about women like you, Erika. There's mutual respect and understanding. I anticipate a long and excruciating partnership. Now let's go look at some paintings."

"You know just what to say to make me wet. Yes, let's." Before we went into the gallery, however, I needed more information. I didn't want to risk an embarrassing or awkward moment. "By the way, who am I to you? If anyone asks."

"Exactly who you are, Erika. A friend who's pursuing an art history PhD at Harvard."

"Perfect." We then buzzed at the door of a low building on Grand Street. It was after-hours, but Noah Tederich himself came to the door and let us in.

"Michael, so good to see you!" Tederich grinned and shook Michael's hand excitedly.

"Noah, thanks for giving us a peek. I missed the Brown show last year, so I wasn't going to make that mistake again." He turned to me, adding, "And Noah, I'd like to introduce you to Erika Grieg. Erika's at Harvard studying art history. You'll want to make her a job offer when she's finished."

Noah looked me up and down and smiled. I was wearing the sleek black uniform of a New York City gallerina, but with a little extra edge. There wasn't much distance, fashion-wise, between me and many of the saleswomen working at the top galleries. He extended his arm and shook my hand. "Wonderful to meet you, Erika. I hope you like what you see. And as for you, Michael, I haven't seen you since the Kruger show. What's been keeping you busy?"

The two men drifted away, and I was pulled to the far wall, where there was a painting that looked like somebody's body had exploded, smearing fluids and parts all over the place, in a fantastic, orgiastic mess. I felt a familiar surge of dopamine, as I took in the work. The combination of lust and love made me want to crawl inside the painting, a feeling I hadn't experienced since my first glimpse of that Picasso collage.

I took in the other works; in a style I had come to think of as my gallery dance. I'd start far back, taking in the piece as a whole, and then I'd saunter forward, getting closer and closer to the work, until all I could see were the details. Other works in the gallery had a pornographic edge, or a use of color and rhythm that conveyed passion, but that first painting vibrated. There were mouths, breasts, an audience watching an orgy of limbs. The pinks were the rich and tawdry colors of pricks and pussies. There were larger works on the walls, but none that conveyed the urgency of this particular piece, or its lewd invitation. Once I'd taken in the room, I stood in front of the object of my lust, soaking in the detail and marinating in its juices. Shockingly, there was no little red dot beside it.

"What do you think?" Michael walked up next to me and took in the painting that had caused my infatuation.

"This is the one." I made a showy gesture with my hand, as if I were one of the models on the TV show *The Price Is Right*. "Put it by your bed, so you can sleep next to it every night."

"That makes my decision very simple." Michael turned to Noah. "I want this one." The two men went to the back office to take care of the transaction, while I stood gazing at the blurry pink woman having an orgasm. Her arousal infected me, heightening my senses and deepening my breathing.

When Tederich came back with his little pad of red stickers used to indicate that a work had been sold, I asked if I could apply the dot. "Of course." He handed me the sticker, and I swear, as I applied it to the note card next to the painting, my body vibrated just like it did when I had an orgasm.

It took me a second to recover my composure afterward, so I decided to own my arousal. I looked at Tederich and said, "Excuse my vulgarity, but that felt fucking awesome."

Tederich nodded knowingly in response. "It does, Erika. Doesn't it?" He knew the power of matching a painting to an appetite.

Michael seized the moment and we went back to the suite at the Soho Prime, only two blocks away, and I squeezed him into the leather body bag and strapped it tight with belts. There was no space between him and the leather, and I proceeded to tease and torment him for hours. I left little red marks all over his body, to match the little red sticker I'd placed next to the Brown. He writhed and panted while my crop and lube worked over whatever body part happened to be exposed. And once he was gone, I lay back on the smooth white sheets of the bed and imagined inhabiting that wild, messy painting. Then I pulled out my Magic Wand. It was the best sex I'd had in months.

11
QUEEN OF THE DAMNED

1998–2001

My last years of grad school had me spending eight hours each day working on my thesis, "Posing for Peanuts: The Coercive Economics of Impressionist Art." Where artists like Degas and Manet had been able to get sex workers to do their bidding for a pittance, I would not make the same mistake. My time was valuable. My fees went up every year I was in Cambridge.

At first, before I understood the market dynamics, I was charging a mere two hundred per hour. It seemed like a lot of money compared to ten bucks an hour from Harvard, but I had so many inquiries to sift through, and that took time. Within a couple of months of turning pro, I had raised my prices to two-fifty, but it hardly changed the level of interest. Boston was starved for dominatrixes, and the area was filled with newly minted dot-com wealth. I was the perfect provider for frustrated nerds with a hunger for the hardcore, and I seized that market and shook the money out of it with as much strength as I could muster.

Someone else would have upgraded their apartment or invested in shares of Apple. Instead, I began buying art. I consumed catalogs and devoured trade magazines. I'd travel to New York, crash at my friend Amy's place if I couldn't find some client to underwrite the trip and then prowl the galleries or the auctions. My first splurge was at a tiny place on the Upper East Side, for a belle epoque oil of a naked woman with bat wings and wild dark hair. Her eyes stared out of the painting, daring the viewer to admire the translucency of her breasts and the perfect swell of her abdomen. The artist made me crave having wings of my own, so I could swoop and soar over the city, and claws, so I could shred handsy clients to bits. The sleazy seller had wanted eleven thousand, but I had talked him down to half that with an off-the-books transaction, paid in hundred-dollar bills.

After the Brown show had closed at Tederich, Michael announced he was shipping something to me. Two weeks later, a van from Gander & White parked in front of my dodgy apartment. I let the white glove movers in only as far as my entryway, before I signed and sent them to their next stop. It was the painting I'd helped Michael select, the one that had practically induced an orgasm. The gift had set him back fourteen thousand dollars. My collection was growing, even as my bank account was not. I had set out to accumulate riches, but instead, I was accumulating paintings. What was the point of being an outlaw, if not to acquire beautiful things?

The next couple of years passed quickly. I was making great progress on my dissertation, uncovering all sorts of juicy stories of exploitative artists dangling the notion of being a "muse" in front of susceptible young women. The women who had inspired so many of the works we now view as revolutionary had not gotten their due, and I was determined to highlight their abuse at the hands of so-called geniuses. My polemics on the topic in the popular press were starting to get noticed.

As my profile grew in feminist art history circles, I worried that my sex work activities might become a problem. I became convinced that in my corner of the industry, those dangers were highly overstated, and the warnings were probably a patriarchal ploy to frighten women out of work where they'd be the exploiters instead of the exploited. All the same, I culled my client base with ruthless precision. I wanted the most lucrative clients, namely those who wanted the most outrageous and lengthy scenes, and those who would be the most discreet.

At first, I was doing lots of hour-long spankings. Boston was awash in men with mommy issues, needing correction. Their butts couldn't handle more time, and neither could my hands. The related foot traffic in and out of my Cambridge apartment for so many gigs wasn't consistent with my desire for a quiet, lucrative business.

My dad had been an accountant, and he'd loved it when I sat next to him while he explained what he was doing for his clients. Without even realizing it, I had internalized many of his business practices. I made up a spreadsheet to analyze my sessions, to see if there were any trends to consider, and to identify which clients were responsible for most of my money or most of my hassles. There were only a dozen men who contributed over half of my revenues, Michael was one of them. I resolved to cultivate them further as they were my bread and butter.

The most problematic clients were the short gigs. None of them were awful, but I wouldn't miss the real estate broker who always pestered me for a second orgasm, saying things like, "Please, Mistress, I've been such a good boy," when he was lucky just to get one while strapped to my rack. And the spanking fetishist who used to taunt me during a session, trying to up the severity of his paddling, was not someone I'd miss, either. He'd grind his cock into my thigh in a way he had to know I hated, and then he'd say things like, "Evilena drew blood when she spanked my ass last year." "Madame de Sade made me cry when I was across her knee." What could be easier than drawing blood? It takes effort to *avoid* drawing blood. And as for tears? If he wanted to cry, he knew what he had to do, which was to book an extended session. Tears were for serious clients, only. Expiation came at a premium.

I tweaked my website and required a two-hour minimum. This would discourage the men for whom five hundred dollars was a stretch, and it would reorient the clients into thinking longer was better.

By raising my fees, I also found that I could seduce the right wallets. What they wanted was usually no more difficult or outrageous than the one-hour gigs, but their egos craved a feeling of scarcity. It was in my interest to suggest my time was precious, and that they were capturing it for themselves, to the exclusion of others. It took a couple of years, but my practice shifted to extravagant sessions involving lots of bondage or role-play.

I had to find a kinky contractor to help me install a chain hoist in my ceiling for suspension. Then, I had to get help installing soundproofing, so that my neighbors wouldn't hear the click of the ratchet. In addition to my classes and my research, I was earning a reliable three thousand a week. It wasn't investment banker money, but this was on top of my grad school stipend, and my earnings were all cash. Sure, some women reported their income to the IRS, but I was putting most of mine toward art, and I wanted no records. In addition to the charms of being an outlaw, I learned an important lesson from my father: if no one knows you have something, they can't take it from you.

Even calamity didn't slow me down. First, there was the dot-com crash. There had been so much money pouring into nerd pockets in the late nineties, that I recognized the mania and girded against it. I had seen that glazed look and the pressured speech in my father, before my family's world underwent its violent correction. So, I rebalanced my portfolio of clients. The MIT graduates who populated tech companies were overrepresented, so I picked up doctors and lawyers in their place. It was a straightforward marketing puzzle, which I solved by suggesting medical and legal role-plays. I created new sections of my website targeted at the clients I wanted. "The judge will see you now." "The doctor will see you now." "Open your legs and say 'ah.'"

My suspicions had been correct. Those swaggering geeks got pummeled in early 2000, when tech stocks plummeted. Their queries ceased, but I had backstopped them with other pervy professionals, and I only needed eight to ten hours a week to meet my financial quotas, anyway.

The failures of the tech bros meant the secondary art market was flush with their impulse buys. I became one of the vultures, swooping down with cash in hand whenever I learned that something spicy was available. Some of the artworks were contemporary, some were not, but they were all erotic—at least to me. There was a close-up of a safety pin pricking a finger that gave me a frisson whenever I looked at it. It was ridiculously expensive for a grad student, but I knew it would appreciate in value, and I adored the feeling I got whenever I thought about possessing it. I wanted it on my wall, above my bed, for me alone to enjoy.

Just like I had no interest in sharing my life or my body with anyone other than paying customers, I had no intention of sharing my artistic pleasures with anyone either. I stuffed my purse with thick wads of hundred-dollar bills and made the deal. And although I was diligent about learning the provenance of the works, no dealer ever asked me where I got the money. The work went up on the wall of my bedroom, joining my burgeoning collection. I'd stare at the pieces, immersing myself in the works, and lull myself to sleep.

This may sound insane, but 9/11 was even less of a setback. Business dried up for a couple of weeks when the city of Boston came to a standstill. Many of the hijackers had boarded their flights at Logan Airport, and the place was awash in rumors that their buddies were still in town. The roads emptied of cars, just like the skies emptied of planes. My inbox was also empty. But within a week, I got sheepish queries from clients. "Is it too early to think about booking something?"

Like everyone, I'd been glued to my television set, terrified about the future, but those awkward emails were signs of our collective resilience. People were looking ahead, and bodies were seeking pleasure. Michael visited as soon as it was possible to leave New York. And while September had been at a standstill, October was one of my best months in the business and November was even better.

Clients were desperate for connection, and we were all determined to prove that we could not be frightened by a pathetic bunch of jihadists with a death wish. Bondage and discipline became a bold celebration of joy, and like everyone, I was eager to partake in something optimistic and decadent. Nietzsche once said, "Without cruelty, there'd be no festival." Well, I was going to crack my whip. I'd be the Mistress of Ceremonies and the Queen of the Damned.

12

BIG CITY

Spring 2002

I'd been lying through my teeth since high school. First about my criminal father, then about my criminal life. I made up lovers and fiancés to explain to my friends why I was busy nights and weekends. I made up consulting jobs to explain away the expensive clothes.

I fabricated fiction to explain my life to my mother, my professors and my friends, because there was no way I'd share with them my secret sideline as Miss E. They wouldn't understand. They might judge. They might say I was going to hell. They might tell. I might lose everything I'd worked so hard to get. Every time you share a secret, the odds shift toward the world knowing. And although I felt no shame for my professional dalliances, I knew being a part of a deviant subculture could scar my reputation and render me unemployable.

Women profiting off their sexuality was a terrifying thought in America. Most men resented the notion they might have to pay for their pleasure, and most women had been conditioned to think that prostitution was dangerous and crass. That an entire sector of the sex industry existed where women didn't even need to fuck their clients would have blown their minds, but that was a conversation I had no interest in having. I knew of other professional dominatrixes who'd shared the stories of their work with civilians and suffered terrible consequences. They'd lost jobs, custody, partners, families. And even though I was identifiable to my clients, they had so much to lose, they would be crazy to share their knowledge with the world.

It wasn't easy, but I was maniacal about keeping a low profile. Once I had achieved a certain level of clientele, I stopped advertising, and my website was little more than a page where a knowing submissive could send a message and pray it landed in the right place. I often wished those measures hadn't been necessary, but there were message boards where the consumers of professional domination would discuss the providers, and they would go into the sessions in lurid detail. It was like a *Zagat Guide* to sex work. Some of the session descriptions were even more complete than the notes I kept after each encounter.

I announced my retirement when I saw this on one of those wretched sites, next to a score of 9.5 out of 10:

> Miss E, and E is short for Erica, is a statuesque brunette with extraordinary legs to match her exceptional intellect. She's a Harvard grad student, so you know she means it when she tells you that you're a stupid, worthless piece of shit. And the way she stripes your ass with a whip? It's straight out of the Inquisition. If Torquemada had a hot little sister, she'd probably be working in a third-floor walkup in East Cambridge. Erica's studio is within spitting distance of the Lechmere T station and there's plenty of on-street parking.

There was so much wrong with that review. I never called anyone a "stupid, worthless piece of shit." I preferred calling them "useless" and "good only for their wallets." Torquemada killed people and oversaw a reign of terror; my torture was ritualized and eroticized. Nobody had died on my watch. He hadn't scored me a 10, where he had done so for at least one of my colleagues. And the indiscreet jerk had all but given my address to anyone who was looking. If the Cambridge cops wanted to crack down, a competitor wanted to fuck with me, or say, if a neighbor put the pieces together, I'd be in serious trouble.

I figured out who LegMan617 was—the pudgy-faced CFO of a local start-up—and invited him over. He knew where I was, so it was just a question of timing.

When he arrived at my place, I was wearing a short black skirt, black fishnet hose, and no shoes, because he was the kind of foot fetishist who was all about the stockings and the toes, and not about the pumps. He clearly had no idea he was in trouble.

The CFO got down on his knees as soon as I'd shut the door behind him, and he placed a well-stuffed envelope on a small table by the entryway that I had trained the clients to use for their tributes. He was blissfully unaware as I playfully removed all his clothes. And even though it was out of the ordinary, he didn't resist when I pulled out two pairs of handcuffs and locked his wrists to the arms of the desk chair in my living room, nor did he object when I wrapped his balls tightly in rope, and clutched the leftover cord in my hand so that I could yank at will. The indiscreet man stared up at me in anticipation, blind to the fact that I was extremely pissed off.

"What would you like, Mistress Erika?" His cock bobbed with anticipation.

"So nice of you to ask, Gary. I'd like my privacy back." I gave the rope a sharp pull, as I balanced in front of him on the desk. My camera was ready, and I took a photo of him while his jaw dropped. My contempt was obvious.

"What the fuck are you doing?" he hissed at me and strained against the handcuffs. I gave his balls a harder tug.

"What the fuck are you doing, *MISTRESS*?" I corrected him. "Where the fuck do you think you are? Who the fuck do you think you're talking to, you useless piece of shit?"

He quickly realized he had to play along, and perhaps he figured it was a game, so his voice changed from panic to playful. "Sorry, *MISTRESS*. You surprised me. What's it gonna take for you to delete that picture?"

"That's the correct question, Gary." I grabbed his face with my hand and brought my eyes within a few inches of his. I imagined digging my fingers into his flesh and flaying his face, but I let go before leaving a mark. "You know how diligent I am about preserving your privacy. This photo feels like I violated you, doesn't it?" Gary bobbed his head. "And it is. A *horrible* violation of your privacy. Who'd do such a thing to someone they like and trust? Who'd take private, personal information, without the other's consent, and share it with the world?"

"You're right, Mistress, it's a violation." I could see Gary squirming, as he wondered where this conversation was headed. I slapped his face hard, and leaned back, pushing my foot into his crotch with a force that had to hurt.

"Only a total asshole would do such a thing. Am I right, Gary?" Gary nodded. "Because the things we do . . . the things we enjoy are vilified by the public, and if it got out that we are, you know, deviant perverts, who knows what would happen? You'd lose your job. You'd probably lose your wife. You love your kids, don't you, Gary? Wouldn't it be awful to lose them, too?" Gary nodded some more. The stakes of our encounter were sinking in. "Like, if it got out I was a grad student at Harvard, and I have a place near Lechmere, I might face repercussions. Isn't that right, Gary?" His head continued to nod, but at a slower pace. "I'm on the verge of finishing my doctorate. And that stupid fucking review you wrote on Dickie's site could ruin my future fucking career. So, I have a choice Gary, and today, I'm veering toward mutually assured destruction. Did you write any other fucking reviews?" I yanked the rope attached to his balls for emphasis. "Anywhere?"

Gary let out a howl, before he replied. "I wrote one for *The Erotic Review*, too. They give you a free three-month membership when you do, and I didn't want any credit card charges."

"That's unacceptable, Gary." I slapped his face again. This time, he was more prepared, and he braced himself for the impact. So I hit him again, harder, before continuing. "The more I learn, the more I'm convinced it's time for me to leave the business. Thanks to indiscreet assholes like you and thanks to these fucking breaches, I'm retiring."

"I'm sorry, Mistress. It won't happen again. I'll delete the reviews. I know you hate those things. I'm sorry."

"That's exactly what I want to hear, Gary. Let's do it now." I grabbed my laptop and let him log into his accounts while I watched.

He deleted the offending comments and replaced them with a simple, "It's Boston's loss, but Miss E has retired and moved to San Francisco. We should all respect Her privacy and cease any further discussions. It's what She wants, and I respect Her too much to do anything that goes against Her wishes." He looked up at me, with his soft brown eyes. "Is that okay? I promise I won't do anything like that again."

"By the way, you gave Goddess Alexa a score of ten, and you only gave me a nine-point-five. What was that about? She's a hack. No gear. No clothes. She's only a hooker with a whip."

Gary looked at me sheepishly. "She lets me eat her out."

"You don't deserve this." I pointed to my pussy. "And you sure as hell don't deserve hers, either. What on earth is that foolish chick thinking?" I slapped his face again.

"I like it. And she says my tongue serves her well."

"I bet she does, Gary. Now let's make you really suffer for your sins." I then proceeded to shove my right foot in his face and rubbed it on his cheeks and across his mouth until I saw his erection return and I felt his tongue probing my toes. "Yes. Lick harder. This is the only place your tongue goes on me, now get to work, asshole. This is your last chance."

At the end of our encounter, after he'd ejaculated on my toes and licked them clean, Gary got down on his knees and kissed my feet goodbye. "Thank you, Mistress. Thank you for forgiving me, Mistress. Are you sure we can't keep in touch?"

"I'm leaving Cambridge. This kind of violation has taken the joy out of the misery of others."

"Oh, are you sure I can't do sessions with you on the sly? I travel a bunch with work. Just tell me your name and where you're going, and I'll keep it to myself."

"One sec . . . You want my name? As in my real name? When you couldn't even be discreet about Miss E?"

"When you put it like that, it sounds crazy. But I promise, I'll do better, now that I know what the problem is." Gary continued, "Where are you moving to?"

"I'm moving away. Sorry, Gary, but that's all you get." Did he really think I'd answer? The gall of these men staggered me sometimes.

"Aw, Mistress . . . I'm truly sorry. I didn't mean you any harm, I just wanted to avoid a credit card charge. But now I understand. This was one of my best sessions ever. The intensity was over the top and I actually wondered what you were capable of."

"Hold that last thought, because I'm capable of so much more . . . and you wouldn't like any of it. So this is it, Gary. Hope you find someone new to serve, and that they find you worthy."

Gary stood up and slowly got dressed. He seemed to understand he wasn't going to be an exception to my rule. "Good luck with your new life. I wish you weren't retiring. Once again, I'm sorry."

As a peace offering, I ruffled his hair and kissed him on the cheek as he walked out the door. It probably didn't dawn on him until he found his car, that I hadn't deleted his photo. It was just a tiny bit of insurance I'd tuck away, in the unlikely event it was necessary. It's not like there was a dominatrix licensing board he could complain to, and what would he even say?

I called Michael after Gary had left, and he laughed at my situation. "You should tell more of these guys you're retiring. You're graduating soon, and I'll make sure you've got proper introductions with Gagosian, Zwirner and Deitch. You don't need these small-timers anymore. You're going to be mopping up in the big leagues."

13

DAY AND NIGHT

Fall 2002

My classmates at Harvard were envious of my offers from Gagosian and Zwirner. Michael had set me up with both organizations for interviews, and all either of them really cared about in their sales staff was charisma and connections. Gagosian attracted more billionaires, so I went there.

Unfortunately, whale hunting is a slow, tedious process, and the salary sucks. My base pay was trivial, and commissions were tough to predict. My days were spent on the phone and on the gallery floor, trying to fulfill the art fantasies of the skittish wealthy, while my nights were spent in a dungeon in Midtown East, trying to fulfill the kinky fantasies of bankers and lawyers. Michael had set me up there, too.

Madame Margot was a living legend in the rarefied world of professional domination. She'd been at it for over thirty years; unfortunately, she looked like she'd been at it for sixty. Her face was leathery from the sun at the St. Bart's retreat of one of her personal slaves. She hid her flab behind multiple layers of leather and corsetry, only this meant her mobility was hindered as she tottered around in the thigh high leather boots that she'd bought in Berlin in the sixties. But I couldn't deny that she was chic. Madame wore her hair in a sharp silver bob, her lipstick was always deep red, and for all her wrinkles and sags, she had the eyes of an ingenue—they always seemed delighted and surprised by what was in front of her.

She had an extraordinary dungeon in a low-key office building in the east thirties. Madame's practice was so discreet, she'd been there for a decade without a single complaint from her neighbors. To the enormous disappointment of her dedicated slaves, she was also looking to retire. For the better part of a year, I worked with her and her clients. The gentlemen adored her and they paid through the nose for her mix of magic and mayhem.

My role was to offer eye candy while doing all the heavy lifting. At first, I balked. I'd had a successful solo practice in Boston. The prospect of doing her laundry didn't thrill me, likewise, cleaning up puddles of lube after her trademark strap-on dildo sessions, but I persisted. She was generous enough. We split the take eighty-twenty. She got the eighty, of course. My goal was to outlast her, and then take over the shop. And besides, I had a day job. Fortunately, Madame was basically a vampire who avoided the sunlight, unless it was to lie like a lizard and absorb its energy. We made it work. Her clients took to me, and I took to them. They weren't all as geriatric as she was. Some just wanted to drink from the source and to be awed by a living legend.

What I most admired about Madame was the seriousness and fastidiousness she had applied to her craft. For instance, she had a top-of-the-line autoclave for sterilizing the various metal insertables she used on her submissives, and once the items were done, I was trained to seal them in a little packet for later use.

"*Non, non. Pas comme ça*," she'd whisper, if I didn't coil the rope the way she preferred. Every day, it was a different lesson: "*Non, non. Pas comme ça*." But like her clients, I adored the way she'd say the most outrageous things in her trademark whisper. "Today, we are going to truss Jean-Pierre like a turkey, and then use a turkey baster to fill him with butter."

"Seriously, Madame, with butter?"

"No, not really butter—we'll use warmed lube, it's more hygienic, but we'll tell him it's butter and that we're going to enact that scene in *Last Tango in Paris* with my favorite bull, that Dutch guy with the enormous cock."

For a second, she had me believing some guy was going to come by to fuck Jean-Pierre in the ass. "Madame, I've never heard of this Dutch guy." I paused. "Who's really getting the pleasure of impaling JP? You or me?"

"This time? You!"

"Perfect. Good thing I need a shower, because it's going to get messy, isn't it?"

"Bien sûr, Erika. Bien sûr."

When Jean-Pierre arrived, he followed Madame's preferred protocol. As soon as the door closed, he placed an envelope on her bookshelf, stripped naked, and then got down on his hands and knees and waited. It was my job to put a collar around his neck and lead him as he crawled into Madame's chamber. Madame sat waiting on her throne for her supplicant. She had the room lit beautifully, so she looked radiant and regal as she drummed her fingers while clad head to toe in leather mufti.

The rule was the slaves only looked at Madame when they were speaking to her, otherwise, they were to look at the floor. My job was to monitor their eyes, to make sure they didn't cheat. Or rather, to make sure that when they cheated—which they always did— there were consequences. "Madame, this worthless slut looked at you without permission."

"Ah, *pas encore?*" She got up and circled Jean-Pierre, careful not to step on his fingers, as he lowered himself as much as he could, toward the floor. I stood nearby, taking in the scene. By day,

Jean-Pierre was the managing director of a French investment bank, torturing his underlings. By night, he was a naughty little slave, being tortured by Madame. It seemed like a life in balance. Torture. Be tortured. I wondered if he needed some art, to add further decadence and beauty to the symmetry of his life.

After a few months of my indentured servitude, when I had proven myself as adept at working the vacuum bed as I was at using the autoclave, Madame announced that she was going to St. Bart's for a few months and that I should take over in her absence. The split would be fifty-fifty.

It was a crazy existence. Thank goodness one of Madame's clients was a doctor who gave me prescriptions for Provigil. I didn't care for coke to fuel my days, but Provigil kept fighter pilots awake so that was my drug of choice. The pace was grueling, and it rankled that I was earning so much money for other people. Once again, Michael helped me put it all in perspective after I had finished a heavy suspension scene with him.

"Has Madame told you when she's coming back?" Michael asked, while sipping from a bottle of apple juice. His blood sugar had to be low from the workout I'd given him.

"When we spoke yesterday, she said she was going to stay in St. Bart's for another couple of months. Who abandons their business and their clients like this?"

"She's left it in good hands. She trusts you. But how do you feel about the situation?"

"*Fucking exhausted.* I'm putting out. My sales numbers at the gallery are solid. I haven't been screamed at in months. But the commissions suck—I only get ten percent. I'm doing crazy things to close deals, and I'm closing them, but it's almost more lucrative to be doing BDSM. Well, it's more lucrative if you're Madame. At least I get half when Madame's away."

"I'm telling Madame she should retire," Michael said. "She should leave the playing field while still at its summit."

"No! You have more guts than I do. I mean, you're right, of course. She's not moving very fast these days, and I worry she's going to hurt herself . . . or someone else . . . She's lost her edge, and this work demands a ton of edge."

"I've had this conversation with many CEOs. No one thinks it's time. They all think they're indispensable. But Madame is no different. She should be enjoying the fruits of her labors. And so should you."

"What do you mean?"

"I've recommended she pass her practice on to you. You'll pay her a percentage of your fees for a year, and then it'll be yours."

"Madame is down for this? I thought paramedics would carry her out of this dungeon." When you've explored someone's darkest fantasies, made them pant and plead, you think you know them well, but Michael had retained the capacity to astonish me.

"Madame is ready to put up her boots. I speak with her almost every day."

"You talk to her more often than I do!"

"We've known one another a long time. And I told her that you are her rightful successor."

"I'm not ready to believe she's retiring. Retirements are a dime a dozen. I lurk on the message boards, and there's someone announcing their retirement every month or two. They disappear for a while. But then they come back. I think the real world leaves them unsatisfied, so they return to the demimonde, as if nothing ever happened."

"You're being too hard on your peers. Ladies lose jobs or spouses. Their lives change. Isn't it wonderful how they can always return to this profession?"

"Working in the sex industry can be an insurance policy, but it's also a trap. The money's just good enough to spoil you. I can't quit it, not that I want to . . . The work is creative, the clients are great, and the money . . . It gives me room to breathe where my day job doesn't."

"Erika, let's sit down sometime and figure out a strategy to inte-grate these two worlds of yours. I know you've been running the numbers . . . Let's figure out how much seed capital you need to launch your own gallery." Michael paused and leaned in conspir-atorially. "But one with a room dedicated to your other interests. Spare yourself the commute."

"Have you been reading my mind, Michael? I've been looking at spaces in Chelsea, and there's a little building that speaks to me. I'm not ready for it yet, but soon."

"Save your pennies, and we can work on the Grieg Gallery together."

"That's even the name I had in mind. You are a fucking mind reader, Michael. So, what am I thinking, now?"

"You're thinking I need to be punished for being so astute."

"You are so right." I couldn't help but roll my eyes. The man was good at getting what he wanted. "Next time, you'll pay with my cane."

"You're the mind reader, Erika. The cane is exactly what I was thinking of."

14
DADDY'S LITTLE PRINCESS

June 2008

Because I'd been in Los Angeles for a week, I didn't realize my father had started haunting the gallery. My assistant, Josh, called me, perplexed. The white-haired man had come back, and he was looking for me. I told Josh to say nothing and then called Michael immediately. He'd been my best client and also, my consigliere for years. He'd even given me the seed capital for the gallery. We spoke almost daily, and I trusted his advice just like he trusted me to get his mind off of giving advice.

"Michael, my father's up to something. He's come by the gallery twice this week."

"Hmmm . . . That doesn't sound good. Does he need money?"

"He always needs money." The man was perpetually broke, which meant he was perpetually scheming.

"Of course. But perhaps his motives are pure this time. Maybe he wants to repay the money he took from you?"

"He could just write me a check, if he wanted to, and put it in the mail."

"Of course. You know him best. Do you know where he's working?"

"No. He must have something going on in New York, since he's around at such random times. I just have a feeling something's brewing."

"Your instincts are solid, Erika. Are you going to meet with him? Do you want a lawyer present?"

"Well, a meeting seems inevitable. As for the presence of a lawyer, it's thoughtful of you to offer, but that would be an escalation. I think it's smarter just to gather information, and then figure out if I need your services." I inhaled deeply. "Oh, who the fuck am I kidding? I always benefit from your services. But this time, I'd rather keep you as my secret weapon."

"Understood. Just know I'll help any way I can. I know how he troubles you."

"Thanks. I'll tell Josh to let Dad know I'm back on Thursday and I'll meet him head on . . . He's my father. Maybe he just wants to reconnect?"

"That's what I'd tell my corporate clients; gather intelligence and then make a decision. Let me know how the meeting goes."

"You'll be the first person who finds out, Michael."

Thursday dragged. There were no clients of any kind to deal with, and there was only so much any of us could do to hustle up buyers for our lingering inventory of works. The markets were in turmoil, and no one was buying anything—from stocks to statues. As we were closing up for the day, my father appeared at the door. Josh offered to stay, but I sent him home.

"Hey princess, you got some time?"

"Of course, Dad. I knew you'd be stopping by, so I left things pretty open. Come in." I led him to the conference area in the back and sat down at the large wooden table.

"Hey, this looks like the table your mom picked out for our dining room back in Brentwood."

"Good catch, Dad. It's a Nakashima. Mom has great taste." I put a notepad in front of me as my father pulled out the chair opposite mine.

"Yes, you're right. Your mother always had an eye. Well, princess, I'm not here to admire your furniture. I need your help."

"You mean, like that time you needed help three years ago and I loaned you twenty thousand dollars and then I didn't hear from you for a year?"

"I feel bad about that. How many times do I have to say I'm sorry?"

"Once, with feeling, along with the twenty thousand bucks."

"I'm sorry. Truly. But I have a way to make it up to you."

"Oh? I know a simple way."

"You're not making this easy on me, Erika, because I don't have a spare twenty thousand lying around."

"Who does?" I could hear an edge creeping into my voice.

"It looks like you're doing okay."

"I was doing okay. But sales are way down. You know there's a crisis brewing, right?"

"Yes, of course I do. That's why I'm here. Everyone is scrambling but I've unearthed an amazing opportunity, and it would make you far more than twenty thousand."

"Oh? Is this another one of those deals where you're going to try and sell my clients some cockamamie art fund investment? Or maybe it's like the time you pretended you were a consultant to the IMF as you tried to hustle my classmates' parents? Or maybe it's like when I was a kid, and you took all that money from every bigwig in Hollywood? Is it like one of those times?"

"For crying out loud, princess, give me a break. Will you ever let me forget how I fucked up your childhood?"

"Probably not. But we might as well cut to the chase. What brings you here?"

"Okay. Did you know that Basquiat had a five-hundred-dollar-a-day heroin habit?"

"Yes. Everyone knows that." Basquiat's drug use was legendary and part of his myth.

"Well, did you know he often traded paintings for drugs?"

"Yes. Everyone knows that."

"Well, I got to know one of his dealers when I was at Lompoc. I can get you several of Basquiat's works to sell."

"Daddy, don't be fencing paintings for drug dealers. It'll only get you in trouble."

"I'm not fencing, and he's not a drug dealer anymore. He's a *businessman*. And these are honest to goodness Basquiats. I reconnected with some of my old, uh, friends a few months back, and he showed me paintings he'd gotten twenty years ago, from some drugged-out painter. I recognized the works immediately and thought of you. The guy needs money, but he doesn't want to deal with some snooty art gallery. If you sell them, everybody wins."

"How do you know the guy's legit? How do you know the paintings are legit?"

"Well, his arrest is in the public record, look him up. Nicky Burns. He sold a shit-ton of heroin in New York in the eighties. He was practically the King of Heroin. As for the paintings, look for yourself." My father threw a few Polaroids in front of me, displaying some larger works in Basquiat's style. I eyed them suspiciously. They weren't part of any *catalogue raisonné* of Basquiat's works. How could they be? They'd have been traded right out of his studio for drugs.

"I don't sell into the secondary market. I don't know people who collect these works."

"Oh, come on, princess. Don't play stupid. Just pick up your phone and tell the story of the drug dealer to a couple of your investment bankers. I could hang the paintings in your gallery, for the prospects to look at themselves. I can even furnish copies of Nicky's arrest record. The paintings are classic. It all checks out."

"Dad, it's never that simple. My clients, the people I know best, prefer young artists. They're like investors who buy emerging markets or penny stocks. They figure they have the foresight to pick winners and get the hundred banger for their investment. In ten years, they want to be able to say they bought out of the artist's first show. The people who buy Basquiats are a whole different animal."

"Think about it? You'd be doing me a huge favor and earning yourself a fat commission in the process. I'd only need your gallery for a day. Hell, I'd only need a wall in your gallery for a day."

"I'm not optimistic. You and your friend should find another outlet. Go get the works authenticated. I can tell you who does that."

"I don't want another outlet. I want you."

"I understand, Daddy. But I'm not the right person for this job."

"I'll persuade you, princess."

"Seriously, just get them authenticated. That authentication will more than double their value."

"That's not how Nicky wants this done. He wants a quick, quiet sale." My father shrugged. "Let the buyer authenticate and double his investment."

"No. I don't want to have anything to do with unauthenticated works, and my clients are not your clients. Find someone else."

"Princess . . . can I just bring the works by?"

"Absolutely not." I didn't want any dodgy paintings anywhere near my gallery. Their presence could only cause problems for me and all my enterprises.

"I'm desperate, princess. I just need one big score, and that's it for me. Please think it over."

"Oh, I'll be thinking about this, but I won't change my mind. Please go." I stood up and pointed toward the door. My dungeon voice emerged. "Now."

"I'm sorry about what happened, you know." My father looked sad and small, but I didn't want to comfort him. All I felt was fear—and rage. How dare he try to involve me in his scheme? I was livid that he had the capacity to wreak so much havoc in my life, but I remained superficially calm. There was no point letting him know just how unsettled he'd made me. "I know you're sorry. And so am I. Let's just call it an evening."

I locked the door behind my father and slowly climbed the stairs to my apartment. As soon as I'd poured myself a glass of Bordeaux, I called Michael. "Have you got any time tonight? I have a big problem."

MICHAEL CAME OVER promptly and listened carefully as I explained what had happened with my father. "How do you know they're fakes?" He had a notepad in front of him and jotted away while I spoke.

"I don't. It's a feeling. And by the way, they're excellent fakes. Everything is right. The boldness of the colors. The strength of the squiggles. The text looks and sounds correct. The primitive figures are skeletal and weird. There's a gold crown somewhere. A couple of the works are on canvas, and some are on found objects. Each work has the Basquiat trademarks, but none of his known works check all the boxes in the same way. It's like he's offering me a trove of Basquiat's greatest hits. The works are pastiche, perhaps. But are they original? I didn't feel or see the artist's hand. There was always a geometry to how Basquiat placed the elements in his works. That logic is gone. The compositions felt off to me."

"Are you sure? You're not a specialist."

"No, I'm not. But when I worked at Gagosian, I spent hours with his works. And the story kind of makes sense. But let's say you're Basquiat . . . and you owe your drug dealer thousands of bucks. And by the way, dealers are not art connoisseurs. Why would Basquiat give some heroin dealer his best works, right out of his studio? You give your drug dealer your shitty pieces on cardboard, or the studies for your bigger pieces. You don't give your fucking heroin dealer the monumental stuff you're working on to show at the Whitney Biennial or that Mary Boone's going to sell at her gallery. Sure, he was drugged out, but he wasn't fucking stupid."

"Is there a way to authenticate these works, Erika? There are experts who do this."

"Well, the artist is dead, and his estate no longer wants to get involved in the messy business of authenticating. You know how litigious people get when they're told they own a fake."

"Yes. A colleague of mine at Patterson Belknap is working on a Basquiat case right now." Michael shook his head.

"It's not like there's a way to prove, forensically, that it's not a Basquiat. You can't do carbon dating on something that's only twenty-five years old. Wavelet decomposition might be able to sniff out a fake but it's still too new a technique and far too mathematical. No one trusts those statistical black boxes. So, we'd have to rely on the opinion of a so-called expert, and they can be wrong. Frankly, it's clever to fake something contemporary."

"I suppose. And the market is hot for Basquiat's work. The best works are selling for over ten million." Michael stroked his chin and paused while that enormous number dangled in the air. "What do you think is happening with your father? Do you want me to get the firm's private investigator to look into things? He might be able to figure out where the paintings came from."

"Let me think about your offer. Serious forgeries like these cost tens of thousands to commission. It's not like there's a factory cranking out Basquiats. There's probably just one guy in a quiet studio in Brooklyn. Probably some MFA buried in debt."

"Debt to his drug dealer?"

"Could be. Or Yale. They have a lot in common. Both traffic in elusive emotions and improbable thrills, but only one of them is illegal. As you know, people graduate from studio art programs with hundreds of thousands of dollars in debt—it's crushing—and the probability of financial success is slim. What's a little drug habit compared to that kind of underlying misery and uncertainty?"

"Good point. Sometimes, I'm amazed any art gets made. Who do you think is behind the paintings? Do you think it was your dad's idea?"

"Given the story my dad's telling, I'm guessing organized crime's involved. His friend, the retired drug dealer, is still a criminal."

"Then so is your dad." I nodded. What could I say? My father hadn't changed, in fact, he may have gotten worse. "It's like being pregnant. You're never just a little bit pregnant. You're never just a little bit into a criminal conspiracy."

"Right."

"You told him you weren't interested, of course?"

"Yes. I gave him a strong no, but I don't think he was persuaded. He's not just going to go away, Michael. He *never* just goes away."

"No, probably not. Everybody is scrambling to do deals at the moment, to bolster their liquidity. My blue-chip clients are no different."

"I'm scrambling too. I have reserves, and I have other sources of income beyond art, thank goodness, but everything has become harder."

"Can you make payroll and your mortgage? As I've offered before, I'll help. All you have to do is ask."

"You've been extraordinary. I couldn't have bought the building without your money for the down payment, but I've got things covered. It's tight, but there's enough in the bank for a few months. And if I go spend some time with Edouard de Grenet, he's offered me a Hirst to flip."

"So, it's feasible, then . . . Make yourself scarce. I wouldn't normally recommend that tactic, but you're dealing with family and you're dealing with a proposition that could destroy you, professionally."

"Yeah. If it gets out I'd sold forgeries, then I'm either a dupe or dishonest. There's no escaping it. That question would hang over me. The stench would never go away. It's ruined people."

"And your name would be linked to your father's. With Google, there's no escaping the past once a story's out."

"Don't remind me. I had no idea Google would exist when I took my mom's surname. That turned out lucky."

"Yes, extremely lucky. Your business is built on trust. If your clients don't trust what you're selling, how can they do business with you? It's difficult, but making yourself inaccessible might be the easiest, lowest risk approach."

"Low risk, perhaps. But easy? I'd have to get out of town for a couple of months. How on earth do I do that?"

"Your team knows how to operate the gallery. They do it when you're away for a week or two. Why not a month or two?"

"It's not so much the gallery as my *other* clients. I've invested so much in getting and keeping them happy. If I disappear for a few months, they may find other diversions. That would be a bigger problem than the shitty art market."

"You need to find a substitute dominatrix." Michael grinned at the prospect while I tried not to laugh.

"I'll put an ad on Craigslist: *Wanted, Substitute Dominatrix, training provided*. Who'd answer a crazy ad like that?"

"Oh, you're making this more difficult than it has to be. What about one of your colleagues? They'd kill for the opportunity to see your clients."

"Yes, and then they'd steal and keep those clients."

"Good point. So, perhaps someone who's retired but who still likes to dabble?"

"Mistress Ariadne retired a couple of years ago. She was hot, and boy did she know how to make a scene sizzle . . . But I'm not sure I'd trust her with my space. I'll have to think about this."

"Okay. Forget seasoned and skilled. Who do you trust most?"

"Oh, that's easy. My friend Amy. But she's no dominatrix. She's an investment banker."

"Amy . . . she's that tall, athletic brunette, right?"

"Right. You've met her."

"Oh yes." Michael paused, clearly savoring the memory. "She's extremely attractive. She even looks a bit like you."

"Oh, did Amy catch your eye?"

"Is there something wrong with that?" Michael winked at me, bringing a bit of levity to the conversation.

"She's a bit mousy, with a borrowed sense of style."

"And this is a problem? You can fix her. You don't need someone amazing. You only need someone good enough. The hard part is finding someone you'd trust with your place and secrets."

I grimaced. "We were roommates at Harvard. I've known her forever. She's the kind of person who, if you dropped a hundred-dollar bill, she'd pick it up, and then run five blocks to hand it back. If she borrowed your car, she'd return it with a full tank of gas."

"She sounds perfect. Is she kinky?"

"Hardly. She's straight as an arrow. I don't even think she's sexual. But she just lost her job in the BFB restructuring, so she'd be available."

"Could you train her? Teach her a few tricks?"

"What do you think I am, a magician? I just wave my crop and a dominatrix appears! There must be easier options."

"Everything is on the table. But in my opinion, you need to get as far away from your father and his cronies as possible. And soon."

"He's tenacious. He'll be back."

"You're pretty tenacious, yourself. Perhaps it's in the DNA? Convince Amy. I'll help with her training."

"Ah, now I understand. You want a bespoke dominatrix; one you've built yourself. You'd be the anti-*Pygmalion*. Turning a proper lady into a sex worker, only one whose talents are fine-tuned to your appetites."

"And what's wrong with that? This would be yet another one of my fantasies you've helped me realize. *You make dreams come true.*"

"Why yes, I do. Do you remember that crazy afternoon during Art Basel Miami Beach, when there were three of us working you over?"

Michael nodded, his mind clearly flashing back on a penthouse hotel suite where I'd presented him with two lingerie models/escorts to provide us with entertainment. "That blonde was magical."

"Yes. She sucked your cock like a hoover while I had you tied down to the bed. That brunette was a waste of flesh though, she was so strung out. Good help is hard to find."

"I don't remember her that way. Didn't she masturbate the whole time she was lying next to me?"

"I hate to ruin this memory for you, but no. She lay there, inert like a rag doll. I just told you she was playing with herself."

"Oh. Well, at least I have memories of the blonde."

"Right. And so do I. That girl was bold. I saw how she stuck a finger up your ass right as you were about to climax."

"Don't knock it. It works. Her jaw was probably tired."

"Probably. But this raises the larger issue, do you really think Amy has what it takes to do this work? Can you imagine yourself as a client?"

"Well, it's worth a shot. And besides, it would only be for a month or two. Worst-case scenario, she's dreadful. In which case the clients who see her will only be too happy you're back. But frankly, I think she's got the spark, and I'd like to try and nurture it."

"This, darling, I want to see."

Michael touched his fingers to his eyebrow, in a mock salute.

PART 2

CREATION

CREATION: The stage where the artist produces her work and brings it into tangible form.

15

LANDING AT THE LAIR

September 2008

Leaving New York was filled with a riot of chores and last-minute decisions. It was nerve-wracking, placing my gallery in the hands of my staff and my dungeon in the hands of Amy. She'd gotten the hang of the basics, and Michael promised to see her regularly. He said it was to monitor her progress, but I knew it was because he had a serious crush on my friend. He'd once had a crush on me, and I felt only a twinge of jealousy listening to a sixty-five-year-old corporate lawyer talking like a girl swooning over some boy bander.

Despite all the stress before departing from JFK, arriving in Geneva was perfectly smooth. The plane landed on time. There was a greeter at the airplane door holding my name on a discreet placard. He ushered me through the airport to a lounge where I would wait for my luggage. And just as I was finishing my espresso, a porter arrived with the large trunks I'd packed full of gear. The customs officer barely flinched at my pile of belongings; it was so unexceptional in size. *"Bienvenue en Suisse."*

I was escorted to Edouard's dark gray Maybach, and we left immediately. "*Monsieur, mes valises?*" I wanted to know what was going to happen to my bags.

"Mademoiselle, there's a van taking your trunks to the house. Monsieur de Grenet thought you might be tired after your flight, so I was told to make your trip as fast and comfortable as possible. We'll be there in thirty minutes."

Upon hearing that, I sank into the thick leather seat and let the universe worry about my gear. I must have dozed off, because when I woke up, the driver was turning into a driveway where a solid gate swung open. We pulled up in front of a modern two-story building, all sharp angles, concrete surfaces and glass walls.

Edouard emerged from the oversized wooden door and waited for the car to stop. Before the driver could get out of the Maybach, Edouard had opened my door and politely held my hand as I exited the car. We quickly embraced and he ushered me inside and introduced me to Herr Boxler, his house manager. Boxler was bald and athletic. His conservative gray suit was cut tight against his body, an unexpected show of vanity revealing many hours spent in the gym.

"Unfortunately, I won't have time to give you a proper tour. I'm in the middle of a complicated negotiation. This is your suite." We arrived at the end of a hall where a large dark wooden door was ajar. Edouard pushed it open to reveal a shimmery gray sitting room, complete with an oversized sofa, a large desk, and several chairs. "The bedroom and bathroom are over there. I hope you enjoy the view of the lake."

I took in the room, with its tasteful decor and luxe furnishings. "This looks marvelous. Your home is spectacular. I can't wait to see more of it once I'm fully awake."

Edouard nodded. "Why don't you get settled, see how you're feeling. I know that red-eye all too well."

"Yes, those flights are hard, and espresso only does so much."

"Precisely. I'll get back to my office and give you some privacy. By the way, I may not be Swiss, but I live a pretty scheduled life. I get up at six to work out, I have a light breakfast at seven, I work till one, when I have a light lunch, and then I work some more. I have dinner at eight. My chef is fantastic. Don't worry, he's French, not Swiss. I hope you'll join me if you feel like it. No pressure. We'll make enough for two, and you can decide."

"Thanks. I should be fine by evening. It's tomorrow when the time change will really sink in."

"I understand. And just so you know, I don't expect to be entertained. You are my guest, not my captive . . . although I hope you'll make me yours periodically." We nodded at one another. "I'll have Boxler leave you a note in the morning about what's scheduled for meals. If you have any preferences, Boxler will introduce you to my chef." He handed me a file folder. "I've made a list of the prominent galleries here, and the names of their owners. Let me know who you'd like to meet first, and my secretary will make all the arrangements. I want this to be a productive and pleasant stay for you."

"I already feel at home. Thank you. But I don't want to be a burden on you, either. And if there's an evening when you need some privacy, let me know, and I'll become very scarce." It seemed prudent to signal that I understood—and even expected—that he might have a romantic entanglement.

"Thank you. I doubt that will be necessary; work has been consuming. Incidentally, I've equipped a room. I hope you find it acceptable. You'll be responsible for its inaugural run."

"Will Boxler give me a tour of that, too?" I couldn't resist the dig, as I imagined Edouard's assistant giving me a tour of his dungeon.

"No. I will, and now I must return to my colleagues." Edouard's face turned red even as he smiled. "Herr Boxler's domain is this floor. He'll make you comfortable and answer any questions."

As Edouard exited, Boxler stood in the doorway and gave the door to my suite a gentle tap.

"Herr Boxler, come in."

Boxler oozed energy and efficiency. Even as he gave me his full attention, he made miniscule adjustments to the room. He straightened the file folder Edouard had given me. He repositioned the large arrangement of pink roses that dominated my desk, moving it to the side, so that there was room for my taupe Birkin. He then presented me with a menu for the evening.

Foie Gras
Côte de Boeuf
Fresh Strawberries

Accompaniment:
Krug Champagne, 1996
Screaming Eagle, Cabernet Sauvignon, 1997
Château d'Yquem, 1900

I had to laugh. We were within spitting distance of some of the best vineyards in the world, and Edouard was offering me wine from Napa. He knew of my weakness for Screaming Eagle; he'd been sending me boxes of the stuff for years. I turned to Boxler. "This looks extraordinary and celebratory. Please convey to the chef my enthusiasm for his choices. But in the future, I prefer something lighter to begin. Say, a small salad, or perhaps some soup. Tonight, however, count me in for this feast."

"Yes, Miss Grieg."

"I'm going to take a nap now. Have someone wake me at one. Whatever the chef is making for Edouard's lunch, please have him make me some, too. I'll eat it in my room. And then I'd like to work out. I'll need someone to show me where the gym is."

"Very good, Miss Grieg."

"Great. While I'm working out, the housekeeper can put away my things." Boxler took notes on a small pad, as I rattled off my instructions. "Oh, there are also two large trunks. Please put them in the playroom, but don't open them. I'll take care of the contents."

Boxler didn't flinch when I alluded to Edouard's dungeon. "Yes, Miss Grieg. Is there anything else?"

"Mornings at eight, I'd like a double espresso, a croissant and some kind of fruit—whatever's freshest—brought to my room. That's all. Thank you for your help."

"You're welcome, Miss Grieg." Within five minutes of his departure, I was sound asleep. The room was chilly, which made it the perfect temperature. I didn't hear the sandwich arrive—it was left on the desk in my living room. I snored through my plans to work out. I didn't wake until after six. It was disorienting at first, I didn't recognize where I was, but then it came back to me. I had run off to Switzerland to avoid my father, only my hideaway had surrounded me with exquisite taste and luxury.

I rummaged through my suitcases and found my makeup bags, my hair accessories and a little black dress for the evening. Following a bracing cold shower, I got to work on myself.

At exactly two minutes after eight, I wandered out of my suite in my favorite black latex dress, custom ordered from the Baroness. Its bodice had strips carefully cut to crisscross my bust, supporting my breasts without making them look vulgar. Its skirt reached my knees and was almost demure in length, even as it was cut close to the body. The matching opera length gloves added to the look. My Alaïa pumps, with their platforms and laser-cut red patent-leather straps, completed the ensemble. My hair was slicked back in a tight bun. I was ready for some foie, and to enjoy the reaction of my host.

When I appeared at the dining room, Edouard jumped to his feet immediately and held my chair as I sat down opposite his spot at the table. "Erika, you look spectacular. This evening can hardly get better."

"This evening has hardly begun. Just you wait." Boxler arrived and poured us each some champagne. I raised my glass to my host.

"Thank you for this extraordinary welcome. But you know what they say, *no good deed goes unpunished.*"

Edouard's face lightened up immediately. "Yes, they do say that, don't they? Do you think it's apt?"

"Absolutely. Especially on days like today. You've committed so many good deeds." I looked over at Boxler, who was holding the champagne, his face impassive at the spectacle in front of him. "The more good deeds, the more punishment required."

"Yes, that makes sense. The onus is on me, then, to commit an abundance of good deeds."

I shrugged and dug into the perfect morsel of pan-seared foie gras in front of me. "Oh, Edouard, I need your advice on something."

"Of course. What can I do for you?"

"Well, etiquette says I should remove these gloves before eating, but it's cold in here. Will you be offended if I violate glove etiquette?" Sitting still at the table had made me aware of the temperature, and I was beginning to shiver.

"It seems obvious to me. You must leave them on unless you prefer to take them off." Edouard waved to Boxler and I could overhear him asking for more heat in the dining room.

"The problem with latex is you're never comfortable. You're either too hot or too cold, and right now, I'm freezing."

As Boxler was clearing our plates after the foie, I turned to Edouard. "I didn't think to pack a shawl or something to keep my shoulders warm. Do you have something I could borrow?"

"Of course." He waved at Boxler, who disappeared and returned a minute later with a cream cashmere wrap.

"It undermines the look, but what can you do? Your dining room is inhospitable to latex."

"Let me work on that. I want all your latex dresses to feel comfortable in my home. Whenever they want to be worn, I want them to feel welcome."

"That's very kind of you. Latex, as you know, hates being hidden away and ignored. It needs to be used. It's desperate to be adored."

"Yes, it's desperate. After dinner, I'll show you *my* desperate latex. I hope you approve."

Boxler brought in the entrées. The beef was perfectly cut and plated, with three gorgeous spears of asparagus and two fat baby carrots adding color to the tableau. Edouard poured us each a glass of the Screaming Eagle, and we sipped at it serenely. For the first time in weeks, I felt like I could relax. There was no one trying to get me to participate in some scam. There were no customers or clients clamoring for attention. There was nothing to do, but make my host feel thrilled to have me as a house guest, because I wanted to be far away from New York for as long as my father was scheming.

Boxler served us each a plate of cut-up strawberries and a graceful glass filled with Château d'Yquem. A little sauterne goes a long way, and I was already feeling giddy. I finished the wine but didn't bother finishing the berries. "Come, let's see this room you've built."

Edouard was about to put a strawberry in his mouth, but he put his fork down immediately, hustled over to my chair and helped me stand. Then he escorted me to the basement of his home, and to the room he'd had equipped for my visit. It was the dream room for a serious latex freak. There was a vacuum bed, an adjustable dental chair, a rack. Two walls were mirrored, as was the ceiling, and there was another wall filled with everything from harnesses to paddles. The floor was polished concrete and every surface gleamed. My two trunks were stacked in the corner. They seemed almost superfluous.

Edouard turned to me. "I hope this is to your liking."

I gave the room a tour, opening drawers, examining the collection of butt plugs he'd assembled and the assortment of whips. "You did a fine job. Who was your contractor?"

"I worked with someone recommended by the owner of Mr. S Leather in San Francisco. Do you know Mr. M in Berlin?"

"No. But he knows what he's doing . . . Except for that phone in the corner. Are you expecting any calls when you're in bondage? Does your mommy want to say good night? Is your broker on speed dial?"

Edouard shook his head sheepishly. "It's regrettable, but necessary. I hope it never rings, but if it does, somebody needs to answer because it's important."

"I can see it now . . . You're wired up on the dental chair and at the worst possible moment, the phone rings. What would you like me to do?"

"Answer it, of course, and then give the receiver to me so I can find out what needs my attention."

"I see. Well, for your sake, I hope it doesn't ring." I looked at my host, and he had that eager puppy look in his eyes, which made me eager to make him suffer. "Now get your fucking clothes off, because we have some work to do."

Edouard smiled as he stripped. "Yes, Mistress." He didn't even bother folding his clothes, he just pushed them into a corner as he got down on his knees and waited, looking up at me, with his lips parted and his eyelids only half open. Fortunately, I spotted a simple black leather collar centered on the top of a gleaming black rolling cabinet, the type auto mechanics fill with wrenches, and we got to work.

"I know you'd love to try the vacuum bed, but I need to experiment with it first. Wouldn't it be awful to lose your cock to some suction malfunction?" I reached down and grabbed his dick. "I don't want anything to happen to this, so you're just going to be strapped to the bench and caned until my arm gets sore, and then we're going to call it a night. Got it?"

"Yes, Mistress!" I pulled Edouard up by his cock and led him over to the bench. It took a minute, and some coaching from my victim, before I found the necessary straps and cuffs, but in short order, Edouard was trussed to the bench, unable to move. Unlike his legs, chest and arms, his ass was the only thing not covered in straps. I explored the toolbox a little more and found a very large gag shaped like a penis. "Is this your way of telling me you want to suck cock?"

"It's up to you, Mistress." Edouard had never expressed any curiosity about men before. I'd always assumed he was as hetero as could be, but perhaps I'd misjudged. Or perhaps this was an easy way of introducing a little edge and uncertainty into our play. Whatever. We could explore the pervy recesses of his mind and body at our leisure, because I had no intention of returning to New York until I was confident my father had moved on to some other sucker.

"I'll take that as a no, for now. But don't be teasing me with toys like this. If you want to suck cock, just let me know and you won't have to settle for latex." I forced the gag between his teeth and strapped it behind his head without giving him a chance to reply. "There. You should be very happy now."

Edouard gave me a grunt, and then soon he was flying on an endorphin ride from the bondage and the discipline. I switched onto autopilot, applying strokes of a leather paddle as a warm-up, and then graduating to the hardcore cane. The strokes were landing with precision, leaving parallel welts up and down his upper thighs and lower buttocks, and I was able to put aside the problems that had brought me to Geneva. My favorite moment was after all the blows had landed. With his chest still stuck to the bench, I lowered my chest onto his back and we both rested for a minute, inhaling and exhaling at the same pace. It was peaceful, and his blissed-out state infected me. It was almost as if we'd both needed something physically intense to clear our cluttered minds.

16
DUNGEON INSPECTION

Edouard offered to help me restore his playroom, but I sent him to bed. This was a guy who had probably never done his own laundry, I wasn't about to trust him with cleaning all the toys and tools, even though they were for his use alone. Also, I wanted some stillness.

There was a closet filled with cleaning supplies. I tried to imagine Boxler stocking it, which was an absurd prospect, even though it was probably correct. There was an obvious order to how the supplies were stowed away—alphabetically—which showed me that someone was being conscientious, even as they had no idea what the fuck they were doing. I set about rearranging things, putting all the disinfectants together, grouping the polishes on a different shelf, and otherwise making sense out of a jumble of random acquisitions someone had probably told Edouard his dungeon required, and in turn, he had told Boxler to buy.

Once every surface had been wiped down, and every toy treated appropriately, I gave the room a thorough inspection. Edouard had done a fine job building things out. It wasn't as chic as my usual play space, but it had items I hadn't bothered to acquire. The vacuum bed, for instance, was something I'd only considered getting. Why not acquire one, right? But its frame was about seven feet long and four feet wide, making it an incredibly bulky item for a very specific purpose. Also, they're noisy. While the submissive could wear ear plugs and wallow in splendid isolation, I could not. Vacuum beds left me cold. I prefer equipment that's versatile.

The bed, however, was clearly something that had captured Edouard's imagination. He wanted to lie between two thick sheets of latex as a vacuum sucked all the air out between them, leaving him trapped and compressed. It was one of the most restrictive forms of bondage. I've known of people having panic attacks at the sensation, and yet he had invested money and space for this specific experience. This was an intense new craving, for a guy whose tastes had been routine. I jokingly called his middle-of-the-road preferences the B&D Buffet. A little bondage, a little discipline, maybe an orgasm if he were good. Maybe the vacbed was a hint that I needed to shake things up.

It took an hour to get the room into shape, and it was only as I was returning to my suite that I noticed the bubble for the security camera in the hall outside the playroom. It was discreet but unmistakable. I returned to the playroom immediately and peered in all the corners and examined the ceiling. To my relief, I couldn't find any cameras chronicling our adventures as I had not consented to being the subject of a homemade porno. Except for the prospect of being intercepted by whoever was watching the video feed, I would have woken Edouard up immediately and asked him about it.

17

HIRST SO GOOD

My morning double espresso helped my mood, which was sour. Between the jet lag and the discovery of the cameras—they were all over the place, once I started looking for them—I wasn't feeling much goodwill toward my host or the world. Unfortunately, there was gallery business needing my immediate attention, so the voyeurs of Maison Grenet would have to wait while I kept my rage in check.

Once it was morning in New York, I called Amy to see how she was adjusting. Even if I had to rent a place in Paris for a couple of months should my stint in Geneva prove untenable, I had no intention of returning to NYC until I was certain things had calmed down with my dad. She had to feel supported and prepared. Amy possessed the skills to address the basic needs of my clients, and if she couldn't provide them with everything, that was fine. She didn't need to be great, she just needed to be good enough to keep the boys from drifting.

Things remained dead at the gallery. The level of inquiries had dropped. Cassidy's works remained unappreciated and unpurchased.

The obvious clients were all in a state of horror, as they watched their stock portfolios wither. Only a year ago, certain collectors bought first and asked questions later. If they decided they didn't want something after they'd paid for it, they'd stick the work in storage or try to find a buyer on the secondary market. Unfortunately, my luck and their money couldn't last.

A bout of fatigue hit me after lunch, and once again I spent my afternoon snoring away, oblivious to the world. Sadly, the rest didn't buoy me. Every camera, the ones in the hallways, the living room, the dining room, made my skin crawl. Intellectually, I understood that he needed to protect his extraordinary belongings, but still I balked at the voyeurism.

Edouard had a magnificent Lucian Freud in his entryway. The first thing anyone would see when they entered his home was an oil portrait of a morbidly obese woman, sprawled on a sofa. Freud called this model Big Sue, and some of his most important works featured the extravagant rolls of her flesh, which dared the viewer to scrutinize her body and to find her anything less than magnificent. Roman Abramovich had just bought a related painting for thirty-four million dollars, so the work merited surveillance, Lloyd's of London probably demanded it, but I had recoiled from putting cameras in my gallery for a dozen different reasons, not the least was that my clients would have freaked if they'd known they were being captured on closed-circuit television, going down into my dungeon. And camera technology had become so advanced, that for every camera I could see, there had to be five that were invisible.

I pulled out a pair of cream trousers and a matching turtleneck from the closet and put them on. Out of habit, I fussed with my hair and makeup, but my glam-level was low when I joined Edouard in the dining room at eight. He gave me a polite smile as he held the chair for me, but his disappointment was obvious, and he wasn't one to say nothing.

"Erika, great to see you. Frankly, I was hoping you'd wear something like you did last night."

"Wonderful to see you, too, Edouard. As for the latex? It's too cold here. And frankly, I'm rattled by your security system. How many cameras do you have and where are they located? I don't like being spied on." I could be just as direct.

"Ah, you noticed. I knew you would at some point." He turned to Boxler and spoke in rapid French and then he turned back to me. "Let me show you what's observed. You should find it reassuring."

Boxler led the way to a basement room, adjacent to the laundry room with its commercial washers and dryers, where a lone security guy sat at a desk, surrounded by computer terminals. Even in this distant corner of the house, Edouard's style and precision were evident. The room was a pale gray, the man had short blond hair, and his white shirt was immaculate. Edouard said to the man, in English, "Show Miss Grieg every view and explain where we do and where we do *not* have cameras."

The security guard pulled up the view from each camera onto his screen—there were over two dozen different feeds he could observe with a click of his mouse. The four-car garage had two cameras— one pointed at the garage door and one pointed at the entry into the house. There was a camera pointed outward, from the front door of the house, similar perspectives offered from every other door to the exterior. Hallways had coverage. Main rooms had coverage.

"*Montrez-moi les chambres.*" I asked to see the bedrooms.

"We do not have cameras inside the bedrooms," replied the guard in careful English.

Edouard confirmed this, and added, "Or in any of my private spaces." He looked at me, waited a second to make sure I understood this included his dungeon, before he continued. "I don't care for all these precautions, but my insurers and my head of security tell me they're necessary. Unfortunately, we live in dangerous times."

We returned to the dining room, while I asked him to point out any cameras as we passed. "I might as well know where they are, so I can give your security guy my best angles."

"But of course, Erika."

By the time we'd finished the bottle of La Tâche, my mood had improved. There's something about a two-thousand-dollar bottle of wine that mollifies me. "Your cameras caught me off guard."

"My apologies. I have so few visitors; I forget how unsettling they can be. How can I make it up to you?"

"Heat your dining room! This is my second meal in this room, and I'm freezing. See?" I pulled up my sweater, to reveal goosebumps. "I'm just a California girl at heart."

"I've told Boxler to work on it, but it is complicated. I'll figure out an interim strategy, because I'd love to see that dress again."

"If you promise me I won't freeze in here, I'll wear something even better. I came prepared."

"You know how to get my mind off work, and I'd like to return the favor." Edouard rang a discreet bell and Boxler arrived with the Hirst in hand. "This is for you." I stood up and gave the painting a hard look as Boxler stood behind, clutching the canvas in white gloved hands. It was one of Damien Hirst's typical works. Nothing exceptional, but nicely executed in his atelier. There were a few butterflies scattered across the black-painted canvas, as if flying in the night sky, and some other odds and ends, to fill in the space. "I hope you can find an appropriate home for it."

"I know just the guy. He'll probably put it in his bathroom above the toilet, so that all his hedge-fund buddies can piss beneath it and think, 'Hey, Johnnie must be doing fucking great if he's got a fucking Hirst in his bathroom.'"

"Perfect. I knew you'd know what to do with it." Edouard nodded at Boxler, who retreated from the dining room.

"The painting's super, Edouard. Thanks. How about we go downstairs?"

"Not tonight. You exhausted me yesterday. I need to get in shape for you and your cane."

"Yes, you do. I won't go easy on you, especially now that I know we're not saving our moments together for posterity."

"No. Nothing is on film." Edouard shook his head and excused himself from dinner. "I'm dealing with some associates in Los Angeles on one of our complicated investments, so it will be a late night and I need to give them my full attention. My apologies for being such an absent host."

"No apologies necessary. I need to get caught up on my work, too, darling. Good night."

"Good night, Erika." Edouard gave me a polite kiss on each cheek, and then headed off to his office. I summoned Boxler and asked him to put the Hirst and its papers in my room. He nodded and disappeared. By the time I had returned to my suite, the Hirst was already mounted on the wall, and the authentication documents were stacked on my desk. I checked the auction results for similar works, and discovered its market value was about four hundred thousand, or enough to keep my lights on for two years. But for my father, lurking around the gallery, and but for the fact Edouard might feel cheated, I could return to NYC immediately. Instead, I made plans to stay for at least another month. Thanks to the collapse of the stock market, my life in New York was in a state of suspended animation, and it made little sense to return to it. There were no buyers. There was a substitute in place in my dungeon. Nothing was going to happen except my dad would try to suck me into something distasteful.

18

PAIN IN THE PORTFOLIO

My jet lag was temporary, and I was able to slide into the rhythms of the house and the pace of Geneva without much difficulty. Boxler set up meetings with several prominent galleries in the city, and although they were pleasant conversations with impressive people, we were all in the same situation. Except for the bargain hunters and the vultures, the art market had all but seized up while people figured out what was going on with their stock portfolios. Sotheby's had had an auction of Impressionists in early October that was a dire omen for the fall. Christie's followed with an evening sale of contemporary art that landed with a thud. If there was little oxygen in the art stratosphere where the billionaires played, what hope did those of us closer to earth face?

Unlike my clients, my stock portfolio hadn't taken a beating, but that was only because I didn't have one. My wealth, if I dared call it that, was in art. Only the art market had also just experienced a sharp decline in value. Thankfully, the Hirst was fungible. As an art advisor once joked to me, "Hirsts are like Hermès bags. They're a way for the wealthy to signal to their peers they have a spare million with which to adorn themselves." Although its value had probably declined by thirty percent since the start of the year, it would still generate a solid sale.

I sent a photo of the Hirst to one of my hedge fund collectors who seemed to be weathering the crisis okay, and he replied with an email filled with exclamation points. I promised to hand carry the piece back to New York for him.

Amy called every day, and to my amazement, she seemed to be getting the hang of the work. My expectations had been modest. I just wanted her to take care of the odd client and keep an eye on the gallery. But ever the good girl, she had immersed herself in the work and tried her hardest. She had created an enormous database of all my gallery clients, and then she'd run it through software to identify who had the most money to help prioritize sales efforts. She'd started a blog. She was experimenting with Twitter. Amy was a truffle pig, let loose in my gallery. In the process, she was whipping my employees—who'd never thought much about blogs, social media and customer relations software—into shape.

Michael, who was both her coach and my spy, was pleasantly surprised by Amy's progress. Then again, he was creating his perfect dominatrix and in Amy, he had found the most dedicated student.

A week had passed quickly. I'd found a Pilates instructor in town, and a manicurist. Edouard's driver had little to do, since his boss had a phone stuck in his ear all day and a Bloomberg terminal on his desk, so I made the driver my own. I liked to think I was giving him and the Maybach a sense of purpose as I ran my errands and explored.

One afternoon, as I was speaking with Josh in New York, Boxler knocked on the door to my suite. He deposited a large box on my desk and left. Curious, I hung up immediately, and opened the note attached to the box.

I hope this will keep you warm. —Edouard.

I untied the large ribbon, opened the heavy cardboard box, and found a fur coat inside. It was from Fendi, probably flown in from Rome or Milan, and it was spectacular. The brown mink hairs had been chemically infused with gold, so that the fur was holographic and dimensional. All the same, the pelts felt soft and sleek against my skin. Edouard had just earned another latex outfit and more welts on his ass.

19

SHARING THE PAIN

"I feel like I should be greeting you with a kiss on the cheek and a martini, every evening. 'How was your day, honey?' We could role-play suburban bliss!"

"That may be the most perverse thing you've ever suggested, Erika." Edouard rested his hand on the table and grinned.

"I know, darling. I'm just trying to stretch my limits. I've never even fantasized about housewife-ing, so it feels particularly taboo."

"You weren't raised like that? I was. My childhood was very conforming. My mother even poured my father a cocktail the moment he got home from the bank. The shaker was ready, waiting for him to arrive and so was she."

"This may surprise you, but I was not raised like that. Well, maybe for the first twelve years of my life I had a dose of that, but afterward, I might as well have been raised by wolves."

"Yes, wolves . . . that makes sense. You seem very predatory."

"Edouard, so do you. Are you devouring any enemies these days?" I liked that my clients were kings in their worlds, and supplicants in mine.

"I wish . . . only sometimes, it feels like they're eating me."

"Sorry to hear that, darling. I'd offer to help, but the thing I do best is getting your mind off your problems."

Edouard sat back from the table, and his lips formed something that looked like a smile. "You and the dress are enchanting. You're distracting me from my miserable Russian aluminum deal. Thank you."

"Aluminum? That's not much of a challenge." I stood up, lowered the Fendi mink, and showed him the emerald-green molded cups and the thin straps holding my latex DeMask dress together.

"May I see the back?"

"Of course." I completed my pivot, so that my ass was on display for my host. "I've been working my glutes. They're hard as rocks. Feel them."

Pushing his plate and cutlery aside, I stretched out on the table in front of Edouard, as if I were an entrée, with my ass in his face while he remained seated. I stared at Boxler, as he slowly backed out of the dining room. Edouard ran his fingers over the material, caressing and cupping the latex. His breathing became deeper and more audible. He kissed my hip and then my butt cheek, pressing his lips into the material so that I could feel them.

After a very long minute, I righted myself and returned to my seat. "Very nice. We don't want to give your security guys too much to think about, do we?"

"No, of course not. You've given me another reason to curse the cameras." Edouard breathed in deeply, straightened himself in his chair and took a sip of wine.

I called out, "It's safe to come back in, and I could use more wine." Seconds later, Boxler appeared with the open bottle of Bordeaux as I restored the mink to my shoulders.

While we each poked at our perfectly composed salads, Edouard asked, "You've been here two weeks. Is Geneva to your liking?"

"I've hit every gallery and museum. Some, I've visited twice. I've exhausted Boxler's list of contacts. I've basically done Geneva."

"You're done here? Will you be leaving me? It's rare that I have guests, and you are easily the best guest I've ever had."

"Am I the only guest you've ever had?" I wanted to know just how low a bar I'd overcome. The house felt like it had always been cold and empty.

Edouard shrugged. "No, but you're the only guest in years."

"Your family doesn't visit?"

"No. I didn't leave them on good terms. They were happy to take the money when I sold the family bank, but they blamed me for the sale."

"They didn't want to sell?" Edouard had never shared details of his personal life.

"They didn't have a choice. The deals they favored had gone out of style. They had no appetite for risk. When I took over, their biggest asset was our name. Fortunately, I was able to find a buyer for that—a Lebanese group looking for a toehold in France. Before my father and my uncle came to terms with the damage they'd done to the firm, I'd closed the deal. My great-grandfather had balls. My relatives did not."

"Oh, I had no idea you sold the family business out from under *papa*. No wonder they don't speak with you. It must gall them how you had the smarts to recognize their mediocrity."

"That's the generous interpretation of what happened. Thank you. So, no, my family does not visit. I left France to make it easy for them and easier for me." Edouard's voice grew hushed.

"When did you last speak with your father?"

"It's been a few years. And you? Do you bring your family to your home?"

"Uh, no. Not if I can help it. My mother married a casino executive in Vegas. She's happy and busy. We speak every month or two and it's always lovely. My father, however, is a different story." I took a big gulp of the Bordeaux and shook my head. "But I'll share that some other time."

"Ah, yes, complicated families."

"Yes. But let's change the topic back to Geneva. Am I missing something? What's the draw? There's nothing to do here."

"You don't come here if you want to live in a metropolis. You come here because you don't. The Swiss take their privacy very seriously. In my twenties, I went out to nightclubs and parties, but not now."

"You went to nightclubs?"

"In my twenties, my favorite was Les Bains Douches."

"I started out in dive bars on Sunset Strip and graduated to expensive nightclubs . . . Sadly, I never got to Les Bains Douches. It was before my time." I couldn't help but needle him a bit. Edouard was fifteen years my senior.

"But of course you did." Edouard shook his head and smiled. "You started young. You were probably still in university."

"High school, actually. I was fucking this guitarist and he got me in. Unfortunately, the guitarist was a little lacking, but his coke was excellent."

"You must have been something. I was a very serious student. I didn't find the nightclubs until after my divorce, when my friends took me out to cheer me up."

"You were married? I had no idea." Once again, Edouard had startled me with a detail about his private life.

"Yes, it was very brief and we were very young. I'd just graduated from HEC, you know, the Wharton of France. She'd just graduated from Sciences Po. My family loved her. Her family loved me. It felt like the right thing to do."

"It's hard to defy gravity, isn't it? When all the forces are pushing you in the same direction."

"Yes. I still regret that it didn't work out. She's someone I admire. She married another lawyer, and she now works as an advisor with the Cour de Cassation."

"That's your supreme court, right? She must be very sharp."

"Yes. Too sharp, perhaps. It was the force of her intelligence that drew me to her."

"She knew how to put you in your place?" I couldn't resist bringing the conversation back to our common interests.

"Yes, although she wasn't kinky. She spoke her mind. She asked for what she wanted. She had high standards for herself and all those around her."

"A vanilla dominatrix! She sounds fantastic. What happened? Why did you end things?"

"I didn't. She did."

"Oh? She found out about your girlfriends?"

"No, she thought I had boyfriends."

"I don't understand. You are *very* straight."

"She found my bondage magazines." Edouard shook his head.

"Oh fuck . . . The best magazines are often the *gay* magazines. I have a bunch of them in my library for reference when I want to come up with a new predicament bondage scenario . . . She got it wrong, didn't she, about what turned you on in the photos?"

"Yes. And then she left. She never gave me a chance to explain, although I doubt it would have helped. She was enthusiastic but conservative about sex."

"Oh Edouard, I'm so sorry. That's a difficult conversation to have . . . What would you say?—'I'm not aroused by the handsome men you just saw pictured in bondage; I'm aroused by imagining *myself* in that same bondage. It's not about the cocks, it's all about the knots . . .'"

"Yes. We'd probably still be married, but for that misunderstanding." And with that abrupt comment, Edouard slid his chair away from the table. "I'm afraid there's a phone call I must take. And to change the subject, I have a question for you."

"Fire away, darling." It was clear the memory of his ex-wife remained a source of pain for Edouard.

"The art in your suite isn't correct. It should be attuned to your tastes. Tell me if there's a piece from my collection you'd like in there."

"What an extraordinary offer. Is there an inventory I could consult?" I was desperate to know what else Edouard had hidden away.

"That would be difficult." Like many serious collectors, Edouard was discreet about his holdings. I might know his sexual secrets, but he remained hesitant to share his other secrets.

"I tell you what, darling. Just put up the filthiest, most erotic work you have. I may not have told you, but that's what's in my own personal collection."

"No, you never told me that. But I have an idea."

The next day as we sat down to our lunch of green salad and poached chicken, Edouard motioned to Boxler who brought in a framed watercolor. "I just got this, from a gentleman outside of Berlin. It wasn't even framed—it was stored in a folder. I think you'll want it in your suite."

"Darling, is that what I think it is?" The image was of a dark-haired woman, wearing only a shirt and stockings. She lay on her stomach, with her bottom bared and covered with red stripes. It was stunning.

"Yes. It's an Egon Schiele that's never been seen before."

"Are you saying Jane Kallir hasn't gotten her hands on it?" Kallir was the preeminent authenticator of Schiele's works. She had compiled the *catalogue raisonné* of his works, and her word was enough to transform a scrap of paper into something worth millions.

"No. Other than Boxler, the framer and the Berliner, you're the only person who's seen it in decades. It was tucked away in a farmhouse for eighty years. The seller believes his grandfather bought it in Austria and hid it away because he didn't want his wife, who was a very devout woman, to know."

"It looks authentic, to me. Her features are angular. Those eyebrows? Their arch is perfect. The signature looks correct and in the right place. And he love-love-loved depicting women in stockings. But there are some troubling details."

"I agree. Look at her ass."

"I see stripes, and that's the rub. Those aren't mere red marks—they are specific and intentional. Cane strokes would be out of place in Austria in 1916 or 1917. That's a British form of amusement, not an Austrian form."

"Yes. But what if they're crop marks? Or whip marks?"

"Oh, Edouard, you've thought about this a lot, haven't you? That would make more sense. Do you think the model was the young runaway who accused him of rape?"

"Perhaps, but he was only with the runaway for a couple of days." Edouard continued to show me his prize. "The girl looks very young—she has no bust—and the dark hair seems right. She's not Edith, Adèle or Wally. Of course, Schiele used many models. I still have much research to do."

I sat back, stunned at his discovery. This was a side of Schiele we hadn't seen before. He had a fondness for teenagers, and he'd been accused of public immorality for bringing young girls to his studio where they could see his works. The father of the runaway, who was only twelve when she found herself with Schiele, had the artist charged with kidnapping and statutory rape. While those charges wound up getting dropped, Schiele spent time in jail for the public immorality charge.

Some critics say we shouldn't apply the lens of the present on behaviors of the past; that Schiele was just behaving like many bourgeois men of his day. Not yet ready for marriage, these men consorted with prostitutes and women of lesser means until it was time to find a proper wife. Schiele, however, did one thing few of his peers could do—he'd captured these sex workers on paper. Unable to afford models, he'd exploited the women around him to pose for his works. He'd even gotten his sister Gerti to pose for him nude. She was so embarrassed; she would only let him capture her from behind. Was this one of the prostitutes Schiele carried on with? And who put those marks on her ass? Did Schiele beat the girl, or was she showing him what some John had done to her? My mind reeled.

"Yes. This is the work I want to stare at every night. I want to curl up next to her and learn her secrets as I fall asleep. Thank you."

Edouard motioned to Boxler to take the painting away. I knew it would be in a prominent spot in my room by the time I had finished my fruit salad. That's how efficient Boxler was.

20

CRUELTY AMONG EQUALS

Having shared with me the secrets about their sexuality, their fetishes, their obsessions, some clients feel compelled to share everything with me. It's a shame I don't trade stocks, because the insider information I've received over the years would have made me a fortune. But between my long-standing aversion to Wall Street, the cause of my family's fall, there's the problem of reliability. The men want to boast and preen, so I can never be sure how much of what they're saying is true, or how much is ego-puffing embellishment. Where does the fantasy start and end?

The flip side of that is I rarely reveal much about myself. Sure, they've all been in my gallery, but I try not to speak about my personal life with any accuracy or candor. It's better if the woman of their fantasies and nightmares remains a mystery. But every now and then, I can't help myself. I'd kept Edouard's curiosity at bay for weeks, but he finally drew me in with a question about my gallery.

"I've often wondered how you wound up showing Axel Gortun's work. He's hardly an emerging artist. The year before yours, he had that memorable show at Hunter and Wells, where he featured close-ups of faces contorted in misery and eyes filled with tears."

"Yes, that show caught my attention as well." I paused, unsure if Edouard had just insulted me. "Are you saying he's too well-known for the Grieg Gallery? That he's out of my league?"

"No, no . . . of course not. It was unusual." Edouard furrowed his brow and shook his head.

"I'm just joking. The whole thing was very unusual. Gortun's no emerging artist. If you promise me you'll keep your mouth shut, I can share a few details. But let me start with this one—he owed me. Contractually and personally." Edouard stared at me with a baffled expression on his face, while I sat opposite him, grinning at the memory of my art slave. The only person who knew the whole story was Michael, who drew up the contracts that bound Axel to me.

"Boxler has nondisclosure agreements prepared for my associates. I'd sign one for you." Edouard leaned forward, eager to do some kind of deal with me, in exchange for serious gossip.

Boxler must have heard our conversation, because two minutes later he appeared with an agreement and a pen for both of us. Edouard signed it with a flourish and then he cocked his head, as if to dare me to open up to him for a change, so I told him the story of my art slave.

"AXEL, I LOVE your eye series. Those close-ups of retinas are stunning, with all the variations in color and the blood vessels. Your precision is perfection. And it's remarkable how you were able to convey all those different feelings in the works."

"Thank you. I worked with some very emotional and capable muses."

"Yes! They were excellent actresses. Or maybe they were feeling what you were capturing on the canvas. Joy? That little bit of reflected light in the corner was the ideal twinkle. Arousal? The dilated pupil was such a great choice. But the pain one? That evoked a different response in me."

"Oh? Did you like it? Were you turned on?" Axel gave me a leer.

I wrinkled my nose. "To be honest, it wasn't your best work. I found it sloppy and self-referential. And what did you do to that poor model? I could feel her anguish. Did you torture her?"

"If you felt something, it couldn't have been too sloppy. And for your information, one man's torture is another man's pleasure." Axel's voice was smug.

"Yes, yes, darling. Of course. But it's clear you were capturing something awful. But it was an inartful kind of misery. What were you doing? Hitting her with a hammer?"

"No. Don't be crass," Axel hissed at me.

"I'm not being crass. I'm expressing curiosity. What was happening behind the scenes?" It felt like I'd touched a nerve, and suddenly I wanted to learn more.

"Nothing I haven't done to myself." His voice was fast and low.

"You've hit yourself with a hammer?"

"No. Not with a hammer."

"Well, give me some specifics. Don't worry, you won't shock me. I'd like to know." I crossed my arms in front of me, daring him to share.

He shifted his weight from his left foot to his right foot as he mirrored my posture, with his arms crossed in front of him. "I used a cattle prod."

"A cattle prod? Oh my goodness." Then I cocked my head and smiled, as I whispered to him, "A real cattle prod, or one of those wimpy stingers they use in kinky porn."

He looked startled as he let his arms fall to his sides. "Those stingers are hardly wimpy."

"If you say so. That hasn't been my experience." I stared back at him. "And your model consented to this?"

"Yes. She signed the necessary forms. And when I pulled out the stinger and explained how I was going to use it on her, she had a look in her eyes. That became my terror image. And then when I used it, I got pain." His mouth formed a tight smirk.

"She really committed herself to your vision, Axel. I'm impressed. Where'd you find her?" I continued to probe, with a breezy tone in my voice, even as I was appalled by his approach.

"She's a drama student at Juilliard. I went looking for someone who took a 'method' approach to her art, just like I take a 'method' approach to mine."

"Axel, I'd love to work with you on a project, sometime." One of my missions was to offer a certain kind of artist a lesson in consent. "Forget mind-fucking young girls, you need a collaborator whose mind is as outrageous as yours and whose imagination is even more bold. Come to my gallery tomorrow night at nine. Bring your cattle prod."

As I had hoped, Axel arrived at nine, lugging a large black leather bag. He was dressed in tight black jeans and a black leather motorcycle jacket. He looked ready to burgle. I had dressed for the occasion in a tight black leather skirt, black bodysuit with a plunging neckline, my highest Louboutins with a serious platform. My lipstick was the color of arterial blood. When I met him at the door, Axel looked me up and down and gave me a lusty smile.

"Come on in. Let me lock the door behind you. I don't want us to get interrupted. We have important matters to discuss."

"DON'T TELL ME you showed him your basement?" Edouard sat there, giving me an intense look. Was it jealousy? Perhaps.

"Of course. And when he said he wanted to be my slave, I locked him in that basement for a month while he painted."

"No." Edouard's mouth was slightly agape. The stories of artists toiling in basements were legendary. Annina Nosei put Basquiat in a studio beneath her gallery, and despite all the drugs and liquor that fueled him, boy did he produce. "How did you keep him there? Kidnapping is illegal."

"Oh, he was desperate to stay. I was awful to him, but in exquisite ways. Frankly, I was appalled by him, but I sucked it up for a few of his eyeballs." I sat back and smirked, while Edouard stared at me. "Did you know that the going rate for psychodrama at any respectable Manhattan dungeon starts at two-hundred and fifty dollars per hour, and for that, the lady makes the gentleman cry. If it's the other way around, the price is higher. Axel was paying these young girls minimum wage while he engaged in serious mindfuckery."

"So, you turned him?" Edouard looked at me with amazement.

"Not exactly. He'd been projecting his own tortured fantasies onto his young models, so I gave him a taste of his own medicine. With his consent, of course."

"Of course. Details, please."

"Oh, I locked up his cock in one of those fiendish metal cock cages, and then threatened to throw away the key. That twisted fellow got harder at the prospect. His flesh bulged when I told him if I lost the key, he'd have to go to the emergency room and have it cut off."

"His cock cut off?"

"No, silly, the cage. The one I put on him was made of stainless steel. Let me tell you, darling, the cage had the desired effect. It really focused his mind. He painted all day, every day, for the four weeks he was down there. The works I showed were his production from that time."

"He gave them to you?"

"Well, slaves don't have property, do they? They *are* property!"

"You amaze me, Erika. Did he get anything from his stay in your basement?"

"Well, he got an appreciation for what his models went through. I made him *my* model."

"What do you mean?"

"Well, as you may recall, the series at my gallery was about emotions, too. There was desperation, frustration, hunger and release. I took the pictures that he transformed into his works."

"That was his right eye, in all the paintings?"

"Yes! You understand."

"Desperation seems obvious. You took that photo when the cock cage went on."

"Exactly. Frustration was after it had been on for two weeks, and I only took it off to tease him a bit. That was tricky. I didn't want him to cum, but I did want him to get aroused. You should have seen him plead for release while I stroked him for a few seconds."

"Indeed. What was hunger about?"

"Exactly what you think. He was hungry. I didn't feed him much for a few days and made him grovel for Goldfish crackers out of a dog bowl."

"Goldfish crackers?" Edouard shook his head and laughed. "Why *Goldfish* crackers?"

I shrugged, and sitting in his elegant dining room eating chef-prepared foods made the crackers seem trivial. I probably should have opened a can of Alpo and spooned it into his reluctant mouth, but the prospect of its smell disturbed me. "Kibble seemed too mean, and I don't think it's very digestible to humans. And I really just wanted to see him down on his hands and knees, so he'd have that particular experience and vantage point. His gaze is very alpha. It needed some reorientation."

"You made an impression on him. His latest set of eyes feature themes like wisdom and doubt. There are even wrinkles."

"Yes. He's using older models now. No more teenagers and no more awful surprises. I mean, who did he think he was, Bernardo Bertolucci in *Last Tango*, tricking Maria Schneider? Did you know Bertolucci didn't tell her they were about to film that anal rape scene? He wanted her tears to be real. It makes for provocative art, but the PTSD cheapens the work."

"Let the artist suffer, if he or she wants suffering. Is that what you're saying?"

"Well, it shouldn't be the viewer who suffers. And really, does it have to be the model? Unless he or she consents, of course. And let's make that informed consent. I've suffered for someone's vision, and I'd do it again, but it's fucking hard. You need to know what you're getting into."

"I'm surprised by your stance on this. Isn't the point to nurture talent and produce the greatest art?"

"Sure. But between you and me, Axel's work is gimmicky and shallow. He's technically proficient, but there's not much to show beyond that."

"I agree about the gimmickry, but the man does know how to paint."

"Yes. but he hides behind his skills. His voice is derivative. I mean, haven't we all seen eyes before?"

"Very true, Erika. Let's face it, Gustave Courbet portrayed despair better."

"Those eyes in Courbet's self-portrait? Magnificent. They just jump out of the canvas, and you can feel the man's anguish in every brushstroke." We both sighed at the thought of superior works to Axel's. "Let's face it, Edouard, for too long we've let talent be a shield. Think of all the assholes who've gotten away with outrageous things, just because their works moved us. Picasso, for instance, tortured his women. He demanded utter submission from them, and when they balked, he did horrifying things. He once branded Françoise Gilot with a lit cigarette. He beat Dora Maar.

He fantasized about having the women fight over him. They were just tools to feed his ego and his work."

"He was an ogre. But he was also a genius. The women around him didn't come close to his talent."

"Picasso's work, at its best, is extraordinary. But he did a lot of extremely mediocre things, too. As for the women, it's their role as muse we celebrate. We ignore they were his victims or artists in their own right. In the public consciousness, they exist primarily in service to him. It's staggering that we're still willing to tolerate these misogynistic bullies, all in the name of art."

"Bullies are celebrated everywhere. Consider Steve Jobs. He's a horror to his employees, but I see you using an iPhone. You also carry a Chanel purse. Karl Lagerfeld is not a nice man."

"Point taken. Dreadful people can make exquisite things, but for me to express that depth of hypocrisy, the things had better be extraordinary."

Edouard laughed and shook his head. "Back to Axel. Do you really think you reformed him? That he went from being a misogynistic bully to being a feminist?"

"No. I'm not a miracle worker and I'm not a fool. But do his models need to actually experience fear to be persuasive? This stance diminishes *their* artistry. It suggests they lack the capacity to persuade, unless they're feeling whatever emotion Axel dictates. Frankly, we women have been faking things—unnoticed—for years. Axel has probably never been with a woman who's having a genuine orgasm."

"Touché. Maybe that's why he's so determined to elicit real emotions?"

"Perhaps. But what makes him think he deserves to elicit these difficult emotions on demand?"

"It's their job, Erika. He's paying these models. They are participants in the creation."

"Yes, but they're getting minimum wage. He's getting thousands."

"Are you turning into a Marxist?"

"No! But he is the experienced person in the room, and he knows what he's going to do to them. Mere consent doesn't always make things acceptable. Some of these young women might even find his process challenging and thrilling. You and I appreciate emotional torment, but we are *not* the norm. The models talk, and I've heard them discuss his 'artistic process' in very unfavorable terms."

"No, I suppose we are not the norm. But surely he's the exception?"

"Sadly, no." So many collectors have some romantic notion of how art is created, but it is often produced under horrifying conditions by ridiculous, abusive people. "There's this one artist in New York—a neighbor of mine—whose atelier is basically a cult. He exploits the youngsters around him. They wear little uniforms. They exercise together. And get this, they get punished—physically and emotionally—if they don't follow his systems to his liking." I paused at the memory of seeing a small squad wearing matching tracksuits featuring his logo, doing calisthenics in a parking lot near my gallery. "To outsiders it seems eccentric. Who cares, if the works sell, right? And some of these assistants come out exhilarated and excited to have been in the same room as a genius . . . But some of these assistants are scarred for life. They didn't understand the deal they were getting. Their consent was not fully informed."

"Many ateliers seem cult-ish; so do many operating rooms and CEO suites. Is it really so different?"

"Yes. Operating rooms are inhabited by trained professionals. They may not all be professional equals, but they have protections. There's always HR, if things get too crazy. Where does an abused model go? My hope is that Axel will think twice before he picks up some wide-eyed little co-ed and takes her back to his studio. In the future, let him pick on models his own size."

"Maybe works need to come with those notices you see at the end of films, or on cosmetics packaging."

"You mean, like 'No animals were harmed in the production of this movie'? Or, 'Cruelty-free.'"

"Precisely. 'No humans were harmed in the production of this painting. This painting is cruelty free.' Maybe the Grieg Gallery should be a pioneer in such things."

"You are very funny. As Nietzsche once said, 'Without cruelty there is no festival.' I adore cruelty . . . I am a connoisseur of cruelty . . . I have monetized cruelty. But cruelty needs to be consensual, and cruelty should only happen among equals."

21

BEATING CLIENTS
INTO SUBMISSION

Having learned some secrets about my business emboldened
Edouard. It didn't surprise me when the conversation turned personal. "Our discussion last night made me curious about something, Erika. Do you enjoy your sessions?"

"Edouard, of course I do." It always shocks me when a sophisticated client asks that question. Does he really expect to hear something sordid or negative?

"But surely some clients are less agreeable than others," he
pressed, unable to help himself.

"Of course. But I get paid to put aside some of my preferences
so I don't just do scenes with beautiful women and men who look
like George Clooney."

"George Clooney?"

"Don't you find him charming and handsome?"

"*Everybody* finds him charming and handsome." Edouard sat
back in his chair and pressed his fingertips together to form a tent
in front of his face. "Seriously, do you enjoy your work?"

"Seriously, do you enjoy yours?" I wanted a moment to collect my thoughts and to decide how much to share. "I imagine it has its good and bad days."

"Of course it has bad days. And right now, I wonder if it's going to be a bad year."

"Well, it's the same for me. I assume we're discussing the domination side of my work, and not the gallery side. And by the way, both sides have much in common."

"How interesting. Where do you find the commonalities? Is it as Baudelaire suggested, that art is prostitution?"

"Well, I'm not sure that all art is prostitution, but some prostitution is certainly art."

"Hah. Point taken, and I agree with you completely."

"But back to what my gallery and my dungeon have in common . . . I have to look a certain way in both environments. Nobody wants a sloppy gallerist or a shabby dominatrix, do they? Before I started my own gallery, I had bosses encouraging me to dress sexier—higher heels, more cleavage—to better satisfy the male gaze, because, let's face it, that's who buys most art. Did you know there are twice as many male collectors as there are female?"

"I certainly see that at auctions. Most bidders are men. So are most dealers."

"Exactly. So, at times I felt like I was working in a brothel, where the owner—and I'm not going to name names—would dangle pretty saleswomen like flashy lures in front of wealthy clients. And we'd be rewarded if we could flatter the buyer and persuade him to open up his wallet and show us how big a man he was. Oops, I mean, how serious a *collector* he was."

"Are you trying to tell me that my pleasant experiences at White Cube and Gagosian were just mercenary saleswomen trying to get me to buy?"

"Edouard, please. You're a different animal. You are an educated and serious collector."

"Go on. You flatter me." Edouard grinned as he leaned back in his chair.

"You own pieces that others envy. Your taste informs what the galleries carry, not the other way around." Flattery is my medium. I can wield it like a scalpel. But flattery without context or constraint can feel insincere. "But they are nicer to you because you *buy*. Don't you treat certain clients better than others?"

"Of course. But what about your private clients? How do you manage them? They can't all be wonderful."

"My job, if you will, is to be so engaged with the client he has no idea he isn't my favorite and that I don't adore everything we are doing together. My job is to listen, to be fully present, and then to create."

"Right . . . Right . . . I've heard your speech before about how it's an expert performance for an audience of one."

"You're a careful listener. I appreciate that."

"You turn critic John Berger upside down, with his idea that men act and women appear. You act. There's nothing ethereal about you. You grab the client and you don't let go until you're finished with him."

"Thank you for noticing. But there's an aspect of Berger I can relate to. He went on and said, 'Men look at women. Women watch themselves being looked at.' I am watching the client watching me all the time, because that's how I learn what works. That gaze influences what I do and how I create. And besides, I enjoy being looked at. I wish I could say I didn't care. At first it bothered me, but now the male gaze nourishes me. Maybe I should have been a stripper!"

"You'd have made an extraordinary stripper, but selfishly, I'm happy you chose this path instead."

"Likewise. After all, it brought us together. Some of the best people I know are perverts."

"Yes, perverts are fine people. Now, back to what we were discussing earlier . . . we've established that you don't let your less favored clients have a clue. But you have had bad clients? Every industry has bad clients."

"Well, at first, I had my share. When you're starting out, you don't know what you don't know, and I was scrambling to earn money. That meant I had shitty clients . . . There were guys who didn't even show up . . ."

"I can't believe there are men who'd change their minds about seeing *you*." Edouard grimaced as his words came out.

"Oh, this is a field that evokes much dissonance." I shrugged. "One minute, they're listening to their libido, the next they're listening to their conscience."

"Of course. And once the conscience weighs in, it must be difficult to override those hesitations."

"At first, I tried, but then I gave up. I didn't want clients who were overcome with guilt. These kinds of men might make stupid mistakes or get angry. I've heard stories about dommes having violent clients. I prefer mine grateful, content and docile."

"Docile and grateful? Of course you want that. I want that from my clients, too."

"Who wouldn't? Do any of your clients balk at paying you?" Why wouldn't Edouard have similar problems? The wealthy can be flighty and flinty.

"It happened in the past . . . it's happening now, in fact. This crisis has left many short of funds and put deals in jeopardy. People are scared and scrambling, which means there are problems and delays when I put out a capital call. Years ago, under different circumstances, investors committed to having money available for when my fund needed it. They'd get a message and immediately wire me forty million dollars, and my fund would acquire a share in some aluminum smelter. Obviously, these capital calls have become more complicated, and yet I see so many opportunities because of the crisis."

"You're seeing opportunities?"

"Of course. Crisis creates opportunity, but it's hard to take advantage of a crisis if you don't have liquidity. Every day I spend hours persuading long-standing investors to be calm and to send me the money they committed to sending."

"I'm sorry to hear you're getting pushback. It must be agonizing and awkward."

"Exactly. And am I supposed to sue an investor who won't fulfill his obligation? Am I supposed to forgo an excellent opportunity because someone hesitated, punishing my more confident investors in the process?" An exasperated edge had gotten into Edouard's speech, where usually, he was measured and calm. "And how about you? Surely, I'm not alone in dealing with skittish clients."

"No, you're not alone at all. It's something I experienced, especially at first. There were guys who balked at paying—and by the way, my rates were much lower then, I was so ignorant . . . it only happened a couple of times, early on. That's why I make the clients pay up front. I even had a client steal his tribute back. He seemed harmless. I'd left the envelope on a shelf and when I went to collect it, it had disappeared."

"That's awful. What did you do?"

"Nothing. I called him, asked him if he'd picked up something *accidentally*, but he said he hadn't. And then I hung up, because there was nothing else I could do except never see him again." It was a memory that pained me, because of the helplessness it evoked. "While I'm venting, let me ask you this: Did you ever have a client try to stick their fingers up your ass?"

"That's easy. No."

"Occupational hazard at my end. I had guys who tried to stick their fingers in my pussy . . . grab my ass . . . lick my breasts, even.

Then there were the guys who nagged me to do things I'd already told them I wouldn't do. It was exhausting."

"How does someone tied down try to stick his fingers in your pussy?" Edouard rested his head on his hand, like Rodin's *Thinker.*

"Well, they can be pretty fast and very handsy. That's how I got so quick at bondage. It started out as a defensive move. I worked by myself from the start, which means I had no backup if something went wrong."

"Very clever. But it sounds dangerous. Why persist? If it's such a taxing job?"

"I liked most of the clients. The work was amusing. I was good at it. And even though the money wasn't great at first, it was still better than what Harvard Dining Services paid. It's different in the States than in France. It's very expensive being a grad student in art history, even at an elite school. *Especially* at an elite school. I had funding, sure, which covered tuition and some basic expenses. But most of my classmates had trust funds and parents who'd fly them to whatever exhibition they wanted to check out."

"Viewing works in a book or on a computer doesn't compare with seeing them in person, does it?"

"And I was researching the use of sex workers as models. I wanted to walk the streets of Montmartre and Pigalle to see how and where they lived. You can't get that from a biography of Degas."

"No, you cannot. Well, I'm grateful you persisted, otherwise we would never have met. Here's a thought: instead of defending the works of the models, perhaps we could role-play that time Napoleon III hit Courbet with his whip because he didn't like a painting. Let the artists suffer, too!"

"Edouard, aren't you twisted. Should I find a handlebar mustache, to make it real? Or can I go bare lipped?"

"You cannot be Napoleon III without a mustache. Or a goatee, for that matter. Perhaps we should find another idea. I know, I'll be your helpless latex slave and you'll be the cruel woman who teases me without mercy."

"Done. Tonight darling, you'll suffer."

22

SPLENDID ISOLATION

The house was large, especially by Swiss standards, but after a few weeks of leaving only to go to meetings or Pilates, it was starting to feel very small. One time, I'd suggested going out for sushi to Edouard, but instead, he brought a sushi chef to the house, and we had an eight-course meal of immaculately plated delicacies, ranging from toro to unagi.

"What's the deal, Edouard? You get to New York. You travel a lot . . . So I know you're not agoraphobic." I was baffled by how housebound my host had become.

"No. Nothing of the sort. Simply put, things are difficult right now."

"It's difficult everywhere. Cologny is no exception."

"Very true." Edouard winced. "How's your business doing?" It felt like he was trying to change the subject.

"There are zero sales. Which is why you're stuck with me."

"Your presence here is the lone bright spot of my crisis. Unfortunately for you, it's better for me if I stay close to home, which makes me a poor host."

"Boxler, more sake, please." I turned to Edouard. "We've known one another for years now, and you need to get out more. I've been here three weeks, and I don't think you've left the house once."

"More sake for me, too, Boxler." Edouard pointed at his little cup, and Boxler poured until the clear liquid was almost overflowing. Edouard stared at the cup and then took a long sip. "When I'm in Geneva, I rarely go out. Frankly, there is little to do."

"So I've noticed. Do you have friends? Colleagues? All this isolation can't be healthy."

"There's not a lot of mingling here. The Swiss don't care for the French, and vice versa. There are still social clubs here that admit only natives." Edouard stared at his glass, and then finished its content in one gulp. "Frankly, I never liked networking."

"Fair enough. The forced socializing of the art market is something I find tedious, too. There are too many people who lack your discernment and dedication, and who just want to waste my time. I can't tell you how many glasses of shitty champagne I've consumed at art fairs and openings."

"Yes. Who wants to waste time?" Edouard pointed at his glass again, and Boxler filled it to the rim. He finished it as efficiently as he finished the last one. My host wasn't treating it like the ceremonial drink it is in Japan. He was treating it like a tequila shot, and yet his face looked unaffected by the alcohol.

"Exactly. Well, I should go call the gallery and make sure Josh and the gang are not wasting time. There may be no sales, but there are things to do."

"Wise." Edouard stood up and followed me as I walked to my room. He gave me the background on some of the pieces on his walls, and when I got to my door, he followed me inside.

"Your comment about wasting time inspired me, and so have you." Edouard had been standing behind me when he pulled me to his body and began to kiss me. He was all lip and tongue, and it was disorienting. It wasn't unpleasant, I'd always found him handsome, but it was unwelcome. This sort of thing had happened before— usually with collectors. And although I don't like to admit it, once or twice early in my career I closed a deal beneath a duvet at the Four Seasons. I'd get caught up in the thrill of the seduction and the excitement of a purchase, and the collector and I would celebrate horizontally.

What pains me to admit is that once or twice I also failed to close a deal while horizontal, beneath a duvet at the Four Seasons. Apparently, my pussy has its limits when it comes to separating cash from clients. Those unsuccessful experiences did not sit well. Even though I'd consented to them, I couldn't shake the feeling I'd been misled or cheapened, and I hated feeling cheap even more than I hated feeling fooled. But what could I do or say? If it's acceptable to change your mind about having sex with someone, even once you're lying with them naked, how is it different if someone changes their mind about buying a painting? Consent can be retracted at any moment.

I spent hours with my therapist going over the play-by-plays, and describing how these collectors had fouled my mood and stoked my rage. It might not have been fair to them, but my anger with myself and with them was real. From that point forward, I kept the amorous collectors at an arm's distance.

These client fiascoes flooded my brain as my mind went into overdrive. If Edouard were to push matters, I'd have to leave Geneva immediately, before these overtures became a habit. While I stood there, wondering what to do, Edouard pushed his pelvis into mine. I could feel his cock hard beneath his trousers. "I'd love to fuck you. You excite me. Let me return the favor."

My relationship with Edouard was murky and messy enough already, the last thing I needed was to add further complexity or entanglement. "Oh, Edouard, I'm not the girl for this." I turned my face away from his, deliberately not making eye contact. I didn't want him to have his humiliation witnessed. I liked Edouard, and I enjoyed his company. Only a few years ago, that would have been enough, but I'd been saturated with sexual desire and my own hunger had been squelched. It was hard to explain to a civilian, but it was one of the ancillary costs of my business. And besides, it would set a dangerous precedent. I didn't want Edouard showing up at my room whenever his erection got strong enough.

He straightened up immediately. "Forgive me, Erika. I had too much to drink."

"We both did. I probably won't remember any of this in the morning."

"Good night." Edouard turned and left the room immediately, while I stood there wondering what to do with him and my otherwise perfect crash pad. If only Josh hadn't told me there'd been another sighting of my father. He'd turned up at the gallery, demanding to see me. Josh told him I was out of the country on a business trip, but the news only seemed to get him more aggravated. When I spoke with Michael, we agreed it wasn't cowardice on my part to stay away, but common sense. But it meant that Geneva was the best place for me to be, even if that meant dealing with an amorous-but-embarrassed host.

Decamping to a hotel would cost me money I didn't have. Amy was ensconced in my apartment. Usually, I enjoyed Edouard's company very much, so I simply had to hope this was just a guy taking his shot and he was mature enough not to hold a grudge, because the last thing I wanted or needed was a billionaire with a boner to pick. Fortunately, I had an idea.

23

HUNTING AT CLUB DIAMANT

At lunch, I told Boxler and Edouard I was going downtown for dinner. Boxler volunteered the Maybach and I accepted without hesitation. I could hardly navigate Geneva's cobbled streets in my Louboutin pumps, because I was getting all dressed up for my jailbreak.

I hit the bar of the Hotel Beau Rivage just as the banking crowd was enjoying its cocktails. There were scores of men, all wearing dark suits, drinking scotch at the bar. It must have been another tough day on the market, because their faces were uniformly tight, and their mouths were pursed closed. Drinking brought them no pleasure.

In the dim light, I looked around as I nursed my gin martini. There was one attractive brunette at the bar, possibly Moldovan, and I waved at her. She wore a fitted navy dress, a discreet gold cross around her neck, and she carried a Chanel bag. She had the perfect mix of flesh and muscle, as if her body had been engineered for the gym and the bedroom. I was sure she was a pro, but when she got closer, I realized my mistake. She was also carrying a black leather portfolio, bulging with deal books and PowerPoints.

She sat down opposite me and nodded. "Joanna Albot. Are you here for the UBD restructuring?" She was just another vulture, dining on carrion.

"Erika Grieg and no. Nothing of the sort." I gave her an appraising eye, all the same. As an escort, she'd have earned money on par with whatever she earned as a management consultant and her conscience would be cleaner. Being part of the apparatus that was destroying the world's economy had to be depleting. It was a shame she wasn't in the sex industry. Most clients would have loved the cross, her demure gold hoop earrings and her perfect, un-enhanced tits. "I'm an art dealer. I don't speak restructuring. Are all of you here for that?"

"Pretty much. I thought you were part of the team. Sorry."

"It's all right. Everyone looks grim. It must be a hard job."

"It's complicated, but we'll get it done." And with that, Ms. Albot stood up and left my table. She must have been prospecting for business or intent on networking, because she was not at the bar to play. It seemed like a sign, so I moved on as well.

There was a cool breeze off the lake as I made my way to the Hôtel de la Paix. The Jet d'Eau in the middle of Lake Geneva was spurting water in a high, steady stream. It felt as though the lake were ejaculating while everyone else in town had gone flaccid.

The doorman nodded as I climbed the stone steps and the host at the wood-paneled bar made a signal, inviting me to sit wherever I wanted. I found a spot at the bar and waited. People drifted in and out, but I didn't see a candidate as I nursed my second gin martini.

Other sex workers could find business in hotel bars like these. When markets roil, potential clients feel crushed or exuberant, and both conditions can inspire time with an escort. Many men are conditioned to feel that sex is both their way to medicate and to celebrate, that it seems only natural when you're on the road to hit the hotel bar. They'll order a glass of expensive scotch, see an even more expensive woman and decide they need a fix.

I had dominatrix colleagues swear they'd found clients in hotel bars. After all, if escorts could do it, why couldn't we? Other colleagues said that shoe sales at Nordstrom were excellent hunting grounds for fetishists. That seemed more logical to me, but if a guy was haunting a shoe store, he wouldn't be out making money and that was the necessary prerequisite for some time with me. Instead of prospecting, I had been content to build my business by relying on word of mouth and the rare advertisement in specialty magazines. It was bad enough I had to talk to these random assholes to sell them art. But to try and pick them up at the bar, too? Excruciating.

A lean, silver-haired man in a sharp Brioni suit made an effort. He sidled up to the bar, ordered me another martini in a move he'd probably practiced in hotel bars from Toronto to Dubai. We chatted pleasantly, and he seemed startled to learn I was an art dealer. We were both hunting the same prey, so he moved on, disappointed I wasn't the escort he was seeking.

I struck out again at the bar of the Hôtel Du Lac. It felt like I'd been traipsing through the entire Geneva waterfront, tottering between fancy hotels in my Louboutins. Finally, I gave in, and asked the bartender for help. He had the look of someone who'd worked in hotel bars for decades, so nothing would shock him.

"Another martini, please . . . and perhaps you can assist me." The gentleman leaned onto the bar, in a move that implied he had my undivided attention, but which also served to block any eavesdroppers.

"What can I do for you, madam?" He had that indistinct accent, that said English wasn't his first language, and it was probably only his fourth or fifth.

"I'm looking for someone . . ." I leaned into the bar and matched his position. "A lady." I tried to convey this was an ordinary request on a typical day. "Can you help me?"

He seemed startled, but only for an instant. He nodded as he rubbed his chin and discreetly scanned the room. "There's no one here tonight." He must have sensed my disappointment. "But you might find one at the Diamant. It's a nightclub downtown. There are dancers who are open."

"Sounds perfect. I'm off." I gave him a hundred franc note, and he gave me a rakish smile in return.

I arrived at Club Diamant on the early side for a sleazy nightclub aspiring to being classy. There were poles, velvet banquettes and several very bored but beautiful dancers waiting to take their turn. It was the kind of place where the dancers wore gowns between dances, but these were skintight gowns that showed lots of tit, leg and tat, and were designed for ease of removal.

Back when I lived in Boston, I sometimes took clients to a gritty little strip club called the Glass Slipper, lodged in the middle of Boston's notorious "Combat Zone." It felt dissolute and outrageous, arriving at the club with some foot fetishist in toe. Before heading to the club, I'd fashion a cock harness out of rope. I'd leave a bit of cord jutting from his pants and give it a hard yank if the client misbehaved. Usually, that was all it took to turn even the most rambunctious fellow into someone obedient.

There was one client I took to the club on several occasions. We'd sit in one of the most discreet booths, where the black vinyl of the banquette seats needed only a few small pieces of duct tape for repairs. One by one, the dancers would come visit us, because I had Jimmy buy a bottle of their cheapest champagne—Taittinger—from each, to satisfy their quota. The real money was in tips, so I had him tip generously. He'd give one a twenty as he gave her a foot massage. He'd give another a fifty, when she'd have him get down on the floor and crawl.

My favorite was Samantha, I'd even time our visits to coincide with her shifts. Jimmy probably figured she was just another leggy brunette with perfect tits and teeth, but she also was a junior at

MIT where she studied chemical engineering. She told everyone she was studying marketing at Emerson, one of the many second-tier schools in the area whose students populated shitty jobs around Boston. It was a lie I could relate to. I told my clients I was a graduate student in anthropology at Boston University.

Samantha would see me, and she'd amble over in whatever spandex gown she was wearing. The dances, even though they were practically gynecological in terms of how much they showed the customers, were basically appetizers. At the Glass Slipper, the most successful women were those who knew how to sit at a table with some guy, sell him champagne, and then work him over conversationally. While Samantha seemed disarmingly low-key, she was charming and effective at emptying wallets. Dancers have one of the toughest jobs in the sex industry. They mostly sell sizzle and the fantasy of steak, so clients can be resentful about paying lots of money to a woman they will never fuck. There are also clients who delight in the prospect of saying no and insulting a beautiful woman. Dancers face rejection on an hourly basis, and yet the best dancers persevere and turn the work into a numbers game. Samantha once shared with me that she expected three nos for every yes. But when she got that yes she was relentless.

In my presence, Samantha always got a yes. But I always got a yes from her, too. I'd invite her to sit down with Jimmy and me. She'd nod, arrange her dress as she slid into the booth, and with no further chitchat, she'd take her black patent Pleaser pump and grind the shoe into Jimmy's crotch. Jimmy's eyes would roll back in his head in ecstasy, while Samantha and I emptied multiple bottles of Taittinger.

As I sat at Club Diamant, eyeing the dancers, I didn't see any with the same quirky humor as Samantha, but I wasn't looking for conversation. After about fifteen minutes, I had picked my favorite. She wasn't the best on the pole, but there was a smirk on her face that worked for me. She had enormous dark eyes, emphasized with excellent false eyelashes. Her black hair was pulled back into a sleek high ponytail, which she tossed around with a riveting grace. I wanted to grab that tail. I wanted to make her do very bad things . . . with her consent, of course.

She must have spotted me watching her, because she moved in on my table before any of the other dancers thought to do so.

"Hi, I'm Erika. Can I get you something to drink?"

"Champagne. I like champagne." Her accent was thick, but her English was solid, and she was prepared to hustle.

I waved over one of the waitresses and asked for a bottle of vintage Dom Pérignon. I didn't want to look cheap; this bottle would set me back over five hundred francs. One lesson I've learned from years in the sex industry is that the best way to get a sex worker's attention is to be polite, to tip ahead of service, and to be extravagant.

"You're very pretty, and I like your accent. Where are you from? What's your name?"

"Viviana. I'm from Bucharest. You're very pretty, too. Where are you from?"

"I'm from New York, but I'm visiting my boyfriend who lives here."

"You should bring him to the club. Or maybe you like it when he stays home," Viviana purred.

"I think I like it when he stays home. Although, I think he'd like to meet you." I could purr, too.

"Oh? I'm here four nights a week. Come by tomorrow." It was hard not to be impressed by her commitment to her job. Every sex worker likes repeat customers.

"Perhaps, but that's not what I had in mind."

And then we got down to business. I told her I needed her help, but that I would pay her well for the opportunity. I pulled out a stack of hundred-franc notes and gave her twenty of the bills. "I'll give you the same amount at the end of the evening, if you'll come with me now."

She grabbed the money and stashed it into her small, faux-Chanel purse. "That would be difficult."

"I know. Your boss probably wants you to stay till your shift ends." She nodded as she gave me an elegant shrug. "Tell him you're not feeling well, and that I offered to give you a lift home in my car. It's tonight, or never. I'll be out front. Look for the Maybach." Viviana arched her eyebrow when she heard the name Maybach, and she excused herself. I went out and sat in Edouard's car and waited. It didn't take long. Viviana was in her black wool coat and out the side door of the club in only two minutes.

While we drove back to Cologny, I called Edouard. "I have a surprise for you. I want you in your robe, and nothing else . . . And get a champagne bucket, fill it with ice and a bottle of your best champagne along with three champagne glasses."

"Three?" The surprise was audible in Edouard's voice.

"You heard me. Now get cracking, because we're only five minutes away."

"Yes, Erika."

24

THREESOME

It was late, but Boxler was there to meet us at the door. I handed him my coat after he'd helped Viviana off with hers. The lights in the house were dim, but more importantly, the paintings were unlit. The driver had probably tipped Boxler off, and he'd done his best to conceal the items of most value. I had no interest in giving Viviana a tour. I had other plans.

"We're going to see Edouard. Good night." I grabbed Viviana's hand, which was clammy, despite the cool look on her face. I turned to her. "I just want to remind you, only do what you feel comfortable doing. But I'm hoping we can both get comfortable. Are you okay?"

She nodded, so I led her back to Edouard's suite. After all, I wasn't her babysitter. He'd heard us coming, so the door opened immediately, revealing Edouard in his thick terry bathrobe.

"Please come in, ladies." Edouard turned to me and gave me a big smile.

"Edouard, I'd like to introduce you to my new friend Viviana. Isn't she lovely?"

Edouard nodded with enthusiasm, but as he was about to stick out his hand, I stopped him. "Put both hands behind your neck. Now." His lips pursed together in a tiny grimace, but he did as he was told. I removed the belt from his robe and tied his wrists together. I then turned to Viviana. "He's very obedient, so if there's anything you don't like, please tell him. And if there's anything you do like, please tell me."

Viviana was quick, and she caught on to the game. She looked from Edouard to me. "Will he get down on his knees if I say I don't like him standing?"

"Yes. Tell him what to do. He'll obey." I gave Edouard a harsh look, to remind him to commit to the scene I was orchestrating.

"Kneel." Viviana's voice was firm. She looked at me as I nodded approvingly.

Edouard carefully got down on the floor, unable to let his bound hands drop or help his balance. He stared at the Romanian intently. She presented her left foot, still clad in a pair of faux-Louboutins, to him. "Kiss it." Edouard bent at the waist and pressed his lips to the toe of her black patent leather stiletto. Viviana cocked her head and shrugged. She'd clearly done this before.

"You're a natural, Viviana. We're going to have fun tonight with this handsome toy." I gave Edouard a nudge that toppled him onto his side on the floor. His robe fell open, revealing that he was naked beneath it.

"Edouard, get up and lie down on the bed." It took him a moment to find his balance, but he clambered up, his wrists still tied behind his neck. And with a flourish, he hurled himself onto the bed and flopped onto his back so that he was centered on the mattress. Sadly, he didn't have a four-poster bed, so I had to settle for tucking the tail ends of the belt securing his wrists, under a pillow.

It wasn't perfect immobility, it was strictly half-assed, but I didn't want to take Viviana to the dungeon or let her see that Edouard's tastes were extreme. Geneva is a small town, and people talk. But more significantly, I didn't want to waste time. "Now, lie there and don't move. I have plans."

25

GENEVA'S DARK SECRETS

After we were through, and Edouard was snoring, I escorted Viviana to the Maybach and gave her the money. She offered to come back if I ever needed more "help." Should Edouard become a sex pest again, I had her mobile number at the ready.

An evening of decadent activity left me wiped, so I crawled into bed only to wake up when my phone rang at six in the morning. It was Amy. It was always Amy. She hardly slept, and she always had questions. I'd spoken to Michael the prior day, who shared with me that she was getting the hang of the work. I tried to hide the irritation in my voice as she confessed to a crush on one of my clients. I'd worried she'd injured someone, not that she had kissed someone.

"We've all been there, Amy. What you're describing is incredibly common. Even therapists can feel something for their patients." And it was true, there had always been the odd client—from the gallery or my dungeon—who stirred something in me.

"Dan's the kind of man I usually like to date." She was discussing Dan Levine, a billionaire with a bondage fetish. He was reasonably good-looking, but hopelessly dull. He was often on the phone at the start of our sessions, signing off on some deal. That kind of showiness was a frequent enough occurrence in my presence that I had determined the men wanted to demonstrate to me how they were at the top of their pile before they became abject at my feet. It was predictable and unnecessary.

"Did you think there'd be something undesirable or wrong about my clients? They're all exceptional men."

"That came out poorly. Yes, you're right. They all seem fantastic. But some are more fantastic than others . . . It's unsettling. I even kissed him. Or he kissed me . . ."

"I get it, Amy. Did you know there's a whole body of literature on countertransference."

"What's that?"

"Countertransference? It's when the therapist projects his or her feelings onto the patient. Do you remember that Harvard medical student who got caught up with his psychiatrist back when we were undergrads? What was her name . . . uhm . . . Dr. Bean-Bayog?"

"Oh my god, yes. That case was so lurid. She fell in love with him, and he called her mommy. Didn't he commit suicide?"

"Yes, you remember. That was an extreme case and its worst possible outcome. I probably shouldn't have mentioned it. At its best, though, countertransference helps enhance empathy. Our feelings are like guideposts for seeing our clients better. Fortunately, dominatrixes can't lose their license if something happens; we can only lose our cool. So be careful. Kiss him if you like. Only do what feels right to you."

"It's dizzying, trying to figure out what feels right and wrong. How do you manage this? The clients are so complicated."

"Amy, listen to me, you make the rules. Different women have different limits. Google 'girlfriend experience.' Those ladies are fucking warriors. Consider dancers, they have to guzzle champagne as they talk to their clients, all the while staying skinny enough to look great on the pole. And those lap dances? Incredibly hot. I couldn't do what they do, and most of them can't do what we do. We are artists and we make our own rules . . . Although I wouldn't make a habit of kissing clients. They'll want more. They always want more." My mind flashed to Edouard and his nocturnal visit to my suite. "You have to know where to draw the line."

"What line? He knows who I am, Erika. He knows everything."

"Amy, the men all think they have more to lose than you do. He knows who I am, and he's never been a problem. You're doing great."

"I don't feel like I'm doing great."

"That's very common among baby dommes. But I've spoken to all the clients you've seen, and to the man, they enthuse about the way you take command during their sessions. Michael is especially smitten."

"Michael is wonderful. And I can tell he adores you."

"We've known each other a long time, and he's an extraordinary judge of character. If he thinks you're doing great, you are. So, relax. Avoid the hard things, stick to where you feel comfortable, and bring your intensity to the work. It's like investment banking, only the clients are baring their souls and offering you their bodies."

"That's not like investment banking. That's nothing like investment banking."

"Point taken. But keep doing what you're doing. I hear only good things."

After hanging up with Amy, I couldn't get back to sleep. Instead, I got dressed and got to work. My gallery might have been on the other side of the Atlantic, but there was always something that needed my attention, so I settled in at my laptop and wrote emails through the morning. My only break was when Boxler knocked at my door.

"Is this a good time? May I come in?"

"Of course." Boxler wasn't the kind of man to simply show up and bullshit. He'd done twenty years in the Swiss military before attending business school. Although he poured Edouard's wine, he was more than a mere flunky. It had taken me a while to realize that he was both Edouard's minder and his auxiliary brain. Boxler had the keys to the wine cellar and the combination to the safe; he was that trusted. If he wanted to speak to me, it had to be important. "What's up?"

"There was a guest last night."

"Yes. Viviana. Edouard seemed in need of a diversion, so I found one."

"I see. Things have been very difficult lately. Last night appears to have improved his mood." Boxler spoke with practiced efficiency, his accent barely noticeable.

"I should hope so. Is there a problem?"

"May I speak with you confidentially, Miss Grieg?"

"Of course. I assume that about all my conversations and encounters. Discretion is essential to my business, too."

"Yes, of course." Boxler paused, perhaps trying to decide which business I was referring to. I assumed he knew about both aspects of my work. "As you know, your American financial crisis has had an enormous effect throughout the world. It's now a global crisis."

"Yes, I know. This has implications in my industry. Art sales have all but frozen." I wasn't going to discuss what was happening in the sex industry. "And it clearly has implications in yours."

"Yes, profound implications. It has unsettled the equilibrium and put our deals in jeopardy. This is true for us, but it's also true for our neighbors, which is why I need to be candid with you."

"Please, go on."

"It's unwise for you to bring anyone to the house spontaneously. There's no way for you to know this, but there have been many break-ins in Cologny recently. One of our neighbors was held at gunpoint for several hours, while the thieves stole millions of dollars' worth of cash and jewelry."

"Oh my, that's awful. I met Viviana at a club, and I never let her out of my sight." It immediately struck me that I'd been nonchalant about Edouard's security, thinking the guards and the cameras were more than adequate, but it wasn't my place to make that assessment, and I suddenly felt very bad.

"The police tell me that Viviana's boyfriend is Romani and a member of a criminal gang."

"He's in a gang?" My heart sank further. "I'm so sorry. I don't think she saw much when she was here. We never left the bedroom."

"I believe we'll be all right, but it's complicated. The club is owned by someone with close ties to Russian organized crime. Regrettably, we've dealt with these types in some of our most contentious business matters. So, for the next month or two, we'll have additional security as a precaution. I've been pushing for this since the crisis began, but now Monsieur de Grenet understands the urgency of the matter."

"What do the local police say?"

"They are very busy. Geneva may have a reputation for being a tidy city of watches and finance, but beneath the surface, it's extremely messy."

"Please, tell me more. I think of it as a place of chocolate and clean sidewalks."

"Yes, most do. But the city attracts people who require the privacy it offers. The house adjacent to this one belongs to an arms trafficker. The next house belongs to a Russian oligarch who earned his billions in natural gas. Russia is a brutal place and that's a brutal industry. Geneva may seem genteel, but it's not. The rest of the country is no different. You'll even find North Koreans nearby."

"North Koreans? Here?"

"Yes. The regime sends its children to Switzerland to be educated. There are several enclaves of North Koreans engaging in insurance fraud and other schemes. Of course, the Montenegrins may be even worse. There's one nearby who is the CEO of a Balkan drug gang." Boxler paused for a moment, telegraphing his distaste for such overt corruption. "Where you find great wealth, you also find the best criminals."

"Sometimes it's the wealthy who are the criminals."

"Yes, that is correct. Like our neighbor, the Montenegrin. But the wealthy also attract criminals who want a share. This has been a problem for us in the past. Monsieur de Grenet is susceptible to a certain kind of woman. I've had to intervene to protect him."

I resisted the urge to roll my eyes when Boxler said "certain kind of woman." The kind seemed clear to me—beautiful and bossy. Edouard was extravagant with me, and I was certainly not the first. It seemed wise to change the subject. "Let me be frank with you. Is Edouard doing okay? He seems stressed. I care for him."

"These past few months have been difficult. Your presence has been a gift."

"Thank you. Well, I'm grateful to be here. Things have been complicated for me, as well."

"Yes, I know. With your father." There were clearly few secrets in a house with a security staff and consultants on call.

"Precisely. I'm also trying to avoid criminals. The art market draws them, and they make life difficult for those of us operating clean galleries."

"I have connections with Interpol if you'd like to speak with any of their specialists in forgeries."

"Thanks, Boxler. I hope it doesn't come to that. I'm really hoping my problem simply goes away."

"Yes, of course, Miss Grieg. Unfortunately, these periods of crisis are periods where people who are frightened do things they later regret. We must all be prepared for surprises."

Boxler was saying aloud to me the things I balked at saying silently to myself. "You're right. These are turbulent times. There's so much uncertainty in the air, it's smothering."

"Yes. And it raises the level of danger. The safety of Monsieur de Grenet, and of you, his guest, are my responsibility. Please let me know if you see anything or anyone odd or unexpected. We all need to be vigilant."

"Certainly. I'm grateful for the warning."

Boxler nodded and stepped backward. "Thank you for your time. Good day, Miss Grieg."

I understood the visit. No more Vivianas. He also wanted me to know he'd been briefed on the situation with my father. But ultimately, I think he wanted me to know that risk was in the air—and not just financial risk. I called Michael immediately, and he agreed, noting that there had been protests, harassment and even kidnapping threats leveled against his clients in the US. I'd thought Geneva would be a place to hide, but given the international nature of the meltdown, there were no discreet places left. All the same, I was in no hurry to return to New York.

26

SIDONIE AND THE TICKLE TORTURE

"Boxler tells me you have some dodgy neighbors." I took a sip of the Grüner Veltliner Edouard had chosen to go with the salad. "Mmm . . . this is very nice . . . a bit acidic to match the dressing, and the pepper notes are delicious." I paused, as Edouard leaned back in his chair. "You're switching things up. Are you abandoning your French wines?"

"No . . . I would never abandon French wines! But I thought you might welcome a change." Edouard paused and sniffed his glass, before taking a slow sip. "Yes, some of my neighbors have businesses some find problematic. Frankly, I don't have an issue with the arms dealer. He sells to everyone; he doesn't take sides. And the more unpopular the business, the better the neighbor. He's invisible."

"You make a good point. I was very discreet when I first worked in Boston. My neighbors never saw me, and I prayed they never heard me either. But my crimes were victimless. Your neighbor's work kills people."

"Erika! Since when did you become an arbiter of morality? Think of all the other distasteful professionals who buy art from you. Hedge funders, for instance." Edouard gave me a sly smile.

"Yes, of course, you're right. It just surprised me, that's all, the prospect that your neighbors aren't as upstanding as you are."

"Oh, I'm sure there are some who find *my* work problematic. Many of my deals are with people I'd never want to spend time with. I'm actually wrestling with one of those situations now."

"I'm sorry to hear that. Then again, I have clients like that as well." Once again, I was reminded that effectively, most of us are just doing customer service, and customers, quite often, are wretched.

"Which kind of client?"

"Gallery clients, of course. I got rid of all the horrible clients as my other work became more exclusive. But at first? I had quite a few problematic, kinky clients."

"Really? I must admit, that astonishes me. My perception is that you're a woman who deals only with those she chooses."

"I learned how to do that, but at first, I didn't realize I could fire clients. It was an enormous leap forward when I began to do that. Initially, however, I needed the business so I couldn't afford to be choosy. I had some crazy situations."

"Tell me! I'd love to hear about baby Erika." I was wary of telling the story in front of Boxler. Sharing stories from my dungeon-life was something I preferred to do only with those who shared my interests. Telling my friend Amy about my secret life and showing her my play space had felt radical, more revealing than standing naked in the middle of the street. To my relief, she had taken it in stride, but there was a constant worry someone might be outraged by what they heard or that the specifics could be used against me. Boxler had earned Edouard's trust, but he hadn't yet earned mine. Instinctively, I looked for him before I spoke, only he had already disappeared. He was a model of Swiss discretion. He knew when to be present and when to be absent.

"Oh, I was never a baby . . . but some of my clients were. I actually had one guy come to my studio who was only sixteen years old." I paused, remembering the moment and how terrified I'd been. "We'd spoken on the phone, and he said he was a senior. I assumed he was a senior in college, but he meant he was a senior in high school. As soon as I laid eyes on him, I realized he was too young. He was barely shaving. Just breathing the same air as him put me in legal jeopardy, so I sent him away. I was frightened for weeks afterward."

"Sixteen? That's so young. Of course, I knew what I liked much younger than that."

"That's very common, in my experience." I wanted to get rid of the memory of my underage almost-client. Turning the tables on Edouard seemed like an easy way to do so. "How old were you?"

"Ten or eleven, perhaps?"

"So young? There must have been an incident. What happened?"

Edouard leaned back in his chair and paused. "It was something that happened one summer at my family's vacation home in Deauville."

"Did a nanny give you a spanking?" This was a common trope in spanking erotica, where governesses took their errant charges to task.

"No! Our nannies were always very proper. It was actually my cousin, Sidonie." It was Edouard's time to look for Boxler. I watched Edouard's eyes dart around, but Boxler remained out of the room. Edouard's glance finally settled on the bottle of wine. He poured himself a glass, and his sense of relief was palpable.

"Your cousin? Oh my. Was she older? What was she like?"

"Yes, my cousin. I should explain . . . my grandfather had a large house in Deauville where we all spent summers."

"That's in Normandy, right?"

"Yes. It's been a very chic resort town for over a century. We all gathered there. My grandparents . . . My parents, me and my brother, along with my aunt and uncle and Sidonie, their only child."

"That house sounds very full. How did you find time for mischief?"

"Well, the place was large and there were a couple of small buildings on the property." Edouard rested his elbows on the table and clasped his hands together. "Sidonie was a few years older than me, and she used to hide in an old barn where she'd read and smoke. I thought she was remarkable; she was so much more sophisticated than either my brother or me."

"The age difference between, what, a fourteen-year-old girl and an eleven-year-old boy is enormous."

"Yes. I was very sheltered, so I probably seemed even younger."

"Probably! So, darling, tell me what happened."

Edouard shifted in his chair, took another long sip of wine, and began to talk about the summer in Deauville that changed his life. "I was bored one afternoon, because there was no one to play with, so I went looking for Sidonie. I found her hidden behind some old furniture. She was in the middle of a novel, and she was very irritated to have been found."

"That sounds about right. But I'm guessing you didn't get lost."

"No! I refused to leave, and I threatened to tell her father she'd been smoking."

"You tattletale! How naughty." I shook my head at the thought of Edouard as a young boy, threatening his glamorous cousin.

"Yes. She didn't like that at all, so she invited me into the little nest she'd made of cushions and blankets, and I joined her. But it was a trap. She sat on me and she began to tickle me. Did you know I'm very ticklish?"

"I'd noticed, but it was never a kink you'd mentioned, so it was never something I pursued. Some people find it an agony, not a pleasure."

"I'm one of those who finds it an agony. She had me pinned beneath her—she was quite a bit bigger than I was—and she wouldn't stop and there was nothing I could do. I pleaded with her. I begged her, but she kept on tickling."

"Oh my. That sounds intense." Tickling scenes were not a favorite of mine. I had one client early in my career request one. I tried for an hour to make him giggle or squirm, but he was inert. He even seemed bored. Finally, I stopped and asked him if there was something I should be doing, when he announced he loved watching tickle porn, but that no one had ever succeeded in tickling him. It was a baffling lesson in the difference between fantasy and reality. "Is there something she said or did that you think about to this day?"

"How did you know?"

I shrugged and smiled.

Edouard continued. "Incredibly. There was one moment, when she paused, and ordered me to say something stupid."

"Like what?"

Edouard's eyes shone as he recounted the moment. "She had me say, 'I'm a disobedient little boy and I will do what my cousin tells me to do.'"

"Oh, now that's interesting. And did you do it?"

"Of course. And when she made me say, 'Boys are stupid and girls are smart,' I complied."

"What else did she do?" There had to be more, and he clearly wanted to share everything about this formative experience.

"She didn't stop with the tickling. She'd pause, every minute or so, and make me say something ridiculous and then begin again. I could barely breathe. I cried, even. And there was a horrifying moment when I wet myself." Edouard cringed as he relived something so embarrassing.

"Did she notice?" Now I was playing with him, wanting to make sure all the sordid details were aired. Having spent hours with the very proper and restrained Edouard, I was determined to explore his messy beginnings.

"Yes and she mocked me for it. But then she said if I told anyone she'd been smoking she would tell everyone I'd pissed myself. And in that moment, we both knew she'd secured my silence."

"Was that the end of things, between you two?"

"No. I adored her even more. I followed her around all summer, and she would tickle me until I cried and pleaded for mercy. But the game became arousing to me. It's when I got my first true erections."

"I can see how those moments imprinted on you. You were at the perfect age for your sexual scripts to get codified. What about Sidonie? Did she notice you were hard?"

"Yes, but she never said anything about my erections. I think it was probably too strange for her . . . but she always pinned me down and tickled me whenever I visited her in the garage. Our relationship had taken a very specific turn."

"It certainly did. How long did that go on?"

"Just that summer. Afterward, she had boyfriends, and she wasn't around much. I think we both outgrew the games."

"That makes sense. Did you ever discuss what happened with her as adults?"

"No." His voice was flat. The answer came quickly.

"No? What a shame. Wouldn't it be fascinating to learn what she remembers of that summer?"

"We haven't spoken in years, and frankly, that's the last thing I'd discuss with her."

"Years? Did you two have a falling out?"

"Us, specifically? No. But I did, with my family." His voice was strained. He had alluded to his estrangement, and it was obviously a source of pain. It was also, clearly, a subject that he didn't want to discuss, which made me all the more curious.

"Understood. Do you know what Sidonie is doing now? Maybe she has a submissive husband doing her bidding? Maybe you changed her as much as she changed you."

Edouard gave me a vague smile. "I don't believe she married. Her work is too consuming. She went to medical school and became a surgeon."

"That's unusual. I thought your family was all about banking."

"Yes. Unlike me or my brother, she escaped. There were few expectations that a daughter would enter the family business."

"I suppose sons—especially talented sons like you—bear extra responsibility. What are you, the fourth generation to go into banking?"

"Fifth. But the third and fourth generations were the least innovative and effective. That changed with me. But unless I want to be in the generation who crashes spectacularly, I have some work to do. Good night."

"What a shame. I was thinking for dessert, I might like to strap you down, sit on your chest and tickle you until you beg. But it sounds like I'll have time to call the gallery, instead."

Edouard's faint smile broadened. "Perhaps tomorrow? Unfortunately, there are some urgent matters I must take care of tonight."

"I understand. Good night." Edouard left, after having only eaten a plate of salad. Once he'd retired, a housekeeper emerged to replace my salad plate with a perfectly prepared chicken breast and some broiled asparagus. I ate alone in silence.

27

DUNGEON AGONY

When I got back to my room, I found a dozen emails waiting for me and my phone blinking. Josh had been trying to reach me, and I'd been busy eating chicken by myself, while feeling reckless about Viviana and chastened by Boxler.

I called Josh immediately. "What's up? Is the gallery on fire?"

"No, it's worse. Michael's in the hospital. He was with Amy." I let the words sink in. Michael, my consigliere, confidant and most favored client was in dire straits. My mind reeled. Had Amy hurt him? Pushed him too hard because she didn't know better? I collapsed into a chair as my body began to shake.

"Tell me what you know."

"They'd been in the basement for an hour when they rushed upstairs. Michael was leaning against Amy. She helped him into his car, and the driver drove him off. I've been trying to reach her, but she bolted as soon as she changed into street clothes."

"Oh shit, so they'd been playing."

"Clearly." This meant it was my fault. I should never have entrusted someone so inexperienced with my dungeon and with my clients. Michael had been enthusiastic, but like most clients, he underestimated the risks he faced.

"Have you been down there?"

"Yes." Josh's answer came without hesitation.

"What did you see?"

"Uh, it's messy. Amy hasn't cleaned up. But there's no sign of blood . . ."

There have been stories of medical catastrophes in dungeons. One dominatrix accidentally ruptured the ball sack of one of her clients during a session, requiring a visit to the local emergency room to get everything sewed back in place. I'd heard of knife scenes gone bad. Clients getting pierced by stiletto heels. I breathed a little easier, knowing that Amy hadn't somehow severed one of Michael's arteries.

"So, Amy hasn't checked in with you? Well, she hasn't called me, either." This was unlike Amy. She was the most diligent person I knew. She had to be freaked out. "I don't suppose you remember Michael's driver?"

"He was dark haired. That's all I know."

"Dark haired? I think I know the guy. I'll call him. And when Amy gets back, tell her to contact me. ASAP."

"Got it. Would you like me to clean up the basement?"

"Yes. And lock it up. I need more information, and I may need to fly back pronto. Shit. Shit. Shit."

"You may want to rethink that. Your father came by yesterday."

"I'm only hearing about this now?" I was now furious in addition to being anxious. Everyone at the gallery knew to be on the lookout for my father, and to call me immediately if he showed up.

"I'm sorry." Josh's voice grew quiet and sincere. "We had a walk-in at the end of the day and I forgot to tell you. I thought we might sell one of Cassidy's works, but it didn't pan out. In any event, your dad came by around four looking for you. He might have been drunk."

"What did he say? What makes you think so?" If my dad had been drinking, things had to be dire.

"Well, he seemed unsteady and his eyes were watery. He just didn't look like a man in control of himself. I know you won't like this, but he proposed renting the gallery for an evening. Said he had an event in a couple of weeks, and he wanted to use your space. Blah . . . blah . . . blah . . ."

"Fuck."

"I'm sorry, it slipped my mind and then things got crazy today. I told him we don't rent out the space and hustled him out as quickly as I could. Did I say the right thing?"

"Absolutely. I don't want him suggesting to whoever he'd be hosting that I approve of whatever he's doing."

"Your father said he'd be back, Erika."

"This is not good. None of this is good. I need to make some calls and figure out if Michael's all right. It's not like I can call his office and ask his secretary . . . And I doubt he'd pick up from his hospital bed . . ." It would be peculiar if the woman who sells Michael the odd painting were to call his office and inquire about his health. I didn't trust his office staff to avoid speculating, because the obvious conclusion would be that I was Michael's mistress . . . I might be his mistress, but I was not his sidepiece.

"Why not try him? He gets calls all the time. If he can't pick up, his phone will be off, or he just won't answer."

"Josh. Let me think about it. And if you hear anything more, call me immediately. I'll have my phone with me, because there's little chance I'll be sleeping tonight."

I tried not to immerse myself in catastrophic scenarios, but my mind gave me no choice. I imagined Michael, helpless in a hospital bed because of something that had happened in my basement. The man had been a near constant presence in my life for over ten years. He'd helped set me up in New York, he'd coached me on the art business, he'd listened to my dreams, and he'd always taken them seriously. He'd given me the seed capital for my gallery, set me up with a mortgage broker, and his frequent purchases helped keep the place in the black. On a purely financial level, he was the difference between misery and mastery.

Michael was more than a mentor. He was better than a lover. He was no longer just a client. I knew what animated him, and he had the same understanding of me. His consistency and constancy was in direct opposition to the other men I'd encountered. He never pushed for more than I wanted to give. And he always offered ideas and solutions to the issues I was facing. He was singular in my life, a beloved, and the prospect of losing him filled me with fear.

For years, I'd been able to dial down my angst and hold it in check. But it was now at a level I hadn't experienced before. I could lose everything I'd built: my gallery, my dungeon, my reputation. Even my freedom was in jeopardy. It wasn't that I was worried about going to jail; it was more that I had earned my way to a certain level of personal freedom. Sure, I had enormous bills to pay every month, but I managed to do so all the while indulging my own whims and appetites. If I wanted to buy a three-hundred-year-old Shunga scroll from Japan because I'd gotten curious about their erotic pillow books, I could do so. If I found a provocative work by Belgian pop artist Evelyne Axell, I could indulge. There wasn't much in the way of art I denied myself. This was the freedom I craved.

My calls, texts and emails to Amy went unanswered. I left one careful email for Michael; in the off chance he was able to read it. There was nothing more from Josh. I put on some burgundy flannel pajamas. They were the opposite of sexy, but they were warm and cozy, and I wanted to be hugged by comfort. All I could do was lie on my bed and wait, because sleep seemed out of the question. I tried to do some overdue research on potential buyers for some of the works lingering in my inventory, but even simple tasks were beyond me given my state of mind.

It was midnight in Geneva, but only six in the evening in New York, and there was still no news. I refreshed my email compulsively, hoping for a message from Josh, Amy or Michael, but the only new messages were spam. Every minute, like an obsessive, I'd press enter on my laptop, only to find a new level of disappointment. I was spiraling downward with each refresh. After an hour of this compulsive and pointless hitting of the enter key, the lump in my throat began to strangle. Michael had been integral to all of my plans, and his loss would first leave me bereft, and then it would leave me broke.

Sex work can be a pragmatic response to catastrophe, but what few people understand about the sex industry is how precarious it can be. Even at my elite end, I often felt like any slight glitch in the work could cause the whole edifice of my life to collapse. Every day, I'd look around and try to guess which path would cause me the least pain and put me in the least jeopardy. A minor change in policy with a credit card issuer, for instance, could jeopardize my income. A whisper to a district attorney could put me in the crosshairs. If the money hadn't been so good, I'd have bailed because the level of stress was stratospheric.

I once had a lock jam at my apartment in Boston. Before I brought in my crosses and my whips, I had a locksmith put a deadbolt on the door to the master bedroom. I'd looked for someone in the local BDSM scene but I'd come up blank, so I found a local guy in the Yellow Pages. What could be more banal than a single woman wanting extra security? I told him I was nervous at night and needed to lock myself in before I could sleep soundly.

He shrugged, as I handed him the cash for the job. A year later, I needed to call him again, when my key broke in the lock, making my dungeon inaccessible.

I sat miserably at my desk, watching him as he worked on the frozen lock. As the drill bit advanced into the mechanism, I pictured having to move again. Had my neighbors ever complained about noise or foot traffic? Nobody had ever said anything to me, but that didn't mean they hadn't said something to my landlord. How much did my landlord know? Was it possible he thought me a prostitute or a drug dealer? Criminals can make the best tenants, because we keep to ourselves and pay our rent diligently. And if he had an inkling that I was doing something unusual in the apartment, would he warn any future landlords away from me?

As the door was about to open and my secrets were on the verge of being revealed to the random young guy who had just lucked into the ultimate bar story, I spoke out, if only to prepare him for what he was about to see. All I could muster was a vague, "It's a bit unusual in there." He looked up at me, drill in hand, and shrugged.

As the lock was breached, he opened the door a crack. "May I? I need to take out the lock assembly. And I'm guessing you'd like me to replace it." He was asking permission to open the door, which I liked, but he was also about to open the door, which I dreaded.

"Yeah. But seriously, it's *unusual* in there. Don't . . ." I struggled to figure out what I didn't want him to do. Don't judge? Don't worry? Don't ask me for a spanking? Don't tell anybody? *Please don't tell anybody.*

He paused while opening the door, and I said nothing as he revealed an assortment of gear that screamed "DUNGEON." There were a dozen whips hanging on the back wall. An umbrella stand filled with canes. A freestanding St. Andrew's cross. A rack. A shelf filled with cock and ball devices, each more fiendish than the last.

The locksmith took a hard look around the room and then set about removing the lock. After ten minutes of silent effort, he had installed a new mechanism. Without saying anything to me, he demonstrated the lock worked. He then handed me the keys.

As the fellow was putting his tools away, he looked me in the eye. "I'm a big believer that what happens behind locked doors stays behind locked doors. But I gotta tell ya, lady, that looks like one fun room."

I nodded, as relief washed over my body. "Yeah, it's one fun room. What can I say, my boyfriend likes this stuff."

"I bet he does. Well, if you two ever have any *other* locks that need to be opened, just holler. Emergencies . . . whatever."

"Will do, and thanks." While his visit could have led to problems, it seemed like it had led to a solution. I'd heard of kinksters who'd had locks jam, and how mortifying it was to bring in a locksmith to open a pair of handcuffs or some intricate piece of metal bondage. I'd read about couples who'd gone to the local police station when a handcuff key could not be found. And while I hoped never to need his services again, he seemed cool. If he could keep his mouth shut, I'd be set. Only time would tell if that had been the case, but I knew that for the next couple of months, every time there was a knock on the door, I'd be on edge. On edge, of course, was my default state.

Desperate to interrupt my catastrophizing, I climbed out of bed and went to the kitchen in search of something potent. I didn't care if it was Lafitte or bourbon, it just had to have an alcohol content high enough to help me sleep.

I'd never really inspected the kitchen before—there was a chef on duty who catered to our needs, and it felt disrespectful to enter his workspace when he was there. I was an established face, and a midnight raid on the well-stocked kitchen had to be among the expected behaviors for guests, so the security people remained invisible.

Edouard had one of those enormous glass-doored commercial refrigerators that was as orderly as every other aspect of Edouard's home. The vegetables were organized by type and stacked in open bins, likewise the fruits. There were tidy jars of homemade yogurt in small glass jars on one shelf, along with cheeses labeled as if in a file cabinet. I spotted some tall, colorful bottles of juice, but there were no wine bottles. I realized that there had to be a wine fridge or some kind of bar area, so I started to open doors.

My mood was growing more anxious with every cabinet, so I jumped when the overhead light blinked on, blinding me temporarily. It was Edouard, wearing slim black jeans and a gray HEC hoodie.

"Erika, can I help you find something?" He stared at me, obviously surprised to find me hunting through his kitchen.

"I'm looking for something to drink. Wine, maybe, or something stronger."

Edouard strolled over to a far corner of the kitchen where there was a small wine fridge I hadn't spotted. "What moves you? Red? White?" He pulled out a couple of bottles and presented them to me.

"Do you have any bottles that are open already? It seems wrong to waste something special when all I want to do is get drunk and go to sleep."

"Oh, is that what you want? Then follow me." He invited me inside his office. There was a small, Deco bar cart in ebony and chrome, with an assortment of liquors on display. He picked up a plain bottle and a cut crystal glass and he began to pour. "Whiskey has always been my medicine of choice."

"Thanks." He poured us both a glass and I immediately took a large gulp from mine. "This should put me somewhere between calm and comatose. Frankly, darling, I'm hoping for comatose."

Edouard tilted his head and motioned to the smooth gray sofa opposite his desk. His office was unknown to me, so I sat down to take it all in. There was wood paneling everywhere, with built-in bookcases across an entire wall. There was even a grouping of sculptures by Giacometti, looking sticklike and elegant, under the perfect lighting. They were there for his own private enjoyment, a bit like me. But what really distinguished the room was its view of the lake. The room was tasteful, perfectly composed and orderly, just like Edouard.

We both drank silently, and I quickly emptied my glass. Edouard was still nursing his first, but he stood up and poured me a second. I wasn't sure how much of an explanation I wanted to give him. It had always felt strange discussing one client with another, and yet Michael and Edouard were more than mere clients. "I just learned that a friend is ill, possibly a heart attack. I may need to go back to New York."

"Oh dear. I'm sorry to hear that."

"Yes. I've been trying to reach him, to find out how he's doing. But there's no news so far. It's exasperating."

"That's a difficult diagnosis." Edouard sat back in his black leather swivel chair. He held the glass in his right hand and stared into the amber liquor. "My father had one, not long after I sold the family bank. My mother still believes I was responsible."

"Did your father survive?"

"Yes, he's in his nineties now. But as you know, my relationship with my parents did not. That's when I moved to Geneva."

"I'm so sorry. These moments of crisis and pain crystallize and prioritize things, don't they? Or at least they usually do. Things seem beyond my control at the moment, and I don't like it."

"No. When people we love are in pain, we feel their anguish. And when we must sit back and wait? It's doubly agonizing."

"This stuff is dangerous. It goes down smoothly." I looked at my glass and realized it was empty. "Pour me some more."

"It's Japanese whisky. I prefer it to the Scottish."

"Ah, is that why I don't taste much peat?"

"Precisely. The Japanese distilleries are at higher altitudes than their Scottish counterparts, and they don't use as much peat when drying their barley. It makes for a lighter, smoother product."

"You have excellent taste, Edouard. I admire how seriously you take your passions." Edouard poured another shot, only this time I sipped it instead of gulped. "Tell me, honestly, you're an expert in what's happening in the finance world. Are we going to get through this crisis?"

"Just how depressed do you want to get, tonight?"

"It's that bad? Seriously? Are we going to make it through?"

"Of course. Well, maybe not everyone, but in most instances, if you're willing to walk away and take your losses, the down-side risk is finite. People will make it through. After all, this is just another crisis . . . One in a long line of crises." Edouard's voice started out as calm and professorial. He continued, "But this ignores the fact that most people cannot just *take* their losses. We hate the prospect of sunk costs with no return, so we do stupid things. And I'm no exception to that phenomenon. It's hard to remain cool and analytical when you're watching your life's work explode in front of your eyes. I imagine there will be many more heart attacks in the months to come." Edouard swiveled his chair away from me, as he began staring out the enormous window at the shadows of Lake Geneva.

"I was afraid of that. It feels as if we're on the verge of something very serious."

"I'm long past the verge. My verge was crossed months ago, and now I'm just trying to right the ship."

"Darling, I'm sorry to hear that . . . I had no idea things had become so complicated. You've hidden it well."

"It's not my preferred topic. What man wants to reveal these kinds of problems to a woman he finds attractive?" Edouard shrugged and looked deep into my eyes.

"I understand." Or at least that's what I said. His work was a mystery to me since he spoke about it so rarely. I had assumed he was exhibiting Swiss-style discretion, but apparently, there was also a heavy dose of avoidance. "If you need a sounding board or a fresh pair of eyes, let me know." We both emptied our glasses of whiskey, and I was beginning to get very drowsy. "Well, it's probably time for me to get back to my room. I hope I didn't keep you up."

"No, not at all. I haven't been sleeping much lately." Edouard stood and gave me a hand as I climbed off his couch. Unfortunately, I needed his help as I promptly fell backward.

"Oh dear. That Japanese moonshine is stealthy." My head began to spin, where only moments earlier I had felt completely sober.

"Let me get you to your room." I would have waved Edouard off, but it dawned on me that a steady arm would be helpful.

Once in my suite, Edouard helped me take off my robe. He even got down on his knees to remove my slippers while I sat perched on the edge of the bed. "Such a shame you're not into feet." I'd had men kneeling at my feet for years, aching to suck my toes or lick my pumps. If someone was kneeling in front of me, they were usually a foot fetishist, but not that night.

"Truly. Your feet look lovely." He stood up beside the bed, and helped arrange the covers on top of me as I began to drift away.

As my eyes grew heavy, I suddenly panicked at the prospect of missing any news from New York. "Where's my phone? I need my phone. Michael might call." Edouard rifled through the nightstand, looking for it. "Check my pocket." I muttered, my eyes starting to close.

Edouard found it in my robe and put it on the pillow beside my head. "Here. If anyone calls, you'll know." Even as I was finally about to crash, I feared that the phone would ring and no one would hear it.

"Stay here in case I sleep through it. Please?" I patted the bed beside me.

"I'm here, Erika. Now go to sleep." The last thing I remember from that night was feeling Edouard lying next to me, as I curled my body into his.

28

EDOUARD SPENDS THE NIGHT

My state of oblivion was interrupted the next morning, when I heard Edouard speaking softly into his phone. I lifted my head up and spotted him seated in a chair opposite the bed, with a large black binder open in his lap.

"Hi there." I was confused by his presence and my circumstances. "What time is it?"

"Eleven. I tried to wake you up a couple of times, but you refused. Once, you even told me to 'fuck off.'"

"Oh, darling, I'm sorry. That was very rude of me." I tried to conceal my bafflement. "But why are you here?"

"Don't you remember last night?" Edouard tilted his head to the side by about ten degrees. "You asked me to stay."

"I did? I don't remember anything after our drink in your office."

"Drink? That was *drinks*, plural. You're fond of Japanese whiskey."

"Am I? Well, I guess I won't drink that again." It took me a moment to recenter myself, and to remember Michael.

"No, perhaps you shouldn't. I even had to help you to your room, and then you asked me to stay in case the phone rang."

"Did I? Did it?"

"Yes, you did. And yes, it did. At around four a.m., I heard it, and tried—unsuccessfully—to wake you up. So . . . I answered and spoke with Michael."

"Oh shit, that should have been me." I was both embarrassed and horrified. The prospect of these two men chatting with one another was bizarre, and yet, it had happened at my request. "Well? How is he?"

"Michael told me he's fine. He said he was being held overnight at the hospital for observation, but he'd be returning home tomorrow, which is today."

"This is such a relief. Did he say anything else?"

"Yes. The doctors think it was a mild heart attack with excellent prospects for full recovery. He attributes this to Amy and his driver as they both acted quickly."

"Wow. Not bad for a rookie." Amy deserved a lot of credit for staying calm when it mattered most.

"Yes, very impressive. Michael suggested you call him on his mobile later this afternoon, once he's back home."

"Got it. And thanks."

"My pleasure. I know this was weighing on you, and now I understand why. Michael is one of your gallery's backers, isn't he?"

"Yes. I adore him. He's been a mentor and a coach. Without Michael, I'm not sure where I'd be right now, but it's unlikely that you and I would be in the same room. I have much to thank him for."

"I should thank him too, then."

I looked at Edouard, who was still wearing the same gray HEC hoodie he wore last night. My memory of our time together in his office was slowly returning. "Have you been here, in this room, since last night?"

He leaned forward in the chair, as I sat tucked beneath my heavy duvet. "Yes. You asked me to stay, so I stayed in case the phone rang."

"Oh." I tried to dredge up the memory but failed. "Did you get any sleep?"

"A few hours after the phone rang."

"In the chair?" The night remained a mystery to me.

"No. In the bed. You wouldn't let go of me."

Edouard was honest and direct. It was one of the things I most appreciated about him. I didn't recall taking any Ambien, but I also knew my behavior as I was falling asleep could be unpredictable and disinhibited; no drug was required. "Did we . . . ?" I couldn't quite bring myself to say the words, but I wanted to know.

Edouard looked at me and laughed, as if I had said something utterly implausible and ridiculous. "No, of course not. I only fuck conscious and consenting women."

I blushed. "Of course. I just couldn't remember . . ."

"Of course. I'm going to change and go to my office. See you later?" Edouard collected his papers, stood and began moving toward the door.

"Yes. It looks like I won't need to run back home just yet. Do you mind if I stick around a little longer?"

"Mind? I was hoping you would. I adore your company." To my great relief, Edouard had put my rejection behind us.

"Thank you, for everything. You're special to me, too." Two crises had highlighted just how significant these two men had become.

29

EVERYONE'S FAVORITE CLIENT

I tried to reach both Michael and Amy, once it was a decent hour in New York. Amy wasn't picking up, and it wasn't until late afternoon that I reached Michael.

"Erika here." I tried to get my voice to sound both playful and concerned, but it didn't sound any different than usual.

"Hello, 'Erika here.'" There was humor in Michael's voice.

"Michael . . . so great to hear your voice. Is this a good time?"

"Yes, absolutely. I'm in my home office pretending to work. My doctors told me to take it easy, but don't they know, I only follow *your* orders."

"You're just waiting to find out what Dr. Grieg will prescribe!" Bantering with Michael was one of my favorite activities.

"You know me well." Michael's voice sounded no different than usual, and certainly not like someone who'd just had a frightening trip to the emergency room.

"Do you need a nasty nurse? Say the word, and I'm back in Chelsea where I'll stick a thermometer up your ass and keep you in line."

"That got my attention, but if I want to recover from this heart attack quickly, there can be no thermometers up my ass *recreationally*, at least not for a few weeks." Michael chuckled at the prospect.

"Such a pity. My thermometer will have to remain in my medical bag. *For now.*"

"Indeed. The sacrifices we make for our health . . . How are things in Geneva?"

"Fine. The same. Nothing to report. My dad continues to pester Josh at the gallery, but there's nothing new. Sales remain dead, so it's not a bad time to be away . . . But I'm utterly serious, Michael, if you want me closer, I'll be there. I feel terrible about what happened. It should have been me at your side, not Amy, when things got scary."

"I'll be fine, Erika. Thanks for your offer, but it's unnecessary. I find all this concern about my health tedious. The doctors have me covered, and if they're not worried, I'm not worried." Michael's voice shifted from confidence to concern. "Do you know if Amy's all right? She seemed pretty shaken."

"I haven't been able to reach her. I told Amy the work was straightforward and safe. I imagine dealing with a medical emergency was not something she was expecting."

"No, I'm sure it wasn't. But I have to tell you, she kept her cool. When I realized I was having a problem, she was decisive and helpful. She even thought of getting an aspirin for me."

"I'm relieved. And quite frankly, I'm astonished that she even knew where the aspirin was. It's not like there's a jar of pills on the bathroom counter."

"Well, if you speak with her before I do, please let her know how grateful I am. Her quick thinking changed my prognosis. Who knows, she may even have saved my life."

"It pains me to think the stakes were that high, and I wasn't there . . ." Michael grunted affirmatively. "Do you have many follow-up visits with your cardiologist?"

"Of course. These emergencies produce lots of billable opportunities. Who am I to get between a professional and his payday?"

"Yes, darling. There's a reason your doctors call you right back. You're their favorite client!"

"Absolutely. And I work at it. I want to be everyone's favorite client."

"You're mine, for sure. But you're so much more than that, too." I paused, unsure how much I wanted to share. "I was really frightened when I learned about your emergency. It made me realize just how important you are to me, and it was a reminder of how fragile things can be."

"Yes, Erika, it was a reminder to me, too. Health can be fleeting, so I need to step up my pursuits of pleasure. You and I need to think ahead to all the outrageous things we might do next year. After all, it's not too early to think about Miami and Basel . . . and all those days in between."

"Amen. Let's plan on being wicked. Soon."

"And let's make your business less fragile. I have some ideas on how to insulate you and the gallery from the ups and downs in the economy."

30

AN UNUSUAL REQUEST

Knowing that Michael was on the mend, I felt like rewarding Edouard. I pulled my most dramatic latex gown out of its drawer and set about buffing it so that it gleamed. It took about twenty minutes to get all the smudges out of my peacock green halter neck gown, a custom piece by Savage Wear in Berlin.

When it was time to join Edouard in the dining room, I had to walk carefully. The long, tight skirt only permitted short strides, and the last thing I wanted was to shred the dress before Edouard had caught sight of it. It felt twice the distance as usual, from my suite to the dining room, but I made it. And once there, I paused dramatically at the doorway.

"Erika"—Edouard's eyes tracked me as I entered his space— "you look stunning." Boxler, however, appeared unimpressed. He decanted the wine and then quietly left the room.

"Thanks. I like how you look at me . . . As if I were a painting you are desperate to mount on your wall!"

"Please, that's not where I'd mount you. And besides, you'd never be a mere painting. You are an artist, the creator of masterpieces. The rest of us are your collectors."

"Well, I definitely feel like creating some art tonight. Let's go downstairs after dinner and be outrageous."

"What mortal could say no to an offer like that?" Edouard paused and gave me an awkward smile. He blinked hard as his lips pursed and his shoulders hunched. In an uncharacteristic stammer, he said, "But I have a small request. Do you mind if we use the vacbed?"

"Do I mind? Absolutely not. Whatever would make you think I'd mind?"

"I know it's not your favorite apparatus. And I have another request I'll explain once we're downstairs."

I tried to conceal my bafflement. I was accustomed to clients sharing things with me that elicited shame or doubt in them. My job was to make the most outrageous and embarrassing things seem possible and intriguing. Edouard had known me for years, and yet there was something he wanted from me that he struggled to articulate over salad. "You know me, Edouard, I'm hard to shock."

"Yes, I imagine you are. But what I'd like to do may surprise you. You may even wish to change into something more comfortable than this spectacular gown."

"Something loose-fitting and cozy?" I threw out that idea in jest, because flannel pajamas were my idea of a perfect scene outfit.

"As you wish."

"Now you have my full attention. I'm prepared to be astonished."

After our dinner, I quickly changed out of the latex dress into a heavy gray cashmere turtleneck and a pair of black yoga pants. If Edouard wanted me comfortable, that's what he'd get. He had gone straight to the dungeon, where I found him organizing the vacbed.

"What did you have in mind?"

"This may sound odd." I shrugged at Edouard as he spoke. "But I'd like to get in the bed and experience a few hours of sensory deprivation."

"Of course." Nothing seemed odd to me anymore, and certainly not an evening spent in a vacbed. "Let's get this organized. I should hook you up to the heart rate monitor first, though. After Michael's experience, we shouldn't take any chances." Edouard began to remove his clothes, as I pulled the electrodes out of a cabinet and began to adhere them to his chest. "I've been thinking an oxygen monitor could be a good addition to this setup."

31

THE WEAPON OF NICE

It was another couple of days before Amy resurfaced. She called at nine in the morning, after I'd been up all night. It felt unfair, Edouard got to snore away contentedly in his latex cocoon, while I stayed awake and did my best to make sure he didn't expire.

My tasks, where vacbeds were concerned, were very simple: keep the vacuum tight and keep the client alive. This was an intimate game of trust and confidence and it consumed me while Edouard floated off, oblivious. And then once Edouard was out of the vacbed, I'd tidy up and head off to my room and fall fast asleep. My alarm wouldn't ring until noon. It was almost like being back in my old time zone.

When Amy phoned, she sounded anxious. Despite my exhaustion, I did my best to soothe her. The prospect of my substitute turning into a loose cannon didn't thrill me. Amy had always seemed so stable and sane, and yet she'd just shown she could be a flake. Running away from Chelsea? Understandable. But not checking in with Josh or me for days? Unforgivable. Sure, she'd had a traumatic afternoon with Michael, but that was no reason to scamper away without notice.

I stayed chipper, but it felt like she was trying to provoke me. She said she'd hooked up with one of my clients—the bondage freak, Dan Levine. I had approached Amy to keep my clients contented, not to fuck their brains out. The prospect of Amy having affairs with them was destabilizing. It's hard enough to establish effective boundaries with submissive men, because they always want more access, time or affection. I'd spent years training my clients to arrive on time and to depart promptly. That one of them could believe full sexual service might be on the menu was regrettable. Fortunately, the client in question was a pampered billionaire. He was fine for an afternoon, but he was far too self-absorbed and needy for much more than that. She'd learn the lesson that so many sex workers have to experience firsthand—there aren't many men worth transitioning from business to personal.

It's one of the paradoxes of professional domination, that dominatrixes need to be extra nice; our perches are so tenuous and we have to be careful not to attract the wrong kind of attention. We deploy niceness like a weapon. We are Machiavellian in our displays of kindness. These gentle moments, after all, are the flip side of the intentional acts of cruelty and pain we inflict on our enthusiastic customers. Each mode—nice or mean—has its moment and each will elicit a certain response. I needed to embrace Amy, to consume her with kindness and enthusiasm. After all, I didn't need her upsetting my clients, whether they were legit or pervy. If I exuded calm, Amy might project calm, in turn. If I seemed confident and serene, she could mirror my mood. I might feel anger and worry, but I had spent years masking my doubts and learning how to convey that mastery to others.

One of my biggest talents is tuning in to the passions of the person in front of me. This knack was something I first developed in the sex industry, where it's efficient and effective to figure out what the client is too timid to ask for, or maybe he lacks the vocabulary to ask for what he's craving. Sex workers learn to watch where the client's eyes land; we spot when the pulse quickens or when the pupils dilate.

Gallery clients aren't that different from submissive clients. If they feel lust for a work, I can feel it in turn. Their eyes glaze over, just like in the dungeon. Their shoulders hunch in a certain way. Their bodies betray their hunger. But even more often, these clients are uncertain and seduction is required. Sex work taught me when to play hard to get and when to move in for the kill. And while I can't always close the deal—some clients are too elusive or determined not to be seduced—the odds of my success are better than average, and in the long run, operating a gallery is a numbers game. If I can turn even a few of the equivocators into buyers, I run a successful shop.

What my time with Edouard had highlighted, however, was how exhausting it was being present for whoever walked in the door. Being an emotional chameleon was depleting. And although I wondered about the eventual boredom of dealing with the same person on a daily basis, it now appealed to me. The emotional contortions of gaining clients, and the roller coaster of two industries that were so uncertain and fraught had left me drained. It had taken a crisis in the form of my criminal dad to make me understand just how tired I'd become. And it had taken me dozens of sessions with Edouard before I finally understood that what he seemed to truly crave was the same thing I was lusting after—a night of peace and restful sleep. He had the misfortune of needing layers of latex and extreme sensory deprivation equipment to accomplish that modest goal, but when I saw the tension disappear from his body as the vacuum was applied, it was clear what he wanted. And truly, who could blame him? I wanted to sleep soundly, too. If only it were as simple as lying in a vacbed for me.

Sleep had become the ultimate luxury good. There were anesthesiologists who'd administer propofol to the affluent and desperate. You could hire a massage therapist to prep you for slumber. For only two hundred bucks, you could hire one to arrive at your place at 10 p.m., and they'd leave once you started snoring. There were consultants in mattress texture and experts in sleep hygiene. Was there much difference in deploying a dominatrix and a latex vacbed? Edouard had innovated in style, but not in substance. I'd give the vacbed a shot, except it wasn't my cup of tea and given the stresses coming from New York, it was clear that deep slumber would be elusive for yet another month.

I'd heard from Josh that my father had been back at the gallery. He'd asked to rent the place the night after the election for a private event. It was easy to say no, but it gave me a clue that my father had found a mark, and he was closing in on his scheme, whatever it was. Josh then gave me another piece of news—there was an email addressed to me in the gallery's general mailbox—that he knew I'd want to check out immediately.

The email landed in my box right away, and it was as awful as Josh had implied.

Dear Dr. Grieg,

I hope this email finds you well. It has been several years since we last crossed paths at your gallery near Lechmere in Cambridge. I was thrilled to learn of your recent successes. I get to New York often, and although I'm not an art collector, I'm open to anything else you might propose.

Yours Truly,

Gary Hall
CFO Insightery

Gary, the jerk who had blabbed about my dominatrix persona on various review websites had found me, in the real world. His message was discreet, but it was unmistakable. As I scratched my head about how he'd tracked me down, I popped onto Twitter. The Grieg Gallery account had already amassed a few thousand followers. Before Michael's heart attack, Amy had been tweeting daily about various shows and collections, and somehow, the gallery had caught the eye of one LegMan617, the same handle Gary had used when he first posted the reviews. I had no way of knowing how he'd made the connection between Boston and NYC, and if he was alone in doing so, but it freaked me out. Managing Gary would be a puzzle I'd have to solve. Should I claim mistaken identity? Should I call him directly, and remind him of mutually assured destruction? Should I ignore him, and hope he'd go away?

Given the problems with my father, it was clear I needed to keep my distance for another month or so, because dates slip and criminals aren't the most organized people in the world, but I could see the emergence of an unobstructed path back to NYC, and also, to the rest I was craving. This would also give me the time and space to prepare a strategy for Gary and his kin. There's never just one guy, after all. I knew of women who'd retired and had clients resurface decades later. I thought I'd been careful about protecting my privacy, but apparently I hadn't been careful enough. Sooner or later, one would pop up; it was practically a law of physics, only it was impossible to predict which client from my old life was going to try to infiltrate my new life. In my head, I made plans to return to Chelsea after Christmas. It would be peaceful in Geneva, and there were far worse fates than a snowy Swiss holiday.

32

MASTERPIECES ON THE MOVE

"Erika, tomorrow I've got a team coming from Natural le Coultre to remove some of the works." Edouard sat opposite me at dinner. We had both taken to dressing casually and comfortably, since the dungeon was our destination afterward, and one of us was going to wind up blindfolded and naked.

"Really? Which ones?" I was startled by the news. Edouard's collection was his pride and it made him the envy of most of his fellow collectors. The last time I'd been in a home where the art was being sold off was when I was a child and my father was liquidating every asset he could to try and avoid financial Armageddon. Although it was possible that Edouard was simply reprioritizing works, it seemed unlikely. His statement set me on edge.

"The Freud and the Rothko." These two paintings were the most significant and valuable of his impressive collection. I was becoming alarmed.

"Are you mixing things up, or deaccessioning?" I kept my voice steady, but I wanted to know if he was selling, or merely putting these masterworks into storage.

"Deaccessioning." Edouard shrugged, as if selling off fifty million dollars' worth of art was of only minor consequence.

"Are you putting them up for auction? I have thoughts on where they'd fetch the best price."

"No, this is a private sale."

He could have asked for my help. I would have quietly shopped the paintings around and gotten him an excellent price, but he'd chosen to keep me out of the loop. This was disappointing, given how much time we'd spent together and the intimacy I thought we shared. "This is my field, so I'm always happy to help. But I can understand why you might want to delimit your personal life from, uh, your personal life?"

"Erika, I hope I didn't offend." His dark brows furrowed in concern. "The prospect of selling didn't occur to me until yesterday."

"Seriously? And you found a buyer that quickly?"

"Well, it was a standing offer from one of Roman Abramovich's rivals. He wanted to establish a collection that was better than Roman's . . ."

"And Abramovich paid thirty-five million dollars for *Benefits Supervisor Resting* by Freud in May at Christie's. I hope you got more than that from your Abrama-wannabe?"

"Close enough. But I need his help, and now we are *friends*."

I was stunned. It was rare for a collector to get rid of his showpieces. It was a sign of taste and acumen to possess pieces by a small set of blue-chip contemporary artists. Owning a Freud was a signal to other collectors that you were serious. Owning a Rothko said you had discernment. I could understand why the Russian wanted a shortcut to such spectacular works, but I was astonished that Edouard would sacrifice his prizes, unless he really needed something. My personal collection was more modest, but I'd never sold a work.

"How's business going for you? Does the shitty market have anything to do with your sale?" If he was cash-strapped, he had plenty to sell, but the market was complicated due to the financial crisis.

"I was afraid you'd ask. I loathe talking about business when we're together, because I'm trying to escape business in your company."

"Let's keep it short, then. I'll be blunt. Do you need the money?"

"No, not at all. But I need a favor." The precision of his answer was a relief. It sounded unlikely there'd be a fire sale of the blue-chip works on so many of his walls. I wasn't going to witness an art Armageddon again.

"It must be one extraordinary favor."

"Yes. It is. Do you know much about how business is conducted in Russia?" Edouard settled into his chair, his hands clasped in front of his chin.

"Not really. I know that the oligarchs own the place and Putin runs it."

"Well, the oligarchs believe they own the place, but actually, Putin both owns it and runs it. The oligarchs are effectively his vassals. This means there's little distance between the oligarchs and Putin. If you cross the wrong person, you wind up poisoned, or worse."

"Right. Like Yushchenko. Do you think he'll ever get over his dioxin poisoning? He was once very handsome."

"He'll never get better. Quite frankly, it's astonishing he survived, but his pockmarked face is a warning to anyone who might cross the Kremlin."

"And what has this got to do with you? Why do you need to co-opt an oligarch?"

"Many of my investments are in Russia. For years, they were fine. The fund was doing well—my niche was very profitable; even my partners seemed solid. But when the markets became uneven, things became strained. This may seem implausible, but I just had a company stolen from me."

"Stolen? How does someone steal an entire company?"

"You need the cooperation of the Russian courts, and more importantly, the Ministry of the Interior." My jaw dropped. "Early this year, one of my companies was raided by the Ministry for not having paid its taxes. The taxes, of course, had been paid. But the search warrants entitled the officers to seize all the company's financial documents and seals. We believe the officers then gave these things to criminals, who later posed as the company and sought a tax refund."

"Didn't the Ministry just say you'd paid too little in tax?"

"Yes, but that was just as fraudulent as the lawsuit to have the taxes refunded. A judge, probably paid by the criminals, awarded the criminal clone of my company over two hundred million dollars in a false rebate. It would have been the largest tax rebate in Russian history, except they pulled the same scam on my colleague, the investor Jan Bakker."

"That's remarkable." I sat there, trying to put the pieces together, his tale was so confusing and bizarre. "Well, what happened to the money? What happened to the real company?"

"The money went to a syndicate operated by a murderer, so he operates with impunity. My company was also sued, *secretly*, and it was found in default, *secretly*. It has taken me months to understand what happened, because, as you can imagine, the Russian authorities are not helpful."

"No, they want to appear open for investment, but this sounds like the boldest, most hostile takeover imaginable."

"Indeed. I had to evacuate dozens of employees because it was no longer safe for them. Bakker wasn't as fortunate. His accountant was just arrested and he's sitting in the Butyrka prison in Moscow *right now*. Poor Sergey. He'll probably have a lot of company."

This news was horrifying. Russian prisons were notoriously harsh. I could understand why Edouard was struggling to clear his head enough to sleep, because his daytime was a fucking nightmare. "I'm so sorry you're going through all this. Why didn't you say something? I can't pretend to understand the specifics of your work, but I can understand its gravity."

"It's been agony."

"I'm sure, darling. I have to ask . . . Are you safe?"

Edouard's mouth turned downward as he took a long sip of wine. "Probably. Bakker has it far worse than I do."

"Probably? That's not a reassuring answer. I'm worried for you. Does this put you in any danger?"

"My life's work has been about assessing risk, and 'probably' is the best I can offer. It's difficult to find the right level between fighting for my people and my investors, while protecting my own interests."

"I see. So, you are *probably* safe."

"Yes, exactly. As you may have noticed Erika, I have security officers."

"Yes, many of them. Are they sufficient?"

"I believe so." Edouard took another long sip of wine.

"That's another not very reassuring answer. Have you been threatened?"

"I'm threatened frequently. That's part of my job. The frequency has risen of late, and it's hard to ignore the violence directed at businessmen dealing with similar types." Edouard shrugged, as if he were speaking to an innocent child. "It's the job of my security officers to determine if the threats are of any consequence. So far, we don't believe they are."

I sat back and shook my head, and the essential truth of Edouard's life at the moment finally dawned on me. "Is this why you never leave your house?"

"Yes. The perimeter is controlled, and I have people in place. But things have been moving very fast in Moscow, too. I've wanted to be by my phone and by my staff, because we've had to make many rapid decisions."

"And so you remain inside your glorious prison?"

"Yes, you understand. It's temporary, but necessary. I expect we'll have these matters straightened out by the New Year."

"I hope so, for your sake. I mean Edouard, your view is spectacular, but your home is still your jail."

"Indeed, but I try not to think of it that way, especially since your company is so enchanting. The arrest of Sergey changed everything. It's been a very complicated and taxing time. I'm sorry to burden you with this."

"No apology necessary. I'm glad you told me what's been on your mind, darling. I've felt your tension, but I didn't understand the severity of the situation."

Edouard drummed his fingers on the table. "To be frank, being with you is the only time when I get this debacle out of my mind."

"Got it. We don't need to discuss it any further. I'll take your lead on your Russian affairs. Let's hope the Freud works some magic, because you deserve it."

"Thanks. I've moved beyond trying to save my investment. Now, I'm just trying to save my people. Lucian Freud's grandfather was the great psychiatrist Sigmund. Perhaps the grandson can bring a bit of sanity to these undertakings?"

"Wouldn't that be amazing? I'm rooting for you and your Freud, darling."

"Well, enough of my grim business news . . . Let's change the subject to something more pleasant." I preferred the playful Edouard to the troubled Edouard. It had taken a while for his silly side to emerge, but he was clearly a man who was comfortable with absurdity and who delighted in the perverse.

"All right. What then? I'm thinking I should write a paper for the *Journal of Sleep Science* about the use of vacbeds to address insomnia. I have a nonrepresentative sample of one. I realize it doesn't offer much statistical power, but I've witnessed how well a vacuum works at calming *you*."

"Perhaps this is your next business. Vacuum beds in the home, as a cure for restless sleepers." A slight smile appeared on Edouard's face, as he mulled his outrageous idea. He liked to provoke me, and I accepted his challenge with gusto.

"You're not the first person who's imagined a therapeutic purpose to BDSM scenes." It was a relief to see the playful side of my host, after such grave revelations.

"Oh? What ailments do you cure?" Edouard's voice changed from somber to sly.

"Well, I've had clients who think of their scenes as psychological therapy. They get a chance to examine shame, for example, and come out of the scene reassured. Sometimes, they experience an emotional catharsis more profound than anything they've achieved with a psychiatrist. I've even had some wonder if they could get reimbursed by their health insurers."

"How extraordinary. They must be Americans."

"Yes, quite right, it's that American obsession with health, I suppose."

"Or an American belief that pleasure isn't sufficient . . . for things to be worthwhile, they must also have a serious purpose. Americans are, at core, Anglo Saxons in how they approach desire."

"If you say so . . . and you French? How do you approach desire?"

"It's at the core of our culture, Erika." Edouard winked at me. "Consider how we approach wine, food, theater." A smile appeared on his face as his shoulders relaxed.

"You'll hear no complaints from me. Your commitment to pleasure is laudable. Look at your *libertins*. They figured out how to masquerade eroticism and the pursuit of pleasure as a form of protest against the king and the church."

"*Libertinage* is the intersection of two things we French adore . . . Social protest and seduction. It hits all our pleasure centers."

"Indeed. And don't we all need more pleasure in our lives? But now back to the vacbed business . . . Do you think these sleep technicians should be dressed as nurses or as dominatrixes?"

"Client's choice, obviously." Edouard shrugged, suggesting there was no other sensible option.

"Obviously. But only the most special clients get their vacbed operator wearing yoga pants and a sweater."

"But of course. And you wear them well. I must ask . . . Do you find these scenes dull? I worry that I'm boring you." It was unusual to hear a bit of doubt or uncertainty in Edouard's voice, but I was charmed that my amusement was important to him. Many clients are indifferent to my enjoyment.

"Don't worry about boring me, darling. I find your scenes calming, practically meditative. And besides, you look awfully cute as you lie there, immobile."

"You're making me blush."

"Good. You need to be off-balance more often, and I'm willing to help."

"But seriously, Erika, don't you wish there was more action, and more for you to do while I lie there?"

"Not necessarily. I mean, there's a place and a pet for every kind of scene. Sometimes, it's amusing getting and giving a workout. But not always. In this case, I enjoy your stillness, and there's something sweet about giving you a few hours of peace." I paused, trying to decide how frank I should be with Edouard. "So, I've been indulging our appetites for almost twenty years personally, and more than a decade professionally."

"I thought so. That's a lot."

"For argument's sake, since I started, I've probably averaged one hundred scenes per year. That's over *two thousand* scenes." I paused so the numbers could sink in. Clients might indulge their passions once or twice a month—if they were lucky—but if I wanted or needed to, I could act out their fantasies on a daily basis. There was an enormous gulf between their frequency and mine. I continued, "I want all the scenes to hit a bull's-eye at the intersection of my counterpart's desires and my whims . . . but does that have to include a certain kind of action? Absolutely not. There are things I'd never do in a scene. I have limits, obviously. But at this stage, I just want to thrill my audience and then stick the landing like an Olympic gymnast."

"Very good. I don't want you to feel obligated or burdened. I guess those numbers shouldn't surprise me, but their magnitude is impressive."

"I don't usually like speaking so specifically, but you asked . . ."

"Of course . . . of course . . . do you worry about your past playmates?"

"Like, will they talk? Is that what you're getting at?" I couldn't help but think of LegMan617 and wondered if I should mention him or not. I opted to paint the rosiest picture possible as I didn't want my worries to become Edouard's.

"Yes. If you've done two thousand scenes, that's a lot of slaves."

"True. I can't run from that number, but what I can tell you is that I've always been very fussy about who I let in the door. I've also been very careful about my privacy. When I moved to New York from Boston, I told everyone I was retiring, and they seemed to have accepted that. Occasionally, I pop onto the message boards, and Miss E—that's how I was known in Boston—is spoken about fondly, but always in the past tense."

"Good for you. I know of women who've had problems."

"Me too, and so far, I'm not one of them. Here's a question

for you. Have you ever heard anything rumor-wise about me from some gossipy gallerist?"

"Nothing exceptional. You're viewed as aloof, although some think you use your sexuality to your advantage."

"Hah. Show me a woman in this business who hasn't been accused of sleeping with her clients! It's the easiest accusation to make. But let me assure you, any rumors are not coming from gentlemen like you. You have too much to lose from talking."

"Those are very good points." Edouard tilted his head and took a small sip of wine. "You may get a chuckle out of this bit of gossip I once heard."

"Oh, do tell? I like a good laugh."

"I had someone tell me that your Dark Mistress of Chelsea reputation was just an act. That you're actually a bubbly blonde disguised as an edgy brunette."

"Fantastic. I'm accused of disguising myself as someone dark and deviant!"

"Yes. It sounded like envy to me, but it made me smile, because I know you are authentic."

I leaned toward Edouard and whispered. "You know that I'm naturally a blonde, right? But someone calling me 'bubbly'? *That* hurts."

"Yes, you don't seem bubbly to me. Now, where your gallery is concerned, you have a solid reputation. You're considered a good judge of talent and not some shallow trend chaser. You nurture your artists; you don't exploit them. You're taken very seriously."

"That's what I hoped you'd say, except for the 'bubbly blonde' business. And let me tell you, that kind of reputation doesn't happen by accident. I built it. Just like you built yours. It's one of the reasons this sleazy business with my father is so troubling. One whiff of something so dubious and criminal? A decade's worth of effort would evaporate."

"Indeed. Forgeries and frauds are the kinds of things that destroy a business . . . as they should. These are businesses built on trust."

"Yes. Trust, taste and lots of intangibles. Sometimes, I wish I had more of a flair for identifying the most profitable works and artists, but that approach feels inconsequential . . . it just doesn't move me. Frankly, my goal has always been to establish long-term relationships with my artists and my clients—gallery and otherwise."

"That's clear. Although you've had some defections, lately."

"Yes . . ." It was my turn to show frustration. "My gallery is viewed as a farm team for the mega-galleries. I do what I can, but they poach my best artists. How am I supposed to compete with the reach of a Gagosian and all the billionaires he has on speed dial?"

"It must be an enormous challenge. But I admire the way you operate both sides of your business."

"That means a lot, Edouard. Thank you. You're one of the only people who can appreciate both worlds. Unfortunately, for both of us, all our worlds are a little shaky right now."

"Indeed. It's a shame you have no interest in private equity. I think you'd be very good at it."

"Right back at you, darling. It's a shame you have no interest in art galleries. I think you'd be very good at that."

"By the way, how is the gallery doing in your absence? And I'm certain your gentlemen must miss you."

"To be frank, my business in New York is focused on only a handful of gentlemen, and that handful has been kept busy by Amy. They probably don't even realize I'm gone."

"Oh, I'm certain they know you're gone. There's no substitute for you." Edouard leaned back and slouched in his chair. "I doubt you know this, but you're the first woman who's stayed overnight in my home. And I hope you'll stay as long as you like. I also hope you'll come back."

"You say the nicest things." But my mind paused on the fact he'd just shared with me. "Am I really the first? You've lived here for over a decade!"

Edouard shrugged. "I'm very private, too. I have a small apartment in Paris where I have received a few *guests*, but never here."

"I'm honored. Thank you for taking the chance."

"You're welcome. This has been an exceptional time for both of us. When I suggested you come visit, I didn't think I'd be fortunate enough for you to accept."

"Well, as you know, your offer was timely. I needed to get away from Chelsea, and I've always enjoyed you. And to be frank, I didn't think I'd stay this long either, but you're the best company."

"Likewise. I've never met anyone like you."

"You are singular in my life, too, Edouard," I said. And I meant it. We'd talked—intensely—every night for weeks. His passions were similar to mine, and he wasn't one of those men who preferred to speak. He actually listened; and not merely when I discussed prurient matters. I had come to look forward to our nightly dinners, and whatever happened after them.

"I'd like to share an idea with you I've been considering for the past couple of weeks."

"Oh? Do tell, darling. What's on your mind."

"Have you considered expanding your gallery?"

"Not with any seriousness. Why do you ask?"

"Well, this downturn will have an end, and I believe strongly in art as an asset class."

"I believe strongly in it too, Edouard."

"Well, Switzerland has one tenth of the world's billionaires, and many of them live in Geneva. Geneva itself is close to Zürich, Paris and Basel. There's even a local free port. What I'd like to propose is the possibility of establishing the Grieg Gallery in Geneva, with me as your partner."

"What are you thinking, a 'Grieg/de Grenet Gallery'?"

"No, of course not. You are the star. You're always the star."

"Thanks, darling, I guess? So, this gallery would be in my name only."

"Of course. My only interest is supporting your work."

"And would that involve closing New York?" I wanted to know just how exclusive an arrangement he visualized. Would he expect me at his beck and call, toiling in Geneva every day?

"That would be up to you, but it shouldn't be necessary. Gagosian has, what, a half dozen galleries? There are rumors he's looking to lease space in the city center. Krugier has a gallery here and one in Manhattan." Edouard gestured as he spoke, animated by the possibility of a Geneva expansion.

"But Krugier's been at it since the sixties." His suggestion had caught me off guard. I'd been in business for several years, but that didn't put me in the same league as the galleries he was discussing. I aspired to be in their league—they had cachet and lots of sales—but it's a difficult business, which is why I continued to see clients on the side. Selling art was a tough undertaking. Selling bondage and discipline was often much easier.

"Yes, he's a veteran. I got my Giacomettis from him twenty years ago. But there's room for you. There are excellent dealers here if your tastes run to the Flemish, but not if they run to young artists. I know of several buildings that could be ideal for your purposes. If you take the long view, this could be an excellent moment for expansion and selfishly, I'd like to help."

"I'm going to be frank with you, the gallery in New York is barely profitable. If not for gentlemen like you, who buy works along with sessions, I doubt it would be viable." I took a long breath, to steady myself. I had few qualms discussing kinks, but finances? It felt shockingly intimate delving into my business. I could happily discuss Edouard's personal predilections for hours without hesitation, but it was quite another to discuss my professional struggles, and yet I continued, "I hate discussing the economics of my business, but if it weren't for my basement, I'd struggle to make payroll. And since I cannot clone myself, the prospect of twice the overhead, while there's still only one of me, is daunting."

"I still don't see a problem. We each have resources we can leverage for the other's success. I can't be bothered splurging on a Bugatti. A project with you, however, would be worthwhile."

"Oh? This would be an unusual partnership." I wanted to know more about what Edouard had in mind.

"Is there any other kind of partnership? At least where people like us are concerned? I've had the opportunity to watch you these past weeks, and every day, you amaze me more. I admire your priorities and I share your passions. Our conversations fuel me through the day, and I can't wait to hear what's on your mind at night."

"What you're proposing sounds extraordinary, but there are so many details and so many ways it could get derailed. And I want to be frank with you, as much as I delight in your company, darling, I'm not wired for monogamy."

"Nor am I." He gave me a brief smile, baring his teeth. "The promise I'd make, and the promise I'd want in return, is that we not embarrass the other. The stakes are too high. In Geneva, nothing happens except between us. It's a small town, and you know how the Swiss can be. They pretend to be discreet, but they talk."

"I'm stunned, but also intrigued." My mind was reeling. Did he want me to move in with him, as his own personal pet dominatrix? Or was this something more equitable and significant. It sounded like something that could take years to play out, which raised flags.

"Good. There will be details. But I trust you, Erika, and I hope you trust me."

"Of course. Let's not get ahead of ourselves, but I can see potential in this."

"Excellent. That's all I ask. Think it over. Take a few months, but if we proceed, it would be smart to get started early next year, to lock up the best space and to find the right team."

I wondered about my unorthodox sideline. "You're not concerned about my Chelsea basement?"

"Not particularly. You've had no problems to date, correct?"

"No. Well, apart from Michael's heart attack."

"Good. My expectation, to be frank, is that you'll be so busy building your gallery empire, you'll have little time for the basement. The crutch it's provided, financially, will not be necessary. Instead of working by the hour, my partnership will let your efforts be scaled and you can dedicate yourself to the art market."

"So, you'd want me to give up doing sessions?"

"No, I'm not a fool. But I don't see how you could do many if you're dividing your time between Geneva and New York. You'll be operating at a different level. You've done two thousand sessions. Do you really want to do three?"

"Why not? I enjoy the work, but I agree, it has been a distraction— a *necessary* distraction—from the gallery."

"That's where I can help. It won't be necessary any longer." Edouard paused, then looked at me straight. "Where do things stand with your father?"

"He's popped up at the gallery, trying for a meeting, but we've put him off. My guess is that he only has another week or two before he tires and figures out another solution to his problem."

"Good. You don't want him damaging your reputation just as you're launching something major. A new gallery will attract a lot of attention."

"Tell me about it, darling. I'm just counting the days until he finds some other dupe to trouble . . . so thank you for sharing your elegant jail with me."

"It's my pleasure, Erika. Please let me know if you'd like to discuss your father with my security consultants. They may have some ideas."

"Thanks. I'm hoping it resolves itself. But Josh is there in case it doesn't . . . and if things escalate, I have some ideas. Families are tough, aren't they?"

"Yes. Families can turn us into children. You deserve better than to be drawn into something unethical and sleazy."

"Let's get back to your proposal, Edouard. Start-up costs for this kind of gallery are high. What does a commercial storefront run in Geneva?"

"You're correct. The cost per square meter is high, but it's also twenty-five percent less than it was last year." Edouard looked pleased with himself. What businessman doesn't like a deal? "Boxler has identified an Art Deco building downtown where a suitable ten-year lease is available at a fraction of what it would have cost before."

"Ten years is an eternity for people like us. And Boxler's been working on this? You amaze me, Edouard. What else have you been thinking?"

"It's Geneva, so the initial build-out will be expensive. I estimate the cost to be a manageable one point seven million francs for the first year, with ongoing yearly overhead of about eight hundred thousand. How does a ten-year commitment sound to you?"

"Staggering. And how does that work with your own cash flow?"

"It's supportable. And quite frankly, I think you'll be profitable very quickly, so it should be worth your time to come to Geneva often. After all, you offer something that the Geneva market craves—aesthetic edge and deep knowledge."

"What would you want in return? I've never given up equity in my gallery before."

"I don't want equity. I want to see more of you."

"Isn't it easier, and less expensive for that matter, to just visit me in New York?"

"Certainly, but it's less satisfying. You've shown me there's a gap in my life. I don't want a wife or even a girlfriend. Frankly, I prefer what we do, to what they require. I want to pursue the things we adore more deeply."

"Oh? You didn't seem bored when we were together with Viviana. You fucked her enthusiastically."

"Yes, of course. Why wouldn't I? It would be rude not to show enthusiasm for a beautiful woman. But it was having you in the room that made it worthwhile."

"It was having *me* in the room while you were tied up and fucking her that made it worthwhile? So, that time you made a pass at me . . . were you just being polite?"

"Of course not. I wanted you. I wanted you so desperately I would have gotten down on my knees and begged." He shrugged and cocked his head to one side. "But usually, I want other things even more."

"You're funny, Edouard. But I understand what you're saying. That's something we have in common . . . don't get me wrong, I enjoy sex, but it's rarely special. Once you've had truly exceptional erotic experiences, everything else can seem banal."

"So true. Well, I hope you'll consider this proposal. I'll have Boxler give you the numbers for various spaces we've identified. I would have said something sooner, but I wanted to do some homework first."

"You don't propose anything in jest, Edouard. I take you very seriously. Darling, I'm flattered and amazed by what you've been up to."

"It may seem presumptuous of me to encroach on your work, but art is just one of our many shared passions. I deal with executives every day, and I've learned what distinguishes the good from the great. You could be the next Zwirner or Gagosian. I'd like to play a role in that."

"You know how to speak to my fantasies, just like I know how to speak to yours. What you're proposing is life-changing."

"It could be very satisfying for both of us. As part of this project, we could coordinate our calendars. For instance, I'd like to join you in Basel and Miami."

"Oh, that sounds wonderful. I can just picture the look of disappointment on the faces of all those gorgeous gallerinas who've been circling you for years. Those ladies will hate me, and I will love every moment of it."

"And then there are the men who've been coveting your company, and you'll be there, next to me. I'll enjoy their envy."

"You know just what to say! This sounds very promising and pleasurable. For both of us."

"And I'd also like it if you joined me at some private equity conferences. I realize they're dull, but they're full of prospective clients for the Grieg Gallery and I'd enjoy them more if you were beside me." Edouard sat back and looked at the ceiling as he stroked his chin. "Hmm . . . how do you feel about Davos? Klaus Schwab owes me a favor. Maybe I could get you on a panel at the World Economic Forum . . . perhaps a discussion on the state of the art market? What are you doing at the end of January?"

"The end of January? My calendar is open, and I'd love to speak at Davos. But Edouard, the benefits seem to be accruing mostly to me. I've been at this long enough that I can't escape the nagging feeling I've missed something or there's some hidden cost that will nail me in two years."

"I want to be completely transparent. You write the terms, then. I believe we'd make an excellent team and I trust you to be fair."

"You want me to write the terms . . ."

"Yes. Or I can write them. Or your Michael can write them in consultation with both of us. Whatever is important to you should be present in the terms. I've told you what's important to me."

"Right. This is very unexpected. I need some time."

"Please think it over. Boxler will show you what we've pulled together tomorrow. And in case you're worried, we could include an exit clause, in the unlikely event that one of us decides things aren't working. You could leave Geneva at any time. But I truly hope you won't want to."

Edouard had given me a lot to consider. As he lay compressed between the latex sheets of his vacbed, probably blissing out to the prospect of regular vacbed encounters while I launched a gallery in Geneva, my fantasies were elsewhere. My mind drifted to the stage of Davos. What would I wear? Who would be on the panel with me? How could I get all the wealthy in attendance to open up their wallets and splurge? Edouard had baited the hook. He had done to me what I routinely did to others; he had seeded my imagination with fantasies that only he could satisfy. This was a more powerful kind of bondage than mere ropes or chains.

33

GALLERIES GALORE

When I got up at noon, just in time for lunch, Boxler had a binder filled with information about the various vacant storefronts available in Geneva. He'd categorized them by proximity to the other major galleries; he'd assessed the suitability of the size and allocation of space; he'd even tried to rank them. The spaces themselves varied in size and cost. One was a jewel box of only a few hundred square feet, while the largest was over two thousand square feet. I'd need to see them in person and walk the neighborhoods to truly assess things. Having already opened a gallery, I knew the features that moved me, and in turn, what moved my clients to buy.

"Boxler, thank you. I'm grateful for all your work. When Edouard mentioned this idea to me, it was a surprise. You're from Geneva. What do you think about the market here?"

"Zürich is the third largest art market in the world. It's already well-served. Geneva has lagged, and this, perhaps, is where the opportunity exists?"

"Does Geneva feel overlooked, like it has something to prove?"

"Of course, Miss Grieg. Zürich's art scene is larger and more established, where Geneva only has the Quartier des Bains."

"Edouard also mentioned he was facing some security issues. Do you anticipate any problems if I go look at some of these properties?"

"No, but I'd like to have one of my men accompany you."

"I see. Please set up some visits for me for tomorrow afternoon. Here's my list of priorities." I handed Boxler a sheet where I had ranked the possibilities.

"I'll revert with a time later." Boxler did an about-face and headed for the door.

I was trying not to let my excitement get ahead of me. Affluent men had promised me extraordinary things many times, and with the exception of Michael, very few had delivered. There was a real estate tycoon in Boston who'd proposed setting me up with a condo. I was still innocent then, not realizing that such talk was just a horny guy verbalizing a fantasy of having me nearby with cuffs at the ready. During our weekly sessions, he talked about the condo, showing me floorplans and discussing how the ceilings would be high enough for a chain hoist, but every time I asked to see the unit for myself, there was always a fresh excuse. It embarrasses me now that I took him seriously for as long as I did. I wasted time and enthusiasm exploring parking options and soundproofing, for when I'd move myself and all my gear into his fantasy unit.

All the same, it would be crazy not to take those initial steps and see what might be feasible with Edouard. He'd proven himself to be marvelous company, and if his finances were as robust as he claimed, Grieg Gallery 2.0 could be my leap into a whole different marketplace. My head was spinning with ideas.

Over the next two days, I spent hours with a commercial real estate broker, exploring units around Geneva's city center. With every appointment, I got more deeply invested in opening a place in Geneva. I did my best to curtail my enthusiasm, but Edouard was a serious guy. He wouldn't propose such a project—and then involve his staff—unless he was willing to see it through. Or at least that's what I told myself.

The beginning of a project is always the most intoxicating phase. Everything is possible, nothing is off the table, and my imagination was desperate to look at those empty spaces and see them filled with potential. Edouard's offer had come at a time when I could see that my fellow professional dominatrixes were about to experience a serious shift in their business practices.

There were sites like Twitter and Facebook offering practitioners and prospective clients the opportunity to mix and mingle virtually. And while this might be good for newcomers, it would be devastating to someone like me. My business thrived on its mystery and inaccessibility. Periodically, I'd lurk on some of the message boards where I used to trawl for clients and see a post from an old client who missed me and who regretted my "retirement." It would be harder and harder for my practice to remain discreet, given how many more places these conversations could take place in the future.

Being able to expand the gallery work without fear of personal consequences, while diminishing the dungeon work that could wreck me reputationally was a prospect I'd been toying with ever since the emergence of social media. I'd barely made a tweet, but LegMan617 had already found me. It was only a matter of time before my privacy would be further at risk.

"You're seducing me, Edouard." I'd worn one of his favorite latex dresses to dinner, after a long day of discussions with an architect and the realtor.

"Are you sure you're not seducing me, Erika?" Edouard had a faint smile on his lips, as he took a bite of salad.

"Who, me? You are impervious to such things. I, however, can be seduced by potential . . . and I'm seeing so much of it here." The more I thought about his proposal, the more I saw how it could protect me from an inevitable crisis. How many more years could I work extra-legally before something bad happened? Amy and Michael showed me that a catastrophe could happen at any moment. And as for the internet, it filled my heart with dread.

"Fantastic. When we ran the numbers for a gallery here in Geneva, they seemed promising."

"Yes, very promising. Although, your numbers are low. The unit I liked the best isn't the most expensive, lease-wise, but it will require more work. Also, the landlord wants a minimum five-year lease." I didn't want to tie myself to Edouard for ten years, but five years seemed manageable. Besides, we could always renegotiate later if things were going well between us.

"Five years? I'm surprised they'd be willing to offer such a short term. Ten years is more common. I imagine there's a renewal clause?"

"Yes. Since I'm a foreigner, there would need to be guarantees."

"Which I'll address. I was thinking of establishing a trust account, which would disburse the gallery's rent, as required."

"Very good idea. To be frank, I never want to ask you for anything. I find that sort of thing unseemly." The prospect of nagging Edouard to pay the rent horrified me. "Instead, I'd like to get these administrative details organized up front. Unfortunately, the estimates you've been working with are a little light. I'm going to have to give Josh a promotion in New York, so he has the authority to act in my place when I'm here."

"I see." Edouard raised an eyebrow but didn't say more. Perhaps he hadn't realized the consequences of opening a Geneva gallery had consequences regarding staffing in New York. And perhaps I was testing him, to see if he'd push back as I pushed for more.

"And another thing, the estimate for the build-out is low. I realize most civilians believe galleries are simple white cubes, but they're far more than that. The details are where identity is achieved . . . and details are expensive. There's the lighting, the architectural features—floorboards, columns, that sort of thing.

The space I like best has a distinctive ceiling, for instance, and I would want to feature it."

"Have the architect prepare a proposal and give it to Boxler. I trust your taste and acumen. I want this gallery to happen. I want this to be the best idea you've ever had." Edouard didn't seem perturbed by my comments, but it was always possible he'd push back later, or have Boxler push back on his behalf.

"I want it, too, to my great surprise. I'm starting to see how it could come together, and how a Geneva gallery could complement New York."

"Tell me more." Edouard leaned back in his seat, with his hands clasped in front of him. He looked at me with the full force of his gaze.

Even though he'd stared at me before, it felt different this time. I was sharing my vision and my dreams, instead of delving into his. Beyond the specifics of the gallery, I wanted to impress him, and I wanted my ideas to seduce him. "Well, I think, given the sophistication of the Swiss art scene, it might be productive to do small, curated shows of underappreciated contemporary artists. Why not highlight women, some of those astonishing African artists, or even the best indigenous artists in Australia?"

"Why not, indeed? Perhaps these are the sectors where more growth is possible . . ." Edouard paused. I worried he might dismiss my ideas, but to my relief, he continued, "It's a bit different from your usual 'young artists,' but I can imagine a certain kind of collector being animated by all the potential."

"I'd enjoy the work of identifying the artists to show, but also, it might be possible to kind of, I don't know, own those sectors if I do it right. White men and their works are overrepresented in the marketplace. All the major galleries specialize in them. In my opinion, there's a hunger for different voices and visions, and that hunger represents opportunity."

"Like stock market investors who want emerging markets exposure."

"Yes, something like that. These are works where there's more financial upside, and I can speak to that. But also, it gives collectors a chance to show how their tastes are dynamic. Anyone with enough money can acquire a blue-chip work. It takes discernment like yours to go beyond the obvious or to get there first."

"You flatter me." Edouard offered up a slight smile. "Your Africa idea could do well here in Geneva, where we have many United Nations offices."

"I hadn't thought about that, Edouard. But yes, you're right—anyone doing business with the UN should be keen on works from underappreciated and underrepresented artists."

"The director general of UNESCO, Kōichirō Matsuura, is someone I know. Tell me if you'd like to have a conversation with him. It might be helpful, because they oversee many programs intended to promote cultural diversity, and also, to assist the 'global south.'"

"You amaze me. Thank you. All those corporate art collections should be interested in these works, too. Seriously, Edouard, this could work out."

"I wouldn't have proposed it if I didn't believe it could. We both have resources, and I'd like to see you succeed, while also seeing more of you." This would be no minor satellite of my New York gallery. His vision suggested that the New York gallery might even become a satellite of Geneva.

"I'd like that. You've really grown on me!" I was beginning to invest mentally in Edouard's idea, and in Edouard, too.

"Grown on you? Like fungus or mold?"

"Don't be silly." I had to laugh. How could I capture what was on my mind and express my heightened affection for the man? "Let me correct myself. You haven't grown on me. Let's think of tailoring, instead. You're a bespoke garment, elegant and refined. Now, we're just working to finalize the fit."

"I prefer the Savile Row reference to mold."

"Me too. So, I'll get going on a proposal based on what I've seen here in Geneva. I fear your estimates are low, but we're talking twenty to thirty percent low, not a hundred percent low . . . which, quite frankly, is remarkable for a team who's never launched an art gallery before. I'm also going to need a different type of PR in Geneva than I use in New York, but the path to profitability may be shorter than anticipated . . ."

"Never bank on that. Projects always take more time and cost more money than we anticipate, but I'm very optimistic about this one. It's great to see that you're gaining enthusiasm for Geneva."

"I am. And tonight, we'll celebrate. Be prepared to be squeezed. Your vacbed is going to be put to the test."

"You know just what to say, Erika."

"Sometimes, I do, Edouard. Sometimes, I do. And just to reiterate, you're not a fungus. You're a most extraordinary gentleman. And now, it's time for this most extraordinary gentleman to go downstairs and submit. Are you ready?"

"Yes, Erika. I thought you'd never ask."

While Edouard snored away in his latex cocoon, I opened up my laptop and tried to get some work done. There were the usual messages from Josh. Although we hadn't sold anything in weeks, he and Amy were trying different ideas to get people in the door. It was frustrating, but I liked the initiative he was showing and it was easy to imagine promoting him once Grieg Geneva was in the works. Josh was capable and creative. Even more important, Josh had always shown he'd suffer for me—and who doesn't want that in a director of their gallery? Smart gallery owners should hire masochists for directors. Anyone could put a job listing with the New York Foundation for the Arts. Only a truly inspired gallery owner would think to recruit a heavy bottom at New York's Eulenspiegel Society.

Edouard's heart rate was low and steady, when mine spiked suddenly. The responsible party was an email from one of my gallery clients.

SUBJECT: Basquiat!!! You remembered!!!

Dear Erika,

Thank you for connecting me with your dad. It's been a few years since I told you how much I wanted a Basquiat for my collection, so I'm thrilled you remembered this conversation and hooked me up. Jake's a real kick, btw. I can see how you take after him. You Griegs have so much style and savvy.

Gonna see the paintings in a few days, and hopefully, make one or <gulp> two of them mine. It all depends on what my broker says, because the fucking stock market remains crazy. Stay tuned.

Jenny

It was all I could do not to scream, but that wouldn't have helped me and it might have startled Edouard. How capable could his newest business partner be if she couldn't even keep her father from stealing a few million bucks? Moreover, he was also leveraging my name and contacts for his scheme.

I wondered how he'd found Jenny, one of my best non-dungeon clients, but then I remembered she'd been featured in an enthusiastic interview for ArtNet, discussing one of my openings. Dad must have found his marks from my most outspoken clients, and in turn, he was exploiting my reputation. I didn't want anything bad to happen to him, but I didn't want anything bad to happen to me, either, and that's the direction this debacle was headed. Jenny might be naive enough to buy a couple of paintings, but she'd seek an opinion on the works, sooner or later. Once that happened, she'd receive some very awkward and expensive news.

Someone else would have called their father and pleaded with him to cut out his schemes, but I'd made that mistake before and it had cost me twenty thousand dollars I couldn't afford in a "loan," and a further ten thousand dollars for shrink visits, to work out why I'd been such a dupe. In one of my more insightful moments, sitting opposite Dr. Klagsbrun, I'd sworn to erect and maintain boundaries. At the time, Dr. K had said that if I felt guilt for saying no to my dad, we could work on that guilt later, but the most important thing was to say no. I'd finally given my dad a very firm no, only this time, he had ignored me and then worked around me.

Instead of wringing my hands and pondering a call to Dr. K, I went into my phone book and found a number I'd never needed before—the head of the FBI's Art Crime Unit. Geneva was nine hours ahead of Los Angeles, so if I called right away, I might catch Special Agent Elizabeth Rigas before she left for the day. After my childhood experience with law enforcement, I paused for a second, but there was really just one thing I could do in response to this emerging disaster, so it seemed sensible just to get going.

"Hello, this is Elizabeth Rigas speaking." Her voice was efficient and gave the kind of no-nonsense accent I craved hearing from a cop.

"Hi, Ms. Rigas. This is Erika Grieg speaking. I own the Grieg Gallery in New York. We met a couple of years ago when you gave a symposium on the looting of the museums in Baghdad."

"Ah, very good. I'm proud of the work we did there." Her voice changed from warm to cool, as if to acknowledge that our niceties were complete, and now it was time to get down to business. "What can I do for you, Ms. Grieg?"

"One of my clients has been offered a private sale of some works by Jean-Michel Basquiat, only I have reason to believe the works are fakes. This would represent a fraud of several million dollars."

"I see. Who's the seller?"

"My father, Jacob Warnock, only he's calling himself Jacob Grieg these days. He was found guilty of fraud in the eighties, from a time when he was a money manager in Los Angeles. I thought he'd straightened himself out, but it seems he has not."

"Why do you say that?"

"Well, ever since he was arrested twenty years ago, I've used my mother's maiden name, Grieg. There's no good reason for my father to use the name Grieg. He's up to something, and the name Jacob Warnock would probably give up too many alarming hits on Google."

"Got it. And who's the buyer?"

"Her name is Jennifer Kowalczyk. She's been a client of my gallery since it opened. She's even been quoted in a couple of ArtNet reviews about my exhibitions."

"I see. And what's her story?"

"She's a partner at Barclays. She's had a hard-on for Basquiat for years, so I fear she'd be seduced by such an unusual opportunity. But sooner or later she'd learn she'd been scammed, and then she'd go postal."

"Got it. So, why do you believe the works are inauthentic?"

"I've seen photos, and the images felt like pastiche. There were too many clichés, and the composition was wrong. I've spent hours staring at authentic works—I started my career at Gagosian—so Basquiat's vernacular is one I know well. These are solid fakes. Their iconography is correct and all the elements are there, but they lack the appropriate tension." I worried I was sounding too hand-wavey for a cop, so I decided to avoid anything that reeked of gallerist-speak. "To be blunt, I don't believe any of the paintings would hold up under scrutiny. When he showed me photos of the works in September, I told my dad to get them authenticated and how to do so, but he balked. My dad simply doesn't have the experience to suss out a fake from an original, and I suspect he needs the money, so he's scrambling."

"Got it. Do you know where he obtained the works?" Rigas wasn't wasting time with small talk. I could hear her typing in the background.

"I have no idea. The story my dad told me is that the paintings were traded by Basquiat for drugs, and that's how they came into the hands of one of my dad's friends and fellow prisoners at Lompoc. I suspect he's the front man for some bad guys. My dad cleans up nicely."

"I see. I'll need to follow up with Ms. Kowalczyk."

"Of course. I'll email you her contact info as soon as I get off this call. She emailed me about the Basquiat just now, and that's how I learned my father wasn't just making idle inquiries."

"So, you and Ms. Kowalczyk are in touch?"

"Yes. She's one of my most serious collectors. I suspect my father saw her name in an article about my gallery and then reached out to her."

"That makes sense. Can you think of any other reason why she might be targeted?"

"No. In her email to me, it seemed like my dad had been playing up our relationship."

"Probably to boost confidence. She trusts you, and he'll want her to trust him. It's a common tactic."

"Right. Of course . . . should I reply to Jennifer? Should I say anything about my dad?"

"Hold off on replying until I get back to you. We've been working on a counterfeiting case that may have some elements in common. I need to talk to my supervisor. Let's speak tomorrow. Okay?"

"Absolutely. And I know you can't promise anything, but it sounds like my father is in the middle of something serious, and I'm afraid for him."

"I understand."

"If you need any information about how to approach Jennifer . . . or about my father, for that matter, please let me know." Once I'd established the parameters of the problem, it was time to make a request. "And one last thing . . . if there's any way you can be discreet about the fact his daughter turned him in, I'd be most grateful. I don't want my father exploiting my clients or getting into more serious trouble, but I do love him."

"No promises, but I understand your nervousness. And if it helps you sleep tonight, just know that you're not the only person to have made a call like this. I'll be in touch if I need more information."

"Thank you. I'm grateful for your time. And I'll let you know if I hear from anyone else about these paintings. There's rarely just one potential victim, and my dad showed me photos of multiple works."

"Roger, that. Goodbye, Ms. Grieg."

I hung up the phone and imagined hooking myself up to Edouard's ECG to see just how fast my heartrate had become. I'd just done the unthinkable and set law enforcement on my own father. What kind of daughter does that? But instead of wallowing in rage or pity, both tempting options, I tuned out the professional perils of my family, settled down with my laptop and got to work, with an oblivious Edouard swaddled in black latex next to me. Work had always been my release and my relief. And if the situation with my father didn't blow up, I'd be extremely busy launching a gallery in Geneva.

PART 3

REFINEMENT

REFINEMENT: The iterative process, evolving from reflection and feedback, is the final stage of an artist's undertaking.

34

MAKING PLANS

November 2008

I'm not tuned to passivity. I want to work; I need to do. The month in Geneva in a "wait and see" posture about my dad had taken a toll. I might have been eating gourmet meals and enjoying other luxuries, but the pressure had been inexorable. Every day, there was some new cause for concern, all the while my personal stakes had been mounting. I didn't appreciate the weight and the worry I'd been shouldering until some of it finally lifted.

After my conversation with Special Agent Rigas, I slept seven hours straight, no Ambien required. I had alerted the authorities. If anyone asked, I had cooperated, and I could then answer any questions about any frauds should they arise. And if my dad were savvy, he could negotiate something to save his ass. My father had a knack for self-preservation. He'd know what to do once the cuffs went on. He was practiced at being arrested. When I woke up, I felt calm and there was a new clarity to my plans. Grieg Gallery Geneva seemed within my grasp.

Michael was still convalescing at home, but I had to speak with him. He'd been the most important man in my life for years, and it was a position he guarded. With Edouard's offer, Michael's primary status was in jeopardy. It was possible he'd feel jealous of Edouard or anger toward me, but I had to trust that he was the man I'd always believed him to be—a man who only had my best interests at heart. As soon as I was confident he was awake, I called.

"Erika, I was just thinking about you." Michael's voice was low and melodic.

"Good thoughts, I hope. Or maybe, I hope they're wicked? Michael, darling, how are you feeling?"

"Better, thanks. My cardiologist is pleased, even though I dread every meal and all the nutritious, tasteless food he has commanded me to eat."

"You're following your cardiologist's orders? Fantastic. That'll spare me the task of ordering you to eat your vegetables."

"Yes. I prefer to connect you with decadent desserts, not with something as prosaic as broccoli." Michael snorted.

"I appreciate that. Thank you." We'd bantered, and now it was time for business. "How are you for time? I need some advice."

"We're good. I'm just reviewing some contracts. Nothing I can't put aside for you." His voice shifted and became serious. "What's on your mind?"

"We've both seen how technology and the internet have changed our businesses. With the gallery, I'm facing competition from online art sites and from other galleries, who aren't as locked in as they used to be, geographically speaking."

"Right. The marketplace is more open, and it's easier for clients and sellers to connect."

"Precisely. Well, this is true with my dungeon, as well."

"I don't follow, Erika. Your dungeon is not online. You've been offline for years."

"Yes. It's been several years since I've even taken on a new client. But let's face it, the way I do business is not sustainable."

"It has sustained you for years. What are you getting at?"

"Well, my core business consists of ten gentlemen like you. You're the best of course, but the other nine are similarly consistent, committed and extremely careful. You're on the shelf while you recover, so that makes nine. Well, I think I lost another one."

"Why do you say that?"

"Amy's having an affair with one." Dan Levine, the subject of Amy's affections, had been my second-best client after Michael. He visited every other week, like clockwork. It was a session that felt like a cross between therapy and kink, as he always wanted to do the same thing. To lose such a straightforward client would hurt my bank account immediately. "Do I think he'll just return to the status quo and his biweekly bondage sessions after that?"

"He could. Why not? Or do you think it's serious with Amy?"

"Who knows if it's serious. But is he going to come back to *me* to scratch his itch? It seems unlikely." Dan had found someone who'd give him more than I would. What neither Dan nor Amy knew is that these kinds of relationships are notoriously unstable. To transition from client to something else succeeds so rarely, I could only point to a few dominatrix peers who'd found life partners from their pool of paying customers. "So, I'm down a couple of clients. I have another dozen who are less frequent, but who've proven themselves over the years. And there's maybe one last dozen who disappear until their need becomes too acute. It's a solid business, and the men are fantastic, but if I lose more than one or two from that first group, I'm screwed."

"Of course. But clients are replaceable. The ocean is deep and vast." Michael spent hours every day soothing clients of his legal practice. He often deployed those talents on me, too.

"If this were a normal industry, I'd agree. But this is the sex industry. I can't replace any of those clients without risking exposure. I don't advertise, my website is dark, and it's been years since I got a referral. As you know, my old colleagues think I've retired."

"I understand. But a lot of that could be corrected with a quiet conversation in the right ears. You got along well with Sabrina Belladonna, right? And Isabella Sinclaire is very discreet. Could you trade referrals with them? They're on the west coast, so they're not your competition."

"They're fantastic, and yes, our client bases are similar. But do I want to be visible again? I took a certain pride when I had my first ad in DDI. But even then, I hardly showed my face."

"Erika, your ads were brazen." Michael seemed to be enjoying my discomfort. He wouldn't be the first masochist who also possessed a sadistic streak.

"Perhaps, but instead of showing my face, I showed my body . . . and even then, my body was always covered in something tight and shiny."

"Ah, yes. Well, they showed enough to catch my eye."

"And I'm so glad it worked! But I had second thoughts as soon as I did it. I hated including a photo, but I had no choice. David Jackson, the publisher of DDI, insists on photos, but I always had nightmares about it, because you never know where a photo might wind up. And now, with the internet? Those photos can go anywhere, and the past will never be forgotten."

"The past may never be forgotten, but it can be buried. You've gotten a lot of serious coverage for your gallery; you should be able to dismiss any unwelcome attention as tawdry gossip."

"I certainly hope so. But we're not addressing the underlying problem, which is that the industry is changing. Clients these days want their dommes to be out and proud. There's just so much shame floating around kinks, so there's a benefit in seeing a domme who's up front about who and what she is. These ladies are daring people to accept their peccadilloes. It's bold and very healthy."

"Yes, I see what you're saying. But there's little distance between your domme persona and your gallery persona. You are integrated."

"True. But Michael, there's a huge gap in terms of the privacy I can expect. Being labeled a sex worker or giggled about as a dominatrix would undermine the reputation I've cultivated for years at my gallery. The dominatrix business would be mentioned in the first or second paragraph of every profile of me or the gallery going forward if it ever came out."

"That's certainly possible, but why would it come out? Your clients want to be as discreet as you do. There's no upside in them talking."

"Okay, I have to ask: Have you been on any of those kinky message boards lately?"

"Not in years, thank goodness. They're not a good use of my time."

"Mine either. I mean, except when I was starting out and I needed to hustle up clients quickly. Well, I've had some time on my hands here in Geneva, so I went to some of those old virtual haunts . . . and they are worse than before. The men? They talk about the nitty-gritty aspects of the session. 'Mistress So-and-So let me lick her tits and her pussy before she raped me with her strap-on,' that sort of thing. It's a nightmare. It's like the guys are in a contest to show one another what bad-ass masochists they are, not realizing they're creating an evidence trail and also, incentives for their compatriots to seek out and report on extreme behavior. It's a vicious circle that could end in disaster."

"It certainly sounds unsavory, but what does it have to do with you? You work far outside of that ecosystem."

"For now, Michael, for now. But that ecosystem is growing in size and importance. Have you checked out Twitter? It's a horror show. Clients whining about costs and services, and anyone and everyone can read it. This stuff used to be contained to a few places read only by our fellow freaks, but now it's getting broadcast to the world. This kind of visibility is only going to make things worse."

"Erika, I don't want to seem unsympathetic, but once again, I don't see how this impacts you."

"It hasn't, much, but I can see it coming . . . I had an old client from Boston find the gallery's Twitter account, and now he's emailed me. I haven't figured out a response yet, and maybe I say nothing, but it would be incredibly easy for him to be indiscreet and write some slobbering and public tweet that speaks of my dungeon."

"Do you really believe he'd do that?"

"I don't think it's likely, but let's say he gets a little drunk one night, and horny . . . these internet forums give clients the thrill of anonymity, but they give us sex workers tons of exposure. The future of these services is going to put us even more at risk."

"I tell my clients all the time that although we can't predict the future, we can anticipate it. What do you want to do to prepare?" Michael slipped into advisor mode.

"Close my dungeon. Not right away, and not for everybody—you'll always be welcome in my shackles—but I need to close it."

"Close it? Can we back up a bit? I hear you're worried about clients posting about you online, and that the internet will worsen the business. But is that what's driving your concerns? This feels sudden to me."

"My thinking just crystallized, and now I see the threat."

"Right. You're sensing that things have changed and you need to adapt. Is there something else?"

"Yes. Nothing gets past you. Edouard and I are exploring opening a second gallery in Geneva. This would give me a higher profile. I don't need people whispering about my dominatrix past every time they run into us at Art Basel."

"That makes more sense. Why do you think there would be speculation about your pro domme work?"

"I already get some. Cassidy, the blonde artist—do you remember her? She came right out and asked if I was a dominatrix."

"Well, you're very commanding. What did you tell her?"

"I told her it was a myth I'd cultivated because it helped me sell."

"The perfect answer. You don't need to be honest; you just need to be ready." Michael made it all seem so easy.

"Yes, but I don't like the ongoing dishonesty."

"Oh, Erika . . ." I could hear him sigh in exasperation. "People just aren't that curious. Tell them whatever you feel like, unless you're under oath. Your business is mythmaking and storytelling. It's rare for anyone to ask the follow-up question."

"I know, and that's certainly been my experience, but times are changing and the risks are shifting. Everybody is going to know everything they want . . . in an instant. The level of scrutiny that's going to be possible going forward . . . it's going to be staggering, and I need to put some distance between me and my dungeon. Can you help me do that?"

"Of course, Erika. Of course. But I need to challenge your underlying assumption, which is that you need to close shop."

"Got it. So, okay, I don't need to. *I want to.* Seriously. I need your help."

"Yes, of course I'll help. You've just caught me off guard. This seems sudden."

"Perhaps to you, Michael, but not to me. I've been thinking about this for a while. And then yesterday, I wound up talking to an FBI agent."

"In journalism, they'd call that 'burying the lede.' You spoke with an FBI agent? What were you discussing?"

"My dad. I got an email from my client, Jennifer Kowalczyk. He's using the name Jacob Grieg these days, and he reached out to her because he'd heard she was interested in getting a Basquiat."

"Ah. That's bad. You had no choice but to call the FBI. I wonder who else he's reached out to. She can't be alone among your clients. She just happens to be the one who gets the most press."

"Yep. That's our Jennifer." I had always been grateful to those clients who enthused about their purchases and who were happy to be interviewed, and it was upsetting how their good deed might put them in jeopardy.

"Have you touched base with any of your other high-profile clients? The ones who've been interviewed, that is?"

"Not yet. I thought it prudent just to hang back and wait for the FBI to tell me what to do. I gotta say, speaking with law enforcement gives me the hives. As I was chatting with the agent, I kept flashing back to when I was twelve and they raided the house. In any event, the agent who heads the art task force took the information and she seemed interested in the case. On the plus side, if anything happens, it should happen sooner rather than later. My dad wouldn't be lining up marks if he wasn't trying to get on with things."

"That makes sense. Is there anything you'd like me to do?"

"Just let me know if he reaches out to you. I have no idea who he's contacted, beyond Jennifer. But if he's called one person, he's called several. When he made his pitch to me, he showed me Polaroids of six or seven works, so there's an inventory to move."

"Yes, and he must be working with a team."

"That's what I told the FBI. This is a multimillion-dollar fraud, involving counterfeiters, money launderers, and who knows what else. It's a cornucopia of criminality. My dad just happens to be the front man. The really interesting people are the ones behind him."

"He's going to wind up back in prison." Michael's voice was flat.

"Probably. You'll help me find a decent criminal defense attorney when the time comes, right?" Having tattled on my father, I still wanted to help him.

"Of course. There's a talented young litigator at my firm who could be right for your father."

"You're the best, Michael. This is all so wearying. But it's also a signal. It's time to emphasize the art business, not the kink business. My dungeon's been a crutch. It's time for me to focus. Help me close shop, please. I don't want to be haphazard about this."

"Of course, so what time frame are you thinking?"

"Over the next six to nine months. Edouard and I are finalizing the details for Geneva, and once that project is underway, I won't have time for the dungeon, but I want to be intentional in how I wrap things up . . ."

"Right. No sudden moves, but the financial implications are significant. You'll have to curtail your spending."

"Yeah. No more raising my paddle at auctions . . . unless it's for a client, and not for me."

"Precisely. And maybe we should go through your collection and see if there are any pieces that no longer move you. That could buy you some flexibility." Michael paused. "The market is depressed, but you could get plenty for that Cecily Brown I gave you when you were still at Harvard. Don't feel like you need to keep it on my account."

"You kill me, Michael. I'm not desperate. And besides, I have only one Brown. I have two kidneys. I'd rather sell one of those."

"That would be illegal, Erika."

"Okay, my eggs then. They're legal and I have thousands of them. I can't sell something from my collection. I'd regret it for years."

"Indeed. So, tell me more about this Geneva business. Do you guys have terms yet?"

"No. But I've been looking at properties and there's one I like. It's in a fabulous location and it requires only a five-year commitment."

"Five years? That's barely a marriage."

"Exactly. And at least it's not ten. Edouard was proposing a ten-year lease."

"That man's not afraid of commitment. How refreshing. And how like you, to want to keep things more abbreviated." Michael chuckled. "What else does he want from you?"

"To be my plus one at Art Basel and Miami. Or maybe, given how much he buys, I'd be his . . . whatever."

"Darn. I'm usually your plus one in Miami." Michael's voice grew teasing.

"I know. It sucks." I dared not mention the time we had an escort overdose in his suite. "Would you consider FIAC in Paris instead?"

"If I must." Michael was just playing with me now. Who'd decline a kinky adventure in Paris? "I'm a creature of habit. I've been staying at the Lancaster for thirty years, and they give me a great rate on the Marlene Dietrich Suite. Would that be acceptable?"

"Absolutely. I think we could make do at the Lancaster."

"The suite even comes with a grand piano. Do you play?"

"No, Michael. Do you?"

"I learned as a child."

"You may want to practice. I'll be very upset if you can't play something for me. And you know how I am when I'm upset . . . I just want to hit something."

"Oh sure, threaten me with a good time." It was a relief that we were back to bantering.

"The Lancaster it is, but first, let me find out if their suites have four poster beds. Posters are nonnegotiable."

"You think of everything, Erika."

"I try. Art is in the details."

"Oh, and let me know if you'd like me to review your term sheet with Edouard. What he's proposing sounds like something with potential. But just know you're giving up a lot for whatever you'd be getting."

"I know, and I believe that Edouard knows that, too."

"So, I assume you two have gotten along like gangbusters?"

"He's a good guy, and we've gotten comfortable with each other. To my amazement, I look forward to his company."

"I'm happy for you. It sounds like a productive partnership." I listened for any hesitation or skepticism in Michael's voice, but I found none.

"We'll see. As you often tell me, a cup of coffee is not a certified check. But he's a serious guy. I don't see much upside to him in making idle promises."

"Nor do I. And back to your internet worries . . . if you think it would help, I know a crisis PR guy you could talk to, prophylactically. Michael Sitrick practices PR like a ninja. When his clients need him, his moves are quiet and fast, with no fingerprints left behind."

"He sounds great. Maybe I could use help crafting a few lines, just in case somebody says something?"

"Right. And just knowing you have him could be sufficient. I like having contingency plans in my back pocket for when my clients go rogue."

"If only we professionals didn't need clients, eh? But in the meantime, if you have any ideas on how to discreetly close up my basement, I'm all ears. I want Mistress Erika to fade away, until she's nothing but a distant memory."

"There will be a chorus of slaves lamenting her disappearance."

"Perhaps. But only if they keep those laments very quiet. If only I could figure out how to monetize my departure."

"Ah, now that's the Erika I know! Let's figure out how to make your retirement pay. Got it."

"You're the best, Michael. Help me find someone to take things over, just like how you found me for Madame Margot. That worked out well for everyone."

"Yes. Madame is busy living a life of leisure in Ibiza." We both sighed at the thought of her luxurious beach manse.

"Madame figured it out. Let's speak tomorrow."

"Yes, let's. Ciao!"

35

NAUGHTY MEN EVERYWHERE

Every day, I'd check my messages to see if there was something more from the FBI or about my father. Even as I wanted to keep my distance, I was desperate for news of what was going down. I spoke a couple of times with Special Agent Rigas, giving her background on my dad. I offered to help figure out some of the specifics of the showing, but it seemed like Rigas and her team had undertaken a few art stings in their day, and they didn't want or need advice from me. Perhaps they preferred to keep me in the dark, in case I tried to warn my father. After all, people are often conflicted about turning in a family member, and I was no different.

The business with my father was so unsettling that I even called my mother for advice. "Oh honey, your dad gave you no choice. He's always been blind to the impact he has on others. Think of what he did to me. To us."

"I know, Mom, but that was a long time ago."

"Have you read anything about pathological narcissism?" my mother continued. "Vegas is filled with them, and I believe your father is one, too. And, darling, they never change."

"Right, Mom. Well, the situation sucks, and I feel shitty."

"Of course you do, darling, and that's what he's counting on. He assumes you'll turn a blind eye, and he'll face no consequences. He never thinks about the consequences others will face or he wouldn't have stolen all that money in the eighties. We're just seeing more of the same."

"I guess you're right." My mother was not the most neutral observer of my dad's character, but there was no denying her logic. "Well, I'll keep you posted. And if you hear anything, let me know. I miss you, Mom."

"I miss you too, darling. Come to Vegas some weekend when Tomas isn't around and it'll be just us girls. We can go for massages; I still get an employee discount."

"We could go cocktailing."

"Yes, darling. Let's go cocktailing. I'd like that a lot. Hang in there. This nonsense with your dad will be over soon."

"Mom, I hope you're right. Because there's so much on pause until this Dad nonsense is behind me. I'm thinking of expanding the gallery."

"Oh darling, good for you. I'm so proud of what you've built. I talk about you all the time. Just remember, there's art and money here in Vegas, too. Maybe you could open an outpost here!"

"I'll keep that in mind. But it would be after I open one in Geneva."

"Whatever you say, darling. Love you!" And with that, my mother hung up the phone. I barely had time to collect my thoughts when my phone rang again. It was Josh. His voice was rushed and anxious. "You got another one of those emails."

"What emails are you talking about?" My brain was still processing my conversation with my mother. It hadn't advanced far enough to take on another crisis.

"You know"—Josh's voice slowed down and he paused for emphasis—"from that guy in *Boston*."

"Oh shit. Not another one." My heart sank. The foot freak was back. I'd tried ignoring his first email, but he had persisted. "Forward it to me, please."

I read it quickly, while Josh stayed with me on the line.

Dear Dr. Grieg,

I'm following up on my email of last week. I shall be in New York shortly, and if you are available, it would be my pleasure to take you to dinner. I have a reservation at Bar Masa for 8 p.m. on Tuesday. Would you be my guest? I feel badly about how things ended in Boston and I would like to make it up to you.

At Your Service,

Gary Hall
CFO Insightery

What do you think, Erika? Bar Masa is a tough table. He's probably had that reservation for months."

"Well, that just means his real dinner date bailed on him this week, and I'm his last-minute substitute."

"You're no one's substitute, Erika. How can you say such nonsense?" The tone had shifted from serious. Out of relief, Josh laughed, and so did I. "Maybe I could be your substitute. I've always wanted to go there. Each piece of sushi is supposed to be a work of art."

"Yes, they're exquisite. But I don't think Gary's your type, and I know you're not Gary's . . ."

"For the perfect piece of toro, I could fake it."

"You wouldn't be the first."

"I looked Gary up, Erika. His company went public a few years ago, and he's killing it. The guy's earning three million a year according to the 10-Ks."

"Since when are you reading 10-Ks, Josh?"

"Amy taught me. She's very smart on this stuff." Amy had a Harvard MBA. She knew how to read an income statement and sniff out wealth better than any truffle pig.

"No doubt. Amy's very smart about a lot of things, but it sure looks like I need to shut Gary down. I'm just not sure how. Any ideas?"

"Uh, no . . . tell him you've done all ten steps?" Josh started snickering.

"You mean all twelve steps, Josh." I couldn't resist correcting such an obvious error. If I were back in Chelsea, this error would entail a visit to my basement and a reckoning with my cane. Over the phone, I had to settle for sarcasm.

"Oh, yeah, right. What the fuck do I know about Alcoholics Anonymous?"

"Hmmm . . . we're reaching here." I appreciated his attempt at levity. Josh always knew how to make me laugh.

"Okay, so you could tell him you had a concussion, and you don't remember anything before 2002?"

I snorted. "Should I offer to show him my imaginary scar, too?"

"Is he into scars?"

"No, just feet."

"Then you offer to show him your scar and he won't take you up on it. How about you tell him you found God and now you're praying for him?"

"Oh boy . . . you're making me giggle too, even as I'm ready to tear my hair out."

"All joking aside, would you like me to write him on your behalf? A terse note from your male assistant could put him in his place."

It felt cowardly to have Josh address Gary. "Let me take care of this, but I have to say, Josh, you've been a real blessing these past few months. When I'm back, let me take you to Bar Masa."

"Now that sounds fantastic, but while we're splurging, I'd like a promotion, too. And a raise!"

"I'm working on it, Josh. If the world weren't crashing around us, I'd give you both in a heartbeat. Because let's face it, what would I do without you?"

"Beats me, Erika. But as you wish—you're on your own with Mr. Hall."

"Understood. In the meantime, I have a request." I had an idea, one that might confuse any of my old clients who might stumble upon the gallery's website going forward.

"Sure. What's on your mind?"

"Take down all the headshots of me on the site and replace them with general shots of the gallery."

"Will do. I'll make sure the site looks good and that you are vanished."

"Thanks. While I'm here in Geneva, I'll get some new shots taken . . . and I'm going to look a lot less like I did when I was in grad school."

"A new and improved Erika? How intriguing."

"Yes, something like that." It would require tracking down a talented colorist and a portrait photographer here in Geneva, but I had the time. "And one other thing, let's pause the tweeting. Tweeting's probably necessary in the long run, but in the short run, it's risky."

"The tweeting was all Amy's doing, and ever since she went AWOL, it's been quiet."

"Good. I don't think she's going to be doing much at the gallery going forward. But if you spot her about to tweet, stop her!"

"Deal. I'll throw myself in front of the keyboard." Josh paused, and we both savored such an absurd image. "Well boss, gotta go. But first, I'm going to think about toro and let my mouth water at the meal you won't be enjoying."

"Gary will have to find another pair of feet to go with him. Geesh, what am I going to say to this guy?"

"You'll think of something. You always do. Ciao, Erika."

Not wanting to disappoint Josh, or to let him see I wasn't the exceptional executive he imagined me to be, I sat down and replied to Gary.

> Dear Mr. Hall,
>
> Your message has caught me working in Geneva. As a consequence, I shall be unable to join you at Bar Masa. Your email has also caught me at a loss. My days as a grad student at Harvard were so intense they remain a blur. Regrettably, I cannot recall meeting you.
>
> All my best,
> Erika Grieg, PhD

I hoped it sounded polite yet firm, and like it didn't invite any further correspondence, because I really didn't care to speak with him again.

36

BASQUIATS AND BASEBALL BATS

The rhythm at Edouard's Geneva lair was more or less unchanged, except now my days included tasks related to my expanded footprint. I turned Boxler into my bitch and had him running around helping me evaluate possible architects and contractors. If this project was going to be a success, I wanted to minimize the likelihood of any surprising charges, because cost overruns are inevitable. There's always something expensive lurking behind drywall or plaster.

At least, in Geneva, the work would be undertaken by architects, builders and engineers. When I was equipping my first studio, I used slave labor. Before I knew better, I had a small crew help set up my dungeon. Sadly, I was more skillful with a cordless drill than the men were, which made my so-called slave labor very expensive because I had to do the bulk of the work myself. It was especially frustrating, because I couldn't even excoriate the so-called slaves, because they would have found that arousing, and they would have gotten humiliated for free. Lesson learned. From that day forward, I only dealt with professionals.

While checking my email one afternoon, I spotted a Google alert for "Basquiat forgery." I'd set it up when my father first proposed the deal, and finally, it had borne fruit. The email included a link to a *Newsday* story about a bust of a Queens garage. It read:

BASQUIATS AND BASEBALL BATS

The FBI has raided the Queens home of New York artist DB Rogers who is suspected of masterminding an art forgery ring of paintings and athletic memorabilia.

The alleged forgeries were sold as works by Jean-Michel Basquiat and Keith Haring. Mr. Rogers also sold baseball bats and gloves that he claimed had been signed by Lou Gehrig and Mickey Mantle.

The forgery ring has been active for several years and included multiple accomplices. Victims of the ring included galleries such as the Knopfler Gallery in New York, which acquired two supposed Harings at auction in 2007 for three million dollars.

Several accomplices have been arrested, with more arrests expected.

"Hey, Special Agent Rigas . . . it's Erika Grieg calling. I saw you just made some news."

"Great to hear from you, Ms. Grieg. And yes, we've been busy."

"I realize you might not be able to say much, but was this related to my father?" I tried to keep my voice neutral, even as my head was filled with angst.

"You are correct. I'm very limited in what I'm permitted to say, but let me express my gratitude. Your call was timely and helpful."

"Got it. Well, thanks." I felt an odd mix of shame and relief as I hung up the phone. What daughter wants to throw her dad to the police? But then again, what father wants to mix his daughter up in a forgery ring? It seemed like the problem had been solved, and I had maintained a protective distance from the drama. I was now free to return to New York, only the pull wasn't as strong as it had been a month ago. Geneva was growing on me, and I had Edouard to thank for that.

37

MAKEOVER FOR PRINCESS ERIKA

Whenever my phone rang, I worried. Although the bulk of the calls were from Josh or Michael, there was the possibility some journalist had connected my dad's criminal activity to me. It took a week, but my body stopped flinching to the beeps. My dad, when he went to show the Basquiats, had been the first member of the ring arrested. The prospect of spending his last good years in jail must have persuaded him to cooperate, because the subsequent arrests were all his doing.

It was the sensible and appropriate choice, to become a witness to the FBI—after all, witnesses get lighter sentences. It was also helpful to me, because the FBI was keeping his participation out of the press. The less said about him, the better it was for me.

Amy had calmed down, too. We were back to speaking every day, even as she was planning her own escape from the dungeon. In an effort to purge a billionaire beau from her system, she'd hooked up with some hot, vanilla guy. She sent me a photo of him, and I could not fault her taste. His hair was prematurely gray with sensual waves, his eyes a vivid blue, and the picture of him shirtless from some triathlon showed a perfectly toned body. The guy was a fucking masterpiece, and he sounded smitten. After her close call with Michael, I was just happy she'd gotten her mojo back, although secretly, I was hoping she'd struggle to find another gig. If Michael couldn't identify someone to take over my dungeon, I was going to offer it to Amy and do my best to persuade her to stay. She'd proven she could do the work, even if things had gone sideways during her tenure. My mind was already obsessed with Grieg Gallery Geneva.

It had been months since I last saw my favorite massage therapist in New York, so I treated myself to a spa day at the Four Seasons. Getting a lift into town in the Maybach made the visit even sweeter, but the goal was really to unknot my shoulders, which were still in a state of clench because of my father's problems. My other goal was a makeover. The less Erika Grieg of Geneva looked like Erika Grieg of Cambridge, the safer I'd feel while growing my profile and my business. It wouldn't be fair to Edouard if his investment blew up in his face because of some minor thing I could have fixed preemptively.

The handful of photos that exist of me in my dungeon gear all featured a dark-haired me. Admittedly, my face was partially obscured, but the dark hair had become a trademark. If I wanted to minimize the possibility of my two worlds merging on the stage at Davos, returning to the hair of my girlhood might help. Fortunately, Swiss colorists have a lot of experience with blonde hair, and the final results had the perfect mix of honey blonde highlights, and dirty blonde lowlights. It was a look that said beach and Bergdorf's, and it was perfect.

As soon as I was out of the salon chair at the Four Seasons, I sat for a couple of corporate headshots with the new 'do. The pics were promptly sent off to Josh to update the site. His response was immediate. "Who's the pretty lady? Should we start calling you Princess Erika?"

"That's what my dad calls me when he wants something." I had to catch my breath at the mention of "princess." Josh wasn't trying to trigger me, he was merely trying to make me laugh, so I did my best to sound amused. "Don't call me that unless you want a title, too."

"Like what? Duke . . . earl?" Josh paused. "No, how about duchess!"

"You got it, Duchess Josh of Chelsea."

"Oh, I like that. Anything more I can do for you, Erika?"

"Well, you'd let me know if there were calls from, say, the *New York Post* about my dad, right? Or really, if they called looking for me regarding anything."

"Of course!" I could hear the irritation in Josh's voice. Did I think he was a moron? "There's been nothing. *Are you expecting something?*"

"Not exactly. And frankly, it's better if they don't call, but I like being ready for these things. No one likes an ambush."

"No, of course not. So, how are things goin'? When ya comin' back?" Josh's voice had returned to its pointed yet playful style.

"Soon, I think. I have some things I need to square away here, but I'll be back in a week or two."

"Great. It's not the same without you. And quite frankly, Amy just drifts in and out, so it's lonely."

"Yeah, this is a wretched time."

"Mostly wretched, but with a few glimmers of hope. We've got a couple collectors circling, but they're on the fence. I think they'd buy if they got a little attention from you. Come on, boss, give them the full Erika."

"I'll call them."

"Great. And if there's any chance you'll be back before Christmas, that's our best hope. They've asked for you, and I've told them you'll be back soon."

"I don't have any specifics, date-wise, but I know there's a ton to do. There are Christmas presents on our walls, and they just need to find the right homes."

"Whatever it takes, boss. This has been a very quiet stretch, and we've all missed you."

"I've missed you, too, Josh. Here's to hoping the economy will improve soon."

"Yes. We all need a reprieve. And seriously, how much worse can it get?"

"Point taken. So, I've been thinking about how we can position ourselves and our artists for next year and beyond. But in the short term, darling, we just need to make some money."

"Yes ma'am. Princess Erika has spoken."

38

VACBED INTERRUPTUS

Edouard and I had a routine. We'd have an indulgent dinner, chat about our day, and then I'd pop him in the vacbed and let him marinate for a few hours. While he stewed, I'd visualize the possibility of talks at Davos and hobnobbing with Swiss billionaires.

I've always believed that the person with the least power in a relationship wasn't necessarily the dominant or the submissive; it was the person who wanted something the most. And I was in deep. I wanted the Geneva gallery, to speak at Davos, to immerse myself in the work of building an art empire. Was it his decency, his enthusiasm, or our shared passions? It was hard to pin down, but I'd caught feelings for Edouard.

I was immersed in my Geneva fantasy one night, when the phone in the dungeon rang. This was jarring—the phone had never rung before—and it took me a moment to register what had happened. It felt rude to include a phone in such a sacred space, but Edouard was not a frivolous guy. If he'd included a phone, it was because it was important. I put down my laptop and hustled over to the noise.

"Hello, Erika here. Can I help you?"

"Hello, it's Boxler. Please put Monsieur de Grenet on the line. It's important." Boxler spoke quickly and with urgency. I knew what I had to do.

"Okay, but it'll take a moment." I didn't want to describe the complications of releasing my captive from the vacbed, but it wasn't something that could happen on a moment's notice.

"Understood. I'll wait."

Releasing the vacuum was the easy part, waking up Edouard was trickier as he was in a deep trance. "Edouard . . . Edouard . . ." I placed my hand on his chest and felt his heart slowly beating beneath my fingers. Edouard's eyes opened, and his pupils changed to adjust to the light. "There's a call for you."

"Oh?" It took another moment before Edouard became fully alert and fully himself. "Please hand me the phone."

Edouard sat on the edge of the table, naked with the electrodes still clinging to his chest. He nodded as Boxler spoke. I could only see Edouard's reactions, but he seemed lighter with every word. His back straightened, and a smile formed on his face.

"Thanks for letting me know. It's much appreciated." He hung up and returned the phone to the counter.

"Good news?" I held my breath. If that wretched phone rang, there had to be a disaster.

"Yes, very good news. The last of my employees is out of Russia. Boxler wanted me to know as soon as the job was done."

"How fantastic." I exhaled and felt Edouard's relief. "This is one less worry for you." I pointed at the vacbed. "Would you like to go back in?"

"No, I'll just head upstairs. Perhaps I'll sleep like a normal person tonight." Edouard stretched and grabbed his robe.

"I'm rooting for you, Edouard. You've really grown on me." I didn't want to share to what extent he had. "But I have some news for you darling, you're anything but normal."

39

AN EXPLOSIVE EVENING

"The call that came in last night means I'm free." Edouard smiled broadly as we chatted in his living room. The Freud had been replaced by Cassidy's *Latex Hood*. It was odd, but not unpleasant, having my own face staring at me.

"Free to liberate yourself from your phone?" I didn't understand what he was getting at.

"No. Free to liberate myself from my house." Edouard gestured at the walls as his gaze swept the room.

"Seriously?" Edouard had stayed inside for two months, following the dictates of his security team. It was a relief they were persuaded Edouard could move about the city freely. "How fabulous, darling. How do you want to celebrate?"

"How does dinner at Hashimoto sound? It's not much to look at, but it has the best sushi in Geneva."

"Count me in. I hope there's some celebratory sake, too. Your jailbreak deserves a toast."

"Absolutely. The sake will flow freely tonight."

I was thrilled. Edouard practically vibrated at the prospect of getting out of the house, and I was eager for a change of scenery, too. The restaurant was low-key, so there was no point in getting all dressed up, but I thought Edouard deserved a treat, so I put on my tightest leather pants and a cream cashmere V-neck that allowed a glimpse of the red lace of my Eres bra if I leaned just the right way. It was cold out, so I threw on the gold-infused Fendi fur he'd gotten me when I first arrived and a cute pair of black Louboutin booties.

As usual, Edouard wore slim-fitting pants in a dark gray wool and a crisp white shirt. Although he wore a brown leather aviator-style jacket over top, he still looked every bit the careful banker. "You look good, Edouard." I said, as my thoughts veered to toro. "Now let's go eat something raw."

Edouard nodded as he grinned. "Yes, let's." He took my arm and guided me into the back of his Maybach, where he took the seat next to me. Up front was the driver and Max, a member of his security team. It was clear that although the situation had improved, the people around Edouard weren't completely relaxed.

As we approached the restaurant, located near Geneva's Old Town, we spotted groups of oddly dressed pedestrians. There were women wearing plain woolen coats with starched white collars and white caps on their heads. There were men dressed in metal breast-plates and shiny steel helmets, while others wore simple medieval jackets and felt hats. I spotted a couple of young men carrying drums. I tapped Max on the shoulder. "What's going on? Is there a Christmas market somewhere with costumes? Are they shooting a movie?"

"No. This is not for Christmas; this is for Escalade," Max replied.

Edouard slapped his forehead. "Of course. It's Escalade." He paused, while I furrowed my brow. "This is a very important day in Geneva's history."

"Oh? This seems out of place in such a sedate city." I was having difficulty reconciling the vast number of cosplaying locals with the Geneva I'd come to know.

Max chimed in, as he was the only person from Geneva in the car. "In 1602 Geneva defended itself from an invasion by the duke of Savoy. The duke's forces tried to climb the walls, but the citizens protected the city in very creative ways. One woman even threw hot soup."

I turned to Edouard. "Now that sounds positively kinky." Edouard shook his head, in mock exasperation.

Max continued, "There will be music, bonfires, lots of fun and dancing. The best part is the torchlight parade. It's a special night."

I turned to Edouard. "I don't want to push our luck, but this sounds wonderful. Do you think we could check things out after dinner?"

Edouard turned to Max. "What do you think?"

"Let me look into it."

"Fantastic. Now, let's get some dinner!"

Hashimoto Sushi was a small place. There were only a half dozen tables, and we were seated immediately in the most remote corner. Even though Edouard's security team was nearby, it felt outrageous to be out of Edouard's dining room, enjoying a meal among complete strangers.

Edouard was relaxed and playful, as he fed me a piece of unagi from his plate. I bit the morsel of eel hard, so that he could watch my teeth sinking into the flesh. "Now give me your uni."

"But that's my favorite, Erika." Edouard grabbed the sea urchin between his chopsticks. "But if you want my favorite, I'll give you my favorite." He presented me with a glistening mound of gold sea urchin, wrapped in delicate green nori. I opened my mouth wide with my teeth bared, like the shark in *Jaws*, as he deposited it on my tongue.

"Thank you for your sacrifice." Edouard gave me a half smile as he placed his hand on top of mine. I returned his smile and rotated my hand so that our fingers interlocked on the table. It felt oddly innocent, but also, welcome.

"I'd love to check out the festival, if you're game . . . and if Max says it's okay, of course." Edouard signaled for the bill and went to the vestibule, where Max was waiting. There was a quick conversation between the two men, then Edouard returned sporting an enormous grin.

"Let's see the fun." Edouard helped me with my jacket, and we went outside where a steady flow of people in Medieval costumes was moving toward Geneva's Old Town. The torchlights had been lit, and they cast a magical glow over the walls and cobblestone streets. The city flickered and pulsed. This time, I took Edouard's hand as we moved with the crowd toward the site of the defense of the city. Max kept a discreet distance, as we all proceeded toward the squads of men sporting colorful tunics and hats decorated with large plumes.

Edouard and I tucked in behind a squad of about thirty drummers, as they marched in unison, the feathers in their caps bobbing in time. A little farther down the street, there were men on horseback, carrying shields and spears. It was as if we'd landed in a Disney version of the Swiss Middle Ages.

"After so much time alone with you in your house, it feels crazy to be around so many people." I whispered to Edouard.

"It feels good. Geneva is rarely this exciting." Edouard picked up the pace; he was excited too.

As we rounded a corner and caught sight of a large gathering of people dressed in period clothes, there was an enormous blast. A shock wave made the street tremble and sent dust and debris flying. Car alarms began to blare. Startled, one of the horses threw his rider and took off downhill. Baffled, I stood in the middle of the street and stared at the man lying on the ground. I tried to understand what had happened as I began to move toward the fallen rider. Edouard jumped in front of me, pulling me off the street and against a stone wall. He stood in front of me, using his body to shield me from whatever was happening.

Where I'd been confused only moments earlier, I suddenly felt a moment of terror. Had we left the safety of the house prematurely? Just when we'd thought it was okay to get outside, we'd found ourselves in the middle of an explosion. My brain shot back to 2001, and the explosions that devastated New York. Had terrorists found Geneva? Was Swiss neutrality under attack?

I clutched at Edouard, as our hearts raced wildly through our winter coats. We stood pressed against the wall, shielded by the shadows, as we took stock of the moment. Edouard whispered to me, "We need to get out of here, fast. Follow me."

We inched forward, compressed against the wall, as people scattered. Edouard went first and I kept as close to him as I could. He knew the city far better than I, even though we were just heading back in the direction of the restaurant.

Racing from shadow to shadow, we traversed the block and hid in a gap between two buildings, with Edouard still shielding me with his body. The sirens were disorienting and frightening; the blaring car horns made things worse. There was another couple hiding with us, as we all tried to figure out what had happened.

Max ran over to us and said, "The car's over here," as he hustled us toward the waiting Maybach. The three of us dove inside. The driver did a quick U-turn and drove the wrong way on a one-way street toward Cologny and the safety of Edouard's home.

Max was on his phone, speaking in rapid French to someone, while Edouard and I sat wide-eyed in the back. I clutched his hand, doing my best not to let my nerves show. Max hung up and immediately turned around to speak with us. "It was just a cannon, boss. They fire them for the party. The police say one misfired."

"Ah, *mon Dieu*." Edouard muttered quietly.

"Oh, that's a little embarrassing. I was thinking it was terrorists, or something." I leaned into Edouard, who put his arm around my shoulder and pulled me into his chest.

"I thought so, too." Edouard didn't move for the twenty minutes of the car ride, as our deep breaths synced in the back seat, and our heart rates slowly returned to normal.

When we got back to the house, Edouard walked with me toward my room. As we approached the door, he stopped. "Back there, on the street, we got interrupted." He gently pulled me toward him, as he lifted my chin and put his lips on mine. His fingers caressed my cheeks and jawline, as my arms encircled his waist.

There's nothing like the feeling of danger to heighten the senses, and mine were still on overdrive. I drew Edouard to me, and enjoyed the feeling of his lips on mine, and our tongues tasting each other for the first time. It was hard not to consider the absurdity of the moment. After all, I'd had an extraordinarily intimate relationship with Edouard's body—he'd spent hours in my presence naked. This, however, was our first meaningful kiss.

"Come in." I opened the door, and Edouard stepped inside the room, where we kissed again, this time with ferocity. There were tongues exploring, teeth biting, hands undoing buttons and clothes falling onto the floor.

I stood before Edouard, wearing only my red bra and panties. He was already naked, as he reached over and stood behind me. Between kisses on my neck and shoulders, he slid the straps of the bra off my shoulders and with the other hand, he undid the hooks. His smooth technique made me smile. "You've done this before," I muttered.

"Once or twice, but it's been a while. I hope I remember what to do." Edouard gave me the same rakish grin he must have given scores of women in his wanton twenties and thirties.

"That makes two of us." I turned around and pulled him toward the bed. "But first, get down on your knees."

I sat on the edge of the bed as Edouard, his body lean and pale in the dim light from my bedside lamp, knelt between my legs and teasingly played with my lace panties. His fingers caressed my inner thighs while parting my legs slightly. He pressed his fingers firmly against the fabric between my legs, and then he paused.

"Do you need an invitation?" I looked down at him, amused and aroused by how he was drawing this out.

"No. I have one already. I'm just making sure you're ready." He looked up at me, expectantly. He'd inched his face closer to my pussy, so there was no mistaking where he was going. He didn't move until I nodded, and then he pulled the panties down to my ankles, and with a quick snap, he threw them aside.

I must confess that I felt a certain dread. Early in my career as a dominatrix, back when I didn't know any better, I'd taken on a couple of clients who wanted to do "oral servitude." This was the euphemism men employed to say they wanted their tongue to meet my pussy. Although I knew it was unequivocally illegal, since it was "sexual contact" for money, I was eager for the money and willing to give it a try. At the time, I figured how annoying could it be, to tie them down and then let some fellow lick me for a moment or two? I'd then move on to the more painful acts that moved me more. It was baffling, how much these guys were desperate to perform oral sex, when surely that was something they could do at home? Then again, what I discovered is that they were invariably talentless. Their tongues couldn't have found my clitoris if it had been lit up like a Christmas tree.

At first, I thought it was a game, that these submissives actually wanted to be punished for being such clods, but then I realized there'd been such a failure in basic sex ed that these guys had no clue. I could only take a few seconds of their poking around, their tongue licking at some part of my labia or my urethra, in a sad effort to find my clitoris, before I started giving a mini anatomy lesson—if only as a service to their future girlfriends or their wives.

"This is the labia majora" and I'd point. "This is the labia minora." I'd point again. "This is the vagina." "This is the clitoral hood," and then finally, when I was certain I had their full attention. "And this is the clitoris. But since you haven't shown any understanding of a woman's body, you'll never get to taste mine. You are not worthy of this."

Rebuking the guy for his pathetic performance worked on two levels. One, I could humiliate him, and a certain kind of gentleman thrills to those harsh words; and two, it gave me permission to pull my panties back up and move on to something less intimate. The games grew so wearying, that after the first few men who'd requested "oral servitude," I stopped seeing those clients altogether, and to my relief, they were replaceable with men who weren't seeking such an intimate form of service.

Fortunately, Edouard had no problems identifying the correct spots, and he had clearly paid attention to what worked on prior women because he inserted two fingers inside me, applying pressure upward on my G-spot, as he began to dance around my clit with his tongue.

Relaxed by his competence and his confidence, I lay back and let him get to work. Edouard was playful and patient. He'd lick a few times, switch to some gentle sucking, and wait for my nerves to get on fire. He had a knack, and it wasn't long before I used my legs to trap him in place, drawing him closer to my pussy, so he couldn't take such long pauses. It took only another minute, as my mind focused on the rhythmic stroking of his tongue, before I was ready.

"Put on a condom"—I pointed toward the nightstand, where I kept a small supply of condoms and other necessities—"and then fuck me."

Edouard said nothing as he followed my instructions, rolling the latex down over his erect shaft. He climbed on top as I wrapped my legs around his waist and closed my eyes to experience the sensations without any other distractions. Edouard then pushed inside me and happily did as I instructed. He found the pace I wanted and needed, and after only another minute, I felt the tremors of an orgasm happening. Edouard didn't let up. He, too, was in a heightened state. Needing more, I grabbed his ass and forced him in me as deeply as possible. I wanted to feel full, while my nerves were set ablaze.

I'd become sensitive and even a bit sore, so it was time to wrap things up. I whispered to Edouard, "It's your turn. Come for me." I opened my eyes, since this was now about Edouard's pleasure, and not my own. He looked focused and unusually handsome. His angular features had softened, and his eyes were full of lust and emotion. It occurred to me that I could get used to this perspective.

After a few gentle thrusts, his arms bracing his body over mine, Edouard increased his pace and then he was done. I held his lean, muscular body close to mine as he relaxed, leaving his cock inside. Once he was flaccid, I pulled my body farther onto the bed, and he joined me, his arm wrapped around my waist, as I lay naked atop the crisp linen sheets.

"Well, Edouard, your memory is excellent. You knew exactly what to do."

"Yes, I did recall what to do. Apart from our encounter with Viviana, it had been a while . . . I hope you enjoyed yourself, too."

"Yes, darling, I did. An orgasm is a strong hint I'm having a good time."

"Fantastic. I feel the same way." Edouard's voice was soft.

"For what it's worth, darling, I haven't been fucked properly in a while."

"What? That's not possible. Why are you denying yourself these pleasures?"

"Denying myself? Hardly. But I'm particular. Why do something if it isn't going to be great? Like, would you bother pouring a wine knowing it would be lackluster? You've had the best. Are you really going to be satisfied with whatever's on sale at your local supermarket?"

"I'm spoiled, so, no. Of course, we don't always know that a wine will disappoint. I'm willing to be surprised by the occasional, unfamiliar bottle."

"Sure, I like surprises, too. But I believe one of the costs of my sideline is I have developed a pretty good intuition about people and their, uh, sexual imagination." I was feeling confessional and cozy. I wanted Edouard to understand me better. "This isn't something I like to talk about, because unless something about them says they are likely to be exceptional, my libido can't be bothered. It doesn't get revved up easily, which means it gets revved up rarely."

"Your poor libido." Edouard shook his head as he stroked my hair.

"Yes! My poor libido. It appreciates the Magic Wand. Why bother with a human when a machine can vibrate at a hundred hertz?"

"Oh, the horror." Edouard brought his hand to his mouth in mock terror. "You say such cruel things! Humans will never be replaced by machines, and this human was only too happy to be of service."

"I hope you're right about those machines. Some days, I'm not sure. But what I am sure of is that the human touch—your touch— was just what the doctor ordered and just what this doctor needed."

"Well, I'm delighted your libido got revved up and then decided to come out and play."

"Likewise. I must say, you were amazing this evening. On the street, when things got crazy . . . you were a badass."

Edouard lay back and grinned.

"Have you taken one of those executive self-defense classes, or something?" I continued. "You never lost your cool. You knew exactly what to do."

"Well, I wasn't that smart. I didn't recognize the threat as merely a malfunctioning cannon."

"Neither did I. How could you?"

"I recognized there'd been an explosion and that was an invitation to get the hell away."

"Absolutely. But you knew what to do, darling. It was impressive." I'd been frightened and he'd been calm.

"I spent a year in the army as a young man. They train you hard for moments like these."

"You were in the army? I had no idea." I was learning more and more about my host. It shocked me to realize there were these basic details that remained unknown. It shocked me further that I wanted to know them.

"It was obligatory. But I was a very good soldier."

"I bet you looked dashing in your uniform. Are there pictures?"

"Somewhere . . . but I must confess, I felt frightened, too. I was responsible for putting you in the middle of something dangerous, and I was worried you'd never forgive me." Edouard held me closer, as he gave my shoulders a squeeze.

"I was worried you'd blame me! It was my idea that we explore the festival." I squeezed him hard in return.

"Oh, I'd never blame you. How could I?" His fingers caressed the side of my face as he kissed my lips again.

"I don't know, but it was thrilling seeing you be so brave and bold. It was a real turn-on." I nestled back into his chest, my fingers playing with the stray dark hairs. "You didn't set up the explosion, did you?"

"If I'd known the effect it would have on you, I might have tried . . . but no, it happened spontaneously."

"Got it. Well, it was quite the icebreaker. I'm seeing sides of you I've never seen before. And I like them. Show me more."

"I'd like to see every side of you, too, Erika Grieg. When will you be coming back to Geneva?"

"As you and everyone else have told me, 'Nothing gets done between Christmas and New Year's.' Unfortunately, I need to head back to New York in a couple of days, because things sound a little crazy at the gallery. There might even be a collector or two ready to buy. But afterward, I'll be back. I don't want you getting into any trouble without me."

"Of course. You've been gone awhile. And no, I won't get in any trouble without you."

"What do things look like at your end?"

"At my end, now that I can leave this fucking house, I have a few appointments scheduled, but the plan is to return to the office—next week, even. My employees aren't as productive when I'm in home confinement."

"No doubt. You must show your people your face as you flex your muscles . . . make them snap to attention!"

"Precisely. Although no one snaps very hard, these days. But at least they look up from their laptops when I'm around."

"Oh, I'm sure they keep an eye on you. I'm enjoying *my* view." My fingers caressed his chest as I nuzzled his neck.

Edouard let out a quiet chuckle, as he changed the subject back to our project. "The contracts for the gallery should be ready for your signature when you get back. And in case you hadn't noticed, I'd like to do this again, and again, and again."

"So would I," I said, and I meant it. He was excellent company, upright and prone. I'd never had a relationship progress like this one, but it felt comfortable and unlikely to explode in my face. Past relationships had ended badly. I'd feel hemmed in, or he'd feel insecure. This one seemed different. "I'm not sure what we have here—it defies easy description—but I really like being with you. It feels reckless to admit it, even. That acknowledging someone is important to me makes me vulnerable. And I really don't like being vulnerable."

"I feel the same way. I was worried you'd come to think of me as someone who just . . ." Edouard gestured with his hands, pushing them flat together, reminiscent of the two latex sheets in a vacbed.

"No. Don't even think about it. The latex business is just a small part of what we do and what we like. There's so much more to it than that." Edouard then pulled me up his body and began kissing my lips and neck again.

40

DOUBTS CREEPING IN

Although everything was progressing smoothly, every day, my conspiratorial brain looked from Boxler to Edouard to see if there was a hint that the gallery project was just a flight of fancy or some scheme to trap me in Geneva. As I grew more and more attached to Edouard and to the prospect of expansion, I looked hard for evidence that something had gone wrong. After the debacle with my father, it had become a challenge for me to believe that Edouard was for real.

I selected a space. I met with an architect, and together we had meetings with my future landlord. I ran around Geneva—once even with Edouard—as we finalized the details of the deal. Everything was progressing in a way that felt sensible and comfortable.

Our term sheet had all the elements I wanted—yearly disbursements, so I wouldn't have to ask for money. The up-front costs to establish the physical gallery would be taken care of as well. We'd all shaken hands, it was just a question of signing the contracts and organizing the funds. While Edouard had local counsel, he wanted to have this particular contract reviewed by a lawyer with expertise in the art market, and unfortunately, that gentleman was busy.

Wary of the delay and yearning for more certainty, I called Michael. "So, Edouard wants the final contract done by Wilhelm Arden. Arden says he's tied up in some case and won't be up for air until mid-January, but I've heard he's on the slopes. I don't understand why he can't wrap up this small deal. Is this cool?"

"We're in mid-December, now. What's one month, Erika? Realistically, nothing gets done during the holidays. Everybody's in St. Bart's. *Even this year.*"

"I dunno, darling. I just hate this state of limbo. I'd like things locked down, so that I can truly make plans. Won't just about any lawyer do? This is small."

"Arden seems like a good choice to me. He's Swiss. He does lots of those Art Basel deals. Getting onto his radar seems sound. In my opinion, Edouard's being strategic. Are you worried Edouard's going to back out?"

"He hasn't said anything along those lines. It's just me. I hate feeling powerless."

"Relax, Erika. This isn't personal. Maybe you need to put a little distance between yourself and the deal." Michael let out a long sigh, as he continued. "I see this all the time. It's the biggest thing in the client's head, but for us lawyers, it's just another task."

"Okay . . . okay . . . I won't say anything to Edouard about the timing."

"No, don't. By the way, I like the term sheet you sent. It feels very fair. I like how he does business, even if it will limit our fun."

"Thanks, Michael. Well, given your advice of putting some distance between myself and the deal, maybe I should head back to Chelsea in a few days. With my dad out of the picture, it finally feels safe."

"Yes, it's been a couple of weeks since the ring got busted. If there was going to be a problem, it probably would have happened by now."

"That's what I'm thinking, too. Also, I'm worried about Josh and Amy; I just want to make sure everyone is squared away. And once I'm back, maybe we can plan something?"

"You've made my day so much better. Let me know possible dates, and I'll be there. After all, nothing gets done over the holidays, so I'll have a little more free time than usual. My cardiologist wants me working out with a physical therapist. Surely, a visit to your place counts?"

"Michael, I hate to break it to you, but I don't offer light workouts."

"Forgive me, Erika. Just don't put me back in the hospital. Okay?"

"Michael, we'll get you back up to snuff in no time. You're just going to be wearing a heart rate monitor the whole time we're playing. They're quite interesting and they let me be incredibly precise. The real-time feedback is a game changer."

"Let me be your guinea pig."

"You are the best lab rat this girl could ask for."

"Dr. Grieg. I shall present myself for study as soon as you're back."

"Thank you. We have some very important science to conduct. Your body will be sacrificed for the good of humankind. But be prepared, these experiments could be excruciating. We'll speak soon." And with that, I hung up the phone and chuckled. Michael adored my mad scientist persona, and who was I to deny him the opportunity to donate his body to science, even if he'd donated his body to science dozens of times in my presence.

41

HOT FOR SCHIELE

"When do you think you'll be back in Geneva?" Edouard sipped some coffee, as we discussed my Christmas plans.

"I have a lot to do. I might even persuade a few collectors to take the plunge. As you can imagine, there are some stray Christmas trees needing gifts beneath them."

"So true. Well, it's going to be quiet here without you."

"It's going to be odd for me, too. I'm going to miss you, darling. Shall we plan on the second week in January? That should give the lawyers time to metabolize whatever it is they're up to regarding our Geneva adventure, and it should give me time to make sure things are solid in Chelsea."

"Perfect. I like knowing I'm in your calendar. And by the way, I have an early Christmas present for you."

"Really?" I was taken aback. I hadn't found anything suitable as a gift for Edouard, and this made me look embarrassingly empty-handed.

"Yes," Edouard replied simply. "I hope you like it. Of course, it's already in your possession."

"What are you talking about?" Now I was confused. What did I possess of Edouard's?

"The Schiele. I want you to have it." He was referring to the Egon Schiele watercolor of a woman, her ass looking red from a beating, which had been hanging in my room for weeks.

"Oh my . . . she's magnificent. I've loved admiring her."

"Wonderful. Then she's in the right hands."

"I don't want to part with her when I go back to Chelsea, so I'm going to take her with me."

"As you wish. Just know that you, and she, have a place here whenever you want it. And I hope you'll want it often."

"Absolutely. I'm already looking forward to Geneva in January . . . and to your company." I wasn't sure what to call him. Was he my lover? My patron? My business partner? My friend? All of the above? I settled on something more general. "You're an extraordinary gentleman, Edouard."

"Thank you. Well, I'm glad that's settled. When will you be flying back to New York? Boxler will make the necessary arrangements once you've picked your dates."

"You've been exceptional. I feel blessed. Thank you for everything." I paused and closed my calendar. "I'll let Boxler know when I'm leaving and also when I'm returning."

Edouard then finished his coffee and retreated to his office. I retreated to my suite and to the Schiele, which I slid out of its frame. I set up the desk in my suite with acid-free tissue paper, glassine paper and cardboard that Boxler had procured for me. The Schiele wound up wrapped in protective papers and sandwiched between two pieces of cardboard. It would be safe in transit.

After my experience with my father and the faux-Basquiats, I wanted to have a friend who's an expert in Schiele's works look at it. It felt authentic to me, but she was the pro. Even though I loathed sharing my new obsession with anyone, I wanted the certainty that came with such an evaluation.

As I was holding up the wrapped Schiele, it dawned on me it would fit nicely tucked into the back of the butterfly Hirst painting Edouard had given me when I first arrived in Geneva, the very painting he'd used to entice me to his place. There was a delicious symmetry to the two works, and it pleased me knowing they'd both be traveling with me.

With the Schiele nestled up against the Hirst, when I returned to the US and went through customs, no one would even know the watercolor was there. As I'd learned years before, if they don't know you have it, they can't take it from you. It seemed almost fitting that the butterfly Hirst would protect the delicate Schiele.

42
HALF TRAP, HALF SAFETY NET

While I was flying back to New York, my thoughts kept returning to Edouard, and I found myself grinning whenever the flight attendant asked me if I wanted something. I really had caught feelings for the guy. I'd spent more time with him these past months than I had spent with anyone in years. I thought of great white sharks, who are usually solitary, but every now and then a couple forms. They swim and hunt together for years. Could this be Edouard and me? Could we enjoy a future together? The prospect appealed to me, especially since his Geneva gallery proposal could change my life. Frankly, I was ready to move out of the dungeon and into the daylight. Is this what love felt like? I had no idea.

When I got back to the gallery and my apartment, I found Amy getting organized. She was moving in with her new beau, having ended things with Dan the billionaire. She was giddy with excitement as we spoke in my living room.

At one point, she asked to see the Hirst. I made a big show of donning gloves before extracting the painting from its egg foam and

Kraft paper coverings. Without touching the Schiele in the back, I placed the Hirst on a ledge and watched Amy's face. She was clearly baffled by the work, because let's face it, it was just a few iridescent butterflies and some glass beads, glued to a black background. She'd spent enough time in my gallery that she knew enough to be underwhelmed, but she never let on. Since landing in my dungeon, Amy had acquired a game face, and it never cracked, not even when I asked her, "Spectacular, isn't it?"

Amy smiled pleasantly as she nodded. "Very nice, you earned it. Something that significant should be enjoyed all the time."

"That's how I feel, too. We should all make pleasure a priority." Thinking ahead to when I would transition to the Geneva Gallery, I wanted to keep Amy around and doing sessions, even though I didn't think she was interested. "If you ever want some extra cash or a few bonus thrills, let me know. I've spoken to your clients, and they'll be pining for you."

"Thanks, but I'm retired from the arena. Amy is back to doing her own thing. Don't get me wrong, I'm grateful for the opportunity, but it wasn't my cup of tea. The danger to them and to me seemed too daunting."

Even as I was disappointed by her firm no, I could respect her limits. "You don't need to explain. It's not for everyone." But one thing I'd learned over the years from working in the sex industry is that people leave it all the time, but often, they return. The business is half trap, half safety net. The work is there when and if you need it; it was just a matter of putting out your shingle and putting on the clothes. A sudden job loss or a failed relationship, and Amy might need the work again to regain her financial footing. It happens all the time. "The offer stands, if the urge strikes."

I'd need to find someone else to slide into my client's lives if I wanted any hope of monetizing this extremely ephemeral asset.

43

THE WINDOW

Josh had gone home, so I was alone in the gallery. It was one of those peaceful afternoons and I was relishing the prospect of that first show in Geneva. My initial instinct had been to go exotic, but the more I played with the idea, the more I decided to go with the familiar. I'd curate a show about young American artists, like Cassidy and her fetish works, giving the artists I already represented a second shot in a new market. As I was figuring out whom to invite, my doorbell rang. I raised my head from the table, where Polaroids of dozens of works were laid out, and was surprised to see Michael standing on the snowy sidewalk as he rapped loudly on the glass.

I unlocked the door and Michael rushed inside, shaking the snow off his shoulders. "Hey, Michael, great to see you. I was just going over a first pass for a possible show in Geneva. What brings you here?"

"You haven't heard?" He took off his snow-covered hat and clutched it to his chest.

"No. What haven't I heard? I've been here all afternoon, working."

"Let's go into your office." Michael was leaving a trail of flakes behind him, as he ushered me into my personal space. There was urgency in his posture—his shoulders leaned forward, and his mouth was set into a straight line. He motioned at the couch. "Sit."

I followed his direction and sat on the leather couch, all the while looking up at him. He inhaled deeply. "There's no good way to say this, Erika. Edouard is dead." His voice was quiet, his breathing audible.

"What? How?" I was astonished and horrified. Edouard and I had made plans. He was backing me. I adored him. I couldn't believe what Michael had said, especially since Edouard was so young and healthy. I'd witnessed how hard he ran on his treadmill. He'd do ten kilometers in only forty minutes; the guy was fit.

"Yes." Michael's face was grim. "He had a meeting this afternoon at the Hotel Nouvelle Époque and he fell out a window."

"That's crazy. Nobody just falls out a window." I sat there even more stupefied and confused. "The guy barely left his house for two months. The first time he left was last week, when we went out to celebrate one of his deals." I struggled to get my head around how someone could go from housebound to out a hotel window in the space of ten days.

"Was this a Russian deal?" asked Michael. He stared at me as he rubbed his chin.

"Yes. He'd been the victim of theft. Can you believe someone tried to steal one of his companies? In any event, he'd written that particular investment off. When I left him, he'd just gotten word all his employees were safe, and so he wasn't stuck by the phone any longer." I remembered the sense of relief we'd all felt once that dungeon phone had rung. "Things had gotten better. We even went out for sushi. It was his first time out of the house since the fall."

Michael flicked some invisible dust off his lap. "Perhaps he didn't want to alarm you, but he clearly wasn't staying at home just to be close to the phone. There were threats against his life."

"He told me that, but he also said threats were common and of no concern." I paused, while thinking through the possibilities. "Fuck. He lied to me . . . or maybe he didn't know?"

"Crossing oligarchs is a dangerous business, and they hold grudges. My investigator contacted Interpol, who said the only fingerprints in the room were Edouard's, but that's typical of the work of certain crime syndicates. It's not clear who Edouard upset, but it was clearly someone tight with Putin. You can't defenestrate someone successfully without a lot of juice."

"Shit, I feel so stupid and sad . . . this is all so unreal." My breathing was quickly becoming ragged.

"I'm so sorry. I know how close you two were." In front of him, I was feeling smaller and more ridiculous by the minute, even as sadness and rage began to roil inside me. Michael continued. "Is there anything I can do for you? Would you like me to stay with you for a little while?" Michael unbuttoned his coat and sat next to me on the leather sofa.

The sincerity of Michael's concern touched me, and then the reality of the situation hit me. All my plans and dreams were for naught. That there'd be no Geneva gallery was the least of my concerns. I had allowed myself to get close to Edouard, and I had gotten drawn into a mutual dream for the future. Was it love? Yes. But it was even more than that. He was someone I admired and trusted, and someone who felt the same about me. There were complementary needs and gifts, and we had both succumbed to their potential.

Michael moved closer to me on the sofa and held my shoulders as I shook. My sobs were noisy and embarrassing. For a moment, I worried if the crying might seem excessive, that my grief might seem feigned or insincere. Fortunately, I was alone with the only other man who'd cared for me in such consistent and meaningful ways. My self-consciousness evaporated as I buried my head in his winter coat and muffled myself with his chest.

We sat rooted on the couch for several minutes, with Michael saying nothing as he stroked my hair and held me tight. His comforting touch—rhythmic and consistent—reminded me of all the times I'd soothed my clients when they were wracked with sadness, pain or fear. Absent-mindedly, I wondered if Michael had picked up that technique from me.

As the shock subsided, the contours of Edouard's circumstances came into focus, and I wanted to understand what I had missed when I had been with him. "How do you know about this?" I asked Michael, baffled that he'd know about a Geneva window.

"My firm represents Jan Bakker. He's also faced threats from the Russians. He forwarded us the alert from Interpol. I rushed over here as soon as I saw it."

"Ah. Well, I'm glad you did. Thank you."

"Yes, I didn't want you seeing it on the news or reading about it tomorrow. I wanted to make sure you're all right."

I looked up at him. "Yeah, I'll be all right. But poor Edouard." I paused, unsure if I wanted to know more. "Did the alert say anything about what happened *before* the window? Like, were there unrelated injuries?"

"There was nothing else in the alert. But for what it's worth, I suspect he didn't have any warning. I doubt he suffered."

It was all so horrible, I started to cry again. "That poor man. He was getting ready to live again. I even have a flight booked for two weeks from now, because *we had plans.*"

"I know . . . I know . . . it's awful."

"We had a space picked out. We had booked a suite at the Trois Rois for Art Basel, even . . . oh god, this all sounds so silly and shallow. But I was looking forward to all of it. Including his company."

"I'm sorry, Erika. I know he was someone special."

"Yeah, he was a straight shooter and a fine man. He deserved better."

"Indeed. Is there something I can do for you? Maybe not right away, but once you've caught your breath?"

"I'll let you know. In the meantime, could you help me gather up these Polaroids? I won't be curating any shows in Geneva anytime soon, so we can put these away." The symbolism pained me, so I didn't budge from the couch. Michael gathered the photos and made a stack of them that he placed on the far corner of my desk. My eyes were still filled with tears.

"Is there anything else?"

"Not unless you can think of what else I should be doing with my life. I sure know how to pick men, don't I?"

"Your taste is excellent." Michael cocked his head to the side. "Your luck is another matter. Can I walk you upstairs? Maybe a nap would suit you?"

"Yeah. Maybe that would help." Michael guided me up to my apartment and waited as I took off my black pantsuit and put on a pair of black pajamas. He then tucked me into my bed, as if I were a child with a fever. With a gentle pat of the covers at my feet, he signaled he was leaving.

Alone in my apartment, I stared at the walls, fluffed the pillows, tossed and turned. For hours, I remained in a state of limbo, stuck in the warmth of my bed but aching throughout my body. I grieved for Edouard while imagining him next to me. And then I hated myself while I grieved for the life I thought had been imminent. For two days, I stayed in bed, ignoring my phone and disregarding the voices coming from the ground floor. Josh and Amy had both climbed my stairs, but I sent them away. I was too awash in pity and feeling too much regret for all the things I should have said to Edouard while he was still alive.

It dawned on me that I'd held back because I was afraid if Edouard knew how deeply I wanted him and what he was offering,

I'd seem weak. It was a folly. Nobody needs to be strong all the time. Nobody needs to be in charge at every moment, and yet that instinct had clouded my judgment. I often told submissives it requires strength to be vulnerable, and only the boldest let others in to help realize their fantasies. Somehow, I'd forgotten that lesson for myself. I had spent so much time searching for a sign that Edouard was like all those other men who made false promises, that I had ignored how he had always been committed and true to his word.

44

SYMBIOSIS FOR THE BOLD

After three days in isolation, I showered, dressed and went downstairs. There was only so much grief I could take. A familiar state of rage was starting to emerge, but that was pointless, too. Who was I supposed to be angry at? I asked Josh for the names of the gallery clients who were on the fence. I retreated to my apartment and returned to bed, only this time my phone was turned on. Perhaps, with a little luck, I could close a couple of deals before Christmas.

While I lay tucked beneath my duvet, it dawned on me there was another way to squelch my sadness. I had debts to pay, payroll to cover, and new plans to establish. It took me a minute, but I found a number that hadn't been used in years. "Hi, is this Gary Hall?"

"Yes, you got him." Gary's voice had an authority and a confidence I had never heard from him before. He'd come a long way since he'd last groveled at my feet.

"It's Erika Grieg from the Grieg Gallery in New York. Is this a good time? I got your emails." I tried to purr into the phone.

"Erika? I can't believe it's you! And yes, this is a good time. Your last message made it sound like you didn't remember much about Boston." Gary sounded enthusiastic, excited and oblivious to my ambivalence.

"Oh, I remember it all right. I remember you very fondly." I paused for a moment to collect my thoughts. The call was going better than anticipated. I had almost forgotten about Edouard for a few seconds. "Congratulations, by the way, on your IPO. It must feel great not to be at a start-up any longer, and to be the founder of such a significant company."

"Thanks. Yeah. I'm really proud of our team and what we do for our clients. It was hard at first, but business is strong." Gary's sentences sounded practiced but true.

"There aren't many executives who can say that at the moment. It's a credit to you. But now that you're at a public company with the SEC breathing down your neck, it behooves us to make sure what we enjoy remains under wraps. I'd like to send you a mutual NDA."

"A nondisclosure agreement?" Gary inhaled while my mind drifted to the review he'd written about me years before. Was he still a blabbermouth, or did he want to guard his own privacy as much as I wanted to protect mine? His answer was a relief. "Ab-so-fucking-lutely, Erika. You're the best. You've always been the best. I still feel bad about that stuff in Cambridge."

"It's been a long time, and we're both older and wiser now. But you scared me." It wasn't a sign of weakness to share that I'd been frightened, I decided. Rather, it was a sign of strength. "I didn't want my plans derailed by accident. Just like I'm sure you don't want your ambitions to go off track."

"We've both learned a lot—and accomplished a lot—in the past decade. So . . . I'll sign it and then I'd like to know more about what's keeping you busy."

"I was hoping you'd say that, Gary. We're both different people now, with more responsibilities."

"Indeed. I visited your gallery the last time I was in New York. I was sorry not to see you, but that Cassidy Smith's work is stimulating. I may need to pick up a painting or two the next time I'm in town."

"I bet I know which of the works got you hot and bothered, too. Tell me, was it the close-up of the Cuban-heeled stockings? That back seam goes up those legs forever."

Gary exhaled loudly. "You *do* remember me. But just to be clear, it was the reinforced toe that grabbed me."

"Of course. Your taste in art is excellent. That particular work is one of my favorites. It would look amazing in your bedroom. Who knows what it might inspire?"

"You've still got it, Erika. You've still got it."

"Don't sound so surprised, Gary. My passion is matching exceptional people with what excites them. Art is one of the best ways to arouse emotion and desire. You should see the look I get when I put a little red dot next to a painting. It means I've connected someone with something they crave."

"But art isn't the only way." Gary's voice became low and husky. I imagined his mind drifting back to my dungeon in Cambridge.

"No, of course not. People are complicated, and so is desire."

Gary was silent for a moment, before he spoke. "I'd like to see that look of yours again. We shared some good times."

"Indeed, we did. Let's make plans once we get this tedious bit of paperwork out of the way. I think you'll be astonished by what's lurking in the darkest corners of my gallery."

"No doubt. Please show me all of it. And by the way, thanks for calling. I'm glad we've reconnected."

"Me too. Check your email and get back to me soon." I could imagine Gary filling the gap in my roster. He was pleasant. His foot fetish was easily addressed. He could afford my services, and he seemed eager. I could almost forgive his stupidity of years ago, although I certainly wouldn't forget it. Perhaps my financial situation wasn't as fraught as I had feared?

After hanging up on Gary, I called a more familiar number.

"Hi, Dan? Have I caught you at a good time?" Dan had been one of my few clients to emerge from the financial crisis in better shape than when it started. Professionally, he was a ghoul, feasting off the carcasses of failed companies. Amy had been turned on by his business acumen and his billions, and they'd had a fling. But that was over, and it had been weeks, I guessed, since he'd last explored his fetish for bondage. Maybe Amy hadn't ruined him? If I could get him back into the fold, I could return to some semblance of normal in New York. Certainly, there were risks in keeping my dungeon going, but they were manageable. The more I thought about it, being afraid of a few tweets was ridiculous. In the past month, I'd faced far worse.

"Erika, so great to hear your voice. How was Geneva?"

"Productive, but I'm back now and we have lots to catch up on."

"Why yes, we do. I was worried you were going to stay in Switzerland, eating chocolates and fondue."

"Those are tempting possibilities, and I did go blonde over there."

"Seriously? You're blonde now?"

"Yes. I wanted to warn you."

"Astonishing. So, no to fondue, yes to blonde hair. Got it."

"What can I say, darling? Chocolates and fondue are not as tempting as what's on offer here." I paused, wondering if I was about to signal that I wanted something more than Dan did, which would put the power in his hands. And yet I asked anyway, because perhaps I did want something more. "I have a question for you."

"Oh? Fire away."

"Did Amy cure you? Or are you ready to get tied up in knots again?"

"I am incurable. You should know that. And I'm so ready to get tied up in knots. What can I say, things are stressful and your knots might get my mind off my latest project."

"We're in the same boat, then. I had the most horrendous week, and I need to take it out on someone. Could that someone be you?"

"Like, tonight? You're never available the same day." Had he felt my need? I'd never proposed a session before.

"Tonight's different. If you're available and amenable, of course." I'd do what I'd always done when confronted by an obstacle or a crisis, I'd get my hands dirty and get to work. If it meant showing an intimate that I wanted or needed something, why deny the truth? It was symbiosis. I needed my clients just as much as they needed me . . . and sometimes, even more.

"Deal. I'll be right over."

"Perfect. You know what to do . . . just call me when you're making the turn onto Twenty-Third, and I'll open the door for you. And when some blonde locks you to the rack and turns out the lights, just know that she's probably me."

"Will do." Dan laughed. "I'm so glad you're back. I've missed our time together." I wasn't going to tell him how three hours sitting in the darkness while he strained against his bonds would help me out financially. But more importantly, it would tune out my sadness and uncertainty.

I might not be able to expand right away, but that Davos dream was now firmly in my head. I needed to find a way to realize it, or some version of it. A first step could be a TED Talk or a panel at South by Southwest. I'd been stalled, and it was time to take on more. Edouard had planted the seed, and by manifesting this dream I would honor him. He deserved so much more than fate had given him, and it was a way to keep him close to my heart. Edouard had made me feel like the person I wanted to be.

"Thanks, darling. I've missed it too. Now roust your driver and get over here. Pronto. The longer I wait, the worse you'll suffer." And I meant it, but for reasons I couldn't explain to the man.

"Deal. See you shortly, Erika." Dan sounded happy and eager, oblivious to the darkness in my head, thinking only of the darkness of my dungeon. And that was as it should be. Whether as a spanker of asses or as a peddler of art, my work was about helping people to express and explore their desires. Sometimes it involved misery, but often it involved ecstasy. In my basement, I would push the buttons to their psyches. Dan's triggers were different from Gary's, Edouard's or Michael's, but they all came to me to realize whatever put a lump in their throat.

"Indeed, Dan. See you soon." And that was how I preferred it. I would see them at their most bold and eager, and they'd see me at my most bold and ascendant.

ACKNOWLEDGMENTS

Although *Bold Strokes* is a work of fiction, it is a deeply reported novel. Writing about the life and work of an elite dominatrix required the cooperation and assistance of some of the most successful women in the business. It was a privilege to meet and observe them while they practiced their magic, including Eva Oh, Lady Bellatrix, Midori, Alicia Zadig, Jo Weldon, Simone Justice, Sarah Valmont, Adreena Angela, Amanda Wildefyre, Anna Rose, Ariel Anderssen, Dia Dynasty, Mistress Diamond Blue, Freya Fey, Inanna Justice, Isabella Sinclaire, Justine Cross, Kasia Urbaniak, Domina M, Mistress Malissia, Marie Sauvage, Natasha Strange, Nookie, Lady Petra, Madame Rose, Mistress Salem, Stella Sol, Stephanie Locke, Sybil Fury, Syn Ariad, Tara Indiana, Mistress Troy, Troy Orleans, Goddess Venyx, and Victoria Rage. Their professional example, bravery, and personal encouragement kept me going after the publication of *Edge Play*. I remain indebted to Ilsa Strix, who inspired the character of Erika Grieg.

There were also many men from the demimonde who were important to this novel. Eric Paradis showed me around the fetish scene in Montreal. Because of Gérard Musy and Tim Woodward, I've been inspired by gorgeous photos and decadent parties. Dominik, with his encyclopedic knowledge of rubber, taught me about the complex dynamics of vacbeds. I am also grateful to submissive gentlemen including Jeffieboy, Irv O. Neil, Slaveboy Smith, "Tweet Slave," and Jon "HiThereCatsuit." Their help with the book was invaluable, all the while showing me how capable and driven submissive men can be.

Thanks to Rob Hall and Kai Ingwersen who showed me the ins and outs of Geneva; from the elevated homes of Cologny, to the naughty nightclubs downtown. I wouldn't have met Viviana's cousin at the local strip club without them!

If I'd been more efficient while writing *Edge Play*, I'd have given Erika a profession where I have expertise—my PhD is in industrial engineering and life cycle management. Instead, I made her an art expert. Oops! Thankfully, art savant Barbara Guggenheim came to my rescue. Her writings and experiences informed my understanding of the art world. And I benefitted from time spent with art advisor Sarah Belden, who let me be her sidekick on a visit to Art Basel. Together with Sarah, I've visited Geneva's free port and then marveled at the intensity of Basquiat's paintings in the Parisian home of one of his first collectors.

Hugo Fortin, my French teacher, was fantastic. He used our twice weekly lessons as an opportunity to discuss French culture and how that would have impacted Edouard's upbringing. Hugo is also a talented photographer with a master's degree from the École des Beaux-Arts in Paris, so he generously shared his art world insights with me as well.

Thanks to Jill Bruce for her thoughtful comments about an early draft of my manuscript. She had ideas and edits that enriched the story.

Judith Regan is an ongoing source of inspiration—for me and my characters. There were moments when Erika was in a predicament that I'd ask, "What would Judith do?" and the solution to Erika's problem became obvious.

My husband, Norm Pearlstine, was my first reader and has always been my most enthusiastic booster. I admire his priorities and his passions. I see every day how fortunate I am that our paths first crossed over twenty years ago.